EMERALD MALICE

KUZNETSOV BRATVA
BOOK 1

NICOLE FOX

Copyright © 2024 by Nicole Fox

All rights reserved.

No part of this book may be reproduced in any form or by any electronic or mechanical means, including information storage and retrieval systems, without written permission from the author, except for the use of brief quotations in a book review.

EMERALD MALICE

I crashed a wedding.

Got caught by the best man.

Now, I'm pregnant with his baby...

It's Katya's fault. (As per usual.)

My BFF despises her ex and wants to hate-watch him marry the woman he left her for.

Problem is, she didn't fill me in on that plan...

Until we arrive at the ceremony.

As soon as I find out, I run.

Hop on the elevator and smash the *Doors Close* button like the Energizer Bunny on a sugar rush.

But right before they shut...

A hand comes shooting through.

And attached to that hand, unfortunately for me, is the most stunning human specimen I've ever seen.

Tall.

Dark.

Handsome.

Dangerous.

Also... the best man.

He takes one look at me and knows I don't belong.

"Who let you in here, little bird?" he growls.

I gulp. Tremble.

Open my mouth to lie...

And then the elevator stops.

EMERALD MALICE is Book 1 of the Kuznetsov Bratva duet. The story concludes in Book 2, EMERALD VICES.

1

NATALIA

"We're crashing your ex's wedding?!"

I don't even know which word of that nightmarish sentence to emphasize. They're all equally horrible.

I rub my wrist—it's burning where I just ripped it from my best friend's death grip. Katya turns to me with a painfully forced smile.

"Oh, come on, Nat! It'll be fun."

"We have very different definitions of what qualifies as 'fun.'" I squint around the glittering foyer of the Ritz nervously. As far as I can tell, no one has yet noticed that we absolutely do not belong here. "I thought you brought me here for your early birthday celebration. 'Drinks at the bar,' she said! 'Just some quality bonding time,' she said! 'No drama whatsoever,' she said!"

Katya grins sheepishly. "Aw, what's life without a little drama?"

I groan as Katya homes in on the bronzed bulletin board that proudly announces the **Wedding Reception of Viktor Kuznetsov and Mila Obnizov.**

"Kat, seriously… this is not a good idea."

In fact, it might be her worst yet—which is saying something. Katya has spent the vast majority of our friendship outdoing herself in the "bad ideas" department.

I'm a good girl by nature. I follow rules. I cross streets at the crosswalk, pay my taxes on time, and I always, always return my shopping cart to the front of the store.

And yet when Kat dreams up a new devilish scheme, I somehow find myself dragged along. The reluctant Robin to her Batman as she goes after vengeance or laughs or whatever the hell she wants.

Today is the first option. *Vengeance.*

Katya never forgets an insult. And especially not the insult of being "discarded like a pair of sweaty pantyhose"—her words, not mine—for "an imported Barbie with a botched boob job"— again, nothing I would ever in a million years say myself.

I have no idea if she's ever even seen the woman Viktor dumped her for. If I thought she could be logical about this, I'd say, *Why waste your time and energy on a man who clearly didn't give a shit about you in the first place?*

But the woman's got tunnel vision when she's wearing her revenge goggles, and they're certainly polished and ready tonight.

If only I'd clocked it a little earlier, I wouldn't be here, standing in a five-star hotel in Midtown Manhattan, in a dress I rented—yes, *rented*—specifically for the as-it-turns-out completely fabricated pre-birthday celebration Katya insisted was necessary to ring in her twenty-eighth lap around the sun.

"Actually, this is a bad idea." I snap my fingers. "Earth to Kitty: are you hearing me?"

"Mila *Obnizov*," Katya spits, clearly and pointedly not hearing me. "What a pretentious-ass name!"

"Your last name is Petrova, babes. You both sound like Russian royalty."

She rolls her eyes and tries to grab my arm again. "Come on, if we go up now, we can—"

"We can what?" I hiss, pulling away from her. "Finish that sentence. What the hell do you want to do, Kat?"

"Nothing crazy, okay?" She sounds deceptively, eerily calm. It does not in any way match her constantly roving eyes. "This is purely a hate watch kind of thing."

"Which serves what purpose, exactly?"

"Closure," she says firmly. "I just need some closure, Nat. Is that so bad?"

"Katya…"

"Listen, I just wanna go up there and drink his open bar dry and ruthlessly mock every detail of his wedding, along with the skank he was cheating on me with. I know it's a petty form of revenge, but I'm a petty bitch, and that's not a crime."

"I'm so glad you brought up 'crime'—because isn't Viktor, like, a *literal* criminal?"

I'm hoping that, if nothing else, self-preservation will get through that thick, revenge-addled skull of hers.

My hope goes unanswered.

"Barely." She flicks her platinum blonde bob. "That was just a lot of talk—"

"From Viktor himself!"

"Exactly." She nods aggressively, eyes huge, probably assuming that I'm not aware of how she's inching us towards the gilded elevators while we argue. "He was just trying to gas himself up to impress me. None of it is actually true."

"First of all, what does it say about you that illegal, shady shit turns you on?" I snap. "And secondly, what if it *is* true?"

She waves away my argument and presses the button to summon the elevator. "If it is true, are you really gonna leave me up there alone with all those big, bad criminals?"

Goddamn her.

The elevator dings. I stand rooted to the spot. I should stay here and leave her to her fate. As usual, this is her drama. My kind of drama involves *True Blood* rewatches with a tub of Ben & Jerry's (Cherry Garcia all day, every day).

Leave her to it. This is not your fight. Just turn around and walk a—

As she walks into the elevator and turns to face me, her left eyebrow arches. That's never a good thing. It's the left one that signals she's about to whip out the big guns. "You know, Natalia, if you stopped being so damn afraid of everything, you'd realize that life is an adventure, not just an unrequited love triangle with Ben and Jerry."

Did I also mention that, apart from being a vengeful bitch, Katya can also be a straight-up, in-your-face, *bitchy*-ass bitch? One who knows exactly which nerves to hit?

Because that's an important detail.

"Oh, screw you." I scowl as I join her in the elevator.

She giggles triumphantly and wraps me up in a hug that I do not return. "I promise, this is gonna be fun."

"For whom? Definitely not for Viktor. Definitely not for Mila. Sure as hell not for me."

She just winks. "You look hot as sin, by the way. Green really is your color."

"You don't have to lay it on so thick. I'm already in the damn elevator."

Ping. Katya steps out on the fifth floor with a confident strut. I follow with a sigh.

Once more into the breach, dear friends.

We emerge into a sweeping ballroom. White-clothed tables range on all sides, a gleaming wooden dance floor in the center. Crystal chandeliers cast gauzy light on the ogre-sized floral arrangements lining the walls. There's no way they spent less than fifty grand on florals alone.

But the obscenely lavish decor is nothing compared to the guests. All of them sparkle like human diamonds in their floor-length ballgowns.

As I try to keep up with Katya, who's apparently become an Olympic track star since our last nearly fatal spin class, I count a who's who of New York Fashion Week's most beloved designers.

Earlier tonight, my rented vintage dress with its flowy midi skirt and a daringly sexy open back—daring for me, at least—made me feel like I was giving *Atonement*-era Keira Knightley vibes.

Compared to these people, I feel more like Fiona from *Shrek*. And not the human version.

Oh, Jesus, where's Kat?

I catch a glint of sequins as she whips a sharp right between two hulking men who look more like bodyguards than party guests.

Which, as I think it, is when I realize they are bodyguards.

The serious-looking kind.

The earpiece-wearing, indoors-sunglass-donning, *I-can-murder-you-with-one-pinky* kind.

"Katya!" I reach out and snag her elbow before she slithers from my reach. "Where the hell are you going?"

"I thought we'd do a little recon," she explains as though we stumbled our way into some sort of bizarre spy movie. "Let's split up and—"

"'Split up'?" I nearly shriek. "Have you seen, like, any horror movie ever?"

She pinches my arm. "Lower your voice! We're trying to go incognito here."

"I've got news for you," I say, dabbing my forehead with the back of my hand. "We're the only ones in here with knockoff dresses and costume jewelry." Instinctively, I clutch the small gold pendant that used to belong to my mother. "We're gonna be noticed."

"Not unless we do something dumb! It's all about confidence. You need to look like you belong."

"First of all, this whole thing is 'something dumb.' And as a matter of fact, I *don't* belong here. I can't believe I let you rope me into another one of your—"

"We don't have time for another Nat Lecture. Let's split up and compare notes later." Before I have a chance to respond, she gives me a wink and shimmies into the crowd.

"Okay," I mutter under my breath as I try to avoid eye contact and find a spot to hide until this is all over. "This is good. This is fine."

"Ma'am?"

I whip around and find myself looking up at one of the scary bodyguards. This one has a knotted scar across his lower jaw and a nose that looks like it's been broken several times in each direction.

Not good. Not fine at all.

I try to smile, but all I manage is a wince. "Er, yes?"

"Can I see your invitation?"

I take a quick, panicked survey of the rest of the wedding guests. None of them seem to be holding anything apart from bespoke clutches and glasses of champagne. They look perfectly at ease.

I, on the other hand, am sweating like a whore in church—and it's very, very obvious to my new friend here that I do not have an invitation.

Instead of going through the indignity of being caught out as a gatecrasher, I go for what seems to be the most graceful of my limited options.

I run.

∼

Admittedly, not one of my finer moments.

This dress deserved a better night out. Hell, *I* deserve a better night out. A better best friend, too, now that I'm compiling a list.

For the moment, I'd settle for a better sprint time than the burly security guard on my tail.

Thankfully, I've got an advantage. The security team following me at a brisk pace across the ballroom seem unwilling to break into a full run so as not to ruffle the invited guests. It gives me enough time to slice through the hall and make it to an elevator.

God must finally be done playing mean tricks on me, because for the first time tonight, I get lucky—one set of doors opens just as I arrive.

I plow into the elevators and start smashing the button that will take me down to the ground floor and to freedom. "C'mon, c'mon, c'mon, you bastard…"

The doors slowly groan closed. Through the gap, I see the security golems rumbling towards me.

"Close faster, goddammit!" I cry out. "You have one job!"

The guards come closer.

The doors keep closing.

Emerald Malice

The guards come closer.

The doors are almost closed…

I'm on the verge of letting out my pent-up exhale—there's only an inch left before I'm scot-free—when, suddenly, a huge hand shoots through the gap.

I can only gape in horror as the doors reverse course and the owner of the hand steps in.

The good news is that he's not security.

The bad news is that I'm pretty sure he's much, much worse.

"At ease, gentlemen," he says to the onrushing horde of guards, who promptly freeze at attention like toy soldiers. "She's with me."

Then the doors glide closed.

He's tall, dark, brooding—a dreamboat plagiarized from every single fantasy I've ever had. He's wearing a tuxedo, so he's probably a legit wedding guest, but the scowl on his face says he's not enjoying himself any more than I am.

"Going down?" His voice matches his appearance perfectly. Raspy and low like distant thunder.

"Trying to."

"It might help if you pressed the right button." He reaches over and smoothly plucks my wrist to redirect my hand to the adjacent switch. His fingers are surprisingly gentle on my bare skin, though they burn like he's on fire.

"Oh." My cheeks go red like *they're* on fire. "Yeah. Thanks."

The doors seal smoothly like they were just waiting for this guy to grant them permission.

"You're sweating."

"You're just full of useful observations, aren't you?" I mumble.

I immediately regret it—he's not the reason I'm in this mess to begin with, so he doesn't deserve my misplaced anger and anxiety.

But if he's offended, he shows no sign of it.

"Here." I blink at his outstretched hand. He's offering me a pristine white handkerchief.

"Thanks," I mumble again, face still flaming. I take it and dab the sweat from my forehead.

"Friend of the bride?" he asks as I give it back to him.

"Uh, sure? Something like that." *Deflect. For the love of all that is holy, change the subject now!* "What, er… what about you?"

The answer comes immediately. "Andrey Kuznetsov. Brother of the groom."

Shiiiiit.

I'm saved from figuring out what the hell to say to that by another, much worse, problem. Because it seems God isn't anywhere close to being done toying with me.

The elevator grinds to a halt.

I gasp, grabbing the rail of the elevator as it lurches to an abrupt, jarring stop. The shock makes me forget I'm not supposed to be making eye contact. I look up and his eyes snap onto mine.

God help us all.

Those eyes are too ethereal to be human. The irises are a light silver, rimmed with charcoal gray. Or maybe they're blue? There's sort of a bluish, predawn hue, like…

But I can't quite decide what to call it before my attention is stolen by the rest of his face. The straight, proud nose. The sharp, hollow cheekbones. The diamond-carved jaw, sporting just the faintest brush of five o'clock shadow.

Each feature is a standalone actor in its own right—but the ensemble… *Muah.* Chef's kiss.

Someone stole this man directly from my spank bank…

And then trapped me in the elevator with him.

"Oh my God." I fall back on my initial strategy of attacking the foyer button like a manic woodpecker. "Oh my God, what's happening? What's—"

I freeze when his hand comes down on mine for the second time. "Once again, you're missing the target." He redirects me to the emergency bell in the bottom corner.

I push it and it turns red. Then…

Nothing.

"What now?"

"They'll get to it." He couldn't sound less concerned.

Meanwhile, I'm wondering what kind of fee the dress rental place is gonna charge for excessive sweat stains. But even that worry fades away, because I'm starting to get light-headed, too. And this time, it has nothing to do with him.

"When?" I croak. "When will they get to it?"

"Are you alright?"

No! I want to scream. *No, I'm not alright at all. My best friend is a lunatic and I should absolutely not be in this place and you are way too good-looking to be real and my throat feels like it's closing up on me and are the lights getting dimmer or is it just me and is it getting hotter and hotter in here or is that just me…?*

I stumble back and my ass hits the wall and I scream before I can choke it back. "I-I-I… don't do well in confined spaces," I manage to stammer.

"You're claustrophobic?"

"I do believe that is the technical term, yes." I feel giddy and insane as I fan myself with one hand. "My Lord, it's hot in here. Are you hot?"

I can't tell if he's amused or completely disgusted by me. "You need to stay calm. Breathe."

"The whole thing about being claustrophobic is that you can't breathe when you want to."

The emergency bell button suddenly flashes. There's some static and then a voice comes through, high and reedy. "Apologies for the inconvenience, folks. We're experiencing some technical difficulties. The elevators will be up and running in the next ten to fifteen minutes."

Great. I'm trapped in a steel box hovering several stories above ground with the brother of the groom whose wedding I was forced into crashing.

Somewhere overhead, God is laughing his ass off.

2

ANDREY

As far as decoys go, she's a damn good one.

Looks-wise, at least. She's a siren with seductive green eyes and dark hair that falls in voluminous waves down the open back of her very sexy, emerald green dress.

Of course, if we're taking into account skills, I'm not sure she meets the standards of Nikolai Rostov's usual go-to for fucking with my operation.

This girl has no skills to speak of.

She's clutching the walls of the elevator, nails digging into the brocaded padding as her chest rises and falls heavily. Either this is all part of the ruse—if in fact she is working for Nikolai—*or* she's genuinely claustrophobic.

"… ten to fifteen minutes," she mutters on repeat. "Ten to fifteen minutes… Ten to fifteen…"

I clear my throat loudly and she flinches, her eyes snapping to mine.

No, she's no decoy. Say what you want about Nikolai Rostov, but his ploys usually have a little more finesse.

Although, considering the call I received from my number-two, Shura, minutes ago—the whole reason I'm even in this elevator with this skittish little *lastochka*—I might need to reconsider that opinion.

Blyat', this wedding has been a disaster so far.

"H-how long do you think it's been?" she asks tentatively. The flush on her cheeks has traveled down to her chest.

"Thirty seconds, give or take."

A whoosh of terror escapes through her parted lips. For a moment, it sounds like she's about to hack up a hairball. "Th-thirty seconds…" She turns her back on me and claws the wall padding a little tighter. "Oh, God, I'm not gonna make it."

The silk of her dress hugs her ass to perfection. If I squint, I can just make out the subtle line of her panties pressing through the fabric.

"Counting down the minutes isn't going to help."

"What will help?" she demands. "And don't you dare tell me to stay calm. Don't tell me to breathe, either."

I suppress a smile as she whirls back around. "Pretend we're outside. Somewhere pleasant. A sunny, open-air café, maybe, and we're waiting for the barista to call out our orders."

"Open air," she echoes as her eyelashes flutter wildly. "Um, okay. I'm… I'm waiting for my order…"

"Describe it to me."

"Chocolate frappe with an extra shot of chocolate and whipped cream," she blurts immediately. "And cherries. Lots of cherries."

I grimace. "Jesus."

She smiles self-consciously, revealing a faint dimple in her cheek. "It's my comfort drink, okay? It's what I order any time I'm sad or nervous or freaked out."

"You're missing the point. It's sunny and breezy and nice. You're not freaking out. You're perfectly calm."

"Right. Calm." She gulps and her eyelids stop their frantic fluttering. For the first time since the elevator ground to a halt, she draws in something resembling a full breath. "My aunt had a cherry tree in the back of her house when I was growing up. We had cherry pies on Friday, cherry sundaes on Saturday, and plain ol' cherries on Sundays, 'just the way God intended them.'" She blushes. "That's how my Aunt Annie would say it."

She's clutching the little gold locket around her neck so hard that the chain is embedding itself in the skin of her neck.

Then her eyes blink open and the tension comes roaring back. "Sorry. I'm rambling. We're at the café. It's nice, it's sunny, it tastes like cherries. What did you order?"

"Whiskey. Neat." Devil knows I deserve something strong after this clusterfuck of a day.

"What kind of café is this?" she laughs deliriously.

"My kind."

"Fair enough." She lowers her attention to picking at her fingernails. "How many minutes do you think we have now?"

"Thirteen, give or take."

"Fuck me!"

The moment the words leave her mouth, she goes bright pink. A gentleman would pretend as though she hadn't said anything.

Unfortunately for her, I've never been accused of being a gentleman.

"I'd consider it, but I'm not sure thirteen minutes will be anywhere near enough."

Her jaw drops.

The flush on her cheeks and chest continues to spread. *Where would it go if I followed it?* I wonder. *If I peeled that dress apart and worked my way down the valley of her breasts, and lower, and lower…*

Easy there, Andrey. You have a wedding to attend.

Not to mention the situation I was on my way to handle when this fucking elevator decided to hold us hostage.

She seems to be working up the courage to say something. I wait patiently.

"You'll have to find another wedding guest to proposition for sex. I'm not interested."

"I believe *you* were the one propositioning *me*," I remind her.

"I wasn't… That wasn't… You misunderstood…" When I chuckle low, her eyebrows pinch together. "Oh. You're teasing me."

"Rude of me, I suppose. Here you are in the throes of a panic attack and I'm screwing with you."

"I can't blame you. I know I make it easy."

I wonder what she means by that. Actually, I'm wondering a lot of things about this little *lastochka*. Like how someone as guileless as her could have ended up on my brother's wedding list. She could be a friend of Mila's, but I met enough of Mila's simpering friends today to confidently rule that out.

"Remind me: how do you know the bride and groom?"

She pales visibly. She looks as though that's the worst question I could have possibly asked her. Which of course means it's the right one to ask. "Uh… just a friend."

"A friend of Viktor's or Mila's?"

She swallows and shuffles from one stilettoed heel to the other. "Um, both."

"If I didn't know any better, *lastochka*—" She flinches when the Russian rolls off my tongue. "—I'd say you were lying to me."

She wipes her palms on the sides of her dress. "The thing is—"

Before I can find out what 'the thing' is, a resounding ring emanates from my jacket pocket. I pull out my phone to find my second-in-command's name on the display.

Cursing under my breath, I answer. "What is it, Shura?"

"Just got to the grounds. I'm standing in front of the intruder right now…" There's something hesitant in Shura's voice.

"Well? Is he one of Nikolai's?"

"He isn't talking—but yes, definitely one of Nikolai's."

I have to be careful how I phrase this, considering the second pair of ears in the elevator with me. "You'll have to convince him it's in his best interest to chat with us."

"Uh, right. The thing is—he's a child."

I make Shura repeat it to ensure I'm hearing correctly. I get the same answer the second time around. "How young are we talking?"

"Teenager?" he guesses. "He's about halfway to a mustache, if that paints a helpful picture for you."

This shit makes me sick to my stomach. What the fuck is Nikolai doing, sending in a boy to do a man's job? Then again, he's also the bastard who makes his fortune profiting off the sale of women and children.

Made his fortune that way, rather. Not anymore, though. Not since a few months ago, when I shut down his human trafficking business for good.

Which, incidentally, is what set off this campaign of retaliation against me.

I check the time on my watch. "I won't be able to get away for another couple of hours. Keep an eye on him until I get there."

I hang up to find my phone blowing up with texts from Viktor.

VIKTOR: *What the fuck? Where are you? Ceremony's about to start!*

VIKTOR: *Bro—you're the fucking best man. Not to mention the goddamn* **pakhan**. *You need to be here.*

VIKTOR: *I can't believe you're not here after* **YOU** *forced me to marry the bitch.*

Sometimes, I forget what an asshole my little brother can be. Luckily, I can always rely on him to remind me.

I ignore all his messages and turn my focus back on the quivering woman in the elevator with me. Good timing, too, because apparently, the two-minute call with Shura is all it took to completely unravel her.

She's back to being a sweaty, clammy mess, scraping at the wall padding like a cat going through withdrawals.

Real or fake? I still haven't fully made up my mind. This could be real. It could also be an attempt to distract me from the fact that she's obviously not supposed to be at this wedding at all.

"Is there something you'd like to tell me?"

Those green eyes of hers go wide and trembly. Then, without any warning, she collapses in a dead faint.

"Oh, fucking hell."

I drop to one knee beside her. I tap her face, but she doesn't so much as stir.

Her chest is heaving, though. Stuttering, almost, like the stitching in the dress where it binds across her chest is handcuffing her lungs.

It's pure survival instinct that moves me next.

Not lust. Definitely not lust.

No, I tell myself as I gather two fistfuls of the fabric. *This is solely to help her breathe.*

Then I rip her dress apart like tissue paper.

Her exposed skin is pale and cold to the touch. When I hover a palm over her mouth to feel her breathing, it's too still.

Only one way to go from here.

But it's not lust. It's definitely not lust.

I lower my face to the girl's. Her lips part as I get close, like she knows what's coming and she wants it.

Closer.

Closer.

Her scent is sweet and my dick has never been harder.

And then, just like that, I'm ripped back in time.

Because I've *been here before.* In exactly this situation, kneeling beside a cold, shivering woman and preparing to give her my breath.

I know how that ended. I feel the grief of it in the pit of my stomach every single day of my fucking life.

This kiss is to heal; that one was nothing more than a belated goodbye.

My lips seal to the girl's. I exhale to fill her lungs. Turn and feel her heartbeat. Exhale again. Check her pulse. I do it all one more time, and just when I'm wondering if I ought to be preparing last rites instead—*why won't this fucking elevator move, goddammit?!*—she makes a noise.

"Mmmm…"

It's a moan. There's no other word for it. It's a *moan.* Low and dreamy and undeniable.

And, like magic, it brings her back to life.

The emerald *lastochka's* eyes fly open and she shoves herself upright, just barely missing cracking her skull against mine. She scrambles backward to a hunched seat in the corner. "Oh my God." She slaps a hand over her mouth like she can shove the moan back in there. "W-what the hell…?"

Before I can explain, the elevator shudders into motion. Like it has a mind of its own, it takes us back to where we came from.

Ping. "Fifth floor."

The doors open onto the ballroom. I can see my brother standing amidst a throng of his useless, half-drunk friends. One of them spots me and claps Viktor on the back.

I feel a blur of motion at my side. In the second it takes me to signal to him that I'm coming, the little *lastochka* has darted out of the elevator, ducked between two security guards, and careened out of sight.

I let her go—for now.

My mind was made up as soon as I tasted her, so her quick getaway is just the nail in her coffin.

I've never met a mystery I couldn't solve.

And she's a mystery I'm determined to get to the bottom of.

3

NATALIA

"Watch where you're going!"

I stumble backwards, wilting on the spot at the murderous glance I'm getting from the six-foot-tall woman I just ran right into. She pulls her white fur stole tighter around her body and skewers me with a disdainful glare.

I follow her gaze to the ruined neckline of my dress. *Is my boob hanging out? Well, would ya look at that? It sure is. Nice going, Nat. Way to be an upstanding member of polite society.*

"S-sorry," I mutter awkwardly as I shove the girls back in place.

The haughty woman rolls her eyes and walks away, talking loudly enough for me to hear. "Honestly, if I'd known they'd be inviting the riff-raff, I'd have stayed home. I expect more from the Kuznetsovs."

Katya would have tackled the snobby bitch to the floor and strangled her with her own chinchilla. But all I can muster in my current state of flustered undress is a pathetic sniffle in her direction before I run off in search of a place to hide.

I keep waiting for the other shoe to drop. My thoughts are as much of a mess as my dress is.

Is security following me?

Is he following me?

Where the fuck is Katya?!

As though I've pulled her from thin air by the strength of my thoughts, a door opens to the side. Katya's slim arm darts out, grabs me, and hauls me in after her like Satan himself dragging me down into hell.

Where the hell have you been?" she breathes in my face. "I've been looking for you everywhere!"

This is so typical of Katya. Usually, I just laugh it off.

But nothing about today is "usual." Today, I've been forced into crashing a wedding, chased by security guards, trapped in an elevator. And the cherry on top of the shit sundae? I completely and totally humiliated myself in front of the most beautiful man I've ever laid eyes on.

That moan will be echoing in my nightmares for the rest of eternity.

"Me?" I explode. *"Me?!"*

Katya takes a startled step back. Only then does she seem to notice that my clothes aren't sitting right. "Your, uh… your dress is a little torn up there, babe."

"Thanks, Captain Obvious." I grab the neckline and try to pull it into place. For a moment, it obeys—but as soon as I let go, it withers right back like a dying flower.

"Okay, calm down. Let me try." She toys with it for a second, then magically produces some safety pins from a box on the shelves at our elbows and works some witchcraft that fixes it right up.

"There! Good as new." She wiggles her eyebrows at me. "You wanna tell me why you're running around half-dressed with sex hair and smudged lipstick?"

"Is my lipstick smudged?" I pivot on the spot in search of a mirror, but of course, the utility closet is fresh out of those. Just as well—I can't bear looking at myself right now.

"Only a little."

I whimper and cover my face with my hands for a three-second pity party. It's all we have time for. "We have to get the hell out of here. Now!"

Katya has the audacity to look puzzled. "But the ceremony's about to start!"

I feel insane. Am I? Or is she?

"For fuck's sake, Kat—you seriously wanna watch your ex-boyfriend get married to the woman he cheated on you with?"

"Yes! Yes, as a matter of fact, I do. Call me a masochist, but I wanna see it and I can't do it alone."

"Since when?"

"Since I decided everything's more fun in twos," she explains dismissively. Like that just about settles things, she opens the door a crack. "Look at all those rich assholes... Is that Leo?"

"As in DiCaprio?"

"What other Leo matters?" she sighs as if I'm a lost cause. "Wouldn't it be just a terrible tragedy if he and I met and we fell in love and got married in a ceremony twice as expensive as this one?"

I roll my eyes. She's joking—mostly. "Hate to break it to you, sweetheart, but you're almost twenty-eight now. You've aged out of Leo's dating pool."

"Have you *seen* my ass?" Katya counters, sticking it out for my benefit.

What I'd prefer to see instead of my insane best friend's posterior is some hope that we can get out of here unscathed.

I peek over Katya's shoulder. I don't see Leo—or anyone else on the A-, B-, C-, or D-lists, for that matter. But I do see a veritable army of security guards herding straggling guests into the main ballroom.

As the crowd filters past our little hiding spot, I pay closer attention to the guests themselves. Some of them look like important, respectable businessmen, but the vast majority look more like what I'd generously call "hardcore criminals." We're talking thick golden chains, tattoos on necks, knuckles, or both, and the kind of furtive, aggressive side-to-side glances that all but scream, *I dare you to fuck with me.*

I shudder.

If this is the company the Kuznetsovs keep, it was a bad idea coming here today.

"Kat… We need to leave. These are not people we want to mess with."

She snorts. "I was wondering when Nervous Nat would rear her head."

I could slap her. I truly could. I love her, but I'm this close to cold-cocking her right across the face and dragging her limp body out of here.

Before I can, she doubles down. "Playing it safe is gonna take you exactly nowhere. Come on—don't you want to have adventures to look back on in your old age? Don't you want experiences to share with your grandchildren one day?"

"That's making the assumption that I even get to old age. Which, judging by the men outside this utility closet, is a stretch."

"You need to stop being so damn scared of everything," she says firmly. It's the same tone she used when she was trying to get me to go skinny dipping in her boss's pool that summer she was house-sitting for him. "You have to stop letting one tragedy be the crutch that keeps you from living your life!"

I should've hit her when I had the chance.

Because her words are as good as a slap across the face in their own right.

Tragedy—that's a funny word for what happened. It feels too clinical, too cold. Then again, what is the right way to talk about your parents getting dragged out of the car and murdered right in front of you?

I bite my tongue to keep the tears from spilling over. There's no way I'm gonna cry in front of her. "Low blow, Kat."

She sighs and clutches my hands. "I love you, you know that. And I just… I don't want to see you stuck in the past, Natalia. Life happens *here*. Now. In the present."

I'm still a little tongue-tied, but the opening chords of the wedding march coming from the ballroom save me from having to figure out what to say.

Katya squeezes my hands in hers once more. "We're just gonna sneak in there, find a couple seats way in the back, and judge from afar. Okay? Nothing risky. Besides," she adds, "if we leave now, we're only gonna draw attention to ourselves. Best to just blend with the crowd until after the ceremony and then we can leave."

"You promise?"

She makes a cross over her heart with her index finger. "Cross my heart and hope to die."

"Oh, you *will* die if you don't keep that promise. I'll make sure of it."

She laughs, grabs my wrist, and pulls me out of the utility closet. We join the last exodus of people streaming through the doors and find seats tucked alongside a looming onyx vase bursting with flowers.

Everyone settles into their places. The conversations slowly dwindle.

It doesn't take me long to spot Andrey Kuznetsov. He's standing at the head of the aisle, looking impossibly huge and impossibly gorgeous. A mountain in charcoal with eyes too bright to be real. My lips tingle with the flesh memory of his lips on mine.

"Damn, is that Viktor's brother?" Katya interrupts my guilty thoughts. "Forget Leo—I'll take one of those, please."

It's weird how instantly my hackles rise. I have absolutely no claim to that man. So why do I care if Katya is attracted to him?

I don't, I tell myself firmly. *I don't care one little bit.*

Luckily, Katya's quickly distracted by the bride's entrance. "Oh my God, look at her dress. My freaking grandma would've encouraged her to show a little more skin. Is she the bride or a nun?"

I shoot her a glare. "Hush!"

Katya rolls her eyes, but falls silent while the bride is walked down the aisle by her short, balding father. People rise to their feet as I try to make sense of the little lump that's forming in my chest.

What the hell is that?

It's only when my fingers reach instinctively for the locket around my neck that it hits me.

I'll never have this. A father to walk me down the aisle, someone to hand me off.

Tragedy. There's that word again.

I hate it more and more every time.

The bride looks like a shrinking violet. She's pale as snow, with strawberry blonde hair styled into a tight chignon.

"We're veering into pedophile territory," Katya jeers. "She looks like she's twelve years old."

Viktor looks bored as he accepts her hand from his soon-to-be father-in-law. Then the ceremony starts. Katya chews at her nails as the officiant goes through the blandest marriage vows in recorded history.

"Is it almost over, do you think?" Katya whispers.

"I sincerely hope so."

She nods once, her blue eyes glowing a little brighter. Up on the altar, the officiant plows into the home stretch. "Do you, Viktor Kuznetsov, take this woman to be your lawfully wedded wife?"

Another nod, like Katya is preparing herself for something. It leaves a sinking feeling in my belly.

"Kat—"

Viktor opens his mouth, "I—"

"I OBJECT!"

I stare after Katya, my jaw hanging to the literal floor.

I'm not the only one. The crowd twists in their chairs.

And just like that, Katya has stolen the show.

All eyes are on her—including Viktor's.

"Katya...?" he stutters in disbelief, while his bride lists to the side as though she's in danger of fainting at any moment.

"Viktor Kuznetsov is a liar and a cheater!" Katya continues loudly. Rather than be deterred by the eyes on her, it's like the audience is giving her life. "He prowls the city at night looking for his next conquest. And trust me, he's made many!"

Andrey Kuznetsov is the only one who looks even remotely calm during this abrupt little detour the wedding has taken. His eyebrow flickers up as he regards Katya with pure, acidic disdain. Then he looks off to the left and gives a nod to someone I can't see. I'm guessing Katya has about ten seconds before she's hauled out of here like the crazy-ass intruder she is.

The thing is—and I know from experience—Katya can do a lot of damage in ten seconds. As it turns out, she doesn't even need that long.

"Viktor has a secret mistress," she cries out. "She's pregnant with his baby. And she's standing right over *there!*"

I blink over at Katya—who's pointing in my direction, for some inexplicable reason.

I actually glance over my shoulder to see this pregnant mistress she's apparently brought along to humiliate Viktor.

But there's nothing behind me except an onyx vase filled with calla lilies.

And that's when it hits me.

I'm supposed to be the pregnant mistress.

I'm the prop.

I'm the naive idiot who let myself get roped into Katya's revenge ploy.

Before I can jump in and correct her lie, Andrey Kuznetsov steps off the raised platform. He no longer looks disinterested or calm.

Now, he looks *pissed.*

Those ethereal silver eyes land directly on me and he growls three terrifying words into the microphone. "Security… grab them."

4

ANDREY

One of Viktor's moronic henchmen is the first to reach them. He grabs the little *lastochka* by her arm and even from where I'm standing on the altar, I can see how she winces in pain.

"Carefully, *mudaks*!" I belt from across the room.

Leif appears at my side. "How do you want me to deal with this, sir?"

"Tell those untrained gorillas to keep an eye on both women until after the reception is over. I'll deal with it then."

Leif bows and scurries off to do as I ordered. I turn to my brother and his almost-bride, both of whom look as though they have no idea what to do next. Whatever is going on with those women, I'm fairly confident it's my brother's fault.

As usual, it falls to me to clean his mess.

So I turn to the buzzing crowd and plaster a fake smile on my face. "What's a Russian wedding without a little drama?"

The crowd laughs and the tension breaks. I nod in grim satisfaction and glance over at the priest. "Father Nevsky, please continue." I lower my voice. "Quickly, though. Skip the bullshit."

As soon as the ceremony ends—without any further interruptions, thank fuck—Viktor is suddenly very interested in playing the gracious host, ignoring my attempts to make eye contact with him. He knows he's in for the ass-chewing of a lifetime once I get him in my grasp.

The crowd swarms me as we collectively drift toward the reception. People asking for favors, paying compliments, or offering gifts in the form of alliances and their daughters' hands in marriage.

It's just shit on top of shit on top of shit, all the way down. This whole day has been a fucking disaster, from Nikolai's teenage spy to the elevator debacle with the gatecrasher to my brother's ongoing attempts to lower the bar for how little I expect of him.

But that's what being *pakhan* of the Kuznetsov Bratva entails: dealing with nothing but shit.

So I duck gracefully past the marriage proposals, negotiate with new partners, and reconnect with old ones. I manage my empire one exhausting conversation at a time.

But an hour later, I spy Viktor skulking in the corner with a bottle of gin in hand and I decide that I won't let him evade me any longer.

I corner him by the wall frescoes and pluck the bottle from his hand.

"A little early in the marriage to be driven to drink."

He rolls his eyes, though they seem to each go in different directions. "Be thankful I wasn't drunk for the actual ceremony. That's when I really needed a bottle."

"You gonna tell me what that was about?"

His gaze is fixed on the bottle I've just confiscated from him. "I'll tell you if you hand over the gin."

I skewer him with a glare that makes him shrink back against the wall. "What makes you think this is a negotiation?"

He coughs nervously. "It's not my fault, okay?"

"It never is. Answer the question."

"The blonde's name is Katya," he says with a weary, simpering sigh. "She's no one. Just this chick I fucked for a few weeks… or, shit, maybe it was months… I can't remember now. She's just sore because I dumped her ass."

"And the brunette?"

"The who?" He shrugs as my pulse quickens. "Oh. Nat something. Natalia something? Natalie? I can't remember. She's Katya's friend, as far as I know. And she can't be pregnant with my kid because I never fucked her. Although, trust me, I tried. Even suggested the idea of a threesome to Katya, but she turned me down flat. Didn't even—"

"Enough," I spit, glaring at my brother in disgust. "God, you are fucking pathetic."

He draws himself up to his full height, though he's a little wobbly on his feet. "This is who I am. It's who I've always been." Then he slumps and casts his eye miserably around at the glittering festivities that have been arranged in his honor. "I never wanted any of this."

"You should have thought of that before you set your sights on Mila Obnizov."

"I didn't set my sights on her—I just wanted to fuck her. There's a difference."

"You 'just wanted to fuck' my top smuggler's daughter, Viktor? What were you thinking? Do you not see how that is problematic?"

"She was a *virgin*, bro," he says, as though that's all the explanation required. "Do you know how rare it is to find one these days? It's a fucking unicorn in a sea full of donkeys. I had to have her. Just once."

"And now, you get her for a lifetime. *Pozdravleniya*."

"The fuck wasn't even worth it. Some unicorns just aren't worth riding." His gaze veers over to his new wife, who's sitting alone at the head table looking like she wishes she were anywhere else.

"Have you talked to Obnizov?"

Viktor nods. "Already explained to him that Katya's a crazy cunt. He seemed satisfied."

"And your bride?"

"What about my bride?"

"Did you explain the situation to her?"

He balks, derisive laughter and gin-laced spit spraying past his lips. "Why the hell would I? I have to keep her damn father happy because he's important to the Bratva. I don't have to keep *her* happy."

This conversation alone is enough to make me feel sorry for Mila Obniz— No, actually, she's a Kuznetsov now.

Forget congratulations; *condolences* are in order.

"You do have to maintain the status quo, however," I snarl. "I'm sick of cleaning up your messes."

"Hey, I married the bitch, didn't I? Just like you ordered." He steals the bottle of gin from my hand and takes a long swig that ends up dribbling down the side of his chin. He wipes it away with the sleeve of his jacket. "Looks like Otets couldn't be bothered to be here."

"What do you care if Slavik is here or not?"

"I don't care. I'm just saying."

Viktor never outgrew his desperation for our father's approval. He was never perceptive enough to realize that, by the unchangeable nature of his status as second son, he'd never mean shit to Slavik Kuznetsov. He took the lack of attention personally, having no idea he got the better end of the bargain.

I was the one who got fucked.

I have the scars to prove just how unfortunate it is when Slavik Kuznetsov takes an interest in shaping you as a man.

Meanwhile, as I was bleeding and suffering in the dirt at my father's feet, Viktor was fucking his way through half of New York, thinking that somehow qualified as an accomplishment.

And after Slavik fled the country in the middle of the night, with no warning and nothing left behind but a scrawled note and a wake of dumpster fires for me to put out, it fell to me to keep Viktor in line.

I thought he deserved a break.

I'm starting to think I've been too easy on him the last few years.

Viktor offers me the bottle, but I shake my head. "One of us needs to be sober for this thing."

"I don't see why," he says with a deranged cackle. "The only way to get through a wedding is to be drunk. Honestly, I don't know why anyone would subject themselves to this—" He breaks off, his eyes veering to me. "Well... *you* did."

"I never got married," I remind him gruffly.

"But you would have." He's always been braver when he's drunk. No way would he dare to bring up this topic if he were sober. "I've always been curious: what was it about Maria? Did she have some sort of golden pussy or—"

In an instant, Viktor is spluttering, his eyes bulging like a toad's as I cut off his windpipe with an elbow to the throat. He keeps trying to choke out words, but I'm done listening to him talk.

"You're fucking wasted," I hiss. "It's embarrassing. If you want to keep toting around the title of Kuznetsov, then you'd better clean yourself up and start acting the part. Look around: do you see any of my men acting like a fucking joke?"

I release a tiny bit of pressure on his neck so he can breathe. A few guests have noticed the fracas, but the smart ones look away.

"I'm done making excuses for you, Viktor. You're not a boy anymore. Get your shit together."

I peel myself off of him and leave him there to lick his

wounds. Anyone with an ounce of sense in their head gives me a wide berth as I stalk away.

"Boss..." Leif approaches me from around the cocktail bar with a grim expression. "I've got news. The girls that you asked Viktor's security to apprehend, they've... they've..."

"Spit it out, Leif," I rasp. "I'm not in the mood for guessing games."

"They've escaped," he finishes in a broken whisper.

"Four soldiers couldn't keep their eyes on two civilian women?"

Leif gives me a look. *What did you expect from Viktor's goons?* "Should I get a few men on their trail? They can't have gone far."

I could just let this go right now. The blonde was nothing but a scorned conquest from Viktor's past and the brunette— *Natalia,* I remember, tasting her name—was a hapless sidekick. Neither one has any connection to Nikolai Rostov, and neither one is pregnant with a Kuznetsov baby.

So what does it matter that I no longer have eyes on them? What does it matter if they got away?

In many ways, it's for the best. They can disappear into the night and I can turn my attention to more important things. Like crushing the last remnants of Nikolai Rostov's dying Bratva.

And yet...

"Find them," I order. "And if it comes down to a choice between the blonde and the brunette... bring me the brunette."

5

NATALIA

"I am too damn old for this shit."

Turns out dumpsters aren't as good of a hiding place as I first thought. I don't think a thousand showers will get rid of the stench oozing into me right now. My soul will smell like rotten vegetables long after I make it through the pearly gates.

I've been in this dumpster for a minute, two tops, but it feels like an hour. Maybe a century.

But I make myself stay put until the sirens pass and the normal buzz of the city returns.

Then, unable to take this hellhole for another second, I shove open the lid and fumble my way out.

My foot catches on the edge and I land face-first in a puddle of something repulsive, because *offuckingcourse* I do. After another minute of groaning in pain and misery that this is what my day has become, I peel myself out of the mystery liquid and get back to my wobbly feet.

Pedestrians glance over at me as they pass the alleyway. But only in New York does the sight of a gaunt, shaky, unkempt woman emerging from a dumpster inspire next to no reaction.

I reach instinctively for my purse. That's when I remember that I didn't have time to grab my purse before Katya and I kicked our bodyguards in the balls and ran through the door of the temporary jail cell where we were taken after being booted from the ceremony (a.k.a., a small, unadorned staff room next to the utility closet).

I want to yell and scream and vent. I'm so beyond out of fucks to give that I wouldn't care if the whole damn city watched me lose my shit.

But I don't have the stamina for that. I can only hang my head in abject misery.

My freaking ID was in that purse. My keys. My wallet. My Metro card. My phone. My *life*.

Now, I'm stranded in the asshole of Midtown Manhattan, reeking of sour cabbage, and I don't have two cents to rub together.

Not only have I lost my purse and my dignity, but I've lost my friend, too. Somewhere in the rush of the chase, I realized that Katya wasn't right behind me anymore.

I'm not even sure I care right now. "Friend" is a bit of a stretch after the stunt she pulled tonight, though. Kat is on probation. Tackling the back portion of this night on my own might be for the best.

How, though?

My best plan is to jump the turnstile and ride the subway home. It'll take forever and a half, but I'm not exactly swimming in options here.

First things first—I need to pee.

I end up in the dive bar around the bend because it looks like the kind of establishment that will accept me in my current state and smell. As predicted, no one stops me when I breeze in, whistling merrily, pretending as though my night is going exactly how I intended.

I head to the bathroom first, which is just as stank as the rest of the place. Honestly, I might be improving the aroma. Once I've peed, I stop in front of the mirror. It's scratched and graffitied to shit, clearly working overtime just to give me back a murky reflection. That's just as well. I mean, do I really wanna see myself clearly right now?

What little I can see looks bleak enough. One thing's for sure, I'm not renting this dress anymore—I've bought it. A hundred and fifty bucks for a gown I'm never gonna be able to wear again.

This night is the gift that keeps on giving.

At least I got a kiss out of it.

I walk back through the bowels of the dive bar, planning on walking right out the door, but my legs suddenly feel like Bambi on muscle relaxants. Those stools at the bar are looking mighty nice.

Five minutes of R&R couldn't hurt, right? I mean, the coast is clear. No scary goons in suits coming after me.

I plant my ass on one and rest all my weight on the lacquered bar top in front of me. If I didn't have deeply-rooted trust issues, I'd fall asleep right here in five seconds flat. I'm *that* strung out.

"You okay, honey?"

The man sitting two stools down from me is wearing a plaid jacket and a smile that's missing at least two teeth. He could be twenty-seven or seventy-seven and I'd never know the difference. But he's friendly-looking, at least. After the night I've had, friendly faces are more than welcome.

"Rough night," I admit.

"I can see that. Boy troubles?"

I snort, wondering where Katya is right now. Knowing her, she's probably back home, soaking in a warm bath and plotting the next day's hijinks. "More like girl troubles."

"Ah, right. Didn't mean to presume. Twenty-first century and all; I suppose I ought to be more careful by now, eh?" He grins pleasantly.

"Oh. Heh. What I mean is, I've had *friend* troubles." I shake my head. "Today was supposed to be a fun, relaxing birthday celebration—"

"Ah! It's your birthday?" The man pounds his fist against the counter. "Max, get this lovely girl a drink. It's her birthday!"

I keep my mouth shut. If this is the universe's way of apologizing to me for this shitty night, I accept.

The bartender slides a shot of something amber over to me. "Thanks." We clink our glasses together.

"The name's Rory," he says. "What's yours, if you don't mind me askin'?"

"Natalia."

"Beautiful name for a beautiful girl." He takes a long drink. "Don't stress, Natalia. Nights like this are the nights that end up making us."

I'll admit, I'm only half-listening. I didn't realize just how badly I needed a drink. It's just the kick I need to power through the rest of this night. Or, better yet, to rinse away the memory of it.

Rory is a talker, and I'm glad for that, too. He babbles uninterrupted for fifteen minutes and gives me the full rundown of the last fifty years of his life. He really does seem to be exactly what he looks like: a kindly older man offering a drink and a chat to a girl who's down on her luck. He makes it surprisingly easy to let down my walls and pretend everyone isn't out to get me.

Easy enough that I muster up the courage to do the one thing I hate doing more than anything else: asking for help.

"Rory, can I ask you for a favor?"

Rory recoils like he'd be offended if I didn't. "Sure thing, sweetheart. Ask away."

"I lost track of my purse after my friend and I got into that fight, and I have no money to get back home. I'm not asking for a handout. Just three bucks for a subway ticket. I swear to God I'll come back tomorrow to return the money."

He looks amused at my little speech. Then he pulls out his wallet and hands me a twenty-dollar bill. "Tell ya what? Take this, buy yourself a t-shirt from Max here, and use the change to get your ticket. There's no need to return the money. We'll call it a birthday gift."

You really can find anything in the boroughs of New York: even kindness.

"You don't have to do that."

"I insist," Rory says, pointing at the t-shirts hung up behind the bar. "Take your pick of the litter. My favorite is the one that says, **SUCIO**. Means 'dirty' in Spanish."

The bartender, Max, hands me an XL tee and I go to the bathroom to change. It's a sweet relief to peel out of my filthy dress and pull the black t-shirt on instead. It's big enough that it covers my ass, albeit just barely. I walk back out and do a little catwalk for Rory's benefit, then give him a kiss on the cheek.

"You don't know how grateful I am."

"Pay it forward, darling. And think of me when you wear that shirt."

"How could I not?" Feeling better than I have in hours, I wave goodbye to Rory and step out of the bar much lighter than when I walked in.

I'm not even five steps from the door when a shadow falls over me.

"What the—" I twist around and find myself faced with two hulking men.

The man with long blond hair gives me a calculated smile. "You left your purse back at the ceremony, miss. Why don't we escort you there now so you can retrieve it?"

"You know what? Keep it. It'd look better on you, anyway."

I try to turn my back on them, but the shaved head goon grabs my arm. "I don't think so, ma'am. You're coming with us."

He steers me towards a gleaming black SUV idling on the curb. It sounds like a purring beast, with two violently white headlights like predator's eyes locked right on me.

I can't see much beyond the glare of the headlights and the blacked-out windows. God only knows what's inside. Once again, I have the feeling He's laughing at me.

The second man opens the back door. "In you go."

I dig in my heels. "My boyfriend is waiting for me," I inform them. "He'll call the police if I don't show up."

The blond chuckles. "He can go right ahead. In our experience, imaginary boyfriends tend not to pose much of a problem."

My body goes cold. They know I'm lying. And the only way they could know that is if…

"So you guys are no joke, huh? The serious kind of baddies?" I say it mockingly to show I'm not scared of them.

But when the blond replies, I have to admit I'm losing the battle.

"Oh, yeah," he says with an amused laugh. "We're the *dead* serious kind."

6

ANDREY

Natalia Boone.

The details of her life are splayed out before me, and I damn near fall asleep reading it. "Mundane" doesn't even begin to describe her.

She lives in a four-hundred-square foot studio in Queens. Works a dead-end job at an insurance company downtown. No loans, no criminal history, not even a goddamn parking ticket.

And yet, somehow, she's managed to find herself on my radar.

"Is this all you managed to dig up?"

Shura paces behind the couch in my hotel room, forever restless. "The girl's clean, 'Drey. There was nothing to find."

Her phone is lying on the coffee table next to her purse. It only took me a few minutes to hack into it. Even that was a disappointment. Apart from a bunch of messages and calls to

"Aunt Annie" and the infamous Katya Petrova, her social circle is empty.

Her Notes app is filled with a list of romance novel titles under the header ***Books to read on the subway*** and a grocery list consisting of exactly two items: boxed wine and Cherry Garcia ice cream.

The girl certainly seems clean. Pure as the driven snow, really.

In other words—too good to be true.

Maybe Nikolai picked her for this exact reason.

Shura's phone vibrates and he ambles over to the door. "They're here, boss."

I gesture for him to let them in. Leif escorts her through, bows briefly in my direction, then steps back out into the hall, closing the door behind him.

The sexy green dress she was wearing at the beginning of the night is gone. She's swapped it out for an oversized t-shirt that barely covers her ass. If my Spanish can be trusted, I'm pretty sure her shirt reads "dirty."

It's a little on the nose, considering she fucking reeks. A corrosive mixture of big city stink and the sweat of fear.

"Natalia—" She flinches when I use her name. "Long time, no see."

Her green eyes are wild as she raises her bound wrists towards me and sneers. "Untie me. *Now*."

The last time I was given a command was from my father. That was years ago.

Emerald Malice

It's kind of funny—almost endearing—that this little bird thinks she can get away with bossing me around, when she's the one with her hands tied together.

She seems to realize the same thing a second later, because her tone softens considerably. "Please."

I pull out my engraved switchblade knife. With one swift slice, her hands are free.

A second later, one of those hands flies out and slaps me.

She shrinks back immediately, gawking in disbelief at the offending hand as though it acted without her permission.

"That was a foolish choice, Ms. Boone," I rasp. Panic drains the color from her face. "The last person who laid a hand on me is rotting in an unmarked grave."

Her green eyes go wide. "Y-you're just trying to scare me…"

"Care to test that theory?"

"Not really, no." She shudders. "I don't want any trouble, okay? I just wanna go home."

"You should have thought about that before you decided to crash my party."

"I wasn't even aware—" She breaks off, biting her bottom lip to hold back the rest of her explanation. "Listen, tonight was just one big misunderstanding. If you let me go, I promise you won't ever have to see my face again."

Now, why would I agree to that? That pretty little face has so much to offer.

"I might let you go… *if* you answer a few questions for me."

She pulls down the t-shirt as if she can miraculously make it reach her knees. "You can't do this! This is kidnapping! And… and… Look, you can't keep me here against my will."

"I think you'll find the only will that matters here is mine." I walk back to the couch. "Take a seat."

"I'd rather stand."

Shrugging, I sit down right in front of her purse and phone. She clocks them right away and makes a grab for them.

I slide her belongings closer to me. "Not so fast. You want your things? You'll have to earn them back." I point at the couch with my switchblade. "Sit, Ms. Boone. I won't ask you again."

She falls heavily into the armchair across from me. The t-shirt rides all the way up, revealing a seductive stretch of inner thigh before she crosses her legs.

"What do you want to know?" She's trying to come off as confident and commanding, but she's failing miserably. I see the signs everywhere—her quivering hands, her wobbly lip, the side-to-side darting of her eyes.

"When did you first meet my brother?"

"I don't know. Just… around."

I sigh and start to stand like that ends that. "If you're uninterested in your freedom, then I'll just leave you—"

"Neon Moon!" she blurts. "We met at Neon Moon."

Fuck me. That shithole is one of the places Nikolai used as a meat market for his "merchandise," his sick way of referring to the women and children he'd sell to his equally sick clientele before I put an end to that business.

Maybe Natalia and her friend are working for Nikolai after all.

"You go there often?"

"I don't go there at all, if I can help it," she spits. "I was forced there one night by my pushy-as-hell best friend because she wanted me to meet the guy she was dating."

She crosses her hands over her chest, causing the t-shirt to ride up even higher. *Is she still wearing underwear or has that gone the same way as her dress?*

"If she'd just listened to me back then when I told her what I thought of Viktor—" There's no mistaking the disgust when she says his name. "—which is that he seemed like a rich, arrogant, narcissistic asshole, I wouldn't be in this mess right now. No offense."

I can't help but laugh. "None taken. You really hit the nail on the head with my brother."

"Yeah, well, I'm a pretty good judge of character. Except, apparently, with you."

"Is that right?" I fold one ankle over the opposite knee and lean back in my seat. "Go on; don't let me stop you. Tell me what you really think of me."

"I thought you were kinda nice when I first met you. Cold and arrogant, sure, but still the kind of guy who'd walk a girl to her door in the middle of the night or… or… offer her a handkerchief when she was sweating…" Those green eyes flicker to me. "Clearly, I was wrong. You're not a nice guy. You're a bully and an asshole. Just like your brother."

I tilt my head to the side as I look at her. "If my brother really is the worthless sack of shit you clearly think he is, why turn up at this wedding at all?"

"That was all Katya!" she explodes. "I thought we were having a girls' night out. I had no idea she was planning on roping me into her insane little revenge plot." She jumps to her feet. "And before you insult me by asking—*no*, I am most definitely *not* your brother's mistress and I am definitely *not* carrying his baby!"

It takes all my effort to suppress a laugh. Who knew interrogations could be so amusing?

"So, you're not one of my brother's many conquests. Congratulations. But your friend…"

She freezes. "My friend has bad taste in men. That's not a crime." She looks around the hotel room. "Where is she?"

"I'd worry about yourself right now."

She sighs. "Listen, I get it: Viktor is a dangerous man. You're a dangerous man. I've got the message, loud and clear. I'm not about to go tell anyone."

I get to my feet, towering over her. "Who would you tell?"

"No one. That's my point."

I stalk around the coffee table. She shrinks more and more with every step. "Ever heard of Nikolai Rostov?"

"Who?"

"You've spent time at the Neon Moon. Surely his name came up."

"I've been at that club exactly once and I did not enjoy any part of it." She wrinkles her nose. "The men looked at me like I was meat and the waitresses had dead eyes and…" She shakes off the memory she's obviously reliving. "I don't know who this Nicholas guy is, okay?"

"Nikolai."

"See? I don't even know his name."

"Or you're just a very good actress."

"Look at me. How likely do you think that is?"

The chuckle nearly escapes before I manage to stuff it back down. "I'll admit: not very."

"Exactly." She sounds relieved. "Now, can I *please* go home?"

"Yes."

Her jaw drops. "Yes?"

I nod. "I'll drive you myself."

The relief in her eyes disappears at once. "That's really, really not necessary." She picks up her purse and her phone. "I can get myself home now that I have my stuff."

"I may not be a nice man, *lastochka*—but your initial assessment of me wasn't completely wrong, either. I am the type of man who feels the need to get a woman back home safely in the middle of the night."

"Why do I get the feeling there's an ulterior motive attached to this act of chivalry?"

I don't bother answering her question, though the obvious answer is that there's always an ulterior motive. I just smile and gesture towards the door. "After you, Ms. Boone."

She scowls, unwilling to turn her back on me completely. "Do I have a choice?"

"No," I say, finally letting loose the laugh I've been holding back. "None at all."

7

ANDREY

"There it is," she says. "The building at the end of the street."

I would've seen it myself, but I was fixated on watching her knee bounce nervously for the last fifteen minutes. When I look up, my face curdles into a frown.

"This is where you live?" I make no attempt to mask my disgust.

"We can't all live in ten-million-dollar brownstones," she snaps back. "Some of us have to make do."

Shura parks and stays behind the wheel as I get out of the car along with Natalia. "I'd call it a rat-infested hole in the wall, but that would be disrespectful to rats, holes, and walls."

"Don't be an asshole." She bats at my arm with the back of her hand.

It's such a familiar gesture that I turn to her in surprise. She must be just as surprised, because she looks away from me pointedly. "Well, anyway... Thanks for the ride. I don't think we'll see each other again, so—"

"You're not going to invite me in?"

"Invite you in where?"

I answer by striding past her and through the front door of her building. After a moment, Natalia groans and follows me.

A lightbulb in what barely passes for a lobby flickers to life for a moment before it thinks better of it and snuffs itself right back out. Bugs and rodents skitter in the ceiling.

"Come on," Natalia orders as she heads for the stairs. "This way. You're in for a hike."

"Let me guess: the elevator's out of order?"

"Has been since I moved in. But on the bright side, I've got great calves now."

On the seventh-floor landing, Natalia leads me to the apartment on the right—*702*. She unlocks the door and flips a switch. Cheap fluorescent light floods the apartment.

"Go ahead," she sighs, sweeping an arm to encompass the room. "Judge away."

It takes me a matter of seconds to get the measure of the place. The bones of it are as much of a disgrace as the rest of the building. Water-stained walls, cracked crown molding, windowsills dripping murky, rust-colored condensation from A/C box units.

But there is life here in spite of all that. A haphazard pile of books next to a couch with a well-worn butt imprint on one of the cushions. Floating bookshelves with carefully arranged knickknacks—shot glasses and coffee mugs, crystal balls, hand-painted watercolors.

And photographs. So many photographs.

Emerald Malice 55

I pull down a framed picture of a young girl with a gap-toothed grin, hedged in on either side by a man and a woman.

"How old were you in this picture?"

"Six," she murmurs without hesitation. "It was right after I turned six."

I peer closer. She inherited her mother's looks—the dark hair, the heart-shaped face, the small button nose. Her father's contribution is limited to those bright emerald eyes.

Suddenly, I'm looking at my empty hands. Natalia has plucked the frame from my grasp and flattened it against her chest. "Let me get you a glass of water."

She walks the frame into the kitchen and stashes it in a drawer.

She's calmer with something to do, but even as she fills a glass with water and slides it across the counter towards me, she's tense.

"When did they die?"

She freezes. Her breath rattles in her chest. "You really need to leave."

"You haven't answered all my questions."

"Ask better ones then."

"Does your friend spend a lot of time at Neon Moon?"

Those green eyes sharpen. "Leave Katya out of it. She may have horrible taste in men, but that doesn't make her guilty of… whatever it is you're accusing her of."

"Spying for Nikolai Rostov."

"Spying?" she splutters in disbelief. "You obviously don't know Katya Petrova very well. If you did, you would know that she's the least subtle person in the world. She'd make a horrible spy."

"Petrova? She's Russian?"

Natalia's cheeks flood scarlet. "Listen, she's not... she's not like you. She's not part of your crowd."

I round the kitchen counter slowly, cornering her against the sink. "And what *is* my crowd, exactly?"

Her eyes slink down to my waist and I realize she's just clocked the gun in my holster. "Oh, God," she whispers. "It's true..."

"You're going to have to be more specific."

Her gaze locks on mine. "You're in some sort of... mafia. The Russian variety. Katya said it's called a... a—"

"Bratva."

Goosebumps spread across her throat. The moonlight streaming in from the window behind her highlights the soft, wispy hairs on her arms, each of them standing on end.

"Your friend seems to know an awful lot for someone you claim is completely out of the loop."

Her jaw tightens and she pushes herself off the sink. "Katya was just repeating to me all the bullshit *your* brother told her!" she cries out. "She didn't actually believe any of it."

"Until tonight. When you two little butterflies decided to fly right into a spider's web. You know what happens when you try to escape a spider's web, don't you?" I take another step towards her and she backs further against the sink. "You thrash and you fight and you scream and you beg. But the more resistance you put up, the deeper you get entangled."

She tries to put a brave face on. "Thanks for the Discovery Channel lesson, but I'm more of an HGTV girl myself."

I put a palm against her slim, trembling throat. Softly. Just to feel her pulse. "You don't get to walk away from me until I say you can, *lastochka*."

She's gone very still. Her eyes are rippling with fear, but she lifts her chin.

"You're good at this, aren't you?" she whispers. "Threats. Intimidation."

"If you want to call it that."

"Are all your victims helpless women?"

I press myself against her, feeling her soft curves meet the hard ridges of my body. "I'm willing to bet you're not as helpless as you pretend to be."

"Yeah?" Her breath is warm. She leans closer. "You're not wrong."

Out of nowhere, she reaches towards my holster.

Before I can stop her, she snatches my gun and aims it right at my face.

I can only laugh. I wonder if she knows that I could disarm her so easily. One swift move is all it would take. But frankly…

I'm dying to know what she'll do next.

8

NATALIA

What the hell was I thinking?

I am literally holding a gun. A *gun*. Not only that, but it's pointed right at a human being.

Forget the part about this particular human being more than deserving of being held at gunpoint. It's still not something I can condone.

Ever since the night of my parents' carjacking, I've seen guns as nothing but ugly, black, metal instruments of death. The tiniest bit of pressure and *bam,* someone loses a father, a mother…

Yet here I am, threatening to use it.

"Threatening" being the operative word, because Lord knows there is nothing in this world that will compel me to actually pull the trigger.

Still, *he* doesn't know that.

"Back up now or I'll shoot."

Andrey's lips twitch, fighting a smile. "First rule of the Bratva: never make a threat you don't intend to keep."

Scratch that. He knows.

In my desperation, though, I double down. "I'm serious. I will shoot."

"Ever heard of Newton's First Law?" he asks conversationally. "'Objects in motion stay in motion.' Shoot me now and it won't stop there. You could hit a neighbor across the hall. An innocent person in the building next door. One stray bullet can do more damage than you know."

He keeps his eyes fixed on me. Not the gun—*me*.

"Or maybe you do know…?" he ponders idly. His gaze flickers to the cabinet where I stowed away the photograph of my parents after tearing it out of his hands. "They must have died suddenly. When you were young enough to be forced to rely on… Aunt Annie, perhaps?"

My stomach roils. How the hell has he deduced so much about me so fast? Maybe it's all smoke and mirrors, part of the illusion of power and control. Maybe he's had a full background search done. Although why on earth he'd even care about my past is beyond me.

"You don't know me."

He turns and walks away from me. *How the hell do you turn your back on a freaking gun?* I follow him into the living room with my arms still raised. They're starting to shake.

"I know enough." He looks over my collection of romance novels stacked high next to the couch. "I know that your life is small."

I grimace. I'd be insulted if he wasn't so on the nose. Katya accused me of the exact same thing a few hours ago, and he's as spot on as she was.

"I know that you like your adventures confined to the pages of saccharine love stories or caged safely behind a television screen." He walks towards me again, completely unconcerned by the gun, even when the nuzzle is scarcely an inch from his chest.

Each word pierces me right in the chest. His mouth is doing more damage than this gun ever could.

"I know that you picked a best friend who's completely different from you so that you can live vicariously through her."

Please be done. Please be done. Please be done. But I know instinctively that he's saving the final blow for last.

"Probably because you're too scared to live for yourself."

And there it is. If I was ever gonna pull this trigger, it'd be now.

"How dare you?" I breathe.

He laughs—*laughs*—right in my face, the bastard. "Am I wrong?"

He's not. That's the problem.

"It's okay, *lastochka*. Just put down the gun and no one needs to get hurt."

Easy for him to say after he's done all the hurting.

"You're not going to shoot," he adds quietly. "We both know that."

I could prove him wrong right now. I could shoot him—just in the leg, nothing crazy, nothing fatal—and watch his smug confidence bleed out of him.

The clock ticks in the corner. Andrey raises his hand slowly to take the gun.

"Don't," I whisper as a tear slides down my cheek.

His eyes lock in on that one tear as though he's never seen something quite as offensive. "Drop the gun, *lastochka*."

A sob slips from between my lips. I'm gripping the gun so tightly that it really is in danger of going off in my hand. Maybe that's what I want…

His hand is inches from mine. Just when I think he's going to grab the gun, his fingers brush against mine instead. In the end, that's all it takes. One moment of skin-to-skin contact and the fight leaves my body. I surrender the weapon.

He tucks it smoothly into its holster before his attention is back on me. "Are you okay?"

I blink stupidly, cheeks wet with tears. "I just held a gun to your head and you're asking me if *I'm* okay?"

"I don't waste my time with fear."

Bullshit, I want to spit in his face. *Everyone is scared of something. I'm scared of guns and rainy midnights—and now, you.*

But this man in front of me… He's not bluffing. He's not pretending. He's immune to all the little things that have kept me in the same small circles all my life.

If only I could imbibe just a little bit of his confidence, a little bit of his fearlessness… maybe then I could have an adventure of my own, instead of piggybacking on everyone else's.

"I'm not like you," I whisper, not really sure myself what's coming next. "But... I wish I was."

He grazes my cheek with his hand. "One of me is more than enough, Natalia Boone. What the world needs is more of you."

Like everything else Andrey says, I believe it immediately. On a bone-deep, cell-deep, soul-deep level. I feel like a tuning fork that's been waiting its whole life to meet the right vibration—and now, I'm just resonating with *him*.

I start thinking crazy things. Maybe, just for tonight, I can be the right kind of person.

Someone adventurous; someone fearless.

Someone like him.

He nudges my chin up, forcing me to meet his eyes. *Blue*. Those little flecks hiding amidst the gray, they're a deep, dark blue. I've never seen eyes like his before.

"Do you want me to leave?" he asks.

My lips tremble with the weight of all the answers I ought to give. *You should. It'd be better for all of us if you did.*

Instead, I say the one thing I never, ever should've said.

"No."

His lips find mine, soft as a whisper. I'm overwhelmed by the scent of whiskey for a moment, then warmth slides over my body like a second skin.

I stretch onto my tiptoes and suddenly, *I'm* the one deepening the kiss. *I'm* the one grabbing the lapels of his jacket. *I'm* the one pressing my body against his and mewling for more.

It feels like the world dissolves. It wilts away around us and all I can see and hear and think is him.

My clothes wilt away, too, as Andrey's mouth trails kisses down the curve of my throat. It isn't until a blast of chilly A/C ripples over my bare skin that I remember just how we got in this position.

Suddenly self-conscious, I peel away from him and hug myself. "I… I should take a shower first."

Andrey is half-cloaked in shadow. "No." He grazes my breasts the same way he grazed my cheek. There's a tenderness in his touch that surprises me. "Once I'm done with you, all you're going to smell like is me."

It sounds like a threat, but my skin sizzles with adrenaline. My hand twitches towards him, desperate to make some contact, take charge in some way.

But any confidence I have melts in the face of his.

He steps free of his clothes. It'd be overwhelming enough if he was *just* chiseled, or *just* bronze and tattooed, or *just* that perfect balance of hairy chest and gleaming skin that any perfume commercial actor would kill to emulate.

But when I see what kind of equipment he's working with, my brain literally short-circuits.

"You can't be serious," I mumble.

Andrey follows my gaze down and smirks. "Don't be afraid. I won't hurt you."

He pushes me back onto the sofa and then he's on top, his weight sinking into me, hot and heavy. I'm excruciatingly aware of one thing and one thing only: how absolutely, thoroughly, shamelessly wet I am.

Andrey realizes it, too, when he drags a single finger between my legs and brings it up to examine. "So fucking sweet," he murmurs as he suckles his own finger.

My brain is fully melted and leaking through my ears now, apparently, because all I can muster up is a monosyllabic, "Wet."

He laughs again. "You haven't even gotten close to as wet as you will be," he promises.

Five minutes ago, I would've bet you every penny I've ever earned that Andrey was a selfish lover. A *get-mine, fuck-yours* kind of lay.

I would've lost that bet.

Because when he slides between my legs, roughly parts my thighs, and devours my pussy like it's the last morsel he'll ever get past his lips, he proves me very, very wrong.

I thrash and moan while he licks up and down my slit and circles my clit in broad, delicious strokes. We'd both be on the floor if it weren't for his huge hands spanning my waist and keeping me trapped in place.

Then he slides two fingers into me and I'm coming.

It somehow lasts an eternity and a millisecond at the same time. Whatever it is, I'm still tingling with aftershocks when he rises up to snare me in an open-mouthed kiss. I can taste myself on him; nothing has ever been hotter.

"I could eat nothing but you for the rest of my life," he snarls.

Without waiting for my response, he lines up his dick and slides into me.

He was right about another thing: as wet as I was before he went down on me, I'm ten times wetter now. My desire slicks the inside of my thighs and there is no resistance as I part for him.

He looked huge before. He feels even bigger now.

Three thrusts in and I'm ready to explode again already. My fingers dig into his shoulders as each thrust knocks another moan free. For the entirety of my pitiful sex life, I've clamped down on my noises, too afraid of sounding foolish to let them out.

But Andrey isn't giving me a choice.

If I don't moan, I'll implode like a dying star. So, as he fucks me into the couch, harder and faster and more brutally with every passing second, I can't do anything but cry out to the ceiling.

Sorry, neighbors—I'm about to come harder than I've ever come before. You'll have to forgive the ruckus.

There's not one muscle I can move without Andrey's permission. He's got me fully splayed open and fully at his mercy. And as I come and come and come— *andcomeandcomeandcomeandcome*—I realize one horrifying truth.

I *like* being made his.

I'm still panting when he unleashes himself deep into my core, then immediately pulls himself away.

His body is gone and cold air invades. I wrap my arms around myself until I'm cocooned in a tiny ball, all the warmth zapped out of me as Andrey hunts for his clothes on the floor. I reach for the nearest blanket to cover myself.

I'm fully alone in my post-sex clarity because Andrey is already dressed somehow, utterly flawless once again.

A single glance in my direction makes it very clear…

Something has changed.

The silver of his irises has turned to steel. There isn't an ounce of softness left in the lines of his face as he stares down at me, cold and merciless.

"Is this it then?" I wish I didn't sound quite so bitter, but I'm not nearly as capable of curating my reactions as he is. "You got what you wanted from me and now, you're done?"

His eyes flash. "You did say I'd never have to see you again after tonight."

"You don't." I hate how my voice wobbles with hurt rather than anger. "This was a huge mistake. After you walk out that door, I can forget you ever existed."

Those glacial eyes betray nothing as he reaches into his wallet and pulls out a couple of hundred dollar bills.

He throws the money onto my coffee table and walks to the door.

I don't even have words for how this feels. *Fucked, paid, and abandoned like some cheap hooker.* If only he was done there.

But he stops in the doorway, the flickering glow of the hallway light illuminating half of his face, and says one more thing to ensure the damage is complete.

"I've already forgotten you exist."

Only then does he finally go.

9

ANDREY

It had to be done.

Natalia was looking at me like she wanted to cook me dinner and tell me about her day. She was looking at me like she wanted me to *stay*.

As I walk down seven flights of stairs, lit by bare flickering bulbs, I tell myself again and again that cold cruelty was the only thing that could correct her deluded notions of who she thinks I am.

Not the man you cook dinner for.

Not the man you share your day with.

Not the man you ask to stay.

I tell myself I did it for her. But the truth is, the moment she stumbled towards me, her eyes bright with hope, her lips pursed up in a shy smile, I sensed danger.

Fucking her didn't scratch the itch like I assumed it would.

On the contrary, when she came down from her orgasm, clutched in my arms, my sweat covering her skin, my cum dripping out of her, and my promise fulfilled because she *did* smell like me, *only* like me, all I could think was…

I want more.

It would have taken so little to convince me to stay. That's exactly why I had to leave.

Because the last time I decided to stay, I got to know the woman behind the pretty smile. And now, I can't think about that smile without also thinking about her cold, gray lips the very last time I kissed her.

Forgive me, Maria.

Shura is sitting patiently in the SUV when I emerge onto the moonlit pavement. I'm desperate for a smoke, but if I indulge, Shura will know something's up. It's a dead tip-off that something's on my mind, and I'm not in the mood to talk about this shit. Not any of it.

Even still, Shura eyes me curiously when I get into the passenger seat. "That took longer than I expected. I'm assuming you got something?"

I control my expression. "She appears to be clean. Did you find anything else?"

He holds up his phone. "Not much. She lost her parents when she was young. Carjacking."

I glance up to the seventh-floor window I know is Natalia's living room. A shadow flickers behind the curtains.

She wears the tragedy well, all things considered.

"I can keep digging into her background," Shura continues, pulling away from the curb. "She certainly fits Nikolai's usual profile—lonely, isolated, no family."

"What would be her motivation?"

He shrugs. "Money. Just like everyone else. Look at that dump she lives in—she obviously needs it."

"For now, she's a dead end. I'm more interested in the kid Nikolai sent to spy on me."

"He's being held in the Moir brownstone."

It's late to keep working, but I need the distraction. There's no fucking chance I'll be able to sleep tonight, anyway. "Fine. Let's go."

Shura changes course and, thirty minutes later, we're pulling into a quiet part of the Upper West Side. It's not the type of place anyone would expect to be hiding secrets and hostages, which is exactly why we use it.

Shura drives into an underground garage. The door closes behind us, trapping every last sound echoing between the walls. I step out of the vehicle and through a door that leads deeper into the basement.

At the bottom of the stairs, Anatoly is snoring softly. His legs are sprawled out in front of him, his head dangling off the back of a plastic chair.

He's facing another chair. This one holds a scrawny teenage boy with a mess of dark brown hair and roving blue eyes that seek me out the moment I walk into the room. He's got a purple bruise snaking up his jaw and dry blood caked around his nose.

Blyat'. He's a child.

I kick Anatoly awake and he comes to with a huffed snort. "Boss," he mutters, lumbering to his feet and vacating his chair.

I dismiss him with a nod and drag the chair over to the boy. Swinging it around, I straddle it. "Do you have a name, boy?"

He glowers. "I'm not a boy."

I snort. "My Aunt Olga has more facial hair than you." His clothes are ripped in places, revealing just how skinny and malnourished he is. I see ribs through the tears of his shirt, like a beaten street dog. "This will be a lot easier if you cooperate."

"I'm no snitch."

"Admirable," I concede with a nod. "But ultimately, stupid. Especially if you're loyal to scum like Nikolai Rostov." Rostov's name gets the desired reaction; the boy flinches and looks away guiltily. "He's not coming for you, you know. He has probably already forgotten you exist."

The words I said to Natalia—*my* words—echo in my head again and it takes everything I have not to grimace. *I've already forgotten you exist.*

"I'm not waiting to be rescued," the boy hisses. "I can take care of myself."

"You're certainly doing a great job of that right now."

Another dark scowl. Somehow, it just makes him look younger. "Go ahead and kill me then. I'm not afraid to die."

"Smart. Being afraid of death is a waste of time." I get to my feet and kick the chair away. "But *pain*... Now, pain is something else entirely."

His blue eyes teeter up towards me. There's a tremble in his jaw. And then… "Do your worst."

I have to give it to the kid: he's got a pair of balls on him.

"Do you know who I am?"

"Yes." The word comes out sharp and loathing. "Andrey Kuznetsov. I've heard enough to know I don't like you."

"Have you now? I'm curious. What have you heard about me?"

The boy's mouth clamps shut as though he's just realized he's said too much. He stares at the stone floor silently.

"Go on," I coax. "You won't hurt my feelings."

Shura takes a step into the room, cracking his knuckles. "I could loosen his jaw for you, 'Drey."

I pretend to think about it. "He might be smarter than he looks. Maybe you won't need to rearrange his face before he learns he's fighting a losing battle."

"You don't scare me," the boy says. "None of you do."

I actually believe him. This kid's been through a lot. I know the look of cigarette burns on the inside of his forearms— God knows he didn't put them there himself. The neat row of them is entirely too organized to have been an accident, either.

"Fair enough. Shura, he's all yours." I start to walk away.

I don't get far before the boy's voice echoes against the stone walls. "Wait…!"

I turn, oozing disinterested. "Yes?"

Emerald Malice

"Wh-what are you going to do with me?" As soon as the words are out, he winces. He looks furious with himself for stuttering.

"I haven't decided yet," I say honestly.

"You're not going to kill me?"

"Not today." I turn to Shura and Anatoly. "I want him moved to my estate tomorrow. He won't get freedom of the grounds, but make sure he's cleaned up and given a proper meal."

Anatoly's eyebrow arches. "You sure you want to waste a good meal on this street rat? He's a dead man walk—"

"Misha."

All three of us turn to the boy. "What was that?" I ask.

His blue eyes are fixed on mine, level and unafraid. "My name is Misha."

"Then I have a question for you, Misha. One that doesn't require you to snitch." He looks suspicious, but he says nothing. "Is the name 'Natalia Boone' familiar to you?"

The lack of any reaction says it's not.

"What about Katya Petrova?"

He shakes his head.

Fuck. I was hoping for a reason to justify visiting the little *lastochka* again, but it seems she really is a dead end.

It's just as well. I have enough on my plate. I may have stopped Nikolai Rostov's skin trade for the time being, but that doesn't mean I've stopped *him*.

We're a long way from the end of this story.

10

NATALIA

THREE MONTHS LATER

I've gotta hand it to Kat: she's trying.

Short of chaining herself to my apartment door like a climate change activist, she's made every attempt to right her wrong—well, wrong*s*, multiple—from the night of the Kuznetsov wedding fiasco.

She's sent flowers, chocolates, skincare products. She even bought a special edition of *Wuthering Heights* that I've had on my wishlist for years. After I slammed the door in her face and told her that my forgiveness couldn't be bought and our friendship was long overdue for a break and a serious reevaluation, she showed up with a neon yellow boombox and a stack of massive flash cards. While The Goo Goo Dolls' song *"Iris"* blasted through the speakers, she flipped one large card after the other, Love Actually style.

I know I've been a bad friend.

I know I'm a stubborn bitch with bad judgment.

I know I crossed a line and I will forever regret it.

Emerald Malice

I took things too far and I'm sorry I dragged you into it.

I can only stand here now and promise to do better.

To be better.

To be the kind of friend you deserve.

Please, Nat, forgive me.

I'll admit, that one made me soften up a little.

It took a lot of nerve and determination to shut my window on the serenade and turn off the lights.

The music shut off a minute later and she started yelling at my window. "Please, Nat! Just talk to me! I'll let you punch me in the face if that makes us even!"

She only let up when Mrs. Drummond from #501—that crotchety old witch—opened her window to scream, "There are people trying to sleep here! Save the drama for daylight, you crazy lesbians!"

I watched from the shadows as Kat gathered her placards and her boombox and slumped down the street.

The whole next day, my hand kept straying toward the phone. *Call her. Forgive her. Go back to the way things were.*

But there was no going back. The soreness in my thighs, even as it faded, was a reminder that things had changed in a permanent kind of way. So maybe it's Andrey I have to thank for this newfound stubbornness of mine.

I see him everywhere in my apartment. Staring at my pictures. Cornering me by the sink.

Fucking me on my thrifted couch…

I don't even enjoy sitting there anymore. Partly because it smells like him now. But also because of what those few minutes of so-called "bravery" cost me.

My pride.

My dignity.

My denial.

And worst of all…

My period.

I don't have to glance at a calendar or check the menstrual cycle app on my phone to know that, as of yesterday, I have missed not one, not two, but *three*—count 'em—*three* periods.

Which means I'm either in early menopause at the ripe old age of twenty-seven. Or…

I'm pregnant.

I spent the first month in a state of blissful ignorance. I spent the second month in complete denial. Now, here we are—month number three, and I'm fresh out of both ignorance and denial.

Which is why my weekly haul from the grocery store includes six pregnancy tests, all of which promise to deliver results that are ninety-nine percent accurate. One even assures me it'll do a happy little jingle when the result is ready. Just what this tragedy needs: a theme song.

It's my own fault, really. Why the hell did I think being brave would actually pay off? I'm not some heroine in a gothic romance; I'm a member of the real world where there are real world consequences.

Emerald Malice

I should've learned that lesson already. My father was brave when he stepped out of the car to confront the carjacker. He got murdered as a reward.

Because in the *real world*, you can't just go around confronting armed men and expect not to get hurt.

And in the *real world*, you can't have unprotected sex with handsome Bratva bosses and expect not to get pregnant.

A fact that I conveniently forgot the night Andrey Kuznetsov darkened my doorstep.

My phone starts blaring, and I grab it, grateful for the distraction. I'm so desperate not to take these tests and prove my worst theories true that I'd be willing to talk to Katya. But it's Aunt Annie instead. Much less problematic.

"Hi, Aunt Annie."

"How's my little Nic-Nat?"

Doing miserably, thank you. But instead of pouring my heart out like I want to, I go for a breezy lie. "Doing fine. How are you? How are things at the hospital?"

"Oh, the usual, honey. People get sick and I do my best to help get them better again." She shuffles around in the background and I long to be back in her tiny two-bedroom cottage with the cherry tree out back. "Is everything alright with you?"

Avoiding the couch, I slump down on the carpet by the coffee table. "Of course. Why do you ask?"

"No reason. It's just, you've called quite a bit the last few weeks. Not that I don't *love* hearing from you," she assures me quickly. "But I usually get a call once a week. And yesterday, I had three missed calls from you."

I cringe. "Oh, yeah, I'm sorry about that—"

"Don't you dare be!" she scolds lightly. "I just want to make sure everything's good with you. I would've called back yesterday, but I had a late shift."

"I figured you were at work. I was just… a little lonely, that's all."

There's a pause. "Everything okay with you and Katya?"

I don't know how she managed to put two and two together so quickly. Although, Aunt Annie knows I have exactly one friend and no one else in my life to speak of, so maybe it's not that big a stretch.

God, I'm pathetic.

"Katya and I are taking a… break."

"Oh, dear."

"It's not a big deal, seriously." I have to play it down. Aunt Annie is a worrier and the last thing I want is to stress her out about my troubles when she has people with real problems to take care of. "We just had a little fight. I'm sure we'll get over it soon."

"Has she been roping you into more of her crackpot schemes?"

I laugh. "You could say that."

"You wanna talk about it?" I can practically see Aunt Annie's brows pinched together in worry. "Or, if you need an outing, you can come spend next weekend with me?"

"Don't you have to work?"

"I can see about moving around a few shifts. Meryl's got her daughter's engagement next month, so she might be willing to swap with me."

My stomach plummets as I realize that I have succeeded in worrying my aunt. "No, no. Totally not necessary," I say as nonchalantly as I can manage. "I'm busy this weekend anyway."

"Busy doing what?"

I poke at the pregnancy tests lying on the glass coffee table. "Fun, exciting stuff! Stuff only a single woman living life to the fullest can do in the big city."

Aunt Annie laughs. "Well, have fun. Just use protection."

Now, she tells me.

I can only laugh before saying our goodbyes and hanging up.

"God," I mutter to my empty apartment. "Kill me. Kill me now."

No higher power seems to want to waste energy smiting me today, so I drag myself off the carpet, scoop up the pregnancy tests, and fumble my way to the bathroom. I pee on one test after another.

Six rounds later, my bladder is empty and my spirits are low.

I arrange the six tests in a toilet paper nest around the sink, but the doorbell rings before I can start my nervous pacing. I dash out of the bathroom to answer, once again grateful for the universe intervening to keep me from my own thoughts.

But my gratitude is short-lived. I open the door, only to come face to face with—

"Katya."

Her smile falters. She's got a beanie pulled down over her eyes. But she can't adjust it because her arms are supporting a huge gift basket filled with fruit, chocolates, and nuts.

I'm in the process of closing the door on her, but her foot shoots into the gap. "Wait!"

I scowl at her expectantly.

"Um… there's a cake, too."

She gestures to the floor, where there is indeed a pink cake box from one of my favorite bakeries in Brooklyn.

"I had it custom-made."

Sighing, I bend down and flip the lid up. Inside sits a beautiful cake in vanilla buttercream frosting with the words ***I'M THE WORST AND I'M SORRY AND I HATE ME, TOO*** in deep blue frosting.

One look in her earnest eyes and my resolve wavers.

How easy it would be to forgive her. How easy it would be to pull her into my apartment and pick up where we left off.

I could tell her about my little secret. I wouldn't have to deal with this on my own.

"Nat…"

No.

We've done this before. Too many times.

"You can keep the cake," I say instead. "I'm cutting back on sugar."

Katya withers. "Nat, please. I know you hate me and I deserve that. But I love you! You're my best friend and I hate that we're not talking. It's been months—"

"I'm not a pushover, Kat!" I explode as the very real pressure of those pregnancy tests in the sink weighs on our friendship. Then my anger deflates. "You know what? I can't even be mad at you for thinking that. Because I *am* a pushover. I *do* go along with things I'm not comfortable with. That's on me. That's not on you."

"Listen, Nat—"

"No, you listen for a change. I'm done being your sidekick, Katya. I'm done being the pawn in your games. I'm just done, period."

Her eyes are filled with tears. "I really *am* sorry."

"I know you are. But it doesn't change the fact that I went through something that night. And I'm not sure it can be undone."

Taking advantage of her shock, I push the door closed and deadbolt it.

I walk back to the bathroom, but I'm so preoccupied with seeing Katya again that I don't understand what the soft, tinny music coming from the sink is until I see the six pregnancy tests…

All winking up at me with big, fat, undeniable positive signs.

11

NATALIA

"... is it gonna be painful?"

The girl can't be older than fifteen or sixteen. She's wringing her hands together as she stares up at the morose nurse.

"No more painful than childbirth," the nurse says. "You should have thought about that before you decided to rut around in the backseat of your boyfriend's car."

The girl pales and her eyes veer to me. I look away, trying—not for the first time—to concentrate on filling out the forms the same bitchy nurse dumped into my lap half an hour ago.

The screech of another ambulance siren drones past, and I sit up taller. *Concentrate, Natalia!* I don't want to be in this dingy OBGYN clinic for a second longer than I have to.

I take another crack at the line item I've spent the last ten minutes staring at: **FATHER'S DETAILS.** Finally, in a fit of spite, I draw a long line through the whole section.

"'*Father*,'" I mutter under my breath. "Un-fucking-likely. 'Sperm donor' barely covers it."

"Done filling out those forms yet?" Nurse Satan barks at me.

I scribble in the last few answers and march the papers over to the counter. "Will I get to see the doctor soon?"

She doesn't look up from behind her desk. "You'll see him when you see him. Sit down until I call you."

Alrighty then. She's lucky the forms didn't ask me to rate her customer service.

I give the young girl a reassuring smile as I walk back to my seat, but she's too busy plucking at her split ends to notice.

I don't blame her. This place doesn't inspire a lot of confidence. But it's the only one I can afford that doesn't require health insurance, and by the looks of it, she's as shit out of luck as I am.

Another siren whistles past. I'm extremely glad I decided to take the morning off work to come here. I definitely wouldn't want to walk back home through this neighborhood in the dark.

The nurse jabs a finger in what I think is my direction. "You. You're up."

I get to my feet, but so does the young girl sitting opposite me. We clock each other and freeze. Nurse Sunshine over there scowls. "Not *you*," she tells me, as though I'm an idiot. "The girl. The scrawny one."

The girl swallows and follows the nurse around the corner, leaving me alone in the waiting area with nothing but the dull fluorescent lighting and four-year-old issues of *Vogue* for company.

My phone vibrates in the pocket of my dress. I pull it out, fully prepared to ignore the call if it happens to be Katya.

It's not. But the person who is calling isn't much better.

I accept the call reluctantly. "Hi, Byron."

"Hey, sugar plum. Guess what?" My boss plows ahead without waiting for an answer. "I'm standing in front of your desk and you are nowhere in sight."

"I asked for the morning off, remember? I filed the request last week."

"You never handed it to me." I can practically see his eyebrow cock playfully. Those wandering fingers of his twitching at his side, so ready to find my knee, my shoulder, my hip…

"I handed it to Mr. Ewes."

Byron tuts. "*I'm* your immediate boss, beautiful. You should have come to me."

"I'm sorry. It's just that Human Resources told us last month that—"

"Human Resources, *poo*-man resources!" he interrupts with a childish cackle. "Just come straight to me next time. I'll clear your morning, no problem."

"Okay. Thanks, Byron. Listen, I have to—"

"Why did you need the morning off, anyway?"

I stare at the door where the nurse disappeared with the pregnant teenager. "Uh… just a medical check-up."

"Lady business, huh?"

"Byron, I've gotta go; they're calling my name."

Relieved, I put my phone away. But it's another twenty anxious minutes before the nurse finally rounds the corner and calls me forward.

Emerald Malice 85

"Third floor. Room 12. There's a gown in there. Put it on."

I wait for her to escort me, but she just plops herself down at the front desk, leaving me to amble upstairs on my own.

It's a dark, twisted stairwell with a jagged chunk of metal for a railing that has almost certainly given more than one unlucky patient tetanus.

When I get to Room 12, things aren't much better. The floor is dirty and something that looks an awful lot like rodent droppings has been lazily swept into the corner.

I shuck my clothes and step into the papery gown waiting for me. I've never been more grateful for the sheet of plastic rolled out over the exam table. It's one thin barrier between my bare ass and whatever nightmarish superbugs are haunting this place, but it's better than nothing.

God, I can't wait to get out of here.

While I wait for the doctor to show up, I count two more sirens in the distance and a few short, sharp blasts that sound suspiciously like gunshots.

Then again, I can't really trust myself in that regard. I've spent most of my life since age seven hearing gunshots that aren't there.

The shrink that Aunt Annie took me to called it PTSD. Whatever it is, it gets worse when I have too much time on my hands and nothing to focus on.

Like, for example... right now.

Thankfully, the door opens a second later and a reedy doctor in a lab coat walks in. He's got about five hairs on his "mustache," which is bushy compared to his beard. He looks like he graduated medical school two days ago.

"Hi," I squeak.

Doogie Howser here doesn't return my cheery greeting. Instead, he consults his clipboard with a squint. "Natalia Boone, aged twenty-seven, three months pregnant."

He doesn't look up, so it takes me a second to realize it's a question. "Um… that's correct."

"Have you been examined before?"

"No. This is my first time. I was hoping—"

"Lie flat."

Before I've fully reclined on the examination table, there's a loud boom and then a scramble of footsteps outside the door. People are hollering in the hallway, but their voices overlap and I can't make out what anyone is saying.

"Is something wrong, Doc—"

"Wait here," Doogie blurts, dropping his clipboard onto the floor. "Just… fuck, just put your legs in the stirrups and wait for me."

He stumbles out the door and I gawk after him in disbelief. Something tells me that none of this is standard medical procedure.

I pry myself off the table and creep to the door, which I crack open just enough to allow me to peek out. I spy two burly men, their back muscles clenched as they support a third man who's slumped lifelessly between them.

There's no mistaking the blood staining his torn shirt.

I jerk away from the door.

I've had enough of guns and mob bullshit to last me a lifetime. Whatever is going on outside that door is none of my business.

Maybe, if I pretend not to have noticed, I can just get on with my appointment and then get the hell out of here when it's over. I'm not exactly flush with other options, so I resume my place on the examination table.

For luck, I even place my legs in the stirrups. Let no one say I'm not a good listener.

Minutes tick past. One, two, five. The sounds quiet down.

Then, finally, the door flips open.

I paste on a forced smile, but it wilts when I realize that the man standing on the threshold is no nervous, sweaty doctor.

This man is tall, broad-shouldered and decidedly *not* nervous.

In fact, he's never looked more in control.

"Fancy seeing you here, *lastochka*."

12

ANDREY

The last three months have been a fucking shitshow.

The campaign I launched against Nikolai the day after Viktor's wedding proved to be a miscalculation. I thought Rostov would have enough pride to fight back like a man. But, as it turns out, he's happy to fire bullets from the shadows and retreat into the darkness immediately after.

His guerrilla warfare has cost me good businesses and good men. I was sick of it the first time—after the fifth, sixth, and seventh episodes, I was fucking livid.

Then, today, I was sure we had them cornered.

It was a bold move on Nikolai's part, daring to strike the textile factory I own that's responsible for producing sixty percent of my drug supply. Fortunately, I increased security around the premises only days ago.

I also put some of my most trusted men in charge of daily operations, which proved to be a good move. Vaska spotted a worker he didn't recognize and sounded the alarm.

But it was too little, too late.

The worker was strapped with a suicide vest that took out him and four other workers. A dozen more were injured. Vaska himself took shrapnel in the gut. He was losing blood fast, and this shithole doctor's office was the closest resource we had.

To anyone with eyes, this seedy little clinic is not a place you'd walk into voluntarily. But I happen to have the doctor here on my payroll.

Which is why my men and I stormed in, Vaska wedged between Yuri and Efrem so we could get him patched up before he bled out.

Of course, I didn't count on spying a certain name on the patient list lying open on the nurse's desk.

Natalia Boone.

What are the fucking odds? Could it just be a coincidence? Or is there some grand design behind her sudden reappearance, three full months after our last encounter?

I don't find any immediate answers to those questions in Room 12. I *do* find her naked from the waist down, feet in stirrups, her face flushing as pink as the glimpse I catch between her thighs.

My first thoughts are depraved. So are my second and third. But once the shock of seeing her again wears off, I'm *pissed*.

What the fuck is she doing in a dump like this? *She deserves better.*

It's not saying much—everyone deserves better than a clinic that requires bulletproof vests and a vaccine just to set your toe in the door.

"Why are you here?" I ask.

"None of your damn business," she hisses like a viper. "Get out of my room."

"Is that any way to greet an old friend?" I scoop up a fallen clipboard and peruse the forms.

She looks like she wouldn't mind carving me up with the closest scalpel. Honestly, a part of me wishes she would try. I'd love an excuse to put my hands on that tight little body.

"'Friend'?" Her green eyes burn like they're on fire. "We are not 'friends.' We're not anything. You're nothing to me but a gigantic mistake. If I could take it back, I'd—"

Her voice dies in her throat at the same moment my heart leaps into mine. She must know it, see it, feel it—that my eyes have come across the reason for her visit today.

Her breath escapes her in a vague, haunted, "No…" Then she lunges forward and snatches the clipboard from my grasp.

But it's too late.

"Pregnant." My tongue feels dry, my lips unnaturally chapped. "You're… pregnant."

She scoots backwards, clasping the clipboard to her chest. "I… No, that's not…"

"You'd do well not to lie to me, Natalia." There's no mistaking the threat in my voice.

"Fine. Yes, I'm pregnant. But it's got nothing to do with you." The sweat beading at her temples says otherwise.

"Is that a fact?"

She backs away, eyeing me warily. "I don't want any trouble."

"Then this is the last place you ought to be."

Judging from the way she bites her cheek and looks around, she agrees with me. "It's none of your business which doctor I go to. You're not the father and this doesn't concern you."

"Who is?"

"Excuse me?"

"Who *is* the father?"

Her jaw drops. "Why do you care?"

I advance on her and she retreats, matching me step for step until she collides with the exam table and lets loose a soft, surprised, "Oh!" that brings my cock to attention.

"Because I can smell the lie on you. I believe I already gave you one warning; this is strike two."

Her chest is rising and falling hard and she's gone pale since I walked in. "Fine! Fine. We didn't use protection that night." She glares at me accusingly. "So yeah, I'm pregnant and… it's yours."

I already knew that.

But hearing the confirmation from her sweet, indignant lips makes it all the more real.

Ten minutes ago, I thought my adrenaline was pumping. With the smell of blood and smoke in my nose, the remnant heat of the bomber's explosion still scorching my skin, I thought *that* was dragging me into the present moment.

But this…

This is something else altogether. This woman is carrying my child.

I'm going to be a father.

I don't have to think back to know that she's three months pregnant; I've been painfully aware of each passing day since our last meeting. I've thought of her in idle moments and felt my body hum to life at the memory. Even when I've quashed those useless thoughts, she crops up again in my dreams. Night after night after merciless fucking *night.*

"You're under no obligation to do anything." She's talking fast, barely pausing long enough to inhale. "I don't need you to be involved. In fact, I'd prefer it if you weren't. I can take care of this baby on my own."

"Can you?" I ask. "Because from where I'm standing, you don't seem to be able to take care of yourself, let alone an infant."

Indignation makes her green eyes pop. "Asshole! That's not true!'

"Look at where you live." I take a step towards her. "Look at where you work. Look at where you've come for help. How can you expect to take care of a baby?"

The fire fades in her face as she fumbles for words. "I'll manage."

I shake my head. "I'm afraid I can't allow you to roll the dice and hope for the best, *lastochka*. Not with *my* child."

Glass crunches in the hallway, and I pull the door open while Natalia stutters behind me. She's babbling about "not wanting trouble" and "dangerous environments."

Little late for that, darling.

Through the crack in the door, I spy several of Nikolai's men emerge from the staircase onto the third floor landing.

Well, that decides it.

She's coming with me.

While she's still gibbering, I roll the doctor's chair over and wedge it beneath the door handle. It'll buy us a few seconds at best. Once that's secure, I pull out my gun and check the clip.

The gibbering stops instantly.

"W-why do you—Is that a—Why gun?" she stammers.

I don't have time to entertain her questions, though. Nikolai's men are coming and they aren't the type to play nice.

I stride to the only window in the room and peer out of it. It's locked and nailed shut, but on the other side of the glass, a rusty fire escape zig-zags down to the alley.

It's not perfect. But it'll have to do.

"Andrey, what the hell is—"

Her words are drowned by the blast of a gunshot in the hallway. She screams and slams a hand over her mouth. I grab her face and force her to look at me.

"Listen to me. That's all you have to do. Just listen." She stares up at me numbly. I have no idea if she's processing a word I'm saying, but that's another conversation I won't waste time having. "Everything is going to be alright as long as you listen to me."

I wonder idly if Vaska, Efrem, and Yuri have already escaped. They know better than to wait like sitting ducks. I won't sit around, either.

Especially not now that I have newfound responsibilities.

"First order: stay back and stay quiet," I bark as I grab the metal trash can from the corner.

They'll hear me once this starts. We won't have long.

I take a deep breath. Then I coil back and hurl the trash can through the window.

Glass explodes outward and Natalia screams. She's still asking me questions—"What are you doing? Where are we going? Who are those…?"—but I don't bother answering. If we escape, there will be time for that later. If we don't, it won't make a difference who is doing what and why, because we'll all be dead.

I scoop her into my arms and carry her across the broken glass to the window. I use my elbow to knock out the last of the shards, not caring when they cut me open, then carefully set her on her feet on the fire escape.

Footsteps outside the room thunder closer. The door handle jiggles and the chair I shoved under it groans in protest.

"Go," I snarl at her. "Run."

Gunshots thud into the cheap wooden door. It splinters, but it doesn't give up the fight quite yet.

She grabs my bleeding elbow. "Come with me."

"Go," I say again, gentler this time. "I'm right behind you."

She hesitates for one more moment. Then, *thank fuck,* she obeys.

Just as she starts maneuvering down the ladder, the door is battered down. I take aim and the first three men who pour through the door swallow bullets to the face.

I seize the momentary lull to haul myself through the broken window and out onto the fire escape. The metal whines beneath my weight, though one quick glance down says Natalia has reached the ground.

When I look up, I see a new face shoving his way into the exam room.

Nikolai Rostov.

He's lost a tooth since I last saw him. Lost some weight, too. His cheeks are hollow and gaunt. He looks exactly like what he is: a shadow dweller, a fucking ghoul of the underworld.

He sees me.

I see him.

I wonder if he knows just how much the stakes have changed —what I'm now willing to do for the woman waiting beneath me.

Then I catch a blur of motion off to the side.

One of the men I thought I killed raises his gun. Fires. I flinch away, but the bullet burrows itself into my shoulder.

Pain explodes instantly, hot and savage. A firebrand digging into my muscle. The power of the blast sends me stumbling backward, backward, backward…

I hit the railing of the fire escape with the backs of my knees…

And tumble over the side.

The last thing I hear is Natalia's scream.

13

ANDREY

I wake up with one hell of a headache.

An arm-, leg-, and torso-ache, too, actually.

Hell, even my hair hurts.

But I start to sit up, because pain has never stopped me before and it sure as fuck won't stop me now. Nothing in my world is different except—

I'm a father now.

That's different.

The realization of everything I found in that shithole of a doctor's clinic sits me right back down in my bed.

"Fuck," I mutter, just as the door opens.

"Oh, stop your whining. It's not so bad."

The whip-sharp words are followed by the sweet old lady who voiced them. Short, grizzled, and hunched, Yelena walks over with a basin full of water.

"I could always push you out of a third-story building and see if you still feel the same way," I grumble.

She sits down on the edge of my bed. "Don't let my appearance fool you. I'm nimble as a cat. I always land on my feet."

"Shut up and pass me the water, will you?"

Chuckling, she hands me the tall glass by my bedside, her brown eyes bright and perceptive behind her horn-rimmed glasses.

"What?" I snap when she doesn't look away.

"Care to tell me about the pretty little guest in the room downstairs?"

At least that saves me the trouble of having to ask. "Just a stray I decided to bring home. Don't get attached."

"Mm. Are you following your own advice?"

I narrow my eyes, but Yelena doesn't so much as blink as she stares back at me. Of everyone in my employ, she might be the least fazed by my temper.

"She's very pretty," she adds.

I put my glass of water aside as Yelena dunks a clean rag into the basin she brought with her and starts to dab at the bandages swathed around my shoulder.

I grit my teeth as pain crackles at Yelena's touch. "More so when she keeps that pretty little mouth of hers shut."

The smile on my housekeeper's face is secretive and knowing. "I'm willing to bet that mouth of hers is exactly what landed her in this house in the first place. You always did have a thing for the feisty ones."

I decide to ignore that as she places another rag against my forehead. It's ice-cold and does wonders for my throbbing temples. "Did you speak to her?"

"She wasn't in a very chatty mood."

I bite my tongue to keep from asking more follow-up questions. I don't want Yelena getting any ideas. Well, any *more* ideas.

As she moves to sponge my arms, I duck away. "I can do it myself."

"You had a hard fall. No one would blame you for taking it easy for a few days."

"I have neither the time nor the luxury of taking it easy."

"Because of Nikolai?" Yelena's gaze is piercing. "Or because of the pregnant little bird you brought home with you?"

I swing my legs off the bed and get to my feet. A little too fast. My head spins and I grunt in surprised pain.

"I told you," she sighs. "You need to take it easy."

I shake off her advice and stumble around the bed to where my clothes are lying on the divan. *Christ, everything hurts.* "She told you she was pregnant?"

"I'm sixty-two years old, *malysh*." She only ever uses that nickname when we're alone. "I recognize a pregnant woman when I see one."

I pull on a fresh pair of sweats and a t-shirt. "It's mine."

Yelena smiles as if she already knew that. "Well, I'll be damned. A little prince in the house—and a queen to go with him. What a nice change."

I skewer her with a glare. "Not a damn thing will be changing."

She laughs, heaving her old bones upright and toddling toward the exit. "How wrong you are, *malysh*. How very wrong you are."

The laughter follows her all the way out the door.

Ignoring the ache in my limbs, I thump downstairs—making liberal use of the banister to keep from falling on my face. Shura and Efrem are both waiting, lingering outside the room where Misha is being kept.

"'Drey," Shura greets with obvious relief. "Doing okay?"

I wave dismissively, even as my arm burns with pain. "Fine. What happened?"

"Reinforcements showed up just in time," Efrem explains. "Nikolai, miserable bastard that he is, got distracted and that gave you the chance to get away."

Shura scoffs. "You forget the part where he knocked you out and made a run for it."

A gleaming scab just above Efrem's right brow confirms as much. "He was running *from* me."

"Yeah, I bet you looked real scary with your ass on the floor."

Efrem scowls, poised to keep defending himself, until I hold my hand up and both men fall silent. "So he got away?"

"Snuck out the back with two of his men," Shura confirms with a sigh.

"The rest?"

"Dead."

"So we don't have any leads or leverage." I gesture towards the door of Misha's bedroom. "The boy giving you any trouble?"

Efrem shrugs. "Kid's all bark and no bite. He just hisses and spits in the corner when one of us walks in with his food. But apart from that, nothing interesting."

Shura takes a backward glance at the door. "Have you decided what you want to do with him?"

"Not yet."

The truth is, I've decided to let Misha live. I have no problem killing as many of Nikolai's men as possible. But Misha's not a man; he's a boy. He deserves better than an unmarked grave.

The only decision is: what the fuck do I do with him now?

"We could let him go?" Efrem suggests.

"What, so he can run right back to Nikolai with inside information?" Shura scoffs. "Don't be an idiot."

I ignore them both. "Releasing him is not an option. We can't trust him yet."

Shura's gaze turns thoughtful. "We could train him."

I've been toying with the same idea for the last few weeks. "It's not a bad thought," I acknowledge. "The boy has potential. He certainly has enough grit to get him through basic training."

"Grit is one thing. Loyalty is another," Efrem butts in.

"He's going stir-crazy in that room. It's not right for a young boy to be cooped up in a cell." Shura's arm twitches—the one with the long, twisting scar that seems to have no end. Shura spent most of his childhood locked in a cage by his abusive stepfather. He knows better than anyone how oppressive four walls can be.

"I'll think on it. Now, where's the girl?"

"Second room on the right," Shura informs me, tipping his head in the direction of the arched corridor.

I go there. The door is locked from the outside, like Misha's, and the curtains have been drawn. It takes a moment for me to locate her on the bed in the corner of the room. She's lying underneath a blanket and there's not even a hint of movement.

Is she sleeping...?

But when I approach, her eyes are open wide, staring at the ceiling above. She barely blinks.

"Natalia."

When I speak, she doesn't so much as flinch.

I move to the edge of her bed and run my hand along her cheek. Again—no reaction.

I pull the sheet off her. Her dress is a tangled mess. There's blood staining one corner—I don't even know whose it is— and a tear in the hem. Her face is clean, though. I'm guessing Yelena gave her the same sponge treatment she gave me.

I touch her hand and her fingers are cold.

Shock is one thing; catatonia speaks to a whole different level of trauma.

Intensely aware of the life inside of her, I grab her arms and pull her upright. She moves like a ragdoll, her weight sinking against my uninjured shoulder.

"It's okay, *lastochka,*" I croon. "You're going to be fine."

I start undoing the buttons of her dress one by one, hoping that inspires some sort of reaction. Maybe she'll bat my hand away or tell me to fuck off.

But she doesn't move as I peel the dress off her shoulders. Then I move on to her bra and panties.

The ache in my body doesn't extend to my cock, because that part of me perks right up the moment I catch a glimpse of her soft breasts.

But my arousal is quickly washed away by worry.

She's *cold.*

Lifting her into my arms, I carry her into the bathroom and settle her in the tub. It takes a few minutes for the tub to fill with hot water, but while we wait, I strip naked myself, grab a hand towel from the rack, and slip in behind her. I pull her between my legs and spend the next few minutes running the towel over her body again and again.

It's immensely satisfying to watch the goosebumps on her skin disappear. To see her begin to move. A finger here, a toe there.

Eventually, her lips part and a tiny sigh escapes. It's a small thing, a fragile thing. But it breaks the spell.

Suddenly, I'm struck full-force with the realization that this was not one of my better ideas.

Before I can find a way to extricate myself from the situation, her eyes blink open as if for the first time. "It's okay, *lastochka.* You're safe in this house. You're safe with me."

Her fingers curl around my arm.

I want to pull her closer. Hold her longer.

I want to make promises I have no business making.

I can't afford to do any of that.

So, reluctantly, I get out of the tub and lift her into my arms again. By the time I've toweled her dry and dressed her in clean clothes, my erection is only mildly painful.

I settle her back in bed and pull the covers over her chest, and she turns to me. Her eyes are filled with dazed awareness.

Which means the fun part is over.

It's time to talk.

14

NATALIA

I still don't know what happened.

It was a chaotic jumble of gunshots and broken glass and rusted fire escapes. Of Andrey's body falling through the air and hitting the ground so, so hard.

Adrenaline and survival instincts carried me through the worst of the nightmare. Then I slipped into this fugue state. When Andrey's men showed up and bundled me into the back of a big, black SUV, I didn't even put up a fight. Because, for some strange reason, I needed to hold Andrey's hand while they drove us to the closest hospital.

Except they drove straight past the hospital.

"What are you doing?" I screamed from the back seat, Andrey's limp hand clamped in mine. "You missed the hospital!"

"That's because we're not taking him to a hospital." The man who spoke had a sharp, aquiline nose and dark, ranging eyes.

"Why the hell not?"

No one answered me. The man—someone called him Shura—and said something in rapid Russian.

"He needs to see a doctor!" I insisted, staring at Andrey's pale, bloodied face.

"Trust me," Shura said. "Andrey Kuznetsov has lived through much worse than this."

I wasn't sure if he was trying to be comforting. If so, he was failing miserably.

When the car finally stopped, Andrey was carried in by two huge men, leaving me to stare up at the gorgeous stone mansion nestled between acres of thickly clustered red maples.

Shura led me to a room on the ground floor and bowed out quietly. I think he meant it to be peaceful—but the moment the door shut, the memories began to unfurl.

I tried to outrun them. I tried to wrestle them back into the special box in my head, the one marked **Repressed Memories: Do Not Open**, but the gunshots grew louder and my heart raced faster.

The next thing I knew, I was lying in a bed, huddled and shivering beneath the blankets, slipping slowly beneath the dark waters.

A kindly older woman walked in with a basin full of water, but I couldn't even summon the energy to greet her.

"Alright there, dear?" she asked.

It's not like I had an answer for her. *A little too much gunplay, I'm afraid. My PTSD is resurfacing with a vengeance. See you in a few hours.*

Sure enough, I was out like a light.

It was God-only-knows-how-much later when I came back to my body. To water. A bath. Warm hands, caressing and stroking feeling into my limbs again.

As the sensation slowly returned, it came with the nagging thought that the person bringing me back was the last person who should have the power to.

Now, Andrey pulls a chair to the side of my bed and sits down. His gray eyes are cloudy as they stare down at me. His hair is plastered to the back of his neck.

Why is he wet, too?

Oh, right. He was in the tub with me. The weight I felt at my back… that was *him*.

I shudder at the thought.

"How are you feeling?" As usual, his expression is perfectly unreadable.

I have no idea how to answer his question, so I ask one of my own. "How long was I out for?"

"Two hours, give or take." He's watching me like I'm a ticking time bomb that could go off at any second. "Does that happen often?"

I shake my head. "Only twice before."

I'm glad he doesn't ask what triggered the previous two episodes. That's a whole can of worms I have zero interest in opening with him.

"We need to talk."

All the warmth I felt in the bathtub has all but disappeared. He's looking at me as though I'm a problem that requires fixing. In his defense, he might not be wrong.

"How long have you known about the baby?"

My hand flickers to my stomach. "I've suspected it for the last few weeks. But today was going to be the official confirmation."

"Why did it take so long?"

"Because, believe it or not, I didn't actually *want* to be pregnant by some random crime boss. Shocking stuff, I know."

He looks thoughtful. It's making me more nervous than if he was simply angry.

"You can't keep me here," I blurt suddenly.

He looks surprised, then amused. "Why would I keep you here?"

"Does that mean I can leave?"

"You're not a prisoner, Natalia. You can leave whenever you want. I'll take you home when you're ready."

He's lying. This is some joke that I'm on the outside of, and I don't like it one bit. "Right," I say bitterly. "Because you're just such a gentleman."

He gets to his feet. "I wouldn't go that far. But I do want to make sure you're safe. If you want to go back to your apartment, I'll allow it. But that requires certain compromises on your part."

"Compromises…?" My throat is suddenly dry.

"You're going to have security around the clock until I've determined that the danger has passed." He continues right over the sound of my jaw hitting the floor. "I understand it'll be overwhelming, which is why I'll only assign two men to you."

"Two?!"

"I will give you my personal contact number. If you need anything, just—"

"I don't need security guards, Andrey!" I say. "It's too much. Not to mention an invasion of my privacy."

"Privacy is the cost of safety. Unless you want to be caught in the crossfire again with no way to defend yourself."

I stare at him, openmouthed and helpless. I would love to tell him I can take care of myself, but let's face it: after my pitiful display at the clinic, even the voice in my head is like, *Maybe bodyguards aren't such a bad idea.*

"Who were those men?"

"Men who will do anything to hurt me. And considering you're carrying my child—"

"They don't know that."

"Maybe they do. Maybe they don't. Either way, I'm not taking any chances."

I have to remind myself that his investment in my safety isn't personal. It's about the child in my belly. Which only inspires more questions.

"So… does this mean you actually *want* to be involved in this baby's life?"

His neatly arranged expression doesn't waver. "Like I said, I'm not in the habit of running away from my responsibilities."

"That's the kind of answer a politician would give. Diplomatic and proper on the surface—but it doesn't really answer the question, does it?" One corner of his mouth turns up and I charge on. "What kind of father do you plan to be? The kind who's actively involved or the kind who sees their kid for fifteen minutes every other weekend before the nanny takes over again?"

He's quiet and thoughtful for a while before he answers. "I hadn't really thought about kids. Nor do I think I'll be the perfect father. Far from it. But I didn't have much of a father growing up; I want to do better for my child."

As answers go, it's not the worst one.

"So… co-parenting then?"

"That seems to be the only way forward."

On the one hand, there's intense and abject fear. On the other hand—unadulterated relief. I'm hoping neither one is visible on my face.

I look around the room. Pretty as it is, it's not *my* space. Right now, I feel a desperate, clawing need to surround myself with familiar things.

"So… I'm free to go?"

"With two caveats."

"Two *other* caveats, you mean. Bodyguards Uno and Dos count."

He ignores the sarcasm. "You need to rest first. After a nap and a home-cooked meal, yes, you're free to go."

Just like his co-parenting answer, it could be much worse. Still, I'll hold my applause.

"And caveat number two?"

"We keep your pregnancy under wraps for now."

He doesn't offer up an explanation. That only leaves my mind to filter through all the possible reasons he'd want to play the Silent Game with regards to the little bean in my belly, none of which are very flattering.

He's embarrassed to admit he knocked up some nobody loser from Queens.

He's trying to figure out how to get me out of the picture after the baby's born.

He's got a girlfriend or a wife he's trying to hide the baby news from.

Instead of asking, I decide to let it go. Who am I gonna tell anyway? I don't want to worry Aunt Annie just yet. Katya is She-Who-Must-Not-Be-Named these days. And aside from that, I have no one.

Whether I like it or not… this secret is staying with me.

15

NATALIA

"There are some dumplings in there. And a little something extra for later," Yelena explains as she hands me a glass container stuffed to the brim with food.

"Bless you, Yelena." I turn to Andrey, who's waiting, all broody and unfairly good-looking, by the door. "Why don't you keep one guard and give me Yelena instead?"

I assumed everyone in Andrey's employ was a lost cause, but Yelena is an exception. The woman might very well be a saint.

He snorts. "This house can't run by itself."

I put an arm around Yelena. "You're a rich man. You can get yourself another housekeeper."

"Or you could just move in here. Save us the trouble."

I have no idea if he's joking or not. There's a glimmer in his eyes that makes me think it's a serious suggestion. But I laugh it off.

"Okay, okay, greedy guts, let's go." I turn back to Yelena. "Thanks for the amazing meal. And the knitting tips. I'll definitely try that loop you suggested."

I clamber into the back of the sleek, silver car parked out front and Andrey slides in after me. As we drive through the wrought iron gates, I peer out the window for a better view of the property.

Like its owner, it's all ridiculously pretty.

Wonder what it's like to live in a place like this.

I shake off the thought immediately. I'm happy with my apartment. What some would call "small,'" I call "cozy." What some would call "white-trash," I call "character." At the end of the day, call it what you like—it's mine.

"So, who're the lucky boys who get to guard me?"

Andrey inclines his head towards the young blond in the passenger seat. "That's Leonty."

Leonty twists around to give me a boyish smile and a wave.

"And Shura," Andrey adds. "He's in charge."

I unofficially met Shura earlier in the day. Unlike Leonty, he has "no nonsense" stamped all over his face.

"Okay, so how does this work?" I ask. "You guys camp out in your vehicle outside my apartment, watching for signs of trouble? Sort of a 'seen but not heard' type of situation?"

Leonty chuckles, but neither Shura nor Andrey crack a smile.

"You have a couch, yes?" Shura asks brusquely.

"Um… yeah?"

"Then that's where I'll be. Leonty will man the vehicle."

My jaw snaps open. "You mean to say you're going to be hanging out *inside* my apartment? *With* me?"

Shura shrugs, completely unbothered. "I can mind my own business."

"Have you seen my apartment? You can't swing a cat in there. There's not enough room for the two of us." I turn to gape at Andrey, who, like Shura, couldn't be less concerned. "I don't want anyone in my way."

"He won't be. Shura just said he'll mind his own business."

"He'll—You—You know what? No. He's not coming into my apartment." I try to meet Shura's eye in the rearview mirror, but he's not even looking at me. "No offense or whatever. I'm sure you're a stand-up guy and everything—you know, apart from the fact that you work for a Bratva crime ring—but I still don't know you."

Andrey sighs like a long-suffering parent. "You don't have to know *him*. You have to trust *me*."

"And what if I don't trust you?"

He clicks his tongue impatiently. "Then you're fresh out of luck, because you don't get a choice."

"Since when?"

"Since that baby came to life in your belly."

Apparently, keeping my pregnancy on the down-low doesn't extend to Andrey's men. Neither of them bats an eye, though.

"That's ridiculous. I get a say."

The aggressive silence from all three men is hugely annoying. Especially because they're all acting as though *I'm* the unreasonable one.

"If you're uncomfortable with the current plan, I can always have Shura turn the car around and take us back to the manor."

"Those are my choices? My place with invasive guards or your place with more of them?"

"Correct."

I scowl. "That's not fair."

He shrugs. "Life tends not to be."

"Fine," I mumble irritably. "Keep driving."

As soon as we get to my building, I jump out of the car before it's even reached a full stop and make straight for the door. I'm expecting Shura to follow me, and he does, but Andrey joins us as well.

"Didn't get a good enough snoop around last time?" I snap at him.

He smirks and says nothing, which is the most irritating thing he could possibly have said.

I open the door and trip on a pair of shoes blocking the entrance. The apartment is looking particularly shabby this evening, what with the empty coffee cups on the counter and the pile of dirty laundry I was supposed to take to the laundromat three days ago.

"It's not always like this," I mumble, trying to stow away the half-finished romance novel lying face-up on the coffee table before anyone can see just how trashy my taste in fiction is.

"Dear God," Andrey mutters in a low voice. "It's worse than I remember."

He picks his way through the mess and stops at the window, staring at the cracked, water-stained paint in the wall just above the radiator. My anxiety spikes watching him judge my living conditions, so I turn to Shura to busy myself with something else.

"You want something to drink? I've got water and... uh, actually, just water."

"Water, thank you."

When I pass the glass of water to Shura over the counter, I realize that his boss is missing. "Where's—"

"Is that mold?" Andrey growls, his voice booming from my bedroom.

"Who said you could go in there?!" I rush into the bedroom with every intention of kicking his ass straight out of it.

He's standing in the corner of the room, squinting up at a patch of ceiling that's covered in a rather artistic constellation of black and green spots.

"Uh... my landlord said he'd take care of that."

He made said claim six months ago when I complained about it, but so far, nothing has actually been done. Not that Andrey needs to know that.

"Do I need to speak to your landlord?"

"No!" I cry quickly. "I'll do it."

He casts one last dark look at my twin bed before he goes back to the living room.

Shura has drained his glass of water and is now hovering awkwardly between the kitchen and the living room. "Everything okay, 'Drey?"

The nickname makes me smile. Andrey is so not a "'Drey." Especially now, with that calculating scowl on his face. If I were less tired, I'd be more concerned about what he's planning.

Andrey barely glances at either one of us as he makes for the door. "No. But it will be."

He disappears without so much as a parting goodbye.

"Is he always so ominous or am I just special?" I ask. Shura's gaunt face cracks into a small, tempered smile. I'm so surprised I applaud. "Wow! You *can* smile."

He ignores that and leans against the counter. "You were right: there's not enough room in here to swing a cat."

"Thankfully, I don't have a cat."

He eyes the pile of books by the couch. "Surprising."

Scowling, I walk over to my lumpy orange couch and fall into it with a grateful exhale. "Tell me: do all Andrey's employees have to pass some sort of Broody, Sarcastic Asshole Test to be hired?"

"Wouldn't know." Shura meanders around the sofa. "I'm not an employee."

"What are you then?"

"His right hand *vor*. And his friend," he tacks on at the end.

"What's a *vor*?"

"Like a lieutenant. Sort of."

"Ah." I throw him a sloppy salute. "Aye-aye to that. And he's assigned you to me, no less. I must be important then, huh?"

I'm only joking—probably because I might just burst into tears if I don't laugh—but Shura's face is serious. "You're carrying the heir of the Kuznetsov Bratva. Of course you're important."

My heart does this weird little jump. "Okay, next vocabulary question: did you just say '*heir*'?"

He just nods.

I shove myself upright. "Let's get one thing straight: I'm not carrying an *heir*." I can barely say the word without cringing. "I'm carrying a *baby*. A baby who's gonna have a normal childhood and a normal life. Free of expectations and pressures and weird Russian titles from the guys who will *not* be following him around everywhere."

Shura crosses his arms. "It's a beautiful idea—"

"It's not an idea; it's what's gonna happen," I insist. "'*Drey* might be used to throwing his weight around and getting his way with you guys. But that's not gonna happen with me. I'm done being a pushover." I stab my chest with my index finger. "This former pushover will now push back!"

His skepticism disappears behind a careful smile. "If you say so."

I can't tell if he's impressed or laughing at me. But I'm done parsing these stone-faced assholes for some semblance of human emotions. Sighing, I abandon my metaphorical soap box for my hosting cap. "You can sit down, you know."

He hesitates for a second before he perches on the opposite end of the sofa, as far away from me as he can manage.

"I hope you like rom-coms, 'cause we're about to have a full-on marathon."

His eyes go blank. "Whatever you want."

I cue up the chickiest of chick flicks I can find, then head into the kitchen for some snacks. I have to admit, it *is* nice to be able to watch a movie with someone.

I don't even mind so much that he's forced to be here.

Man, I really need to make some friends.

16

ANDREY

"Why the hell am I here again?" Natalia demands as soon as I open the door.

"Good morning to you, too."

She squints at me. "Seriously, Andrey—I was barely conscious before Shura was banging on my door, telling me I was 'wanted' at the manor."

"Because you are. Follow me."

I stride off, forcing her to hurry after me. We pass through the foyer and into the living room. French doors open directly to the garden. I ignore the zig-zagging stone path in favor of cutting across the freshly mowed lawn towards the pool house.

Natalia huffs along behind me, struggling to keep up. Somehow, she finds enough air to mutter under her breath all the way there.

"… 'wanted at the manor'… like a dog… honestly, how do I get myself into… male version of Kat…"

The pool house is surrounded on three sides by sycamore trees whose leaves have just begun to change color. The house is red stone, elegant and cleverly designed to blend seamlessly into the landscape.

Natalia gasps when it comes into view. I watch her take it all in. As soon as she catches me looking at her, though, she schools her face back into the same surly frown she's been wearing since Shura deposited her on the doorstep bright and early. "Why am I here?"

By way of answer, I lead her into the pool house.

The exterior is understated, but the interior doesn't have any problem reminding you how flawless it is. It's like a secret garden—bristling with plants, beams of golden light pouring through countless windows and skylights. Wooden beams run across the ceiling and ornate carvings dance along the crown molding. Forest green tile adds a splash of color in the kitchen. She hasn't seen the bedroom yet, but I have no doubt she'll have to suppress another gasp when she sets foot in there.

"Okay, it's official," she mumbles. "You win; I lose. Is that what you want to hear?"

"No—"

"Even your *pool house* is leaps and bounds above my—what did you call it—'shit hole in the wall'? Rat's nest? Some other equally insulting phrase?" She sags. "You win this HGTV contest I never asked to be in. So, y'know, congrats or whatever."

I fold my arms over my chest and lean against the closest wall. "Are you done?"

She bites her lip and considers it. "Yes. For now."

"Good." I nod. "You'll be moving in here for the time being."

Her mouth drops open. "You said I could stay in my own apartment!"

"That was before I realized it was a breeding ground for disease and Netflix murder documentaries."

"I told you I would get my landlord to take care of the mold!"

As entertaining as she is when she's teasing me, she's equally delightful when she's rattled and ready for a fight. I can't decide which riled-up version of Natalia I like best.

"I did some digging and it turns out your so-called 'landlord' is a liar and a thief. He's had complaints from every single tenant this past quarter alone and he's seen to exactly none of them."

"How did you…?"

"Mold is not a small problem, Natalia. Do you think I'd let my child breathe poison for the first years of its life?"

Her jaw snaps shut and I know I've landed the winning blow. She spins in a slow circle, taking in the pool house with fresh eyes.

"Well, what about all my stuff?" she snaps at last.

"I'll have Leonty bring everything over today. It shouldn't take more than one trip. You're not exactly flush with belongings."

"How long do I have to stay?"

She asks like I'm trapping her in a four-by-two cage with no windows. "That remains to be seen. For now, this is the best place for you."

She mutters unintelligibly under her breath. Uncrossing my arms, I advance on her.

"I'm giving you the pool house because you said you wanted your own space. You'll have your privacy and freedom of the grounds. The only place I'm requesting you stay clear of is the east wing."

"What's in the east—"

"It doesn't concern you."

She sighs. "How very *'Beauty and the Beast'* of you."

"What?"

"You know, *Beauty and the Beast?* Beast tells Belle to stay away from the—" She cuts off mid-sentence when she sees the blank look in my eye. "Never mind. That's an uphill battle I will never win."

I clear my throat. "You'll also find that the commute to work is much easier from here."

"You're letting me go to work?"

"Like I said, I'm not interested in dismantling your whole life. I just want to make sure you and this baby are comfortable. *Safe* and comfortable."

Her face softens. "Okay. Right. Thank you." She says it like she's not sure she should be thanking me at all.

I'm not sure she should, either. Because as much as I like her teasing and as much as I like her feisty…

I think I like her submissive and grateful best of all.

Before I do something I regret in the quiet, sun-drenched

privacy of the pool house, I leave her to her new home and saunter out into the garden.

Shura is pacing on the upper deck, talking to someone on the phone. He wraps up the call when I approach. "Vaska woke up this morning," he informs me.

"Excellent. He'll make a full recovery?"

"He needs a few weeks and then he'll be good as new," he answers. "Just another scar for the collection."

I nod with satisfaction. *Fuck you, Nikolai.*

"How'd it go last night?" I ask.

Shura's restless eyes slip over to the pool house. "You know I'm not a big talker."

"I'm aware."

"She is, though." I suppress a smile, but to my surprise, Shura continues. "It takes a lot for me to like a woman," he admits, shuffling in place like he wants to sprint away from this conversation. "A civilian woman, no less. But I do like her. She's nice."

"High praise, coming from you."

He clears his throat uncomfortably and changes the subject. "She agreed to stay in the pool house?"

"I didn't give her much choice."

"I'm sure she loved that. Do you have a plan?"

I spent most of last night ruminating on precisely that. I went around in circles until I fell into a distracted sleep. When I woke this morning, though, I was no closer to figuring anything out.

"Not yet."

Shura jaw twitches, a telltale sign that he wants to say something but he's not sure if he should.

"Go on. Spit it out before you choke on it."

"Marrying her would make quite the statement."

The exact same thought passed through my head last night. "It would also make my child legitimate." I lean against one of the huge marble plinths that ring the garden. "But I'm not a fan of the timing. Nikolai's still a real threat and he seems to be getting bolder—"

"A mark of desperation."

"Perhaps," I concede. "But it just means he has nothing to lose." My gaze veers to the pool house. "That's no longer the case for me. Touting around a pregnant bride would only goad him."

"A marriage would help you shore up some power, though," Shura points out.

"Not if I married Natalia. The little *lastochka* will make a pretty bride, not a powerful one."

"I wasn't necessarily suggesting Natalia. Unless of course..." He clears his throat again. "... you *want* to marry Natalia."

I wave away the whole messy subject, as if my heart isn't in my throat at the mere suggestion. "It's immaterial. Political motives or not, I have no interest in marriage right now. I have only two priorities: stabilizing the Kuznetsov expansion—which includes getting rid of Nikolai—and making sure my child arrives safely."

A window opens in the pool house. I catch a glimpse of Natalia as she opens the blinds.

"Which means keeping an eye on his mother," I add in a weary murmur.

"Extra security?"

"When she leaves the manor, definitely. I want a four-man team put together. Their sole responsibility is going to be all things Natalia Boone."

Shura nods. "I'm on it."

"But ask the boys to be subtle. We'll get pushback if she feels stifled."

"I have a suggestion," Shura proposes, glancing towards the pool house. "What if we got her a guard dog? It would serve a dual purpose."

Sunlight streams through the tree branches. I have to squint to get a clear view of the pool house, but Natalia has disappeared from the open window.

"'Dual purpose'?"

"Well... I think it might help her to have a companion," he admits. "I just got the feeling last night that her life is... lonely. Empty. Babies grow best when their mothers are happy."

It's sentimental advice coming from Shura. Perhaps that's why he's having trouble meeting my eye.

"Thank you, brother," I clap him on the back. "I'll think on it."

He retreats into the house, but I stay on the patio, facing the pool house. A guard dog isn't a bad idea—especially since we already have a half-rabid stray trapped in one of the guest rooms downstairs. I glance over my shoulder, towards the east wing where Misha is being held.

Perhaps, if I gave the boy some trust, he'd offer me some of his in return. Although, exposing him to Natalia feels like a big risk.

I table the decision for another time. For now, I'm content that she's under my roof.

Right where she belongs.

17

NATALIA

It's annoying how well I sleep in my new bed.

I wake up at quarter to six, bright-eyed and bushy-tailed. Then I remember who's responsible for my record-setting night of REM, and I get grumpy all over again.

But it's fine. It doesn't matter.

Andrey Kuznetsov sure doesn't.

I'm ready to take on the world today—or, well, if not quite the world, then at the very least, I'm ready to take on the evil ne'er-do-wells of Sunshield Insurance, my employer and enemy du jour.

Armed with all my things—another item to be grumpy about: Andrey was right that it took only one trip for his men to bring my stuff to my new residence—I do some light yoga on the deck, followed by a twenty-minute dip in the pool.

By seven, I'm dressed in my favorite black slacks-white shirt combo, and it's go time. All I need is a little breakfast pick-me-up—preferably something buttery and sweet—then my nemeses at Sunshield should prepare for the worst day of their lives.

My cheerful mood hits a snag the moment I step out of the pool house.

Andrey is standing on the patio, clearly waiting for me. *"Dobroye utro,"* he murmurs as I freeze in the threshold.

The surprise isn't Andrey—it's the four tall men surrounding him, all staring at *me*.

"Come to audition your boy band for me?" I point at one of them with a head of tight, curly ringlets. "I'd go with *Permed and Dangerous.* Or, wait, wait—*New Curls on the Block.*"

Leonty, the boyish blonde who drove me to my apartment, is the only one I recognize. He's also the only one who laughs.

"Call them what you want; you'll be spending a lot of time with them," Andrey says drily. "You've already met Leonty. This is Leif." He points to a man with long, dirty blond hair. "That's Olaf—" Olaf sports a teardrop tattoo under his right eye. "—and finally, Anatoly."

Anatoly, the curly-haired butt of my not-all-that-funny opening joke, grimaces in my direction.

I stare at the motley group of charmers with a wry rendition of *It's Raining Men* playing in my head. Somehow, even my thoughts are off-key.

"Okay, well, nice to meet you all." I give them an awkward wave. "But I think four bodyguards might be a bit of overkill."

"Don't worry," Andrey assures me. "They'll be discreet."

"Look at them. A giant might not crush you underfoot, but it's still a giant. People are going to notice."

Andrey turns with a dismissive wave. "You leave that to them. Now, come on—you need breakfast before work."

"Andrey!" I yell, racing after him.

He doesn't slow down, so I have to jog across the grass to keep up. Not exactly the easiest thing to do in heels.

"Andrey, hold up. I need to speak to—"

I manage to fall into step with him, but before I can finish speaking, he turns to me with a disapproving glint in his eye. "Is that what you're wearing to work?"

I stare down at my favorite—and let's be honest, nicest—outfit. "Yes. What's wrong with it?"

"It's—" His eyes trail up and down my body. "You know what? Doesn't matter. You look fine."

With that, he turns and heads into the house.

"You're an ass!" I throw at his back.

I'm fairly sure I catch a chuckle before he disappears through the double doors.

When I finally catch up, he's in the garage, holding open the passenger door to a sleek red convertible coupe. I'm so distracted by the pretty car that I get in without a word. The door slams shut and, the next thing I know, Andrey's getting in the driver's seat.

From the side mirror, I spy my bodyguards climb into a huge black Escalade. "This is insane," I protest. "I don't need a whole army following me around all day."

"They won't be following you around; they'll be watching you from a comfortable distance."

"Whose comfort: theirs, yours, or mine?"

His answer is a secretive smirk. "What would you like for breakfast?"

My stomach growls. "Something that will soak up all this anger and resentment boiling inside me."

"I know just the place."

～

"Just the place" ends up being a gorgeous patisserie nestled in the heart of Little Italy. My mood improves—slightly—when a tray full of croissants and cherry danishes hits the table. The pastries are accompanied with the richest hot chocolate I've ever seen.

At my first bite, I let out a very loud and very inappropriate moan.

Andrey's eyes snap to mine and my cheeks turn as red as the cherries on the Danish. "Sorry. They're just so good."

He pushes the plate towards me. "Eat up."

When I die, I want to be buried inside a croissant, I decide. It is frustratingly hard to hold onto any kind of anger when you're eating food this good. I happily plow my way through half the tray before Andrey interrupts my gorging.

He slides a small envelope onto the table beside my empty cup of hot chocolate. "This is for you."

The night we slept together and he tossed money on the coffee table comes back to me in a rush. "If it's money again,

I'm gonna order another hot chocolate just so I can fling it in your face."

"It's a credit card. Technically not money, but I'll brace for the hot chocolate anyway."

Opening the envelope, I find a gleaming black credit card with my name on it. I'm hesitant to touch it; it just *looks* rich. "What's this for?"

"For anything you may need. I'm happy to buy you anything you want, of course—but this way, you don't have to ask."

I'm struggling to figure out exactly what I'm feeling. It *is* thoughtful.

But cards this thick and heavy don't come without strings attached.

"Is this a power move?" It's blunt, but there are no prizes for beating around the bush.

"No." He signals the waiter for the check. The moment the bill arrives, Andrey slips a fifty-dollar bill between the cover and hands it back. "Come on. You don't want to be late for work."

Stuffing the credit card into my bag, I follow him out onto the sunlit pavement. To my surprise, he's holding the passenger door to the convertible open for me.

"I thought my boy band was responsible for dropping me off at work?"

The Escalade is parked across the street, although I can't see any of the men through the tinted windows.

"I'll drop you off today. It'll give me a chance to check out where you work."

He says it so casually that, for a minute, it seems almost reasonable. I despise that little magic trick of his. "What does that mean, *you want to check out where I work*?"

"Wherever you go, my baby goes," he explains coolly. "I need to make sure it's safe."

"You have got to be kidding me."

"I never kid about safety," he deadpans.

I plant my feet and cross my arms over my chest. This is the last straw. He's spent the whole morning telling me how things are gonna be.

Sure, it's a pretty pool house—but it's *his* pool house. *His* bodyguards following me around all day. *His* credit card. *His* damn rules.

"There is no way you're coming to work with me."

He gives me a cocky smile. "Why don't you just get in the car, *lastochka*?"

"I think I'd rather walk."

I'm about to give him the hair-flip of my life when he shoots his hand out and grabs hold of me. The next thing I know, my back is pressed against the convertible and Andrey is breathing over me, those bewitching gray eyes boring into mine.

"I think not."

A few people titter as they walk past us on the street. I even hear a wolf whistle from a gaggle of passing men.

"Get off of me."

He doesn't get off of me—he does the opposite, in fact. He leans in a little more forcefully, trapping me between the car and his body—which, in the interest of being fair, isn't *not* attractive. His knee is wedged between my legs and the pressure he's putting on a certain part of my anatomy is definitely not appropriate for polite company.

"Andrey!" I hiss. "Stop it."

"Why? You seem to be enjoying it."

"People are *watching*."

He shrugs nonchalantly. "Let them."

"You're just gonna bully me until you get what you want, aren't you?"

"What I want is your safety, Natalia. I take care of what is mine."

My arms prickle with goosebumps. I try to swallow the unwelcome surge of pleasure that races through my body at his words.

"Except I'm not yours."

He grinds his knee harder against my pussy, kneading slowly in soft, teasing movements. We're gonna get arrested for indecent exposure if he keeps this up.

The problem is my protests are getting breathier and less earnest.

My cheeks are getting hotter and redder.

And my pussy is definitely getting wetter.

I'm so scared of letting out a moan that I have no choice but to clamp my mouth shut and pray that he finishes with me soon.

A pair of older ladies walk past us. Their casual smiles turn to shock and they avert their gazes fast. "Oh my…" I hear one gasp.

Bastard.

I bite down on my tongue and, just when I feel like I'm about to explode, he releases me and steps back.

I sag against the car, suddenly exhausted. Andrey, on the other hand, looks effortlessly calm and utterly composed. But a lopsided, borderline cruel smile simmers on his lips as he leans in, his breath hot against my cheek.

"Oh, you're mine, *lastochka.* You just haven't accepted it yet."

18

NATALIA

The nerve of that man.

You just haven't accepted it. I've been repeating that in my head the entire drive to work, getting more pissed off every time.

The problem is, I'm also getting more and more turned on.

Pissed off.

Turned on.

Pissed off.

Turned on.

It's as much of a headache as it sounds, believe me.

I'm still fuming when we pull up outside the ugly brown building that's home to Sunshield Insurance. As soon as I step foot out of the car, my four new shadows swarm me, a wall of man-meat in every direction.

"So much for being discreet," I mutter, loud enough for Andrey to hear.

If he notices, he gives no sign of it as he climbs out of the car.

I greet the receptionist, Marge, with a quick "Good morning" and breeze past so I don't have to introduce her to the cavalry at my back.

Thankfully, only Leonty follows Andrey and me into the staff rooms where my desk is. But I don't have to look around to know that every pair of eyes on the floor is directed right at Andrey and me.

Well, mostly the female eyes.

And mostly at Andrey.

Abby Whitshaw actually jumps to her feet when we pass her desk, but I keep it moving. I have zero desire to introduce her to Andrey. Particularly not in that blouse she's decided to wear today, which is about three buttons shy of professional.

My pitiful cubicle is wedged against three others, only thin half-partitions separating us. It's never looked more miserable than it does today.

"Well, this is it. Where the magic happens." I point to the glass doors in the far corner. "That's where the senior staff works. Lunchroom is through that door by the water filter and that's the filing room. You can go now."

Andrey doesn't budge. "As it turns out, I've met your boss before. I'm sure Richard won't mind me dropping in and saying hello."

Richard. I cringe like a kid being dropped off at school by an embarrassing parent. "Please, for the love of all that is good and holy, don't go in there and speak to Mr. Ewes."

"It won't take long."

Emerald Malice 137

"Andrey. Andrey!" I turn to Leonty. "Can't you stop him?"

He snorts. "That a trick question?"

Sinking into my swivel chair, I groan and drop my face into my palms. How the hell do I explain this to everyone else? How do I explain *any* of it?

"You get used to him, you know," Leonty adds in his rumbling baritone.

I drop my hands to glare at him. "How long did it take you?"

"I've known Andrey my whole life. So it took me... well, pretty much my whole life."

"Ha-ha," I quip as Leonty snickers. I throw a nervous glance at the senior staff room. "Your whole life, huh?"

"I'm his cousin. Once removed, but it counts."

"Does that come with perks?"

"Please. Andrey doesn't play favorites."

"Shocker."

"I'm gonna go scope out the rest of the place. Just—"

"No," I interrupt, using his elbow to draw myself up to my feet to see if I can spot Andrey through the frosted glass. "Stay right here and keep talking to me. I don't want Abby coming over here."

He glances over his shoulder. "Is she the one with the low-cut blouse?"

"The one and only. Don't make eye contact!"

The glass doors open and Mr. Ewes steps out, laughing

loudly. Andrey is sitting in one of the chairs behind him, looking all too comfortable.

"Natalia!" Mr. Ewes calls over. "Join us in here for a moment."

I plaster on a fake smile and slump my way into the office. "Good morning, Mr. Ewes."

"You didn't tell me you knew Mr. Kuznetsov!"

"She never tells anyone we know each other," Andrey remarks with a wicked smile in my direction. "Embarrassed of me, I think."

"Ha!" Mr. Ewes guffaws. "Embarrassed of Andrey Kuznetsov… imagine."

I've heard that laugh before. It's the one he uses when he wants to schmooze a client.

"Well, don't you worry, my dear—Mr. Kuznetsov has explained the situation to me and I'm sure we can accommodate the security measures you need."

If my cheeks get any hotter, I just might burst into flames. "Are you sure it's not an imposition, Mr. Ewes?"

"Not at all, not at all! Happy to." He turns from me back to Andrey. "It's a little early for a drink, but my office has just been fitted with a new cappuccino machine."

Andrey rises and waves him off. "Nothing for me, Richard, thank you. I need to get going."

"Anything at all you need, just let me know, Andrey."

They shake hands. "I'll send word through Natalia."

Mr. Ewes doesn't look in the least bit put off. "Wonderful. Of course. Whatever you need." He practically bows us out of the office.

"Jesus," I mumble. "I think I threw up in my mouth a little."

We haven't even reached my desk before our path is blocked by none other than Abby. "Arch nemesis" is a slight stretch, but only very slight. She certainly annoys the crap out of me. Now more than ever.

Her gaze is fixated on Andrey. I thought she was already operating on too few buttons, but she's proving that there is no bar she isn't willing to stoop under, because I could swear another button has gone missing since we arrived.

"Can I get you anything, Mr. Kuznetsov?" she croons without bothering with an introduction.

To his credit, Andrey looks at her as though she's a wet piece of toilet paper stuck to the bottom of his shoe. "Nothing, thank you."

That frigid tone would have sent me backing away, because I'm not a moron. Abby, however, is undeterred. "Are you sure? It'd be my pleasure to help out in any way possible." And just in case she was being too subtle, she strokes a hand along Andrey's arm and bats her eyes for effect.

I'm *this* close to pushing the bitch right out of our way when Andrey drawls, "Kindly remove your hand from my arm before I remove it for you."

Damn.

I could freaking kiss him.

Abby blinks, clearly bewildered that her magic boobs haven't done the trick. But at least she drops her hand. "I could show you the rest of the office, Mr. Kuz—"

I don't know what comes over me. I grab Andrey's arm possessively and pull him towards my desk. "If anyone's showing him around the office, Abby, it'll be *me*. You can go back to your desk now."

I can feel his smirk burning the side of my face. "Shut up," I snap under my breath.

My desk isn't empty when we approach it, because bad news comes in threes, apparently. Byron is leaning against my cubicle wall with a takeaway cup of coffee from my favorite café down the street.

My God. The whole damn circus is out today.

"Hey, beautiful," he greets in his usual inappropriate fashion. "I brought your favorite."

He extends his hand, but before I can grudgingly accept it, Andrey beats me to the punch. "It's not her favorite anymore," he says coldly, dropping the entire cup into the wastepaper basket under my desk. "She's off caffeine."

I glare at Andrey. "That was unnecessary."

Even if it wasn't entirely unwanted. I wish I'd had the guts to do that ages ago.

Andrey is staring at Byron with an intensity that's causing Byron's smile to malfunction. The man looks like he's having a stroke.

"N-no caffeine, huh?" Byron asks, trying desperately to gloss over the awkward moment. "New diet thing, or…?"

There's something about Andrey's sudden smile I don't trust. I trust it even less when he wraps an arm around my waist and pulls me to him.

"Natalia's pregnant," he explains. "We're having a baby."

19

NATALIA

I'm gawking at Andrey.

Andrey is smirking at Byron.

Byron is bouncing his wide eyes from Andrey to me and back again.

It's the worst—and, just to be clear, *only*—threesome I've ever had. I would like to get off this ride immediately, please and thank you.

"Pregnant?" Byron stutters. "You're pregnant, Nat?"

Swallowing hard, I plaster a smile on my face. "Surprise."

"Jesus," Byron exhales. "That's... crazy."

"For you and me both." I duck out from under Andrey's grip, but not before pinching him under the arm. "Excuse me for a second while I walk Andrey out."

I march straight for the exit without waiting for Andrey to agree. To my surprise, he follows without complaint. The moment we're away from nosy coworkers and in the lobby, I twist around and stab a finger into Andrey's chest.

I was hoping this finger was the first point of pain in a devastating series of takedowns both verbal and physical that I was about to unleash on his ass. Unfortunately for me, his chest is so obnoxiously muscled that I hurt my poor finger and wince in pain.

"What the hell were you thinking?" I clear my throat and rephrase. "What happened to keeping my pregnancy under wraps?"

He doesn't look in the least bit apologetic. "I pivoted."

"Clearly! My question is, *Why?*"

"You're already three months along," he says sensibly. "You're going to start showing soon. This was inevitable."

"So it had nothing to do with the fact that you were trying to mark your territory?"

He checks his watch like I'm wasting his time. "I'd have thought you would understand."

"What is that supposed to mean?"

"What was her name… the pretty blonde in the red blouse?" He takes a step closer to me as my face goes blotchy with involuntary anger. "When it comes to marking territory, let's not beat around the bush: you're as guilty as I am."

Leonty is chuckling by the door and Marge has abandoned any attempt to pretend like she's not eavesdropping.

"Leave," I hiss in his face. "Now."

"I will—as soon as you let me go."

His eyes fall between us and I realize my hand is wrapped around his wrist. I drop it like it's on fire and spring away immediately.

Andrey winks. "Have a good day, *lastochka*."

It takes a few seconds after he's gone before the angry blush on my cheeks finally fades. Feeling completely unmoored, I head back into the office, shrinking under the weight of the curious gazes aimed my way. Most of them stop at that—gawkers, nothing worse.

But not all my coworkers can take a hint.

"Oh my God! You're having a baby with *him?*" Abby pops up from behind my desk like a Whack-A-Mole I would dearly love to smite with a hammer. "Where did you even meet a man like that?"

"I'm curious about that, too." I peek up to see that Byron has joined the inquisition.

"Guys, I'd love to chat, but I have so much work to do." I shuffle some papers around to make my point, but neither one shows any interest in leaving.

"No, but, c'mon…" Abby cajoles. "How'd you get your hooks in him?"

"There were no 'hooks' involved. And we're not even together." I'm not sure why I choose to share that information with them—it doesn't exactly paint me in the best light—but I'm angry and it shoots out before I can think about it.

"You're not?" I don't like that glint in Abby's eyes at all.

To be fair, Byron has the same hopeful glint, albeit for

different—and arguably worse—reasons. "How does that work?"

"Haven't you people ever heard of a one-night stand?" I ask. "You know what? Never mind. All I can say is, if you ever choose to have one, use protection."

Abby scoffs. "He's rich *and* gorgeous. You can bet your ass I'd be poking holes in that condom."

"Classy," I mutter.

She smiles salaciously. "So what I'm hearing is, he's single?"

I have the sudden urge to cold-cock Abby right in the head. I allow the fantasy to play out for a few short seconds before I force a nod. "Sure. Yeah. Something like that."

"Excellent!" She does a little shimmy that makes her breasts jiggle. "Hope he drops you off at work every day." Having got what she came for, Abby turns around and struts back to her desk.

"I have to admit..." Byron's voice cuts through another little fantasy I'm playing out in my head, this one involving Abby and the freshly loaded stapler on my desk. "I'm relieved, too."

"If you want Andrey, you'll have to fight Abby for him."

He ignores me. "It means I still have a chance with you."

He might as well have poured a glass of ice water down my back. "Erm, Byron... Did you miss the part about me being pregnant?" I remind him gently. "I'm having a baby with another man."

"But you're not *with* said man." He shrugs and backs away from my desk. "There's hope for me yet."

"No, there's not!"

"Just you wait and see," he promises with a devious chuckle. "I'm gonna wear you down."

I hide in my cubicle for the better part of the morning. Turns out, trying to avoid your coworkers can make for a productive day. I'm done with all my work by four and frothing at the mouth to get back to the secluded calm of the pool house.

I manage to duck past both Abby and Byron on my way out. Leonty is standing just outside the building when I step onto the pavement.

"Ready?" he asks.

"I've literally never been more ready in my entire cursed existence."

Chuckling, he opens the back door for me and I clamber inside the car. Olaf is in the passenger seat, but my other two bodyguards are nowhere in sight.

"Where's the rest of the band?"

"We're taking it in shifts," Leonty explains. "They're on night duty."

I roll my eyes. "Ridiculous."

"How was work?" Leonty asks as though he hasn't heard me.

"Fine. I mean—no, not fine. But at least it's over."

"If the tall guy's giving you any trouble, I can take care of it for you," he offers. I frown at Leonty in the rearview mirror, so he clarifies, "The douchey one in the pinstriped shirt."

"Byron?"

He shudders. "Even his name is douchey."

I cross my legs and turn to the window. "He's harmless."

"Not from where I was standing. He's interested in you."

I wave away his concern. "He's a flirt and sometimes, he goes a little overboard. He's actually pretty nice. And he's a decent boss."

"I'm sure."

"I don't like that tone."

Leonty shrugs innocently. "I'd be careful there, that's all I'm saying. Andrey's not gonna like your friend sniffing around."

I sit bolt upright in my seat. "Andrey can kiss my ass. I'm not his property. And I'm certainly not his girlfriend. He has no right to dictate who can or can't 'sniff around' me."

Leonty and Oleg exchange a glance.

"What?" I demand. "What was that look?"

Oleg shifts nervously. Leonty, on the other hand, gives me a carefree smile over his shoulder. "You're new, so maybe you haven't caught on just yet: Andrey gets what Andrey wants. Always."

"Always," Oleg echoes.

"Yeah, well, mark today's date on your calendars," I declare. "We're making history."

They share another amused glance.

"Screw both of you!" I cry.

"Oh, don't get all touchy," Leonty implores. "I'm just calling it like I see it. Things will go easier if you just accept what's obvious to everyone else."

Despite my best efforts, I'm curious. "Okay, I'll bite. Tell me what's obvious to everyone else?"

"That, whether you want to admit it or not, Andrey's already got a hold on you."

I'm so rattled that I don't even respond. We spend the rest of the drive in silence. The moment we arrive at the manor, I unbuckle myself and streak out of the Escalade.

To my ongoing frustration, not even the peace and solitude of the pool house calms me.

I tear off my clothes and run myself a bath, hoping to drown the chorus of voices in my head.

So what you're saying is, he's single?

Andrey's already got a hold on you.

You're mine, lastochka*. You just haven't accepted it yet.*

And under all these fresh memories, under all these confused emotions, a tiny drop of doubt creeps in, tremulous and unbidden.

Do I have feelings for Andrey?

There's no doubt I'm attracted to him. He's handsome and confident. He has a fearlessness about him that I find incredibly hard to resist. It's the whole reason I talked myself into sleeping with him that night.

But attraction doesn't equal affection. Lust doesn't equal love.

I'm tempted to give myself a little release. But the only face circulating in my head right now is Andrey's, and I refuse to masturbate while thinking of him. He's already dictated too much in my life; he doesn't get to invade my fantasies, too.

It's with a sinking sense of failure that I pull the plug on my bath and climb out of the tub. Wrapped in a fluffy bathrobe, I walk into the living room, only to discover Yelena setting out pasties on the coffee table.

"You're like my fairy godmother, Yelena," I sigh. "You always seem to appear when I need you most."

She laughs. "That's the mark of a good housekeeper."

"Why do I get the feeling you're so much more than just a housekeeper?" Sitting down on one of the cushy armchairs, I gesture for her to sit, too. "Join me, please. I can't eat all these pastries alone."

To my surprise, she doesn't protest. She takes the sofa and helps herself to a danish.

I spend the next few minutes of quiet chewing, debating whether or not I should pry into Andrey's life or not. *Why the hell not? He's pried into my life plenty.*

"So how long have you worked for Andrey?"

"A very long time," she replies. "Truth be told, I can't remember what I did with my life before."

"So you know him pretty well then?"

She shrugs. "As well as an employee can know her employer."

She's downplaying it, but I'm willing to bet anything that someone as sharp as Yelena has noticed a lot in her time in the manor.

"Does Andrey have someone… special in his life?"

She stiffens so slightly that I almost miss it. "I'm not in the habit of discussing Mr. Kuznetsov's personal life."

Her refusal is polite but firm. But in the end, it doesn't really matter that she hasn't given me a direct answer. Her reaction is answer enough.

20
ANDREY

A flash of emerald green catches my eye.

That's how I know that day three of this guerilla war has begun.

Since I took over this Bratva when my father fled the country in the middle of the night, I've been to war again and again. I've fought Greeks and Armenians, motorcycle clubs out of the Midwest and seedy Baltimore gangs toting sawed-off shotguns and attitude aplenty. I've sent them all packing, whether in coffins or police body bags spread across the five boroughs in tiny, bite-sized pieces.

But this… this is one war that might not end so cleanly.

Through the window of my office, I see Natalia unrolling her yoga mat on the patio. Her high-waisted leggings are skin tight and her sports bra is bright and revealing.

This is the third day in a row she's walked her green yoga mat over to *this* side of the house.

The first day, I told myself she was here for the scenery. This location offers the best view of the grounds. From where she's stretching, I know she can see the red sycamores bending over the pool house, forests of birch and pine rolling down the hills, the skyline the backdrop for all of it.

On day two, I had my doubts that the view was the only reason.

Now, on day three, I know it's bullshit. She's here for one reason and one reason only: to win the war in my head.

I wonder if she even knows she's fighting, though, or if it's just a primal kind of warfare. Is she aware of how easily she can be seen through my office window? Does she know that, when she bends to touch her toes like she's doing now, the sunlight lets me see straight through her leggings?

Is she doing it to tease me? Punish me? Seduce me?

Fuck if I know. And fuck if I'm gonna dare to ask her. So far, I've managed to keep my distance. A minor miracle, considering how many times a day the woman crossed my mind.

An annoying number of times.

An unacceptable number of times. And that was even before the yoga.

She's in the middle of downward dog, her ass arched high and pointed directly at me. I rip my eyes away and force them back down to the computer screen in front of me.

But scarcely two minutes pass before I'm risking another glance. Profit and loss have never seemed less interesting. Territory, empire-building, imports and exports and guns and drugs and gambling—the bread and butter of my work is utterly meaningless bullshit compared to Natalia in a—

Fucking hell, is she doing a split?

Caught between desire and frustration, I unzip my pants and pull my erection out. I'm concerned about the integrity of my blood flow, to be quite honest. I'm on the verge of exploding.

There's only one way out of this predicament.

Well, two ways, really. But only one that doesn't involve leaping out of my window, pinning Natalia down to that sweaty yoga mat, and fucking her to within an inch of her life.

Option number one it is.

I grab hold of my cock and start jerking myself off, my gaze trained on her perky tits as she stretches.

Her moans from the night we met are still fresh in my ear. She sounded shocked that any man could make her come so fast. Much less do it again.

She switches position and lowers into a squat with her back to me. Her ass cheeks curve beautifully and I imagine my cock sliding between them, ready to coax another orgasm from her.

Rubbing harder now, my jaw clenches from the stirring inside me. A series of images shoot through my head like a picture slide.

My mouth clamped down around her nipple.

My cock sliding between her slick, wet folds.

Her ass bouncing wildly as I milk moan after moan from her pert, soft lips.

I come with a shudder into my hand.

But the relief is short-lived. The high isn't nearly as intense or as satisfying as it was the night I fucked her for the first time.

Instead, coming into my own fist has left me feeling like a disgruntled teenager stuck watching his porn buffer.

This isn't enough. This isn't even *close* to enough.

She turns suddenly.

I freeze, only a few stray beads of sweat betraying the fact that I've spent the last few minutes indulging in shit I swore I'd steer clear of. My sins are drying on my hand as she peers up from below.

The windows are too high for her to see anything. In any case, my desk blocks the bottom half of my body from view. There's no way she knows. She can't *possibly* fucking know.

But something flickers across her face.

Abruptly, she gathers up her water bottle and her yoga mat and speed walks towards the pool house.

Blyat!

Grabbing a handful of tissues, I wipe myself clean and duck to the bathroom to rinse off. When I return to the office, the door is wide open and a pair of nervous eyes are aimed directly at me.

Not the eyes I was hoping for, though. Or was it "dreading"? I can't quite decide.

Emerald Malice

"Mila," I greet without revealing my surprise at seeing her here. My new sister-in-law doesn't usually venture out of her wing of the house. "What brings you here?"

She slips into the room and closes the door, eyes downcast. "I need to speak to you."

Considering this evening has been a bust anyway—no pun intended—I gesture her in. "Take a seat. What can I do for you?"

She wrings her hands as she approaches. But the moment she sits, the nervous twitching stops. She takes a deep breath and makes eye contact for perhaps the first time since I met her.

"I need to discuss Viktor." She's still as soft-spoken as ever, but there's a grit to her words that I don't recognize.

"What about him?"

"I just caught him in our bedroom—with another woman."

I can't say I'm surprised. But I *am* annoyed. Any regular fool would have had the sense to keep his affairs outside of the marital bed.

Viktor is no regular fool, though. He's turned that shit into an art form.

"It's not the first time, either," she continues. "He didn't come to our bedroom on our wedding night. When I went looking for him, I found him in a guest room with one of the singers."

One can always count on my brother to do the classy thing.

"I am sorry, Mila," I say evenly. "I'll speak to him."

Her eyebrows arch and something remarkably close to defiance flashes across her face.

I'm fast getting the feeling that the delicate little wallflower Viktor thought he was marrying is anything but. Honestly, part of me is rooting for exactly that.

Give him hell, Mila. The devil knows he deserves it.

"Actually, I was hoping for more than that."

I'll admit, I'm intrigued. "This conversation might be a lot more productive if you just tell me what you want."

"Freedom," she blurts immediately.

I wince. "I'm afraid it's a little late for that, Mila."

"I'm not asking for a divorce or a separation," she hastens to clarify. "I'm happy to play my part—happy, submissive wife—just as long as I get to have my fun, too."

My own eyebrow drifts upward. This is definitely not what I was expecting. "You want to be free to have affairs of your own. Is that right?"

She shrugs. "Why should the men get to have all the fun?"

"You could just do it. Why tell me?"

"Because you are the *pakhan*. Because I'm living in your house. And because if, one day, Viktor happens to walk in on me and my paramour… I'll have a big shield to hold in front of me."

"I'm your insurance policy, you mean."

She smiles cryptically. "I'd say you're rather more than that. You're my brother-in-law. Maybe one day, we can even be friends."

There's no trace of flirtation there. It's more strategic than anything else. An alliance.

"And if I refuse to protect you?"

Her smile remains unchanged. "Then I'll do what I want regardless. But I'll do it loud and proud, out in the open for the world to see. I'll make a cuckold of your brother and I'll enjoy doing it. Either way, I win."

"It seems I've underestimated you, Mila."

"People frequently do."

"Very well." I nod in permission. "You have my support."

Her cheeks burn. "Thank you."

"Don't thank me yet," I warn. "Even favors amongst family have a price."

She leans back against the armchair. "What do you need from me?"

"Information." My head swivels in the direction of the pool house. Its sloping roof can be seen over the grass of the lawn. "I have a guest at the moment. I need you to befriend her, make sure she has company."

Mila rises to her feet and walks towards the window. "And report back to you?"

"Precisely."

She smiles, and again, I'm struck by the depth in her I never bothered to notice before. I can't say I hate it. It's nice to know there are other cunning people in the world—especially when they're willing to play along.

"I'll be in touch."

21

NATALIA

"Do it, Natalia!" I scold myself. "Just freaking do it!"

I've spent all day trying to drum up the courage to rip the bandage off and tell Aunt Annie about my pregnancy.

She raised you after your parents died. She took you in and loved you like you were her own. You owe her the truth. Don't be such a wuss!

I've known for a week now; I've been living in Andrey's pool house for almost as long. Enough is enough.

I need to tell my aunt.

I dial Aunt Annie's number and spend the next five seconds hoping—like the coward I am—that she won't pick up.

"Nic-Nat!" she greets. "I was wondering when you'd call."

"Sorry, Aunt Annie. I've been busy."

"I was worried you took me too seriously the last time. I wasn't complaining about all your calls, you know."

"I know, I know," I assure her. "This is on me. I really have been busy."

"Well, then, that's a good enough reason to ignore your batty old aunt," she chuckles. "I want you to live your life, my darling girl. If you're busy, that's good news."

I find a shady spot under one of my favorite red sycamores and slide down the trunk to the soft ground. "So, um—" *Just do it!* "—how are you?"

I slap my forehead with the palm of my hand while she launches into everything going on in her neck of the woods. "… Meryl's daughter's engagement party was quite the affair. They had a string quartet and everything."

"Jeez. If that was just the engagement party, what's the wedding gonna be like?"

"My thoughts exactly," Aunt Annie agrees with a laugh. "But I'm happy for Meryl. It really does something to a parent when your children find their forever partners. It's kind of like you can relax at last."

I pull my feet up to my chest. "Is that how you feel, too?"

She hesitates. "Well, I would be thrilled, if and when you meet your forever partner. But really, I just want to know that you're happy and settled. No matter where you end up in life."

The pressure mounting in my chest makes it hard to concentrate. But I know I can't end this conversation without telling her.

"Aunt Annie… I have some big news."

"Uh-oh! You sound serious."

"Well, it's serious news. But… happy, too," I tack on. "I mean, I'm definitely happy about it." It's not that simple, but she doesn't have to know that. "And I hope you will be, too."

"Honey, you're scaring me."

"I'm… I'm pregnant."

A long stretch of silence. And then—

"Oh my God!" Aunt Annie exclaims. "Oh my goodness gracious! Are you really? This is… this is… unbelievable. How?"

"It just sort of happened." That's an understatement, but again, we're operating on a need-to-know basis. "I've decided that I want to have this baby. I'm ready to be a mother."

That last part is more wishful thinking than confidence. Maybe if I repeat it enough times, it'll start being true.

"Wait…" Aunt Annie's enthusiasm dips considerably. She sounds worried now. "Sweetheart, are you doing this alone? Is the father not in the picture?"

It wouldn't be a lie to say that I'm doing this alone. Andrey and I aren't together.

Then again, I have a black card and a pool house with my baby daddy's name written all over it.

"No, the father's in the picture. Sort of."

"So you're having the baby together?"

I bite my lip. "Um—yes?"

"Ah!" Aunt Annie is back to sounding thrilled. "You can't know how relieved I am, sweetheart. Parenthood is hard enough with a partner. I don't want you to have to do it alone."

"Well, no need to worry. I'm not alone."

"Who's the man?" she asks eagerly. "And when do I get to meet him?"

Okay, there might be a small need to worry.

"Soon," I lie. "Very soon."

In typical Aunt Annie fashion, she launches into a barrage of questions without giving me any time to answer. I wait for her to finish before I offer the extremely sanitized version of Andrey's biography.

"Uh, his name is Andrey. He runs a business in the city. Several businesses, actually. And he's... he's good to me."

"Are you two planning on living together or are you waiting until the baby's born?"

I glance over at the pretty pool house that's all mine. "Um, actually, I've moved in with him. He wasn't happy with my apartment. The mold in the ceiling nearly gave him a conniption."

"Goodness me, I like him already."

I'm not sure why I'm selling him so hard to Aunt Annie. Maybe it's because, for a little while at least, I kind of want to live the fantasy.

I want it to be this easy. Like I'm just a girl having a baby with a boy who loves and dotes on me.

Forget about the girl's PTSD and shitty job. Forget that the boy is a terrifying Russian *pakhan* who collects toxic red flags like they're Pokémon. Forget that the baby is routinely referred to as "the heir."

Forget all that, and this really is a fairy tale in the making.

"Oh, honey, I'm so happy for you. Sometimes, the best things in life are unplanned." Her voice has turned teary. "I'm gonna be a grandma!"

"I… I wish Mom and Dad could have met their grandchild." It's hard to get the words out past the sudden lump in my throat.

"Me, too, sweetheart," she croons. "Me, too."

We talk for a little while longer before I hang up, a bittersweet feeling tucked between my ribs. The weight of telling Aunt Annie is gone, but it's been replaced with something else.

Fear of the unknown.

Worry about the future.

Trepidation about my co-parenting situation with Andrey.

Take your pick—no matter what you call it, it doesn't feel good.

I'm so lost in my thoughts that I don't notice a woman approaching until she's standing right over me. "Jesus!" I gasp, hand on my chest.

The woman smiles sweetly. "Sorry! I didn't mean to startle you."

"Have we met before?" The moment I ask the question, I'm hit with an image of her in a modest white gown swathed in lace. "Oh my…"

"If I recall correctly," says Mila Obnizov with a wry, amused laugh, "you crashed my wedding."

"I'm—We—You—I never slept with your husband," I finish in an idiotic stupor. "Just so you know. Like, for the record. That was—It was—It's just a long story, okay? But I never slept with him. I swear."

If she wasn't laughing, I'd probably pee myself in fear.

She sits down beside me and spreads out, perfectly at ease. "Well, that makes you one of the few women who hasn't."

Her face is tilted towards the sun so I'm not sure how to interpret that statement. Is she joking?

She peeks over at me with one eye. "But your friend—the blonde—she has slept with him?"

"He dumped her to marry you," I admit awkwardly. "The interruption was her idea of revenge. You know, now that I'm saying it out loud, I guess the story's not really that long, after all."

To my surprise, she just shrugs. "I get it."

"... Do you?"

She shrugs. "I wouldn't have gone about revenge that way. But I understand the need for it. Viktor drags it out of people."

None of this is what I was expecting. Mila might look like a porcelain ballerina, but I'm getting the feeling she's got claws under that pretty little facade.

"I'm guessing marriage is not all you hoped it would be?" I venture cautiously.

She leans back on the grass, balancing on her elbows. "My expectations of marriage were always pretty low," she explains in a matter-of-fact kind of way. "It wasn't something I ever really wanted."

"Why would you agree to marry Viktor, then?"

"It's a long story." She winks to let me know she's messing with me. "It involves a stubborn old man, a stubborn, *evil* old man, and a girl who wasn't willing to put up with either one."

"I'm hooked. But promise me there's a happy ending?"

"That remains to be seen." She looks me right in the eyes. "I believe in making my own luck, Natalia. You can't just let life happen to you."

I observe her with fascination as she turns her face back towards the sun. "I wish I'd met you sooner," I say. "That advice would've come in handy. I've spent pretty much my entire existence letting life happen to me."

She squints at me, her eyes gleaming with mischief. "Well, then, I guess we have to change that, don't we?"

22

ANDREY

It's almost midnight when I get home, but the light is still on in the pool house.

I spied Mila and Natalia talking in the garden before I left. According to Leif, they spent hours gabbing on the grass before Natalia invited Mila into the pool house. Mila has already retired to her wing of the manor, so I can't ask her how the first meeting went.

Shadows skirt past the windows of the pool house every so often. Natalia isn't just awake; she's restless.

I spend an inordinate amount of time by the window, waiting for her lights to turn off. If she goes to sleep, the temptation will be gone. Then, pitched by the glow of artificial lights, another shadow shoots across the curtains.

Stay away, stay away, stay away...

I chant the refrain in my head even as I exit the house to walk down to the pool. As I get closer, I can hear music.

Edging towards the open window, I peer inside.

Natalia is dressed in a light-pink tank top and white panties that show more than they conceal.

"... yeah, I wanna dance with somebody... with somebody who loves me..."

As she twists in circles, eyes closed, mouth parted, her tank top rides up, revealing her still-flat stomach.

Her dancing is chaotic and uncoordinated, but there's a look of rapture on her face that I've never seen before. It's dreamy and uncaring, totally free.

Her hair whips around her head as she spins. She twirls, allowing the music to distract her from whatever it is that's kept her up this late.

I have the urge to take out my phone and record her.

Not to be an asshole—well, not *entirely* to be an asshole. But just so that I have something to remember this by. Something I can look back on when I'm alone in my bed. Yet the thought of going back to the main house and taking care of myself again is in-fucking-tolerable.

I don't want a fucking video.

I want to bury myself balls deep in her and make her moan again.

Which is why I step right up to the window so that she can't miss me.

It takes a long time for her to notice. Whitney Houston ends on a high note and, as the next tune starts, Natalia turns. When she sees me, she lets out a strangled gasp and fumbles for the robe lying on the bed, making spitting noises like a cat.

"*Whatthehell?!*" she screeches without pausing between words. She snaps off the music. "How long have you been standing there?"

"You've got some nice moves."

She careens through the door and onto the porch. "I've got a mean right hook, too!"

I spread my hands wide. "I'm right here. Swing away."

"Don't tempt me," she snarls. "You have no right to spy on me, you creep!"

"I wasn't spying. I was taking a stroll through the gardens when I heard the music," I lie. "I thought I'd come by and say hello since you were up."

She pulls the robe tighter around her body. "Since when have you been interested in saying 'hello'? The only time you seek me out is to bark orders at me."

I tilt my head to the side. She's beautiful in the pale moonlight. The shadows tease me with hints of what's beneath the gap in her robe. "I trust you're settling in well."

"I was—before I knew you spend your nights skulking around the gardens like a perv."

"I suggest you close the windows if you don't want to be observed."

She scowls, but it doesn't hide the blush on her cheeks. "What do you want, Andrey?"

Without answering, I push past her and walk into the pool

house. She follows me inside, still fussing to make sure that her robe is cinched properly at the waist.

"Having trouble sleeping?"

She eyes me warily, clearly still flustered. "You told me I'd have my privacy. You shouldn't be here." Her eyes dart around like she's worried I'll spot something she doesn't want me to see. Of course, that just draws attention to the small pink device lying next to the bed.

"Is that—"

"It's a *vibrator*, okay?" she snaps before I can even finish the question, marching over and plucking it off the floor. "I needed to de-stress and I thought… Anyway, the batteries ran out just when I was getting—It doesn't matter. I just needed to release some steam, so I thought maybe dancing would…"

I watch her squirm. My God, how I love the way her skin goes pink.

"Did it work?" I ask.

She frowns. "Did *what* work?"

"The dancing. Or are you still horny?"

Her jaw drops. "Oh my *God*. You did not just—This is completely inappropriate!"

"We're both adults." I shrug, shifting closer. "And you're carrying my baby. I don't think discussing your arousal should be off the table."

Especially considering my arousal is definitely on the table as we speak. A few more exchanges like this and I might put *her* on the table, too.

She clears her throat. "No. It did not."

"Then maybe I can." I'm close enough to reach out and stroke the expanse of bare thigh where it peeks out from beneath the hem of her robe. I only get a fingertip worth of contact before she smacks my hand away.

"What's the harm?" I bite back my smile. She's so flustered, so riled up. *I fucking love it.*

"'The harm'?" she gawks. "There's plenty of harm!"

"It's not like you're in danger of falling in love with me, are you?"

Those words have the desired effect. She flinches back. "Definitely not."

"Then I fail to see the problem."

Her jaw squares. "The problem is that I don't want to sleep with you again."

"So, your thighs aren't dripping right now with the thought of me inside you? If I reached under that robe and touched you, would my fingers come away wet?"

She takes a small step back as though she's worried I'm going to pounce on her. To be fair, I'm not far from doing precisely that. My cock is in danger of snapping off at this point.

"N-no," she says shakily.

Bigger lies have never been told.

But as fun as this cat-and-mouse game is, I'm done with it. No more banter, no more quips, no more back-and-forth. I didn't know what I was coming here for when I first left my office.

But I know now.

With one hand on her throat, I pin her against the wall next to her bed. "You know what I think, *lastochka?*" I whisper in her ear. "I think you're a filthy liar."

I pull at the cord holding her robe together and it parts easily. She's trembling, goosebumps running up and down her arms despite how warm it is in here.

"Andrey…" she whimpers.

"Let's see if I'm right."

My fingers delve past the band of her panties. I drag a knuckle through her throbbing lips and find her absolutely soaked.

I fix her with a cold glare. "Are you done lying to me now?"

"I… I can't want someone like you," she admits through gritted teeth.

Can't. She *can't* want someone like me. It's a far cry from saying she *doesn't.*

I part her legs with my knee, just like I did in front of all of her coworkers the other day. "Let me show you what you can have." My lips trail the soft skin of her cheek. "Let me show you what happens when you tell the truth."

My lips come down on hers like a sudden storm. I kiss her until she melts to putty in my hands. When she's breathless, I slide to my knees, ripping her panties off with one tug so I can feast on her sweet, wet pussy while she stands skewered against the wall.

She cries out, muffled screams tearing out of her even with

her lips clamped shut. Her nails dig into the wallpaper, looking for something to hold onto.

Grabbing her ass, I hoist one leg over my shoulder and thrust my tongue into her dripping slit. Her hands curl around my head, her fingers weaving into my hair, simultaneously trying to push me away and pull me deeper.

She comes in record time, drenching me in her pleasure and losing her battle to be quiet.

I take her limp body into my arms and carry her to the bed. I rip the tank top off her—the robe fell off somewhere during my pussy feast, long forgotten—and gaze down at her tight little body, glistening with sweat and wracked with fevered pants.

Her eyes are glazed, and she stares up at me dreamily as I take my clothes off.

When I'm standing naked in front of her, her eyes fall to my engorged cock. Her pink tongue darts out of her mouth to run a straight line down her bottom lip, and I know what she wants.

Hungry little bird.

Lucky for her, I'm happy to provide.

I climb over her body, straddling her chest. Then I feed her my cock. She takes me into her mouth, letting me set the pace even as her tongue lashes out enthusiastically to wrap around my shaft.

As much as I want to explode down her throat, I want to explode inside her even more. The thought of my seed filling her up, marking her as mine, is too powerful to ignore. I'm seconds from finishing when I force myself out of her hot, wet mouth and slide down her body.

I align myself with her dripping opening… and wait. Because, as much as I tell myself this means nothing, I know as well as Natalia does that there's no coming back from this.

We're crossing a line. Letting a genie out of the bottle.

But fuck it.

Some things are born to be messy.

Appropriately enough, when I drive my cock inside of her, "mess" is the only thing I have in mind. Natalia's gasp is messy; my thrusts are messy; and by the time I finish emptying myself in her, I've made an absolute mess of her.

The only things messier than what I just did to her body are the words that came out of my mouth as I did it.

"… I'm gonna fill you up, baby…" I snarled as I erupted inside her. "… all mine… *all fucking mine…*"

I roll off of her immediately after the last drop of desire has left me. For a few seconds, all I can hear is the sound of her heavy breathing layered with mine.

When I turn my head to look at her, she does the same.

"This is all it is," I announce quietly. "All it can be. Just sex. Nothing more."

Natalia turns her gaze back to the ceiling. "Understood."

With the agreement sealed, I get to my feet and put my clothes back on. "Goodnight."

I'm almost to the door when I hear footsteps. She's in her

robe again, something clutched in her fist. It isn't until she shoves it at me that I realize what she's holding.

She grabs my hand and folds something against my palm. I don't need to open my hand to know she gave me two crisp hundred-dollar bills. The same amount I threw on her coffee table the first time we slept together.

Her emerald eyes are trained on me with smug satisfaction. "Goodnight, Andrey."

Then she slams the door in my face.

23

NATALIA

As it turns out, throwing a fistful of post-sex cash at a smug asshole and kicking him out the door is one hell of a turn-on.

I mean, I knew it would be for *me*.

I just didn't expect it to be a turn-on for *him*, too.

But as always, Andrey Kuznetsov takes me by surprise.

I expected to see little of him after that. I didn't, at first. I spent most of the day at work and then, when I was back home, Mila and I decided to have dinner by the pool. Afterward, still no sign of Andrey, Mila and I watched *Pretty Woman*—always a classic, though never quite so applicable to my life as this time around—and then said goodnight around ten.

I swapped my sweats for an oversized t-shirt and my favorite pair of granny panties. With the windows thrown open for some cross-ventilation, I was ready to nod off to sleep.

That's when I heard footsteps on my porch.

Eyes opened, I waited with bated breath. Then the lock turned in the door.

There's only one person who has a key to the pool house.

Andrey was framed by moonlight as he strode into my bedroom. He pulled his shirt over his head, and I caught the faint whisper of cigarette smoke that clung to his clothes.

Inconvenient though it was to accept, I was, God help me, *excited.*

"Been waiting for me, *lastochka?*" he growled as he slipped into bed beside me. He coiled his body around mine, his heat making my head spin.

"I was already asleep."

"Liar." He pulled me against his chest. "But you weren't expecting me, that much I can tell for myself." I tried to squirm away from him, but he just gripped me tighter. "No need to be embarrassed, little bird. All the sexless underwear in the world wouldn't have kept me from your bed tonight."

Rebelling against every instinct of self-preservation I've ever had, I let him pull me back into the circle of his arms.

"You looking for more pocket money?" I couldn't help but taunt. "Because I'm fresh out."

To my surprise, he laughed. "Maybe I'll pay *you* tonight."

I pulled out of his arms and straddled him. My hands ran up and down his ridiculously sculpted chest, all the while trying desperately not to let his masculine perfection distract me.

"How about we call it even?" I suggested as his hardness ground against me from below. "You don't pay me; I don't pay you. No point in just passing the same handful of cash back and forth, right?"

"Sex without money changing hands?" he mused. "Sounds boring."

I slapped his chest and he grabbed me around the waist and threw me down on my back, then ravaged me until I saw stars.

As it turns out, I am indisputably a screamer. Apparently, it just took the right man to show me that.

I never in a million years would've considered Andrey Kuznetsov to be the "right man" for anything. But if we're talking hot, passionate, wild sex… If we're talking *claw-marks-on-his-back, bruises-on-my-ass, mind-numbing, toe-curling, stomach-exploding* sex…

He's sure as hell right for that. This last week is proof in the pudding.

He's visited me every night—usually around midnight, when the leaves of the trees turn an inky black to match the skies. I've started leaving the door open so he can just slip inside without bothering with the key.

And as for my granny panties—comfortable as they are, reliable as they've been—they are now relegated to the bottom drawer, along with all the other clothes I've abandoned without a second thought.

Who needs clothes where we're going, right? They'd just get in the way.

If I have one complaint about our nightly escapades, it's that they're limited to sleeping hours. I wake up each morning—

my body raw, spent, freshly bruised, and comfortably achy—to an empty bed.

I feel it when he leaves me at night. The sudden absence of his weight and warmth makes my stomach twist with disappointment.

Just sex, I repeat to myself each time. *It's just sex.*

The thing is, if I've learned anything from *Pretty Woman*, it's that sex is never *just* sex. And human beings aren't capable of doing casual for very long without someone wanting more.

And let's face it: between Andrey and me, I'm fairly certain who that "someone" is going to be.

It's a thought that's been nagging at me for the last few days now. I've been swatting it away easily enough—until this morning.

I wake up to find his side of the bed empty again and a slight bump in my stomach that didn't exist before.

I try to work off the growing frustration by doing some yoga out on the porch. But all my inner serenity keeps getting knocked sideways by the same old internal arguments.

You're not his damn marionette—he can't just play with you and then toss you aside when he's done having his fun.

Except that you agreed to this.

Because you were horny. Not because you actually thought this through. Andrey isn't right for you anyway.

Then why do you get those fluttery little butterflies in your stomach every time you think of him?

I'm driving myself slowly insane. Since yoga is a bust, I decide to work off my excess energy in the pool.

I'm swimming useless laps, the voices in my head still going at it, when Mila shows up. She's wearing a halter midi-dress with cheeky cutouts in the hemline.

"Hey, Nat!"

The nickname triggers me. For one painfully lonely moment, I think of Katya. I wonder what she's doing right now. *Is she missing me as much as I'm missing her?*

"Hi, Mila," I sigh.

She stops a few feet from the pool so she doesn't risk getting water on her shoes. I don't blame her; the pair she's wearing are six inches tall and look like they're made from the skin of some exotic animal.

Her smile flips into a concerned frown. "Why so blue?"

I'm sorely tempted to crack my head open and share some of the torrential thoughts that have taken up residence since Andrey started visiting me at night. But as sweet as Mila is, she's Andrey's sister-in-law. As nice as she's been, there's no telling where her loyalties truly lie.

And even if she was the damn Dalai Lama, would I want to admit what I've been up to once the sun goes down? The mistakes I've been making? The moans I've been burying into my pillows?

Answer: *No, I do not.*

I miss Kat. She would understand. But I shove that thought right down in the trash can of my heart.

"Nothing," I mumble, unable to pull myself out of my funk even for Mila's benefit. "Just having a blah day, I guess."

"How about we kick those blues in the ass by throwing some money at the problem?" She claps her hands. "There isn't a single blah day I've ever had that couldn't be cured with a little good ol' fashioned retail therapy."

Considering the jewels glittering on Mila's wrists, I'd say she's already indulged in her fair share of retail therapy.

Then again, the woman is married to Viktor Kuznetsov—retail therapy is probably barely scratching the surface of her issues.

"Okay," I relent. "Let's set Andrey's credit card on fire."

∼

In twenty minutes, I'm clambering into the back of a shiny gray Rolls Royce with a fresh blow-dry and a very excited Mila—although her excitement has more to do with the fact that Leonty and Leif are my designated bodyguards for this little outing.

"Lucky you," she whispers to me as she straps herself in. "My bodyguards look like the 'Before' versions in those makeover shows."

I guffaw as she gives Leonty a smile that has "bad intentions" stamped all over it.

I wonder what Viktor would have to say about it. Then again, I don't really care. The Kuznetsov men are not worth a single inch of my mental real estate today.

An hour later, Mila and I are circling the mannequins in a nauseatingly high-end boutique store.

"What about this, Nat?" she suggests, fingering a gorgeous, midnight blue sheath dress. "It would look amazing on you."

"I thought so, too, until I saw the price tag." Sidling a little closer so the hawkish saleslady hovering in the background doesn't hear me, I whisper, "It's two thousand dollars!"

"Exactly! It's a freaking steal at this price."

It's a shame Mila and Katya have the whole Viktor thing in common; they'd probably get along great otherwise. The irony that I took a break from my friendship with Kat and ended up with another friend just like her isn't lost on me.

"Mila, I'm not spending two thousand dollars on a single dress. I barely have two thousand dollars to my name."

"Babes, not sure if you've fully grasped this yet, but Andrey is richer than God."

"Not the point. It's his money, not mine."

The defiant flash in her eyes is a far cry from the innocent baby blues I thought she possessed on her wedding day. "That is precisely the point. Where's the fun in having a rich man if you can't buy yourself pretty things with his money?" She turns and says to the saleswoman, "My friend will be trying this on."

"No, I won't. Mila. Mila!" She waves away my objections and drags me to the dressing room. I'm still protesting. "There's no point in me trying on the dress. I'm never gonna buy it."

Mila rolls her eyes. "Didn't Andrey give you a credit card?"

"He told you about that?"

She shrugs. "No, but I assumed. I got my own shiny black credit card when I married Viktor. It's part of the package. If you're gonna be with a Kuznetsov, you've gotta look the part."

"Okay, I feel the need to clear something up." I glance sideways at the saleswoman, who's followed us into the dressing room with the blue dress draped over a golden hanger and dollar signs flashing in her eyeballs. "I am not 'with' a Kuznetsov. Andrey and I are not together."

Mila dismisses the saleswoman with a somehow polite flick of her wrist and turns to me with those deceptively sharp eyes of hers. "So, he just sneaks into the pool house at night for a chat, does he? A little light conversation before bed? Couple hands of Go Fish, maybe?"

I'm so caught off-guard that I don't have the presence of mind to bluff my way through an answer. My jaw drops and I start blushing like an idiot. "Uh…"

Mila laughs. "That's what I thought."

I collapse on the white sofa in the dressing room and bury my face in my hands. "It's just sex, okay? There's nothing else going on."

One of her perfectly plucked eyebrows arches. "But you wish there was more going on?"

The blunt question sends a paralyzing wave of uncertainty surging straight through me. Because the natural next question I have to ask myself is…

Do I?

"No, I mean, maybe… urgh… I don't know!" I melt deeper into the couch. "I don't know what I want."

Mila sits down beside me and gives me a sympathetic pat on the knee. "It's okay. You've got time to figure it out."

"Do I, though?" I look down at my belly, which is no longer

as flat as it used to be. "Because from where I'm sitting, I have a few months at best before I have to get my act together."

"I'm sure this is all very confusing for you. And the hormones can't be helping—"

"I lied," I interrupt. "I lied earlier when I said I didn't know what I want. I *do* know what I want. I've known since I was five years old and I watched my parents dancing in the living room when I was supposed to be sleeping."

Mila smiles. "Did they do that often?"

I nod. "Most nights. Sometimes, I used to stay awake just so I could watch them. They looked at each other like they were the only two people in the world."

"I imagine that's exactly what it's like," Mila murmurs. "When you're in love."

Sighing, I pull at my locket. "I know this is an odd question, considering you're married, but… have you ever been in love?"

Mila laughs, but it's sad. "I thought I was in love once. I was sixteen and he worked for my father. It was very clandestine, real hush-hush. First time I ever fancied myself a rebel."

Judging from the bite in her tone, her clandestine romance didn't have a happy ending.

"My dad found out, of course. Turns out we weren't as subtle as we thought we were. My father paid him off and he decided that five thousand dollars was worth more than I was. He took the money—and all the promises he made me—and ran. Never saw him again."

"I'm sorry."

"Don't be sorry. It was the hard knock I needed to clear my head of all those romantic notions I had. I learned to be practical, independent. I learned to take care of myself." She turns to face me. "You've got to rely on yourself, Nat. There's no point in putting your faith in men. More often than not, they turn out to be disappointing."

I nod as though I understand what she's telling me. And I do —to a point.

It's just that my own experience has taught me differently. It's a hard thing to unlearn hope when you've grown to rely on it.

"My father wasn't, though," I hear myself rasping. "He was an amazing husband. He would have died for my mother. He—" I just stop short of saying, *He* did *die for my mother.* Instead, I finish, "—would have done anything for her."

Mila presses her lips into a tight line. "Must have been a nice childhood."

Sure. What I had of it, at least.

"They were great parents." I take care not to let my voice falter. I have no desire to trudge into my parents' tragic demise today. It's neither the time nor the place for that kind of mood killer. "They used to squeeze me between them at the piano. They stole kisses over my head while I practiced."

Still, to this day, it's one of my brightest and most vivid memories of them. I can smell the wood of the piano, my mother's perfume, my father's cologne. All of it in one perfect mélange.

"You play the piano?"

"I used to."

I haven't played since I was a teenager. And that was only because Aunt Annie used to insist I play every time we got within a stone's throw of one. Once I was out of her house, though, there was no one pushing me to play.

Sometimes, it's easier to forget than it is to move on. The difference between the two is enormous.

I sigh, relapsing back into my forlorn mood from this morning.

"So that's it then? You want what your parents had?"

I wince. "Is that asking too much?"

The look on her face is an unequivocal yes. But she takes pity on me and shrugs one shoulder. "You want real love. That's no crime."

"I'm not gonna get that with Andrey," I say softly.

"Who knows? Maybe, for right now, you should concentrate on what you can get from him."

Glancing at the blue dress in the corner, I frown. "Expensive dresses I don't need?"

"More like getting your rocks off!" She shoots me a wink. "He's good in bed, isn't he?"

"Err…"

"Okay, let's cut the bullshit, woman to woman—do you want to keep sleeping with him?"

I blush scarlet but nod.

Mila doesn't look surprised in the least. "Great. Then keep sleeping with him. The man got you pregnant; the least he can do is be on call for nightly orgasms."

I snort, but my amusement is short-lived. Almost as though she can read my mind, Mila adds, "You're worried about developing feelings for him, aren't you?"

I really need to work on my poker face. "I'm living in his house and carrying his baby," I point out. "Sleeping with him on top of all that feels a little bit like asking for trouble."

Mila gives me a wink that reminds me a hell of a lot of Kat. "What's life without a little trouble, huh?"

"Oh, boy. You might be a bad influence, Mila."

"I'll take that as a compliment." Then she bounces onto the balls of her feet. "Mind if I give you some advice?"

"Go right ahead."

"As long as you're risking the chance of catching feelings, why not make it as difficult for him as you can?"

I look at her, perplexed. "I'm not following."

In answer, she twirls towards the door and gestures for the nearby saleswoman. "Forget the dresses, Rosetta. We're looking for lingerie—the sexier, the better."

Just like that, my heart dives off the high board and plummets into the swimming pool of my stomach. "I'm not sure about this, Mila."

"Good thing I am, then." She fixes me with a stern look. "You're hot, Natalia. You need to use what the Good Lord gave you. If Andrey is determined to give you up in the end, make it the hardest decision he'll ever have to make."

I have to be honest: as strategies go, it's not bad.

In fact, it might just be brilliant.

"What the hell?" I decide on the spot. "Bring on the edible thongs."

Mila beams like she couldn't be prouder of me. "That's what I'm talking about!"

∽

Two hours later, Mila and I duck back into the Rolls' spacious backseat with at least a dozen bags between us. To be fair, most of them belong to Mila. But I've managed to come away with two of my own.

Yes, I used the black credit card.

And yes, I felt guilty as hell doing it.

But apparently, master plans don't come cheap.

The real kicker: by the time we get back to the pool house, I realize that, quite apart from feeling better, I've actually had fun.

So much so that I end up inviting Mila to stay for dinner. Somewhere between that invitation and putting my bags away, I discover that Mila has expanded the invitation to include Leonty.

"Bodyguards have to eat, too," she tells me with a wink. "Men like that have appetites."

"Mhmm." I wag my eyebrows at her. "I notice you didn't invite Leif to join us for dinner."

"He disappeared before I could," she insists innocently, spinning around on her bar stool so she can watch Leonty pace across the porch, talking to someone on the phone.

We end up ordering Chinese and congregating around the coffee table.

Leonty is just as charming as he looks. Although he certainly doesn't have to try too hard where Mila is concerned. She laughs at all his jokes, even the subpar ones. And when I grab everyone's plates and slip off to the kitchen, neither one seems to notice I'm gone.

I wash up quietly, observing them the whole time. There's undeniable chemistry in their banter, an easy back-and-forth that leaves me feeling hollow.

Will I ever get to experience that with somebody?

Taken by a sudden urgency, I leave the dishes half-done in the sink, grab my perfumed shopping bags, and slip into the bathroom.

I have five new pieces of lingerie.

I pull out the most conservative of the lot and hold it up to the mirror. It's a lace nightie that falls around my upper thighs. The cups cover my nipples, but the rest of it is delicate lace. The only coverage it offers comes in the form of a matching pale pink thong with tiny bows on the straps.

I've just stripped down to nothing when I hear Mila and Leonty's laughter wafting towards me through the crack in the bottom of the door.

It makes me feel lonelier than ever.

Aw, hell—if I'm gonna do the thing, I might as well do it right.

Armed with a new and almost certainly short-lived sense of boldness, I swap the pink gown for the most daring of my new purchases—a crotchless, cupless, black lace teddy, complete with a built-in thong. Mila bullied me into buying it with a snippy, "Don't be a fucking wuss, Nat. You might as well wear these things while you have the body for them."

With my heart hammering madly in my chest, I put on the black teddy—which takes a surprising amount of time, considering there's so little to work with—and stand breathless in front of the mirror.

My jaw drops.

It's giving fallen angel turned dominatrix.

I turn this way and that, like I'm flickering back and forth between two different versions of myself.

There's the old me who thinks all of this is ridiculous and dangerous and very much a bad idea.

And then there's the new me, who looks damn good in this shit and thinks bad ideas sound like exactly what ought to be on the menu.

New me takes charge.

Shaking off my nerves, I grab my phone, open my pitifully blank text thread with Andrey, and open the camera. I angle the screen down just enough so that my face is cut off.

And just like that, the show begins.

I take a few pictures, making sure Andrey can appreciate all the features (or lack thereof) of the teddy. Every curve is on display. Damn near every inch of skin.

I scan through the barrage of photos, pick the two that make me the least nauseous, and load them into the message.

My finger trembles over the **Send** button, suddenly wracked with fear.

Once I send the pictures, that's it, there'll be no bringing them back.

Don't do it. It's too desperate, too pathetic, too much.

You're being a wuss.

No, you're being sensible.

Chicken.

"Fuck," I mutter to myself.

Then, as if by its own accord, my finger pulls the trigger.

With a little *shoop* noise, both pictures are sucked into the ether and transported to Andrey.

Goosebumps pimple my skin as I try frantically to reverse course and delete the pictures before he's seen them. But just as my finger hovers over the first picture, **Delivered** changes to **Read.**

No going back now, is there?

I close the thread and put my phone face-down on the bathroom counter. Stripping off the black teddy proves to be an easier task than getting it on.

Once I'm back in respectable clothes, I join Mila and Leonty in the living room. Neither one seems to have even registered my absence.

I slip into an armchair just behind Leonty and wonder if, at this very moment, my phone is lighting up with texts from Andrey.

I purposefully avoid the bathroom for the next few hours. We play Uno, though "we" continues to be kind of a superfluous word, because neither of my two game-mates seem to be aware of my continued existence.

Only after Leonty and Mila have left the pool house do I allow myself to slink back into the bathroom to retrieve my phone.

I see a text notification on my lockscreen.

I take a deep breath and open it.

ANDREY: *I won't be coming over tonight.*

24

ANDREY

I should be happy. It's just past midnight and we've done twice the normal volume of sales.

Sure, a few small-time dealers tried to muscle in on my turf. And a few working girls slipped under the radar and into the club, prowling for clients. But both annoyances have been dealt with.

The quarterly numbers are high. The time is ripe for expansion and Ivan Obnizov, freshly mollified by his daughter's marriage to my shit-heap of a brother, is ready to throw his support behind me.

Everything is going exactly according to plan. I ought to be celebrating. And I would be—were it not for the two little alerts that popped up on my screen an hour ago.

Two images from Natalia.

She's never sent me pictures before, so naturally, I was curious. I even blocked out Shura's extensive club report in order to open the thread and see what she'd sent me.

As it turns out, what she sent me was blue balls and a fucking mountain of distraction.

My initial reaction was surprise—I had no idea the woman had it in her. The lingerie is nothing short of scandalous.

Fuck me—what I wouldn't give to spread her out right now and devour every inch of her body. Lick the desire off her silky skin and replace her sweat with mine.

I've spent the last hour trying to forget. But even when I'm not sneaking a peek at my phone, I'm imagining her waiting for me in the pool house, her sweet, pink pussy bared and glistening for me.

If that weren't enough, Mila has been blowing me up with dutiful reports.

MILA: *She plays the piano but she's conflicted about it. There's definitely some stuff in her past she's not opening up about.*

MILA: *She loves caprese salad. And pink lemonade. And anything to do with cherries.*

MILA: *We're getting along great but I get the feeling she's lonely.*

MILA: *Really fucking lonely.*

Really fucking lonely. If Mila is right and Natalia is choosing to channel her loneliness towards me, that is a problem. Much as I'd like to be, I can't be her savior.

"Everything alright?" Shura asks. "You've been distracted all night."

Reluctantly, I put my phone away. "All good."

But Shura's eyes linger.

Luckily, I spot Viktor across the club. Shura's attention flickers to him and both our faces fall into near-identical scowls.

"He's plastered," Shura hisses in disgust.

My brother has each of his arms draped around a different woman, both stumbling under his weight as they ferry him across the dance floor. They're as much of a mess as he is: eyeliner running like black rivers down their cheeks, smudged lipstick smeared across their faces and his alike.

I snap my fingers and my men converge around the three of them.

Viktor looks up and squawks in amusement. "Aw, look, ladies—an honor guard, just for me."

I dismiss the women with another snap and two bodyguards hustle them out of the limelight.

The soldiers who commandeered my brother pass him off to Efrem, who supports Viktor one-handed but angles his face away from him as though delinquency and cheap liquor are contagious.

"Heyooo, broski," Viktor garbles. Efrem dumps him in the seat opposite me and he hiccups. "Yo, someone get me a drink! The stronger, the better."

Everyone ignores him.

"What the fuck do you think you're playing at?" I ask calmly, one arm thrown over the black leather armchair.

"Huh?" *Leave it to Viktor to slur a single syllable.*

"You've only been married a few months, *brat*. And yet here you are, loitering around with…" My eyes drift toward the back entrance where my men conveyed Viktor's girls away. "… with distractions that are beneath even you."

He tries to smile but his face is so paralyzed by alcohol that it comes out as a sort of awkward grimace. "Just having some fun. If it's good enough for Otets, it's good enough for me."

"And you want to be like him, do you?"

"Easier than being like *you*," he hisses bitterly.

What he has to be bitter about, I have no fucking clue. Nor do I have the patience or the interest to find out.

"Ivan Obnizov is my top smuggler," I remind him, not for the first time. "You almost fucked up that alliance once before. Doing it again will have consequences."

Viktor sits tall for a second, only to fall sideways into the armrest. "You say that as if the last time *didn't* have consequences. In case you forgot, you forced me to marry the fuckin' ice queen."

"That 'ice queen' was promised to another man. A fact that you conveniently forgot when you decided her pussy meant more to you than my trust."

Viktor rolls his eyes. "I married her, didn't I?"

"Your duties don't end there. Marrying Mila is one thing; keeping her happy is another."

"That was never part of the deal," he grits out.

"The 'deal' is whatever I say it is." I nod at Efrem and he proceeds to haul Viktor to his feet. "Go home to your wife, Viktor. And stop embarrassing yourself."

"Men have affairs, Andrey!" he barks. "It's natural. It's expected. My wife needs to fucking fall in line."

Efrem tightens his grip on Viktor, making him wince with pain.

"I'm your brother!" he bellows, spit flying through the air. "Not the shit under your boot you want to get rid of."

"At the moment," I say, "I can't tell the difference. Now, get the fuck out of my sight." Drained by the conversation, I get to my feet, ready to put this whole miserable day behind me.

Shura reads my mind as the last of Viktor's roars fade away. "Shall I bring the car around?"

Unbidden, Natalia's pictures flash in my mind. If I go home now, I won't be able to stop myself from slipping into the pool house and ravishing her the way I've been fantasizing about since the moment I opened her messages.

"No," I answer. "I'll take a room upstairs tonight."

"You sure?"

It's not in his nature to question me. The only time he ever does is when he's sure I'm making a mistake. "Very sure. You're free to go."

"She'll be expecting you."

My fists tighten at my sides. "That's exactly the point—she shouldn't."

"I thought you'd changed your mind?" Shura's brow puckers.

"About what?"

"Natalia," he explains. "I guess I expected… an announcement to be made soon."

I step close so that only Shura can hear me. "Just because I'm fucking her doesn't mean I have any intention of marrying her."

His eyes go purposefully hooded. "I wasn't suggesting a marriage announcement. I was talking about the child." My jaw clenches, but he's not done. "It makes sense to get on top of this, 'Drey. She'll start showing soon and then Nikolai is bound to find out."

He has a point. I'm just too exhausted and frustrated to admit it.

"Stop thinking so much," I slap a hand on his shoulder. "Leave that to me. Now, go and get some rest. You look like you could use it."

I turn from him before he can ask me any more inconvenient questions and make for the spiral staircase in the corner of the VIP section. I'm accosted by half a dozen eager women on my way there, but I shake them off impatiently and head for the quiet of the second floor.

I rarely spend the night here, but even still, the suite is always reserved for me. The linens are changed daily and fresh flowers are on the nightstand.

I expect the inky black comfort of unconsciousness to take hold seconds after my head touches the pillow. But fifteen minutes later, I'm still awake and staring, wide-eyed, at the textured ceiling overhead.

Painfully aware that there's no green-eyed brunette beside me.

25

NATALIA

"I notice your baby daddy hasn't dropped you off in a while."

Abby materializes over the top of my cubicle like the Wicked Witch of the West, her eyes glimmering with a hunter's instinct. She's wearing a thin white blouse today, all the better to show off the lacy red bra underneath.

Honestly, she should just come into the office with nipple tassels. It'd be a hell of a lot more subtle.

"Trouble in paradise?" She doesn't even have the decency to pretend like she's not hopeful for that to be the case.

"Everything is fine. He hasn't been dropping me off because he's busy. And—" I stand abruptly, forcing her to back up a few inches. "—so am I."

Striding around her, I head for the copy room.

A woman who possessed a little more dignity might just leave it there. But not Abby. She's a shark and I, unwittingly, chummed the waters the day I brought Andrey into the office.

Not that I had much of a choice, of course.

"Is he picking you up today, by any chance?" Abby asks, clomping along close behind me on those ridiculous stilettos she's taken to wearing.

"No."

The copy room is empty. I use the desk in the corner to open my file and pull out the documents that I need to scan. The whole time, Abby hovers around me like a bird of prey, ready to swoop down at the slightest sign of weakness.

"Well, what about the company cocktail party next week? Are you bringing him to that?"

I throw her an impatient glare. "That's only for the senior partners."

Abby shrugs. "I'm sure they'll make an exception if I go to Mr. Ewes and ask—"

"Would you excuse me?" She's blocking the damn copier now and I'm losing the will to be polite.

She steps out of the way with an ignorant little titter. "Maybe you could give him my number?"

I put in the first document and close the lid. "I'm not giving him anything."

"Why not?"

A dozen spiteful answers spin through my head, each and every one laced with a scathing insult.

Because he has absolutely no interest in you.

Because he deserves a woman who wants more than just his money.

Because he's not interested in another gold-digger with more boobs than personality.

Instead, what tumbles out is the truth: "Because I don't see him much anymore."

It tastes as bitter as bile coming out of my mouth. And it only makes me want to headbutt Abby all the more for making me admit it.

She smacks her glossy pink lips with unfiltered satisfaction. "You don't?"

Before I have to answer, my phone rings. I'm so desperate to get out of this trainwreck of a conversation that I answer it immediately without checking to see who's calling.

"Hello?" I wave for Abby to give me some privacy. Surprisingly, she takes the hint and skulks back to her desk.

"Hi, Nat." Kat's voice is small and nervous. Clearly, she didn't expect me to pick up.

I freeze for a moment, contemplating whether or not I should hang up or be an adult.

"H-how are you?" she squeaks into the silence.

I close my eyes. Angry as I've been with her lately, hearing her voice again makes me realize how much I've missed her.

Be an adult, it is.

"Okay, I guess."

"That's good to hear."

The silence stretches on. She doesn't say anything, and I'm certainly not about to. I pull my fresh copies out of the machine. "Well, if that's all you called to ask—"

"No!" she yelps. "Nat, wait. Please." She sounds miserable. She sounds exactly how I feel right now.

The loneliness inside me expands tenfold.

Sure, Mila's around. And so is Yelena.

But there are moments—like right now—when neither of them counts.

Because neither of them has met Aunt Annie. They don't know that *Celebration* by Kool & the Gang is one of my sad, *I-need-a-good-cry* songs or what a cherry tree means to me. They don't know to grab my hand every time a car backfires and they haven't watched me cry myself to sleep in the second week of October on the anniversary of the night I lost my parents.

I'm acutely, agonizingly aware that the only person who knows all those things about me is on the other side of this phone.

And she's calling because she hasn't given up yet.

"Okay. I'm waiting."

"I can't stand the silence anymore," Katya says. "You're my best friend, Nat, and I want you back. Just tell me what I need to do to make it up to you. I'm done being a bad friend. I'm done bullying you into my crackpot schemes. I'm done being an obnoxious bitch who thinks the world revolves around her. I just need you to take me back and I will spend the rest of our lives being the perfect friend."

She's panting when she finishes.

Just like that, my anger slips away, eclipsed by bigger, more pertinent emotions. Most of which have Andrey's name stamped all over them.

"Okay."

She gasps. "Really?!"

"I've given you the silent treatment long enough."

"Oh my—*hallelujah*!" she exclaims. "Nat, you have no idea how happy I am."

My face actually cracks into a smile. It feels like it's been a long, long while since I had anything to genuinely smile about.

"When can we meet? Are you free now? Are you working?"

"My lunch break is in half an hour."

"Let's meet at Burning Bird in half an hour then?" she suggests. "It's right down the street from Sunshield. If I leave now, I'll be there on time."

"We can always meet after work if you—"

"No!" she interrupts. "Lunch is great. Can't wait to see you."

She hangs up and I walk back to my cubicle feeling much lighter. The weight in my chest hasn't disappeared by any means, but at least it's manageable now.

∽

I'm so looking forward to lunch that I actually forget about my pretty-boy bodyguard until I see him standing out front with an unlit cigarette dangling from his mouth.

"You smoke?"

"Used to. Best days of my life, really." Leonty puts the cigarette away and sighs. "Now, I just pretend. Where are you off to?"

"Burning Bird for lunch. It's right down the street; no need to follow me. Literally just a block aw—Oh. Okay. Got it. You're walking with me. Still walking. Still walking. Stiiiiill… goddammit, Leonty."

He grins. "Who're we meeting?"

"A friend."

"You don't have friends." I glare at him so hard, he flushes with regret. "Er, what I mean is…"

"Save it." I twist on my heel and resume striding in the direction of the restaurant. "Just stay out of sight, okay? She doesn't know about you people yet."

"'Us people'?" Leonty repeats with amusement.

"My own personal boy band."

I know I'm not being fair to Leonty or any of the others.

They're not the ones ignoring me.

They're not the ones using me for my body.

They're not the ones treating me like a possession instead of a person.

In fact, all of them have been really sweet to me lately. Leonty is always kind no matter how snippy I get. Leif makes sure I have everything I need and then some. Olaf has taken to bringing me flowers in the morning for the vase I keep by my bedside. Even Anatoly has learned to smile at me like he means it, which, given where we started in the facial expression department, is leaps and bounds of improvement.

"It's Katya," I admit.

"Made up with her then, did you?"

It's not something we've ever really discussed, but Leonty's no fool. Katya's glaring absence from my life obviously signified a breakdown in our friendship.

"Sort of. Don't tell Andrey anything."

Leonty gives me a shifty look that I decide to ignore, but to his credit, he doesn't press any more.

When we approach Burning Bird, Leonty tells me he'll be hanging out by the window counter. True to his word, he saunters off to give me some privacy.

I'm waiting only a minute or two when Katya flies through the door in a camel-colored mini-skirt and a white tank. It looks like she sprinted all the way here.

"I'm here!" she announces, rushing up to the table and throwing her sweaty arms around me.

"Why are you so sweaty?"

"I ran down the street. Stupid cabbie dropped me off two blocks over." She slips into the booth opposite me. "It's so good to see you. You look great."

She's laying it on thick. But she does look legitimately happy to see me.

"Thanks for agreeing to meet me," she adds. "I was—We were —I mean, I'm just glad. Yeah. Thanks."

The last few months' worth of distance is thick right now. I'm not used to not knowing how to act around Katya. I hide my awkwardness behind the menu while she catches her breath.

"Nat?"

When I look up from the menu, Kat's looking at me with wide, earnest eyes. I know we're gonna skip right over the small talk.

"The last time we spoke face to face, you said something—" Her eyes dart around the table nervously. "—and it's stayed with me. Tortured me, really."

"What did I say?"

"You said, and I quote, '*I went through something that night. And I'm not sure it can be undone.*'"

My throat clams up.

"Were you just fucking with me or did you mean it?"

I feel immediately guilty—but I didn't lie to her. "I…"

Kat leans forward and seizes my hands between hers. "Oh my God—does it have anything to do with the Kuznetsovs?" she asks. "Because I swear to God, Nat, I genuinely didn't believe Viktor's bullshit about his family. Crime ring, guns, drugs, all that shit—yeah fucking right, you know? It wasn't until later, until you said what you said, that I started digging into the Kuznetsovs. And I realized how wrong I was."

Her cheeks are a blotchy red now. She raises her hand to her chin and I spy the picked-to-pieces nails that she's tried to conceal under layers of bright red polish.

"You've started biting your nails again."

Too late, she tries to hide her hands under the table.

"Because of me?" I ask.

She sighs heavily. "No. Because of *me*. Because I've been an idiot lately and I'm woman enough to admit it."

"Since when?"

She deflates for a second. Then I smile.

Our eyes meet, for perhaps the first time in months. She puts a hand over her heart and sighs in relief.

Just like that, we're friends again.

26

NATALIA

"It does have to do with the Kuznetsovs."

There's no point in dragging out the suspense. I've given Katya enough to worry about these past few months without adding to it now.

"Oh, God." Her bottom lip trembles. "I was worried about that. Was it Viktor or the other one? Did… did one of them catch up to you that night when we made a run for it?"

"The other one," I admit. "Andrey."

"Nat…" Katya looks like she's on the verge of tears. "D-did he hurt you?"

I'm so shocked that I let out a snort of laughter.

Katya pulls back. "So—that's not what happened?"

"Not quite. I actually slept with him."

Her jaw drops.

"But it was totally consensual."

Her eyebrows fly up. "You are kidding me! Why, you little—" She stops short of saying what I know she was going to. Apparently, she's worried that our freshly renewed friendship is still too fragile to withstand a joke.

I launch into the story with as much detail as possible. It feels great, to my complete and total surprise. With every passing minute, my chest gets lighter and lighter.

"... so that was that. He threw a couple of hundred-dollar bills on my coffee table and walked out with the last laugh."

Kat looks furious on my behalf. "How dare—"

I shake my head with a triumphant smile. "He walked out with the last laugh... or so he thought."

"Oh?"

"Well, after I moved into his pool house—" I don't pause even for Kat's shocked reaction; her mouth has already dropped so low it's nearly hitting the table. "—and he visited me for a quickie in the middle of the night, I'm the one who had the last laugh."

Kat gawks at me. "You don't mean... You paid him after sex?"

I understand her surprise. It's not the kind of thing I would normally do. Truth be told, it's a page right out of *her* book.

I give her a smug smile. "And then I slammed the door in his face."

"I couldn't be prouder of you." Grinning from ear-to-ear, she starts to applaud.

A big burst of laughter explodes out of me. Heads swivel in our direction—including my curious, blond bodyguard manning the window.

I ignore him and focus on Kat's admiring expression. "Such a legend. Such a *fucking* legend. Didn't know you had it in you…"

"Being on my own helped some," I admit. "I had to rely on myself."

Kat's face falls. "I let you down."

"It's okay, Kat." I reach for her hand. "You've apologized enough."

She looks doubtful for a moment before she shakes off the guilt and pushes on. "Wait—back up. Why are you living in Andrey Kuznetsov's pool house?!"

And just like that, we've left the fun bit of the story and sailed straight into murky waters. "Erm…"

"Are you with him? Like, *with him* with him? I know you're sleeping with him, but…"

"That's just for convenience." I wince at how that sounds. "What I mean is, it's a no-strings-attached kind of setup."

"But you're not a no-strings-attached kind of girl."

"Yeah, well—things change."

"Like what?"

"Like the fact that he got me pregnant the night that we slept together the first time," I say in a rush.

If I thought she looked shocked when I revealed that I'd slept with Andrey, it's nothing compared to how she looks now. Her mouth flutters open and closed. For the first time in her life, she's speechless.

Finally, she wiggles a finger in each of her ears. "Did I hear that correctly?"

"I'm pregnant, Kat." I lean back and lay a hand on my tiny baby-bump. "Just over three months now."

"And you knew? When I came to the house that day, you already knew?"

"I had six positive pregnancy tests waiting in the sink for me after I closed the door on you."

She runs her hands over her face. "I can't believe it. Does Annie know?"

"She knows I'm pregnant and she knows I'm living with the baby's father. Apart from that—" I bite my lip. "—I don't want her knowing anything else. I don't want her worrying about me."

Kat's hand tightens around my wrist. "Should *I* be worried?"

For a second, the question stumps me. I'm not sure myself.

"What I mean is, maybe we can think of an escape plan?" she suggests. "We can pool our savings, quit our jobs, make a run for it. *Thelma & Louise* style. I can help you raise the baby far away from all this mob bullshit… and then…"

Katya keeps talking, plotting out the next eighteen years of our lives. It means so much to me that she would blow up her entire life just to try and save mine. It reminds me why we're friends in the first place.

She gasps when I launch myself at her from over the table, tears welling in my eyes. "Nat…?"

"It's good to have you back, Katya."

"Does this mean we're changing our names and making a run for it?" she ventures when I finally release her.

I glance at Leonty, who's busy watching me over the rim of his strawberry smoothie. "It's not that simple."

Kat follows my gaze and narrows her eyes at Leonty. "Do you know him?"

"He's my bodyguard."

"He's your *what* now?"

"One of four, actually," I confess. "They accompany me everywhere, including work."

Kat looks more than a little lost. "So, you're in danger… but not from Andrey himself?"

"Andrey—apart from being a raging asshole most of the time—is actually just concerned with my safety. And the safety of the baby, of course."

Kat exhales. "But then—"

"He has enemies, Kat," I reveal, lowering my voice. "And those enemies are probably going to come for me if they know I'm carrying his baby."

"This is some serious *Sopranos* bullshit."

I nod. "My best chance of keeping this baby safe is with Andrey."

Keeping myself safe from Andrey is another matter entirely.

"But—one more time, just to clarify, because I'm a little slow sometimes—you're not together?" Kat asks with a look of intense concentration like she's trying to put together a thousand-piece puzzle. "Even though you're sleeping together?"

"Pretty much."

She falls into a thoughtful silence. "Okay... okay..."

I leave Katya to her ruminations and order us some drinks and tapas. The waitress looks decidedly less disgruntled now that we've finally ordered.

Leonty, on the other hand, is looking more and more restless. He's already finished his drink and he's back to scanning the menu.

"You're not worried?" Kat asks, looking around as though she's paranoid someone might be listening in on us.

"Of course, I am. All the time." *For more reasons than the obvious ones.* "But what can I do? I have a shitty job, a shitty apartment, and no way to raise a child on my own. At least this way, I don't have to burden Aunt Annie with a screaming infant. Not to mention a twenty-seven-year-old with no prospects for a happy future."

"You're selling yourself short."

"No, I'm being realistic."

Leonty leaves his chair by the window and signals to me that he's going to take a call outside. I give him the thumbs-up while Kat watches with interest.

"I mean, as far as bodyguards go, you could do a lot worse," she mumbles appreciatively.

Her ogling of Leonty is interrupted by a sudden crash.

Someone collided right into the waitress who was bringing

us our drinks. Now, they're in a puddle on the floor. The man responsible is apologizing profusely.

"… my fault, I'm so sorry. I should have been looking where I was going."

The waitress looks pissed until she sees that the man who nearly ran her down is tall and handsome. Then she smiles, assures him it's fine, and promises to come right out with fresh drinks for us.

The man turns his hazel eyes on us, and, if I didn't have a pair of steely silver eyes to compare them to, I might be feeling a little weak at the knees.

"I'm so sorry, ladies. That was all my fault." He grins, and I'm sure that smile has gotten him out of more than a few tight spots.

Kat's responding flirty laugh is even more confirmation. "Don't worry about it. It could happen to anyone."

"But it didn't happen to anyone. It happened to me, and right in front of two beautiful women. I have to make it right." He presses a hand to his heart. "I insist on paying for your drinks."

"Totally unnecessary, but highly appreciated," Kat trills before I can say a word.

His eyes flicker to me for a moment. The smile is polite, but curious. "As I said, I insist. My motivations are selfish, anyway. I just want you to leave a better first impression than 'the klutz who ruined your afternoon.'"

Both his smile and his words are smooth as silk. Apparently, it's working wonders on Katya.

"Who doesn't love getting bathed in pineapple juice?" she teases.

He chuckles. "You and I must have different hobbies."

He smiles and backs away from our table as though he's sad to leave. Katya turns to me with those bright man-eater eyes of hers. "Yummy."

"I'm surprised you didn't ask him to join us."

"We've just been reunited. I can't let some rando interrupt, even if he is incredibly sexy." She watches the man leave with a wistful sigh.

The waitress approaches our table bearing a fresh tray of drinks, as well as the food we ordered. "The whole meal has been taken care of, courtesy of your 'clumsy friend,'" she says with a slightly put-out sniff.

I can't really blame her. She's the one who nearly got bowled over and we get a free meal. Doesn't seem fair. I resolve to leave her a fat tip, even as an oblivious Kat helps herself to a steaming empanada.

"Great start to our rekindled friendship, huh? Like, good omens." She chews happily. "If only he'd stuck around for a bit."

I scoop up an eggroll and smile. Pretty as the man was, I'm glad it's just us.

I've got enough boy trouble without adding another to the mix.

27

NATALIA

"I don't want it, Leif!" I cry. "Take it away!"

If I wasn't so damn pissed off, the image of my hulking bodyguard blushing as I brandish a massive pink dildo like a weapon would be hilarious.

I could probably make this easier for him by putting the sex toy down, but as it turns out, I'm more of a misery-loves-company sort of gal.

If I'm suffering, he can suffer right along with me.

"Natalia—"

"Don't you *'Natalia'* me!" I seethe. "I don't want his gifts. I've already told all of you that if Andrey sends me another gift, send them back!"

"He insists—"

With a wordless, frustrated scream, I lob the pink dildo directly at Leif's head.

He could catch it easily—I've seen the man snatch an arrow out of mid-air when he and Anatoly were shooting bows at the archery range in the backyard—but he chooses to duck instead. Guess he's afraid of getting his hands wrapped around a wobbly pink penis. *Coward.*

I stomp back over to the black box I just opened and start tearing out all manner of other sex toys. "*'To help you through all the nights—'*" I read off the handwritten note as I send a sapphire blue vibrator flying, "*—I'm not available!*"

Next goes the diamond-studded butt plug.

"Who the hell does he think he is?"

Then a small purple something that's got me stumped.

"Does he think I can be bought? That I'm some baby oven that he can placate with expensive gifts?"

I grab the biggest bottle of lube I've ever seen and raise it above my head. Leif shields himself like Mt. Vesuvius is about to erupt. "We're just following orders here, ma'am."

"You are *my* bodyguard," I remind him icily. "You should be following *my* orders."

He squints at me from the open window on the patio. "That's not exactly how it works."

Having emptied the box of sex toys, I storm out onto the patio.

Leif scurries back a few more steps. Leonty and Olaf are already hiding way out by the pool. "If you cowards won't stand up to him, then I will. Where is he?"

"Uh…"

"Leif!"

He points towards the main house with an exhausted sigh. "In his office."

I set off, guns blazing, for the main house. Man, does it feel good to direct my anger at the very person who's been steadily raising my blood pressure these past few days.

It's all been from a distance, though. Guerilla emotional warfare. He hasn't visited me at all the past four nights. I haven't seen so much as his shadow.

Despite that, I get several packages every day.

Like the black-knitted Prada dress he sent me on Friday.

And the pair of jewel-adorned Jimmy Choos the day before.

But a box of sex toys is the last straw. It stops now.

I have to check with Yelena where exactly Andrey's office is. The house is like a labyrinth on the inside. Even still, by the time I find myself in front of the brass-studded gate to his inner sanctum, my anger hasn't abated in the slightest.

My goal was to barge right in for maximum effect, but annoyingly, the door's locked. So, I settle for thumping my fists against the surface.

"Andrey! I know you're in there. Let me in."

There are a few seconds of silence before I hear footsteps. The door swings open. I open my mouth, ready to let him have it.

Except, it's not Andrey looking down at me with his usual broody calm. It's Shura.

"Natalia. Is there something I can do for you?"

I spy Andrey in the background, shielded partly by Shura's sharp shoulder. *Cowards.* All of them: Andrey, his men—hell, the whole damn male species. *Cowards.*

"I want to speak to Andrey."

"He's in a meeting at the moment."

I pretend to accept that answer. "Oh! Oh, he's in a meeting, is he? Well, then I guess I'll have to just come back—" I scowl and push past Shura, forcing myself into the office.

Andrey doesn't even bother rising to his feet. He just fixes me with a deep, probing glance, as he addresses the person he's talking to on the phone. "I'll have to call you back, Ivan... Yes, yes... See that it's done."

He hangs up with an exasperated sigh. "Natalia." His tone is cold as ice. His eyes, even more so.

Somehow, it cuts differently in the daylight.

Or maybe it's the absence of the post-sex high that usually softens all those rough edges of his.

"I want you to stop sending me gifts."

Not one muscle moves on his face. "I haven't sent you anything you can't use."

"I don't want to 'use' a single damn bit of it," I snarl. "I'm not some empty hole you can just hurl sex and cash into so it stays quiet. I'm not a midnight distraction. I'm not a fucking *leech.*"

I hear a soft click. When I glance back over my shoulder, I realize that Shura left. We're alone. *Fine.* Better not to have witnesses for the ensuing homicide, anyway.

"I'm sorry you feel that way," Andrey rumbles. I wait for him to say something else—anything else, really—but he keeps looking at me with that coolly detached expression.

"That's it? That's all you have to say to me?"

"To be perfectly honest, Natalia, I'm willing to say whatever I need to if it means I can continue with my day."

Heat rushes to my cheeks. I feel as though my head's about to explode.

"You're busy? Poor thing. It must be hard to be so darn important. Well, guess what? I'm not busy at all. I've got nothing to do except sit around and wait for gifts I don't want and visits I want even less. I'm—I'm—I'm *sofuckinglonely.*"

The words tumble out before I can stop them, and *shit.* I would give my left kidney if I could just take that last part back, please and thank you. I'd give the right one, too, if necessary.

Andrey runs a hand over his stubbled jaw. "I've given you everything you need."

"I don't need expensive gifts," I croak weakly. "When I'm not at work, I'm stuck in that godforsaken pool house, staring at empty walls with nothing to do and no one to talk to."

"You seem to be spending a lot of time with Mila. Or does she not count?"

"She… she counts."

"And Leonty mentioned that you've renewed your friendship with the blonde troublemaker who crashed the wedding."

So much for having bodyguards that keep my secrets.

"Does she not count, either?" he continues.

"I... She does... That's not—"

He rises to his feet, those silver eyes flashing dangerously. All the anger that carried me across the lawn and through the house deflates now that I'm here.

"What I'm hearing is that you're lonely for *me*."

I can't help the gasp that falls from my lips. "That's not true."

"No?" he ventures with a raised eyebrow. "Then tell me again, *lastochka*: why are you here?"

Say something. For God's sake, say anything.

"It just feels bad," I admit in a tiny whisper with my eyes rooted to the floor, "to have you slip into my bed at night whenever *you* want to. And then disappear immediately after. It makes me feel... used."

There's no regret or apology in those heartless eyes as he walks around the desk towards me. "I was under the impression that we had an agreement. One that you entered into of your own free will."

"Yes, but—"

"We both agreed: just sex."

"I'm aware, but—"

"Then it seems you misunderstood me," he says smoothly. "I offered you sex, not companionship."

I bite back the tears threatening my vision. I cannot—*will not*—allow myself to break down in front of him. "Let's be honest: you didn't offer me anything. You made sure I had no other options and then you took what you wanted."

I don't stick around to wait for his reaction. I turn on my heel and speed out the door, yanking it closed behind me.

Shura is standing in the sunlit hallway. His face twists in concern when he sees me. "Natalia, are you—"

"Fine! Fine! Everything's fine!" I shriek as I rush past him.

But the tears are already running down my cheeks and there's no way in hell he didn't see them.

I'm so desperate to get back to the relative safety of the pool house that I make a sharp left as the corridor narrows and run headlong into Yelena.

She exclaims in Russian but reaches out to steady me at the same time. "Natalia!" she gasps, "Are you… Are you crying?"

"No," I lie through a choked sob.

Her face hardens as she tightens her grip on my arm and pulls me deeper into the house.

"No," I try to protest. "I'm going… pool house… I don't want to…"

"Hush now, child." Her voice is soothing, and I find myself falling silent as I let her lead me into the kitchen.

She seats me in one of the chairs around the breakfast table. The bright light sweeping in through the sunroof stands in cruel contrast to my mood. All I want to do is get in bed, curl into a fetal position, and stay there until the pain in my chest disappears.

If it ever disappears, that is.

"Come now, *malysh*, it can't be all bad," Yelena insists in a murmur. "Don't cry now or the baby inside you will be born sad."

It's the kind of old wives' tale that makes me roll my eyes and dry my tears at the same time. I wonder idly where Yelena heard it. Which wizened old woman sat her down in a kitchen, dabbed away her tears, and gave her that pearl to one day pass onto me?

With a jolt, I realize that she can't be much older than my mother would have been if she was still alive.

"Now, tell me: what's wrong?"

I look up at her kind face and try to imagine that she *is* my mother. The problem is, I can't see my mother as an older woman. To me, she's frozen in place at thirty-four—dark-haired, blue-eyed, beautiful as ever.

"I-it's… not important," I mumble.

Yelena makes an impatient click with her tongue. "It's him, isn't it?"

"Doesn't matter."

She lets out a long-suffering sigh. "I wish I could tell you something different—but the truth is, *malysh,* this is who Andrey has always been."

My heart plummets.

"He just doesn't see that what he's doing is hurting you."

I wipe away a fresh wave of tears. "Yes, he does. He just doesn't care."

"I've known him a long time, my dear. Andrey's the type of man who will put himself in front of a bullet if it means protecting you and that baby. But I'm afraid when it comes to feelings, conversation, intimacy…" She shakes her head. "That's never been his strong suit."

"How did he get to be that way?"

Dropped on his head as a baby. Vitamin deficiency. I want it to be something easy and straightforward like that, if only so I can tell myself that he's not actively choosing to break my heart.

"Necessity, perhaps," she suggests, which dashes all my hopes. "Or maybe it's just self-preservation. All I know is that he'll never give you his heart, my dear. There's no point in coveting it."

She's righter than she knows. You can only covet something you have no right to. Something that was never yours.

And God knows Andrey Kuznetsov has never, ever been mine.

28

NATALIA

I'm almost at the pool house when I hear something... A scream? Or...?

No. Couldn't be that... could it?

"Hello?"

There's the rustle of leaves and then: "Just me!"

Mila appears from around the corner, running a hand through her messy hair. *Is her blouse on backwards?*

"What happened to you?" I ask.

She continues to try to pat down her hair. "Uh, I might ask you the same thing. Have you been crying?"

"Uh… maybe." I plop down on the porch swing, still looking towards the bushes she emerged from. "What were you doing back there?"

Her cheeks are pinker than normal. "Just taking a stroll."

"And why is your hair so messed up?"

"Got caught in a strong wind." She joins me on the porch swing. "Leonty mentioned something about a little, erm, temper tantrum you had earlier."

"Leonty talks entirely too much."

I can make out Mila's arched eyebrows from my peripheral vision. "If you don't want to talk about it—"

"It wasn't a temper tantrum!" I snap. "I was just pissed about all the stupid, expensive gifts Andrey's been sending me."

Mila's jaw drops. "Why? I'd never be mad at a Hermes bag—"

"I'm not some empty-headed bimbo who can be bought with a pretty purse. I want *more*!"

The air between us crackles in the silence that follows. Mila goes back to ironing out her hair, pointedly avoiding my eyes the entire time. "A bimbo like me, you mean?"

"No, of course that's not what I—"

"No, you're right: I did marry a rich man I don't love for the convenience of a comfortable life. And I do enjoy spending his money on every extravagant purchase I can get my hands on." Her blue eyes are cool when they meet mine. "I understand why you would feel you have the moral high ground."

"Mila—"

"And while I agree that my choice is definitely not the most morally superior, I disagree with the insinuation that I'm a—what was your phrase—'empty-headed bimbo'?"

I wince. "I wasn't talking about you."

"Maybe not directly." Her hands are folded in her lap. I can't tell if she's pissed off or not. "Did I ever tell you that I was home-schooled my entire life?"

"No. You never mentioned that."

"Yup. Until I was eighteen. I had no friends, except for the ones my father approved of. And I wasn't allowed boyfriends, which is why my first 'relationship'—" She puts it in air quotes. "—had to be a secret. And you already know how that turned out." She pauses to blow out a breath. "Most eighteen-year-olds expect to go off to college after high school. But not me. Right after I turned nineteen, my father told me that he'd already arranged my marriage."

My jaw drops.

"Archaic, isn't it? But that's how my world functioned. The real shock was learning who my future husband was going to be."

I wrinkle my nose. "Did Viktor make a good first impression at least?"

"Viktor wasn't the man I was initially promised to," she explains with a bitter laugh. "My father planned to marry me off to this ancient creep named Vladimir Solovev. He was an arthritic seventy-year-old with eight children and eleven grandchildren. I would have been his fourth wife."

"Jesus *Christ*, Mila."

She actually laughs. "I was horrified. I also knew quite a bit about Vladimir Solovev. You see, his granddaughter and I were friends. And through her, I learned that dear old Vlad had a very specific kink. He only ever married virgins."

From the smirk spreading across her face, it's painfully clear that Mila was certainly not anything of the sort.

"So, when the Kuznetsovs were over for a little tete-a-tete with dear ol' Daddy, I decided to stage a loud conversation with my maid and see which Kuznetsov brother would take the bait. Of course, Viktor slipped the group and found me in the drawing room, where I knew my father always brought his guests after. It's where he keeps his cigars."

Wide-eyed, I gawk at Mila. "They walked in on you talking about not being a virgin?"

"Bingo. Did I mention that Vladimir Solovev was part of the group?"

I actually smack her arm. "He was *not!*"

She nods with satisfaction. "So, I got myself out of what would have been an abusive and miserable marriage to a seventy-year-old pervert who was accused of murdering his last three wives as soon as they started to bore him."

"But you got yourself *in* a miserable marriage with a young asshole," I point out with a frown. "What's the difference?"

"The difference is that Viktor Kuznetsov, asshole though he may be, doesn't have a reputation for mutilating his brides after they've lost their virgin status."

I grimace as unwanted images pop into my head.

"You may look at me and see a kept woman—a vapid idiot who spends her days shopping and ignoring her husband's affairs. But me? All I see is freedom. That's what I set out for when I did what I did. And that's what I got."

Despite myself, I am impressed.

Uncomfortable, horrified… but impressed.

"You want my advice, Nat?" she asks, her voice softening. "Stop looking for perfect. Stop looking for fairy tales. Stop looking for happily-ever-after. You've got your freedom. From where I'm sitting, that's all you need."

"It doesn't feel like I'm free."

"You're free to work where you want and be friends with who you want. You're free to buy what you want whenever you want it. You never have to worry about bills or expenses or whether or not you can afford to send your child to a prestigious private school. You can even have mind-numbing orgasms at the click of your fingers, without the hassle of a relationship to tie you down. What is that if not freedom?"

God, how I wish I could just copy-paste that mentality into my own stupid head. She seems so confident in it, so *freed* by it.

But it just doesn't feel like me.

∽

That night, I make sure to close all the windows and lock all the doors.

No more midnight visitors for me.

29

ANDREY

"That's it?"

Leonty's face falls. His fingers are twitching for a smoke in the same way mine do when I need a release. "I wish I could give you more, but she's not exactly talking to me at the moment."

"What's that got to do with it?"

"Every time I enter the damn pool house, she kicks me out again and asks for Leif or Olaf. This morning, she actually said she preferred that Anatoly be on guard duty today." He shoves his fist through his blonde curls. "Anatoly! No one prefers that miserable bastard to me. She hates me."

"And this is a problem because…?"

"I don't get invited to dinner or movies anymore," he complains.

"You are this close—" I hold my thumb and index finger an inch apart. "—to being thrown out of here on your ass."

"This is your fault, you know. She wouldn't have turned on me if you hadn't slipped and said I was the one who told you about her rekindled friendship with the blonde."

"It wasn't a slip. I want her to know I've got eyes on her at all times." Leonty crosses his arms, ready to keep bickering, but I ignore his sullen mood. "What's going on at Sunshield? Anything to report there?"

Leonty shifts uncomfortably. "Uh… no?"

"If you want me to replace you with Anatoly, too, then—"

"Okay, okay," he protests. "That Byron dude is getting out of hand."

"What's he doing?"

"Flirting, mostly. Never misses an opportunity to approach Nat's desk for a conversation. Brings her stuff all the time—smoothies, cupcakes, cookies. And he's asked her out a few times, too. 'No' is apparently not a word in the *mudak's* vocabulary."

I rise to my feet, fists already clenched and ready. "He asked her out?"

"The whole damn office knows that he's been trying to get in her pants since she started working there."

"And what does Natalia do when he flirts?"

"Er…"

My eyes narrow. "Leonty."

He slumps in defeat. "She always turns down the dates but, well… I mean, it's not like she encourages him; it's just that she doesn't exactly *dis*courage him, either. Especially not lately."

"What does that mean?"

Leonty is looking downright miserable now. "It's no secret that she's kinda pissed at you."

Of course that's not a secret. She nearly brought down the whole house the other day when she stormed into my office.

And if I was in any doubt about just how pissed off she was, it was cleared up later that night when I went to the pool house and found the windows shut tight and the doors locked.

Impregnable Fort Pool House has stood strong the last three nights.

"Go on," I encourage when Leonty pauses.

"Well, lately, she's been a lot more accepting of Byron's advances. Mind you, she hasn't actually *accepted* a date with him—"

"Nor will she," I snarl, heading for the door.

He leaps up and dashes after me. "You're not gonna do what I think you're gonna do, right?"

I ignore him and pull out the keys to my Bentley. "You're off-duty today, Leonty. Relax. Go have a swim in the pool."

"Brother, do you really think this is a good idea? This is only gonna make her angrier."

"I know. I'm counting on it."

～

Sunshield doesn't close for a few more hours, but everyone in the office is deep in their mid-afternoon slump.

There's a bearded man playing *Tetris* on his computer. Another sleeping at his desk. Two women lean over their cubicle wall, heads bent together as they gossip about all the mundane fools around them.

"Mr. Kuznetsov!" a shrill voice calls, cutting through the afternoon lull.

I turn to find Natalia's presumptuous, breast-forward coworker, whose name I've already forgotten and whose face I'd hoped never to see again.

"How wonderful to see you in the office again! Have you come to meet Mr. Ewes? Because he's not here right now, but I can show you—"

"Do you have an off button?" I spit.

That seems to take her down a couple of notches. She stares at me blankly.

"Thank God," I sigh. "Point me to Natalia."

There's no mistaking the pout that turns down her red-smacked lips. "She's over there, through those doors." She aims a manicured finger towards the wall of glass where the senior staff resides. "In Byron's office."

My knuckles crack.

I stalk off in the direction she indicated, fully prepared to break bones if I have to. Thankfully, Abby seems to have gotten my less-than-subtle hint, because she doesn't follow me. She may be an empty-headed moron, but at least she knows to stay out of the range of splashing blood.

Through the glass walls, I can see both Byron and Natalia. They have their backs to the door. Thanks to the carpeted floor, my entrance goes unnoticed.

"... you're being ridiculous," Natalia insists.

I can get behind the words just fine; it's her tone I object to. It's entirely too teasing to have any real sting behind them.

She doesn't talk to me like that, that's for damn sure.

"Trust me: I read it in a pregnancy magazine once. It's totally legit. Pregnant women need regular sex to maintain a healthy pregnancy."

My hands ball into tight fists.

"And why would you of all people be reading a pregnancy magazine?" Natalia asks incredulously.

"My sister was pregnant at the time. I wanted to be a supportive brother."

He moves his hand to Natalia's lower back. I take another step into the room.

You could kill him right now, suggests a voice in my head. *He'd never even know who did it.*

"That's the reason for the glow, you realize," Byron is saying in a serious voice. "If a pregnant woman is not getting enough sex, she doesn't glow. And you, my friend, are not glowing."

My fist twitches. It's going to feel so fucking good to bury it in his face.

But it does beg the question: why isn't she beating me to that (literal) punch? Why isn't she telling this creepy fuck to stay the hell away from her?

I shower her with amazing orgasms and expensive gifts and she despises me. This pompous horn-dog effectively insults her and she's still cackling in his office.

"All I'm saying is that I'd be totally prepared to step in and help bring back that glow."

"Byron!" Natalia exclaims. "Stop."

"Yes, Byron." My tone contains all the acidity that Natalia's lacks. "Stop."

30

ANDREY

"Jesus, Andrey!" They both whirl around, but only Natalia takes a step closer. "What are you doing here?"

Byron clears his throat. "Mr. Kuznetsov, I—we, uh… weren't expecting you."

"That was the point." I step further into his pathetic little office, noticing the sad collection of employee awards displayed like big game animals on the wall opposite the window. "Tell me, Byron: is it a common practice of yours to sexually harass your female employees? Or is Natalia special?"

Natalia's flushed cheeks burn even brighter. Byron just opens and closes his mouth like a goldfish.

It's Natalia who recovers first. "You shouldn't be here."

I ignore her, keeping my gaze fixed on Byron. "I'm waiting for a response, Byron."

He swallows hard and tries to smile, but the corners of his lips don't seem to want to obey. The effect makes him look constipated. "I was only j-j-joking. Just a joke... no harm done... Natalia and I—" My fists are squeezed so hard now, I can practically feel the tendons threatening to snap. "—have a rap-p-port."

"What you call 'rapport,' I would call 'a very viable lawsuit.'"

"That's enough!" Natalia snaps, striding forward and putting her hand on my chest. Only then do I realize I've been slowly advancing on them. "Andrey, you have no right to barge into my workplace and cause trouble with my coworkers."

My blood is heating to a boil. It's a wonder I haven't set off the damn fire alarms in this shithole.

Her defense of him has given Byron some false confidence, because he draws himself up to full height and looks me dead in the eye. "I think it's clear that Ms. Boone would like you to leave."

I brush Natalia aside and take a step towards him. Every inch I get closer to him steals another inch from his posture, until he's slumped and cowering in my shadow.

"Oh, and you know what Ms. Boone wants, do you?"

I can smell his sweat. Can see it trickling past his temples. But he's either much braver or much dumber than I realized —my money's on the latter—because he turns his back on the safe route and decides to stand his ground instead.

His chin juts out stubbornly. "More so than you, apparently."

"No, Andrey!" Natalia clings uselessly to my elbow as I take another step forward. "Stop!"

It's something in her voice that does the trick. A tiny crack— almost unnoticeable, really—but a crack that opens just wide enough for me to glimpse inside...

And see darkness that goes a long, long way down.

I remember reeling her out of that catatonia after the shootout at the doctor's office. It's clear that the prospect of violence turns Natalia's blood to ice. Even now, the bright pink embarrassment on her cheeks is completely gone, replaced by a ghostly white fear.

I *hate* that look on her.

I *hate* that I put it there.

So, as satisfying as it would be to punch a hole through this moron's vapid face, I decide—for her sake; not his—that there are better ways to remind him what I'm capable of.

"Byron," I growl in a low voice. I keep my eyes on Natalia. "Would you excuse us? Natalia and I have things to discuss."

He gapes at me open-mouthed. "This… this is *my* office." He turns to Natalia, clearly expecting her to back him up and kick me out.

But Natalia's chewing her lip and avoiding his eyes. "Byron, would you mind… please?" she asks. "We won't be long."

He looks like he certainly does mind. But in the face of Natalia's hushed plea and my scowl, he has no choice but to nod and retreat.

"O-okay." He eyes me apprehensively as he backs his way to the door. "Nat, if… if you need me…"

"I'll be fine, Byron."

The door shuts, but the walls are still glass. He can see us.

I could use that, I think.

"What the actual fuck do you think you're doing?!" Natalia cries. "How dare you—"

Her angry words fade off as my eyes rove up and down her body. She's wearing a tight black pencil skirt and a powder blue blouse that hugs every curve to perfection.

"Hey!" She snaps her fingers in my face. "I'm up here."

"You look good, *lastochka*."

That puts some color back in her cheeks. But there's still a muscle twitching in her jaw that says, *Beware.* Unfortunately for her, I have no intention of doing that.

"Don't," she warns. "Don't even start."

I look around. "He calls this an office, does he?"

Natalia glances back over her shoulder. Byron has slunk off into the far corner of the hallway, but I can still spy him, peeking around the corner like a nosy child. "You've got balls," she seethes when she turns to face me again.

Smirking, I reach for her. "You would know best."

She slaps my hand away. "Don't! What do you think you're doing?"

"I could ask you the same question."

"I'm at work."

"Certainly didn't look like much work was getting done."

Her face contorts into rage. "You have no right to—"

Before she can finish her sentence, I've grabbed her around the waist and walked her backwards into Byron's rickety desk.

"'Right'?" I snarl so vehemently that she falls silent. "You want to talk to me about rights? What makes you think you have the right to stand here flirting with sniveling *mudaks* when you're carrying *my* child?"

"I wasn't… That wasn't…" Those perfect green eyes of hers are star-bright, sparking with a mixture of confusion and anger.

And maybe something else.

The first flickers of a wildfire.

"I thought I made myself clear, *lastochka*." I hoist her onto the table and knock her legs apart with my knee. "You're mine." She opens her mouth to argue, but I cut her off at the pass. "And if you need any more proof of that—" My hand slips up her sexy pencil skirt and grazes along her inner thigh. "—I'm only too happy to provide it."

"No, Andrey," she protests, squirming against me in a way that doesn't do a damn bit of good to convince me she means what she's saying. "Stop…"

She tugs on my arms again and again, but each is weaker than the last.

I push aside her panties and slip my fingers into her warm slit. To nobody's surprise, she's dripping wet.

Her eyes pop open. For a moment, she's lost in the feeling. Then her gaze flickers to the glass walls behind us.

"No, we can't! Byron will… *Fuck*, he'll see."

"Good." I growl. "He needs to understand how pointless it is to pursue you."

Emerald Malice

She opens her mouth to say something, but I never discover what, because her words are lost to a moan.

I lean in and catch that moan with my lips, sliding my fingers deeper inside her while my thumb strokes her clit. The closer she gets to orgasm, the more desperate and panicky she becomes. "Andrey… please… please…"

But I'm about as capable of stopping as I am of inducting Byron into the Bratva. Natalia shudders, biting her bottom lip so hard that she draws a thin line of blood.

I lick it away.

Then I unbuckle my pants.

"No!" she gasps, trying to push me away. "No, Andrey… not here… not on Byron's desk."

My fingers curl around her throat as I lick the side of her neck. Her breaths are coming hot and fast. "Don't worry, *lastochka*," I assure her. "He's not watching."

It's a lie, of course. I can see him, peering around the corner every few seconds to try to see what we're doing.

Let him watch.

No one can say Andrey Kuznetsov isn't generous.

Pulling my cock free, I shove her skirt higher around her thighs. Natalia doesn't try to stop me. I thrust myself inside her and—

Fuck.

My mind goes blank.

It's like all the noise, all the worries and doubts that have been rolling around in my head since I became the fucking *pakhan*… It all fades away.

Nothing and no one exists.

Except for *her*.

Except for *me*.

She bites down on my shoulder, one hand scraping across my chest as we start rocking back and forth. "You see?" I murmur in her ear. "You see now who you belong to?"

She doesn't reply apart from a breathy moan here, a hitched gasp there.

"And if you're ever in doubt again, just come to me—" *Thrust.* "—and I'll remind you all over again." *Thrust.* "I'll remind you as many—fucking—times—as—it—takes!"

She falls apart again just as my hot cum fills her up.

I stay there until I have nothing left to give, fully sealed hip-to-hip with her. Natalia's eyes are still hazy when I pull out and zip myself up.

When she reaches for a tissue, I stop her. "No, *lastochka*. You're not allowed to wipe it away. You're going to spend the rest of the day walking around with my cum dripping down your thighs. And you're going to fucking love it."

She pushes herself off the desk onto wobbly legs and, for a moment, I think she's going to defy me. But she leaves the tissue where it is and pulls her skirt down.

Despite her compliance, the post-orgasm euphoria has drained off her face almost instantly. She's back to looking pissed.

"Satisfied now?" she demands icily.

"I believe I made my point."

Her eyes flicker savagely. "That's all I am to you. That's all I've ever been: a point. You can have me whenever you want. But I can only have you on your terms, when you want."

She walks around Byron's desk, leaving behind a faint, sweaty imprint of her ass on the wood. It's disappearing already. Pity—someone should frame that and hang it in the Louvre.

"You make a huge deal about meeting my needs and wants, but the truth is, they don't matter at all. I don't matter to you at all." Her eyes have gone misty again. "I'm nothing more than a plaything to you."

There are a dozen or more snide jabs I could think of to lob at her feet and walk out of here victorious. But strangely, the need to come out on top feels much less important than the pain in her eyes.

On instinct, I reach forward, moving to cup her face with my palm.

But she flinches back like I might hurt her.

I drop my hand with the sudden realization that, quite apart from not trusting me, Natalia doesn't feel safe with me. It sends a jolt of something very much like regret coursing through my gut.

"This is what you agreed to, Natalia," I remind her softly.

She whips away from me to face the far wall. If she's crying, she doesn't want me to see it.

"I know exactly what I agreed to," she whispers back, so quietly that I almost miss it.

The words she's left unspoken come through loud and clear. *But maybe I shouldn't have.*

Resisting the urge to touch her, I sweep out of the office, leaving behind the mingling scents of sex and sadness. I'm so deeply preoccupied by that hurt look in her eyes that I don't even notice Byron until he's slipping around the corner to face me.

Before he can so much as open his mouth, I grab him by the front of his shirt and slam him hard against the same wall he was hiding behind this whole time.

"This is your first and last warning," I snarl. "Go near my woman again and you *will* regret it."

I shove him against the wall once more for good measure, just to make sure the message sinks in. Then I stalk away, happy at least that I can put some distance between me and that sniveling rat.

I ignore the curious looks Anatoly and Olaf toss my way as I storm through the lobby. Outside, I throw myself into my car, the memory of Natalia's dejected face burning itself into my retinas.

The last time a woman looked at me with that kind of disappointment, I lied and promised her everything would be okay.

Which makes me realize with an uncomfortable jolt—

Maybe that woman is due for a visit.

31

ANDREY

Drogheda Psychiatric Institution doesn't look as bleak as it sounds.

I spent a huge amount of time and money making sure that the place I chose would be calm, comfortable, and most importantly, comfort*ing*. Still, some of the people who need this place are long past comfort.

"Mr. Kuznetsov!" The head nurse, Kathleen, greets me with a smile as soon as I enter the foyer. "How nice to see you again. It's been so long since your last visit."

Don't fucking remind me.

"How's she doing?"

"She has good and bad days," the nurse gushes. "But she eats well most days and she loves the gardens. I take her for a walk at least twice a day. You're just in time for that, actually. We're due for our evening stroll. She'll be so glad to see you."

Unlikely. It's been four months. I'll face some wrath for that.

Kathleen leads me across a lush courtyard full of lavender and honeysuckles and into a covered corridor on the far side. Tall, stained glass windows block the view of the highway at the bottom of the hill while splashing colored light down the hall.

"Third room on the right," Kathleen informs me. As though I could forget even if I tried. When I don't reach for the door immediately, she sighs and pushes the door open. "Look who's come to see you today, Arina! It's Andrey."

From the hallway, all I can see is the clean, white room, utterly devoid of sharp edges. The locked window looks towards the central courtyard, but when I walk into the room, my mother is staring at her feet.

"Hello, Mama," I greet, lingering in the doorway. "How are you?"

The woman sitting in the yellow armchair beside the bed barely looks like the Arina Kuznetsov I once knew. Her receding eyebrows pinch together as she drags her gaze up to squint at me. "You look… like someone I know…"

I know exactly who I remind her of. If she's forgotten who, that's a good thing.

"I know you," she concludes uncertainly. One bony finger quivers in my direction.

"Of course you know him," Kathleen chimes in. "He's your son. One of them, anyway."

Arina looks pleasantly surprised by this revelation. "I have a son?"

"Two of them. Good-looking boys." She fluffs the pillows and rearranges the fresh flowers in the vase, making things neat and tidy in the room. I stand still and gaze at my mother.

"Two sons," Arina repeats. "I don't remember them."

"How about we take a walk?" I suggest in an uncharacteristic croak.

"Wonderful idea!" agrees Kathleen. "Arina, doesn't that sound like a wonderful idea?"

My mother's hazy eyes rotate from me to Kathleen, then back to me. "Are you going to walk with me?"

"That's the plan."

She nods slowly in acceptance. Then, with Kathleen's help, she gets to her feet.

Her nightdress covers her from the base of her neck to her ankles. She looks so much older than her fifty-six years.

That's what marrying a Kuznetsov will do to you.

Natalia may hate me now, but if she saw what became of the women unlucky enough to land themselves a Kuznetsov man, she'd be happy I'm keeping myself at arm's length.

"Shall I accompany you?" Kathleen mutters to me as we move into the hall.

I shake my head. "I've got it."

She gives me an encouraging smile and disappears back the same way we came.

Arina looks after her and then her gaze flits to me. "Who did you say you were again?"

"Andrey," I tell her patiently. "Your son."

"*Son*," she whispers softly. "My son."

She doesn't talk again for a long time. I accompany her through the gardens, down to the pond where a gaggle of ducks paddle along in the water, dipping their curved necks beneath the surface.

"How have you been?" I ask when the silence gets to be too much.

She looks at me with an irritated frown, as though she'd rather be watching ducks instead of answering stupid questions. "Can't remember."

"Fair enough."

Another five minutes before she turns to me with a start. "I know who you remind me of." She scowls. "My husband, Slavik. Do you know him?"

"We've met."

"I thought you were him for a moment. But then… you're younger."

And a very different man.

"Do you know him?" she asks again.

"Yes."

"How?"

I concentrate on two ducks venturing close to the bank. "He's my father."

She winces, and I almost laugh. Disease is chewing away at her brain, but she still knows enough to pity me for drawing that shitty card in life. "That must be hard for you."

"You have no idea."

"He's not a good man, that Slavik." Almost as soon as the words pass her lips, her face flushes with fear. "But don't tell him I said that! He'll beat me for it."

In her panic, she grabs my arm. I place a hand over hers, shocked at how papery-soft her skin feels. "I won't breathe a word."

"He has spies, you know?" she tells me conspiratorially. "They watch me wherever I go. He killed my favorite brother, too. He denies it, but I know he did." She looks around the garden with wide eyes as if she expects Slavik himself to jump out of the rose bushes. "He killed Leonid because he knew we were close. He doesn't want me to have anyone."

"You don't have to worry about Slavik," I assure her. "He's gone now."

Her eyes snap to mine. "Gone? Gone where?"

"Russia. He's not coming back."

"He left… He really left?" She sounds astonished. "If he left, he would have put me in a cage first. He always puts me in a cage when he leaves."

You are in a cage, Mama. An invisible one, but a cage nonetheless.

My throat is so dry, it's painful. "You're free now, Mama." She flinches when I call her that. "You don't have to worry about Slavik. He can't hurt you anymore."

She starts tugging at the ends of her long, gray hair. It used to be a luxurious chestnut brown. But in the last few years, it's gone thin and wispy. "… evil man. I'm glad he's gone. I'm glad!" she hisses, as if talking to someone standing directly in front of her. She turns suddenly and grabs my arm. "My boys! What about my boys? Did he take them with him?"

I stare into her eyes and for a moment—one solitary, heartbreaking moment—I see the woman who raised me. The woman who ran her fingers through my hair to wake me in the morning. The woman who sang out-of-tune songs to put me to bed at night.

"No, he didn't take the boys."

She sighs in relief. "Oh, thank God. At least they'll stand a chance now." She pauses, taken by a sudden realization. "Although, they must be bigger now? They must be men."

I nod. "Viktor is married."

She draws in a startled breath and her eyes fill with tears. "Oh, how wonderful. My baby, married!"

It's hard to look at her, but I refuse to turn away. This is the sanest I've seen her in a long time.

"And Andrey?" she demands in a rush. It's as if she's aware that her memory could slip away at any moment. Time is of the essence. "Has he found someone?"

The weight on my chest gets heavier. "He's… going to be a father."

Tears shine brightly in her dimmed eyes. "He'll be a wonderful father. He was always such a kind boy. So patient and thoughtful. So unlike his father." Her gaze drifts towards the ducks. "He looks the most like Slavik, you know. Sometimes, I was afraid…"

I wait for her to continue, but her voice trails away.

After a long stretch, she turns back to me, her face slowly creasing into a frown. "You look like my husband."

I get to my feet and resist the urge to offer her my hand.

"Come, Arina," I say gently. "Let me walk you back to your room."

32

NATALIA

My new plan is simple.

DO NOT THINK ABOUT ANDREY KUZNETSOV.

DO NOT FANTASIZE ABOUT ANDREY KUZNETSOV.

DO NOT WASTE TIME FEELING ANYTHING FOR ANDREY KUZNETSOV.

It's been three days since the disastrous office incident, and I haven't seen or heard anything from him. Which I've decided is a good thing.

What's not such a good thing: still having to show my face at work after climaxing on my boss's desk.

Abby cornered me by the copier this morning and demanded to know what really happened the other day. Did I actually fuck Andrey Kuznetsov on Byron's desk? Or was I fucking Byron when Andrey walked in on us?

Lola and Kate from accounting gave me super nasty stink eyes while I was eating my lunch. Even Marge, the sweet old receptionist who has always been nothing short of lovely to me, pretended to be busy both times I walked past her desk today.

The one saving grace in all this has been—shocker of all shockers—Byron.

He's the last person I would've expected to have my back, especially after what I let happen, but not only did he refrain from firing me, but he also refused to accept my resignation.

"No way, Nat," he said fiercely. "You're a good employee and I'm not going to lose you over something like this."

"But—"

He shook his head. "You're staying. And furthermore, I'm not taking this to the higher-ups, either. But just so you know, there *is* talk in the office. I'm only telling you because I want you to know it didn't come from me."

"Then how—"

"Leslie caught a glimpse of what happened when she was walking to the restroom. You know what a gossip she is."

Forget our company—the whole building will know about it by the end of the week. "Why do you want me to stay?"

"Because you're a good employee," he insisted. "And because I don't want that asshole to win."

I didn't tell Byron that there was no hope of that; Andrey Kuznetsov always wins. The only thing we can do is ignore him.

Which is why I repeat my new three-step plan to myself as I get home from my extraordinarily long day.

Do not think about Andrey Kuznetsov.

Do not fantasize about Andrey Kuznetsov.

Do not—

I freeze in the doorway to the pool house, a tight knot forming in my belly.

Nestled in the alcove between the sitting room and the kitchen, right under the window, is a baby grand piano.

I approach it cautiously, like it might grow legs and run away if I spook it. When I'm close enough to be sure it isn't going to flee, I brush my fingers over the smooth, glistening surface. Tears jump to my eyes. When I touch the keys, a C-sharp rings out, clear and pure.

For a tenuous moment, I feel my father and mother in the room with me.

I hear my father's booming laugh.

I smell my mother's perfume.

And then it's gone. *They're* gone.

And I'm standing alone in a lonely pool house with a piano they never played.

Which is how I find myself thinking about Andrey, fantasizing about Andrey—and most definitely, feeling things for Andrey.

Some of them are angry and bitter. For making a mess of my work life. For making me think about my parents, miss them even more than usual.

Most of the feelings, however, aren't angry or bitter at all. That's the worst thing he could've done.

The floorboards creak and I whip around. It's like he could feel the shift in my thoughts, and decided to strike when I was at my weakest.

"Do you like it?" he asks.

"No." I'm still touching it, I realize. I peel my fingers away. My lips are trembling as I try to maintain composure. "I told you I didn't want any more gifts."

"I know you used to play with your parents."

I manage to put my finger on the constricting feeling in my chest: *disappointment*.

And this time, it has nothing to do with Andrey. I told only one person in this house that I used to play piano with my parents. And that person was definitely not him.

"Yes, I did. But since my parents are *dead*—" I hurl the word at him, even though it still hurts me just to say. "—there's no one left to play for."

His gaze flickers to the baby grand. "If you want me to remove it, I will."

I should let him. *Burn it to ashes; see if I care.*

But the moment he suggests removing the piano, I shift closer to it. Now that I've seen it, touched it and felt my parents in the room—I can't possibly let it go.

"Don't bother," I snap. "It's here now. Just leave it. But I want you to know that this is the last thing I will accept."

He inclines his head and leaves.

If I've pissed him off, he does a good job of hiding it.

I drop onto the piano seat and exhale. After a long time has passed, I place my hands on the silky keys and begin to play.

To my surprise, it comes easily. My fingers remember where to move, how much pressure to apply to make the music sing. I play through my complicated emotions, channeling all my frustration and resentment and uncertainty into the chords. I play until the sky turns dark and shadows creep into the pool house.

I'm still playing when my phone lights up with a text message from Mila.

MILA: *Hey, whatcha up to? I thought we could order a pizza and watch a movie together*

I answer without hesitation.

NATALIA: *So you can report to Andrey afterwards? Thanks, but no thanks. Let's agree that you stick to your wing of the house and I'll stick to mine.*

I send the text and put my phone face-down on the stool next to me. A few seconds later, it lights up with incoming messages.

One. Two. Three. Four. Five.

I ignore them all and keep playing.

33

NATALIA

"Nat, please. Just open the door—the window, even! I just want to talk."

Talk about déjà vu. Not so long ago, I was in this exact same position with Kat. What is it with me and the people I'm drawn to? I sure know how to pick 'em, don't I?

The longer I think about it, the louder the little voice in my head gets. *It's you. You're the problem.*

"Natalia!"

My hands crash down hard on the piano keys. The chord that comes out is so cringeworthy that I immediately apologize out loud to the instrument.

This piano deserves better.

I abandon my attempt to play and walk over to the stereo, fully prepared to put on some music and drown Mila out. But she's still shouting at the top of her lungs, and not even Bon Jovi at his best could top that.

"Okay, I know it was a dirty, rotten, no-good, lowdown thing to do. But I thought—at the time—it was harmless. I didn't know you. I figured spending time with you and letting Andrey know how you were doing wasn't such a big deal, y'know? It wasn't that bad, right?" She groans. "But then I did get to know you, and I really, really like you. But I'd already agreed to report back to Andrey. Plus, he was just using my info to give you nice presents. Is that such a crime?"

My hand is poised over the play button, but I can't bring myself to start the music.

"And yes, I had something to gain from agreeing to do what he wanted me to do. I had to look out for myself, Nat. You know my position. I just—"

I'm as shocked as Mila seems to be when I lean forward and wrench open the window. "*What* did you have to gain?" I demand.

"Uh, well…" She looks around surreptitiously, no doubt trying to determine just how many shadows are lurking in the darkness with their ears peeled. "Can… can I come in so we can finish talking?"

"No."

"Okay. That's fine." She fidgets in place. "Andrey is basically my… my shield, I guess you'd call it."

"Is that Bratva speak? Because I don't get it."

She takes another cursory glance over her shoulder. "You know who I'm married to."

"Yes. We've crossed paths," I say coldly.

"Well, he's been cheating on me since the night we got married."

It's a little harder to maintain my frigid composure. But I do my best. It's not that I'm biting back jaw-dropping surprise—leopards don't change their spots, after all, and cheaters don't change their bedsheets—it's more that I'm stopping myself from spitting in her face, *No fucking shit, Mila. He's an asshole. That's what assholes do.*

"And after we moved here, he's become less and less subtle about it," she continues. "I've walked in on him with, like, four different women in our bed already."

Okay, I'm still mad, but my heart also hurts for her. Even when you hate your husband, it can't be easy to catch him red-handed like that so many times. Or, I dunno, red-penised or whatever.

Mila brushes hair out of her face. "I confronted him the last time. I kicked the bitch out of my room and told Viktor that I wouldn't let him make a fool of me."

Despite myself, I lean in. "How did he react?"

"Badly." When I flinch, she rushes to reassure me, "He didn't get violent or anything. But he did tell me that he wasn't about to stop. Actually, he told me that he was the boss and I would have to get in line because 'Kuznetsov women obey.' If they don't, they end up where his mother did."

My heart is hammering in my chest. "Where's that?"

"I have no fucking idea," Mila admits. "But it didn't sound good. I wasn't exactly rushing to ask follow-up questions."

"How does Andrey fit into all this? Is he going to stop Viktor?"

"There's no stopping Viktor, Nat. I didn't expect that from Andrey. But I explained everything and asked for the freedom to conduct my own affairs without fear of retribution."

My jaw drops. "Oh my God. *Mila.*"

"You can judge me if you want. Lord knows I deserve it. But Andrey agreed."

"I'm not judging you."

"Yeah, well, maybe you should." A contemptuous laugh explodes out of her mouth. "I've made a mess of my life, and I have no one but myself to blame."

She's blinking hard, trying to fight the tears turning her eyes misty. It's a far cry from the easy, breezy, *life-is-doom-and-gloom-so-just-accept-it* philosophy she'd recently tried to convince me of.

"I was wrong, Nat!" she wails suddenly. "I was wrong when I told you not to look for a happily-ever-after. You were worried that you'd never get to experience something real, and I just waved it off as unimportant. But you had it right all along. I was jaded and pessimistic and so used to disappointment that I thought it was easier to have a fling rather than a relationship."

Tears roll down her cheeks, and at the sight of that, the last of my anger fades. "You just didn't want to be hurt again."

Mila wipes away her tears with a grimace. "Yeah, well, I was a fool to think I could outsmart my heart. Turns out, when you fall, you fall. And there's nothing anyone can do about it."

"Mila," I ask softly, "do you have feelings for someone?"

She looks at me through damp lashes.

Then I catch a tall shadow in the far distance. My first few nights here, it scared the shit out of me. But I'm used to the patrol now.

"Why don't you come inside?" I offer.

Mila gives me a watery smile and nods. She looks guiltily at the piano as she passes before she sits in the armchair that faces the other way. "I know I betrayed your trust when I told Andrey all those personal things about you playing piano with your parents. For what it's worth, I regretted it the moment it was out of my mouth."

I sit on the sofa across from her and tuck my feet under me. "But you kept informing on me."

"Less and less," she mumbles. "I told him stuff that I thought was inconsequential. But…"

"What?"

"Nothing was inconsequential to him," she says. "It doesn't matter how small or superficial the tidbit I gave him was, he wanted to know everything."

"It's not because he cares," I snort. "He just wants to control me."

"Is it so hard to believe that he might want to protect you?"

"Yes," I insist. "It is."

Mila falls silent. But I know it's not because she agrees with me. She just doesn't want to say or do anything else that will cause me to kick her right back out on her ass.

"I didn't lie to you about my past, Natalia. I wasn't kidding when I said I had no real friends growing up. The truth is, you are my first real friend. I get that it started out as something else," she admits ruefully. "Something pretty ugly and self-serving. But it turned into a real friendship for me. I don't want to lose you."

"How can we be friends if I know that everything I tell you is going to be reported back to Andrey?"

For the first time since I let her inside, she raises her chin proudly. I see a flash of the devil-may-care Mila I know. "Every woman deserves to have some secrets. And I'll keep yours. Anything you tell me from this point on is off-limits to Andrey, I will take to my grave."

"That requires a lot of trust on my part."

Mila nods. "It's asking a lot, I know. Especially after what I've done. But you can trust me, Nat. Like I said, every woman is entitled to her secrets."

"Including you?" I ask slyly.

"Yes, including me."

I can't deny that it makes me feel a little lighter hearing her say that. It also gives me the courage to broach the little secret I've suspected Mila of keeping for the last few weeks.

"So… is it Leonty?"

Her smile gets a little wider. "How did you know?"

"No offense, but the two of you aren't exactly subtle."

She giggles and I'm amazed at how young and innocent she sounds. It's not such a bad look on her. She's too young to be so jaded.

"It started with flirting. And then—" Her eyes turn dreamy. "—he walked me to my wing of the house one night after we had dinner here. We had our first kiss right outside my bedroom door."

"Must have been some kiss."

"You'd think, but no." She sighs. "He was such a gentleman. Just a little peck and then he walked away."

It's painfully obvious that very few men have ever walked away from Mila satisfied with something as innocent as a goodnight kiss.

"It was only meant to be a fling, you know? It was never meant to be…" Her eyes go misty again and the smile slides off her face. "I finally understand what you meant when you said you wanted something real, Nat. I just didn't get it before because—well, I'd never had serious feelings for anyone. Until now."

"Your husband's cousin," I can't help but whisper. "You sure picked a doozy to start with."

"I know." Her eyes flit once again to the open windows. "Like I said, I've made a mess of my life."

"Marriage doesn't have to be forever, Mila. You can divorce Viktor if you really want to."

Mila is shaking her head before I've even finished speaking. "Maybe that's true for some people, but this is the Bratva. Marriage is for life."

"What if you asked Andrey—"

"There's no point. He'll never allow me to divorce his brother in order to be with his cousin." She sounds so damn sure, so resigned to her fate. I hate that for her.

"So, you're just gonna stay married to Viktor but continue to have an affair with Leonty?"

Mila looks at her lap dejectedly. "It's the most we can hope for. We've both agreed: if we can't have each other wholly, then we'll settle for parts. We'll live for stolen moments rather than nothing at all."

How my heart aches for her, for them...

But even as I acknowledge the hopelessness of their love story, I register a stab of something piercing the center of my chest.

At least they're both in it together.

At least they have each other.

"Nat," Mila's voice is barely audible. "Are we okay?"

Swallowing my own heartache, I nod. "We're okay."

"Thank—"

I raise my hand to stop her. "Oh, don't thank me just yet. I have one caveat for our friendship."

Mila arches a brow and waits for me to finish.

"Katya. She's my best friend. We're a package deal."

"Does she hate Viktor as much as I do?" Mila asks.

"My money is on her hating him more than you do."

She laughs. "Then we'll get along famously."

34

ANDREY

As Natalia steps out onto the pavement, sheathed in shadow from the Sunshield logo above, her eyes fall on my vehicle. The scowl that settles over her face is actually quite amusing.

I'd worry she'd run, but considering those pretty heels she's wearing, she has no choice but to skulk to the car and buckle herself into the passenger seat, all the while avoiding my eyes.

"Did you have a good day?"

She mumbles something unintelligible under her breath. I decide not to press her for a clarification, because I'm fairly certain it involved sticking several unpleasantly sharp objects in certain orifices of mine.

"Is there a reason you're picking me up today?" she demands.

"I have something to show you."

"It's not another gift, is it?" she asks. "Because I already told you, I'm not going to accept any more—"

"How about you keep your panties unbunched until after you see what it is?" I suggest.

Her mouth snaps shut and she crosses her arms over her chest. I don't mind in the slightest—I much prefer this snappy, feisty version of Natalia to the quiet, sad iteration I've seen too often recently.

"Whatever it is, I don't want it."

"Now, now, don't say that. You'll hurt his feelings."

"*His* feelings?"

I just smile, enjoying the way her teeth grind together.

The silence grows as I navigate out of after-work traffic and head for home. "You didn't bring me a *man*, did you?" she blurts out of nowhere.

I almost swerve us off the damn road. It takes everything in me to stay between the lines. "Excuse me?"

She shrugs. "You know. Like, a gigolo."

My disgusted expression only deepens.

"A male prostit—"

"I know what a gigolo is," I snap.

She throws up her hands in defeat. "Just asking. Jeez. You did send me a box of sex toys not so long ago."

"Self-pleasure is a far cry from paid sex. And just so we're clear—" I take my eyes off the road just so she understands how serious I am. "—I'm not about to spend *my* money so *you* can get off with another man."

Is it my imagination or is she actually fighting a smile?

"Alright, alright," she mumbles. "No need to get *your* panties in a bunch."

I accelerate hard, causing her to clutch the corners of her seat. Did I really think snappy, feisty Natalia was better?

I stand corrected.

∽

By the time I pull up outside the manor, Natalia is all nerves again. Her eyes keep skirting around the property like she's waiting for something to jump out at her.

"He should be waiting with Leonty by the pool house."

"Who should be waiting with Leonty?"

I ignore her and walk briskly through the house.

"Slow down, will you?" She pauses at the threshold to kick off her heels and then follows me, barefoot, into the garden. "Pregnant woman walking here. I never walked this fast even when I wasn't knocked up."

I take the steps down to the pool two at a time. Natalia follows, complaining under her breath until Leonty tears around the pool house with a leash in hand.

"… just cleaned your damn poop and this is the thanks I get. Ungrateful little fucker." He glances down at the beast by his side. "Ungrateful *big* fucker, actually."

Natalia stops, breathless, at my side.

Staring at her parted, perfectly plump lips, I realize I'm actually nervous about how this reveal is going to go down.

"What is...?" She trails off as a German Shepherd leaps into the air, grabs his leash with his teeth, and shakes Leonty off. Free, he bounds in big circles through the grass.

Natalia laughs, clapping a hand over her mouth when the dog turns to her, ears pricked.

He drops the leash and sniffs at the air as though he can smell Natalia in the wind. He should be able to. It's why I brought one of Natalia's shirts for him to sleep with on the flight back from Russia.

Shura wanted to kill me when he found out I left him in charge so I could go pick up a dog. Mostly because it meant he had to deal with Misha's latest outburst solo. When Shura went to check on the boy, Misha tried to attack him. My response was to give the boy a little more freedom.

"A woman rejects you, you buy her gifts," he muttered. "A boy attacks me, we set him loose in the house. It makes no sense."

Shura would change his mind if he could see Natalia's face right now.

She drops to her knees, wearing the most magnificent smile. "Who are you, you beautiful boy?"

The dog approaches her slowly—cautious, but not in the least bit aggressive.

"Careful now," I instruct her. "Make sure he has the chance to check you out."

Natalia sits cross-legged on the grass and waits for him to come to her. He observes her coolly for several seconds and then, decision reached, he bounds happily right into her extended arms.

"Hey, handsome," she coos. "You're such a sweet boy, yes, you are, such a sweet boy."

Leonty stares at the scene, open-mouthed. Clearly, he had about as much luck with Remi as I did.

Natalia seems to have forgotten that anyone apart from her and the dog exists. She plucks the leash from Leonty's grasp and unhooks the other end from his collar. "You don't need this, do you? No, you don't. You're too good of a boy to need that."

The dog is whining happily, licking Natalia's face and rubbing himself up against her.

Lucky little runt.

"Does he have a name?"

"Remington."

"Remington," she croons, kissing him between the eyes. "What a lovely name."

I walk around them, marveling at how easy that was. As I venture closer, Remi jumps to alertness, watching me with his hackles raised.

As if the dog needs to be worried about *me*.

"Whoa, buddy," Natalia whispers sweetly. "You're okay."

He eases back down, and I resist the urge to roll my eyes. "He's yours."

Her hand freezes on his collar. "You are shitting me."

"I most definitely am not."

She looks at Remi in disbelief. He looks right back at her. I watch it happen right before my eyes—true fucking love.

Which brings me to a new all-time low.

First, I was jealous of that deadbeat numbskull, Byron. Now, I'm jealous of a goddamn dog.

A dog who's staring daggers at me, oblivious to the fact that it was my damn money that bought him the golden ticket to his cushy new life.

"What's wrong, pretty boy?" Natalia murmurs fondly. "Why are you so worked up?"

"He's a guard dog," I say. "He's doing what he's trained to do: protect you."

Natalia looks over at Leonty, who's slinking away in the direction of the big house. "I already have a four-man security detail for that."

"Yeah, well, this security guard—" I gesture towards Remi. "—is the only one I will tolerate in your bed."

She smiles and continues to pat the dog's side.

"I figured you could use some companionship," I add, throwing caution to the wind. "I was hoping he'd make you feel less… lonely." Her eyes meet mine and something unreadable flashes across them. "He's also been trained as a support animal. Specializing in PTSD."

Her cheeks go scarlet. This is the first time I've ever brought up her catatonic episode. She shuffles from one foot to the other, focusing on Remi every time she wants to avoid looking at me.

"Okay," is all she seems capable of saying.

I take a step towards her, ignoring Remi when he bares his

teeth at me. "I know you've been struggling, *lastochka*. I'm not ignorant to your pain. I want to do what I can to help."

Reluctantly, she drags her gaze to mine.

"My priority is that you are safe—but you should know that I want you to be happy, too. I don't want you to feel so alone."

Her face softens. The resentment in her eyes dims behind a tentative smile. "He's a beautiful dog," she says softly. "Thank you."

I clear my throat. "At the moment, he only follows commands in Russian. But it shouldn't be too much trouble to ask Leif or Leonty to teach you some basic phrases. Why don't you take him for a walk around the grounds, show him his new home?"

Her face falls—or at least, I think it does—but before I can double check, she's bending to fasten the leash back around Remi's collar.

"Um... would you like to join us?"

I want nothing more. Which is why I wave her off. "You go ahead."

She nods sadly, as though she expected nothing else. "Come on, Remi. Let's take a little walk, shall we?"

"Maybe another time," I hear myself call after her.

She stops on the spot and glances at me over her shoulder. Her face is unreadable for a moment.

Then, to my surprise... she smiles.

35

NATALIA

"There is no way in hell she agreed to this," Katya announces loudly. "You're trying to get me killed."

I tuck the phone between my chin and shoulder. "I've told you a dozen times already: I cleared it with Mila. She has no problem with you hanging out in the manor."

"Right. Sure," she snorts. "More like, she's trying to lure me into her house so she can poison me while your back is turned."

"Dramatic, much?"

"She's a Bratva wife, Nat!"

"She's not like that."

"They're all like that."

"You ever consider that maybe it's you? 'Cause I'm not a Bratva wife, and I kind of want to kill you right now."

She doesn't bite on my joke. "Seriously, Nat, I don't see the point in Mila and me meeting. We aren't gonna be all buddy-buddy."

"Mila is my friend and so are you. I would like for the two of you to get along."

"Um, I slept with her husband! Then crashed her wedding! She has to hate me. I'd hate me."

"Technically, you slept with him before he was her husband," I point out. "And she understands why you crashed the wedding."

"Just like I understand why she's letting me into her house." Katya lowers her voice to a whisper. "To poison me."

I roll my eyes. "Just trust me. Mila's cool."

There's a beat of silence on the other line. Then Katya lets out a frustrated sigh. "Oh, dammit, alright. If it means that much to you."

"It does. How about this Saturday?" I suggest. "We can have a girls' day. And you can finally meet Remi."

"Can Remi taste-test my food before I eat it?"

"Kat."

She lets out a dramatic moan. "You'll be sorry when I'm choking on arsenic. I hope you have a great eulogy planned. Those tears better be real, bitch."

"Don't worry: Remi actually is trained to sniff out dangerous substances."

"How reassuring," drawls Kat. "Guess I can look forward to a steak knife through the ribs instead."

I curl my fingers through the soft fur on Remi's head. He's currently tucked on the sofa next to me, his head nestled comfortably against my belly, like he's protecting both me and the baby at once.

"And what about the other alpha in your life?" Kat ventures. "How's he doing?"

My fingers stiffen on Remi's head and he gives me an encouraging whine. "He's, er… the same," I admit. "He's been a little more present lately, but I think that's for Remi's sake."

"How do you figure that?"

"He wants Remi to get used to him. And it's kinda working. Sort of. The last time Andrey joined us for a walk around the grounds, Remi didn't growl at him when he got too close to me."

"Ah, he's trying to get *close*, is he?" I can hear the eyebrow wag even over the phone.

For Kat's benefit, I pretend to find it amusing. "Oh, don't worry: he still gives me a wide berth."

"Hm. Do you think there's someone else?"

The mere question has my heart sinking. Remi seems to sense it. He lifts his head and looks at me with those deep blue eyes. *I'll kill whoever's hurting you,* that look says.

I kiss his nose and pet him until he drops his head again. "I have no idea. Andrey's life is a complete and utter mystery to me."

"Maybe you could, like, ask him out or something?" Katya suggests. "Just go in for the kill, you know?"

I bound off the sofa so abruptly that Remi yelps. "Andrey has made it very clear that I'm nothing more to him than the mother of his child. And I'm not about to chase after a man who isn't interested."

"But what if he is—"

"Sorry, Kat," I interrupt abruptly. "Remi needs a walk. See you this Saturday!"

I hang up before she's even gotten her goodbye halfway out.

The mere thought of asking Andrey out on a date is enough to give me hives. Not that I haven't imagined a few different scenarios… especially since he gave me Remi. It was just such a thoughtful gesture.

"I want you to be happy," he told me. For once, I actually believed him.

There was this look in his eyes as he said it, too. Something suggesting that, beneath that cold, austere Bratva mask, is a man who has feelings just as thorny and unwelcome as mine.

He just hides them a little better.

Okay—a *lot* better.

I wear my heart on my sleeve whether I like it or not. Andrey, though? Andrey has *secrets.*

And I might just be one of them.

Ignoring Remi's leash, I open the door and let him bound freely out onto the grass. As I follow him out, I practice the Russian commands quietly under my breath.

'Sidet means "sit."

Nyet means "no."

Bros 'eto means "leave it."

Tikhiy means "quiet."

And *ataka*—I'm not a fan of this one, but Shura insisted I learn it—means "attack."

I'm trying to get my pronunciation of *tikhiy* right because I keep butchering it, when Remi lifts his head and freezes. His body is rigid with tension and a menacing growl emanates from his muscular chest.

"Rem—"

Before I can even finish his name, he bursts forward in a blur and disappears around the corner.

Then I hear three angry barks.

And a terrified, high-pitched scream.

Just like that, I forget I'm pregnant. I forget I hate running. I forget all the commands I've learned over the last few days as I sprint around the side of the house.

I find him hunched over someone whose legs are flailing helplessly between Remi's hindquarters. Remi's got a skinny forearm locked between his jaws.

"Stop, Remi!"

Remi growls louder while the person wails.

"*Nyet,* Remi!" I say desperately, all of the commands coming back to me in a rush. "*Nyet! Bros 'eto. 'Sidet. 'Sidet!*"

He looks up at me, that pale arm dangling between his bared teeth. Reluctantly, he drops it, backs away, and sits.

I blow out a breath and rush to the man on the ground. "I'm so sorry. Are you okay?"

The man is shielding his face with his forearms raised like shields. It takes a moment before he peers at me from between them.

"I'm sorry," I repeat. "I'm—"

I pause mid-sentence when I realize this isn't a man at all. He's a child. He can't be more than twelve or thirteen years old.

"Are you okay?"

He glances nervously over at Remi, who's now licking at his fur like nothing whatsoever is wrong. "Will the dog attack again if I sit up?"

"I'll make sure he won't," I assure him, turning to Remi and giving him one more firm *"Sidet."* I reach over to help the boy right himself.

He flinches away from me the moment I touch him, but I ignore it and help him anyway. "I should have had him on a leash. It's just that I thought he'd been introduced to all the staff by now and—"

"I'm not staff," he snaps. Remi growls and his tone softens. "I'm not staff. I'm—"

"Misha!" Shura's angry snarl cuts through his answer. "What the hell do you think you're doing?"

Remi barks, though there's no threat in it. He and Shura have made their peace.

The boy, however, jumps to his feet and tries to limp away.

"Get your ass over here," Shura bellows, grabbing the still-shaking boy by the scruff of his shirt and twisting him around.

"Shura!" I exclaim. "Stop."

He ignores me altogether. "I give you trust and you betray that trust by sneaking out of your room!"

"*Trust,*" the boy spits aggressively, matching Shura's tone. "You call that trust?"

"You can forget about your morning walks now." Shura wheels the boy around by his neck.

"Shura!" I explode, causing Remi to start barking behind me. "Let him go right now or I will set Remi on you."

That gets his attention. He spins back around, but he doesn't let go of the boy. "Natalia, this doesn't concern you."

My eyes narrow. "Let him go or I will give Remi the command. Thanks to you, I know it well."

He looks at me, waiting for me to take it back. When I don't, he sighs and drops the boy's collar.

"Thanks. Now—" I turn to the boy. "—what was your name again?"

"Misha." He massages the back of his neck and gives Shura a scowl.

"Well, Misha, I'd say you're lucky you weren't eaten, but I doubt you'd even make a filling snack for Remi. C'mon, Skin & Bones, let's get you a good meal."

Ignoring Shura's incredulous expression, I grab Misha's arm and pull him towards the manor.

36

NATALIA

"Did he hurt you?"

Misha snorts. "I can take that old man any day."

I push the plate of roast beef and potatoes towards him. "I was talking about Remi."

"Oh." He eyes the meat with obvious hunger, but doesn't touch it. He turns his attention to the torn sleeve of his forearm instead. "I'll survive."

I can't help marvel at how quickly he shook off the shock of his attack—by both man and dog.

"You're not hungry?"

He stares at me. "Who are you?"

It doesn't take a genius to figure out that this kid isn't an average teenager. He's got all the signs of a child who's had to grow up fast. His every muscle is tense and rigid.

"My name is Natalia. I live in the pool house."

"Why?"

I put my hand on my slightly protruding belly. "Because I'm going to have a baby and I've been told it's the safest place for me."

"Told by whom?" he asks shrewdly.

"Men who think they know better than me." I sound as resentful as he does.

"Let me guess: Andrey Kuznetsov?"

I raise my eyebrows. "Maybe."

Misha eyes my stomach with something resembling wariness. "Is it his baby you're having?"

This conversation is making me more than a little bit uncomfortable. But I figure, if he's smart enough to ask the question, then he's mature enough to hear the answer.

"Yes. It is."

"Then I feel sorry for you," he declares suddenly.

I pull my own plate closer, taking a bite. When I look up, he's still watching me. "It's rude to let a pregnant woman eat alone, you know."

He waits another few moments before he caves and spears a piece of roast beef with his fork.

His eyes flutter on the first bite. The second and third go down even faster. By the fourth, he's holding the plate up to his mouth and shoveling food directly in.

The more I observe him, the angrier I get.

His clothes aren't threadbare, but they're not exactly clean, either. His arms and legs are covered in scratches, wounds, and scars, not all of them healed. And he's jumpy, like he's scared of the very men who claim to want to keep me safe.

It doesn't make sense.

Doesn't it, though? These are dangerous men playing dangerous games.

The shuffling of feet in the hallway has Misha dropping his fork loudly and twisting around. Yelena enters, carrying a heaping pile of laundry.

Her cool gaze falls on me first. Then Misha.

She doesn't say a word, but I hear a low hiss escape her throat as she storms past the kitchen to the laundry room without another word.

Strange.

"So, Misha," I say, ignoring the little interruption, "what would you say to spending the evening with Remi and me? You don't have to worry about him anymore. He's a big softie once you get to know him."

Misha eyes Remi, who's frolicking around in the gardens outside of the window, snapping at passing butterflies. "I'm not supposed to leave my room," he mutters.

"Says who?"

His eyes fall to my belly. "Everyone."

I wave away his worry. "You let me deal with 'everyone.' So what do you—"

The sound of heavier footsteps sends Misha springing to his feet. I follow suit and, acting on some instinct I don't have any idea how to explain, I slide in front of Misha just before Andrey enters.

He freezes at the sight of us, his eyes flickering from my face to Misha's.

"What's going on here?"

"What does it look like?" I counter. "We're having lunch."

It's been a while since I saw that much ice in his gaze. For some reason, it ignites something in me that gives me the courage to stand a little taller.

"And then Misha's gonna come and hang out with Remi and me in the pool house."

Andrey's scowl is as terrifying as it is puzzling. "Like hell he is."

"Why not?"

"Because I said so. That's why."

I glare at him for a moment. Then I call out, "Remi!"

My furry protector zooms into the kitchen from the garden, looking delighted to be summoned.

Someone who doesn't look quite so delighted? The impossibly tall, dark-haired Adonis standing in front of me.

Bet he's regretting the gift now, I think with wicked satisfaction.

"You want to get to him, you're going to have to go through Remi and me," I announce firmly. "I'm not about to let you hurt him."

"I'm not planning on hurting anyone," he says. "I'm just going to show him back to his room where he belongs."

I glance over at Misha. His face gives nothing away. "He needs a change of scenery."

"Natalia." Andrey's voice is hard and impatient. "This doesn't concern you."

"Yeah, well, there are parts of my life that don't concern you, either. Doesn't stop you from getting involved, does it?"

His jaw clenches and he takes a step closer, but Remi bursts into fresh growls, forcing him to a standstill.

I'm not gonna lie—this is *fun*.

Andrey seems to realize that reasoning with me is the only way he's gonna make some headway. He sighs. "You don't understand, but allow me to explain."

"Go ahead.

His eyes shift to Misha. "Not here."

"Alright then. We'll talk in the pool house. We were headed there, anyway."

Andrey fixes me with a sharp gaze that promises retribution for my current sass. "Let me first show Misha back to his—"

"No."

"Natalia," he bites out, "I don't trust him."

"He's just a boy, Andrey."

"I am not," Misha insists from just behind my shoulder. "I'm fourteen!"

"Regardless, I think he can be trusted to walk around the gardens by himself. What are you afraid he'll do?" I demand. "Pull out your begonias?"

One corner of Andrey's mouth twitches upwards. "I wouldn't put it past him. And since I am fond of my begonias, I'll have Shura keep an eye on him while we head to the pool house."

"Why bother Shura when Remi's right here? I didn't finish walking him anyway." I bend down and pat Remi between the ears. "Misha, you don't mind walking Remi for me while Andrey and I talk, do you?"

Misha stares at the dog uncertainly. "Er…"

"Don't worry; he won't attack you again." I call Remi forward and have him sniff Misha's hand. "You can pet him if you want."

After a few tentative pats, Misha relaxes and so does Remi. I fasten Remi's leash onto his collar and pass it to the reluctant teenager.

"Are you sure?"

I gesture towards the gardens. "Go enjoy the fresh air."

Remi gives me a backward glance as Misha guides him nervously towards the French doors.

Without waiting to see what Andrey thinks of my plan, I charge ahead towards the pool house. It might technically be his property, but it no longer feels that way. It feels like my space now—and I intend to use that to my advantage.

Neither one of us says a word until the door to the pool house is shut tight.

"So," I ask congenially, "you wanna tell me why you've kidnapped a fourteen-year-old boy?"

Andrey runs a hand through his windswept hair. "He may look like a kid, but he's a spy, Natalia."

I snort. "Give me a break."

"You already know I have my enemies."

"Are all of your enemies in middle school?"

He narrows his eyes. "Nikolai Rostov sent Misha to spy on me."

"Nikolai uses child soldiers, so you decide to kidnap them? The high road must have been under construction." Andrey's eyebrows rise, but he says nothing, so I press on. "Why on earth are you keeping him here?"

"I can't very well let him go," Andrey sighs. "He knows too much."

I spread my hands wide. "Andrey, do you hear yourself? We're talking about a boy. A fourteen-year-old, whose arms and legs are covered in scars!"

"That was not my doing."

"I didn't say it was," I clarify. "I'm saying that he's been through enough without the adults in the room looking at him like the perpetrator instead of the victim!"

"He's not some run-of-the-mill teenager, *lastochka*—"

"I know that! Which is why he needs more attention, not less. He needs to be able to talk to someone."

"I have tried to get him to talk," he grits out. "He's remained stubbornly silent."

"Were you trying to talk to him?" I accuse. "Or were you trying to interrogate him? I'm not sure you're aware of the difference, but it's a pretty big one for us normal people."

Again, I think I see the corner of his mouth twitch upwards. But when he speaks, there's no trace of amusement in his tone. "This is Bratva business, Natalia. This doesn't—"

"Yeah, yeah. Nothing concerns me. You've made that clear a billion fucking times." I huff out a sigh. "I'm not asking you to let him go. All I'm asking is that he be allowed some freedom."

"Freedom to spend time with you, you mean?" Andrey asks shrewdly.

I shrug. "Would that be so bad? He needs company. And, come to think of it, so do I."

"You certainly have a habit of collecting strays, don't you?" he remarks as he moves towards the door. "You've already got a dog to train, *lastochka*. You don't need another."

"Andrey!"

He stops abruptly and turns to me with arched eyebrows and a pained look on his face.

"What is it about me that makes it so hard for you to listen?" Before he can answer, before I can lose my nerve, I walk right up to him, painfully conscious that my breathing is racing as hard as my heart is. "Apparently," I continue, "the only time I can make you listen is when sex is involved. So, if that's what it takes… fine."

His carefully controlled mask slips for a moment. I register a kernel of confusion; he has no idea where I'm going with this.

But a second later—when I lower myself to my knees in front of him—it can't be any clearer.

37

ANDREY

"Get up," I growl. "Natalia, goddammit, get—"

She ignores me and forces down my zipper.

My cock practically jumps out at her, nearly hitting her across the face. She raises an amused eyebrow. "Looks to me like you don't really want me to stop at all."

"Natalia. I said that's enough."

But the warning rings hollow even to my own ears. She clearly agrees, because she cups my balls in one hand and hums appreciatively.

"Why?" she asks innocently. "You're obviously having fun."

"This changes nothing."

Her lips purse. "We'll see about that, won't we?"

I have to admit, this new, devious side of her is definitely intriguing. Not to mention, a huge fucking turn-on.

Before I can assure her that, apart from my cum, she's going to have to swallow disappointment, she's taken the entire length of my cock down her throat.

What. The. Fuck.

Bright pinpricks of light float across my vision, obliterating everything else from sight. My blood roars in my ears, drowning out everything else.

My body doesn't even feel like it belongs to me anymore.

It feels like it belongs to *her*.

She's taken me so deep that the urge to unload all my pressure into her ravenous throat is already overwhelming. But it's been so long since I've been with her, so long since I felt her sweet warmth, her pulsing heartbeat, the slickness of her desire—I can't possibly finish this early. I need to savor every second.

I grit my teeth and cement myself to the wooden floors as her head bobs.

Then, much too soon, she pulls away. Her hips sway hypnotically as she walks to the sofa and removes the pale pink t-shirt she's wearing. Her breasts pop out of the half-cups of her bra, seeming to have doubled in size since I last laid eyes on them.

She fixes her eyes on me as she peels off her pants, revealing red lacy panties.

I have no clue where all this confidence came from—but I fucking love it.

She beckons me forward with a curl of her finger as the other reaches around to unclasp her bra. When was the last time I came when called? Like a fucking dog?

And yet, I find myself walking to the sofa.

I cup one of her breasts, squeezing as my erection throbs hungrily. She plants a hand on my chest and shoves me down onto the sofa.

When she's satisfied that I'm seated where she wants me, she slides the panties down her slim thighs and then she's straddling me, her hands on my shoulders, her breasts bouncing inches from my mouth.

There's no time for me to take charge because she does it first. She grabs my cock, aligns it with her wet slit, and slides down my length, swallowing me into her inner depths.

I see the pinpricks of light again.

I hear that rush of my own blood.

Goddammit, this woman will be the death of me.

She rides me fiercely, her ass rising and falling hard as she takes her pleasure, using me like I'm one of the toys I once sent her.

Looking back on it now, I can't believe how idiotic that was. A dildo would be wasted on a woman like her. She needs a strong, capable cock attached to a strong, capable man. One who can appreciate every line, every curve, every contour of her body.

She needs someone who can worship her the way she deserves.

When I try to cup her breasts, she grabs my hands instead. Entwining her fingers through mine, she pushes our hands against the sofa's headrest and bounces on my cock harder still. Small, fluttery moans escape from her parted lips. She rides me faster and faster until we both reach our breaking point.

The second I feel her pussy contract around my dick, my own orgasm explodes inside her. It's not a conscious decision on my part. I wouldn't have been able to hold myself back for all the money in the world.

Her hips rock, milking me for all I'm worth, before she finally goes still.

My hand snakes towards her stomach. It's not so flat anymore. It strikes me with a pang of white-hot guilt that I've missed the last two doctor's appointments. I never even asked her how they went. I spoke directly to the clinic and left it at that. I wonder what's changed inside of her. How big the baby is. What's fully formed, what's in the making, what is still to come?

Before I can truly appreciate the changes in her body, she's wrenching herself off me and reaching for her discarded clothes on the carpet.

She turns around, giving me the perfect view of her perfect ass before she pulls her clothes on. Then she drops down on the edge of the coffee table in front of me, the faintest sheen of sweat coating her skin.

"I want Misha to be released from whatever room you're keeping him locked in," she says, all business. "I'll keep an eye on him."

"Natalia—"

"Remi will be with me the whole time. Not to mention my own personal boy band, per usual."

I grimace. The roller coaster of sensations is bringing on a migraine brewed up by the devil himself. "How long are you prepared to fight for this?"

"As long as it takes. I will not let you mistreat that boy. He's a child. Children deserve to be protected, no matter the circumstances."

The fierce determination glowing in those fire-bright eyes of hers is almost touching. She's a mama bear if ever I saw one.

"Very well," I agree.

"He gets freedom of the grounds?"

"Yes."

"And you won't lock him in his room anymore?" she verifies.

"Not all the time."

She hesitates for a second, but then thinks better of arguing the point. "And he can hang out with me whenever he wants?"

"If that's what he wants, yes." I rise to my feet and sigh, pinching the bridge of my nose. "Enjoy your victory, *lastochka*. It may well be your last."

She smiles. "I wouldn't count on that."

As I walk back to the main house, I'm torn between the desire to check Natalia's newfound confidence and the desire to lock the pool house door, throw her in her bed, and never let her leave.

Before I can decide either way, I hear a scream. "*Mudak*! You'll kill her!"

"Yelena!" I roar through the house. "What's going on?"

Yelena rushes clumsily around the corner, gasping. "It's Viktor. He's gone mad!"

More screams echo from deeper in the house, and I follow them to the sitting room.

There, I find my brother, walking wild-eyed and wrathful across the room, dragging Mila by the hair behind him.

38

ANDREY

"Stop!"

Viktor freezes where he stands. All the sound drains out of the room, but his fist is still curled in Mila's hair.

To her credit, Mila doesn't look scared. She's *pissed*.

Her cheek is red from where he must've slapped her. Judging from the scratch marks scored into Viktor's cheeks, she gave back as good as she got.

"Let her go," I snarl.

"This is a private matter between husband and wife, brother. This is for me to—"

"You have three seconds to release her or I will cut your hand off at the wrist." My deathly quiet warning has the intended effect; he drops his hand at once.

Mila scrambles to her feet and glares at Viktor with an expression that gives new meaning to the phrase, *If looks could kill.*

I look back and forth between the glowering couple. "What happened?"

"I'll tell you what happened!" Viktor seethes. "I walked into our bedroom and—"

"I was talking to Mila," I interrupt.

Viktor flushes scarlet and his hands ball into fists once more. His knuckles are split and bloody.

Mila takes a deep breath. "Viktor walked into my bedroom—"

"*Our* bedroom!" Viktor inserts.

"I had no idea you considered it '*ours.*' Especially given the number of whores you've entertained there."

"I don't need to pay for sex! Just because you have no interest in fucking me anymore doesn't mean—"

"Enough," I snap. They both fall silent until I nod at Mila to continue.

"He walked in on me and—" She drops her gaze to her feet. "On me and Leonty."

Viktor's eyes are trained on me, watching, waiting for my reaction. I keep my expression carefully masked as I process that.

Do I wish Mila had chosen someone other than my cousin to have an affair with? Obviously.

Am I going to intervene? Not a fucking chance.

"Well?" Viktor demands when I don't say anything. "What do you have to say to that? She was fucking our cousin in my fucking bed!"

I glare at my sniveling brother. "Let's get one thing straight right now: this is my house. Therefore, it's *my* fucking bed."

Viktor's eyes bulge wide with outrage. "Did you not hear me? She was fucking Leonty!"

"Unlike you, brother, I'm not slow. I heard her the first time. Speaking of…" I glance towards Mila. "Where is Leonty?"

"*He—*" She inclines her head in Viktor's direction. "—knocked him out! He clubbed Leonty on the back of the head while he was checking on me."

"You attacked a man while his back was turned?" I ask in disgust.

"He attacked me first!"

"Because you slapped me!" Mila cries.

Viktor's face is red and mottled. "You fucking deserved it, you treacherous bitch!"

"She has done nothing more than you deserve," I interject, causing them both to go silent again.

Viktor gawks at me. "You're taking *her* side?"

"You've been conducting your own affairs out in the open since your marriage. Why shouldn't Mila do the same?"

"Because I won't allow it!" He sounds like a child. I half-expect him to stamp his foot.

"Maybe you didn't." It's only with some effort that I keep the smirk off my face. "But I did."

The color drains from Viktor's cheeks. His mouth opens and closes, but he can't find the words.

I turn to Mila. "Go check on Leonty."

She scurries out of the room without looking back.

Viktor shakes his head when she's gone. "What do you mean, 'you did'?"

"I gave Mila my permission to have her own affairs."

"You... You what?" His fists tremble at his sides. "You had no right!"

I take a step forward and Viktor stumbles back into the sofa. "I have every right. Do I need to remind you who I am? The crown I wear?"

He gulps, and I wonder for a moment if Viktor is smart enough not to run his mouth in the face of my wrath.

But I'm overestimating him once again. "You are my brother."

"A title I grow more and more ashamed of every day."

"You'd let her make a cuckold of me?"

"It won't be the worst thing people say about you."

"I have a reputation—"

"You have a reputation as a drunk, a liar, a bully, a slacker. It will surprise no one that your wife is distracting herself with other, more worthy men."

Viktor scowls and straightens up again, though the inches of height between us have never been more glaring. "I will not let this stand. You might be happy to make me a laughingstock among the underworld, but I will not tolerate it."

"Do your worst, Viktor." I smile. "But if you lay one hand on Mila's head, you will answer to me."

"Is she fucking you, too?" he mutters.

If I hadn't just spent some of my pent-up energy with Natalia, I might've knocked him across the room for that. I've flayed men alive for saying far less. As it is, I pretend not to have heard him. "The same goes for Leonty. If I find you've so much as whispered an insult in his direction, there will be consequences."

He sags. "Why protect him?"

"Because, like Mila, he's more valuable to me than you are."

"He's nothing more than a *vor*," Viktor hisses. "You have plenty more where he came from."

"He's a *vor* with a critical mission. I won't trust just anyone to protect the mother of my child."

It's only when Viktor's jaw drops that I realize he didn't even know.

Idiot that he is, he's paid no attention to the chaos of the last month. I hid nothing—he's just too stupid to have seen the signs of change coming.

"Fuck." His eyes dart to the window, through which a sliver of the pool house can be seen. "When did this happen?"

"Probably while you were drunk and balls-deep in a woman who wasn't your wife."

Before Viktor can respond, Shura sticks his head in the room. "Everything under control here?"

Viktor storms off, brushing into Shura as he leaves.

"Make sure someone keeps an eye on Viktor," I order in a weary rasp. "He's angry; it makes him even dumber than usual."

"I've got you covered," Shura says. "And if you're looking for Leonty, he's in the medical room upstairs. They're getting him checked out as we speak."

I make my way there, intent on seeing just how much damage my cowardly brother managed to inflict on our cousin. But before I push the door all the way open, I hear Mila's voice.

"… already bruising." I shift forward and can see she's next to his bed, her fingers tracing along the contours of Leonty's bruised forehead and swollen jaw.

"I'll be fine. The bruises are nothing." He touches her red cheek with the tips of his fingers. "It's this bruise I'm worried about. I should have killed him."

"He's not worth it."

He drops his head, regret pooling in the corners of his mouth. "Was this? Worth it, I mean?"

"If you're asking me if you are worth the chaos my marriage is currently in, then yes," she snaps. "Yes, it most certainly is."

"I will walk away if that's what—"

"It's not what I want," she insists. "And fuck you for even suggesting it, Leonty. You are the only thing I want. Viktor's just gonna have to deal with that."

"And what about everyone else?" Leonty presses. "What about your father? What if it gets out—"

"Then it gets out." Mila grabs his face and rests her forehead against his. "And we endure the consequences."

Leonty sighs, but there's no mistaking the proud smile hidden behind his bruises. He leans in to kiss her.

I pull the door closed the rest of the way and walk back downstairs, my head so crowded that it's almost painful.

What I just witnessed wasn't a man and a woman entangled in a complicated affair, but a star-crossed couple who are genuinely in love. The same thing is threatening to bloom between myself and Natalia… if only I let it.

But can I? Should I?

When I stand to lose so much more?

39

NATALIA

"*Prygat'*," Shura orders.

Remi runs towards Shura, and, with one final burst of speed, coils and launches himself up until the tip of his nose grazes Shura's outstretched palm.

"Well done, Remi!" I clap and Katya joins in, but she's clearly distracted.

"So cute," she mumbles, almost to herself.

"And the sweetest dog in the world."

Katya turns to me like she forgot I was here. "Oh. Right. But I was talking about..." She gestures over to Shura, who's got his back to us now.

"Shura?" I gawk.

"He has this raw, magnetic sexual appeal." Katya licks her lips.

All I can do is shriek with increasing incredulity, *"Shura?!"*

"You can't tell me you don't find him attractive."

"Watch me: I don't find him attractive. Honestly, I'm surprised you do. He's not your usual type." Then again, that might be a good thing. Her usual type is Andrey's fuckboy little brother. Straying from the standard might be exactly what the doctor ordered.

"I don't know. He's wiry, but strong. And broody. The whole package is… sexy as hell."

I groan. "The last time you described a man as 'sexy,' I was forced to sit through a dinner with Viktor Kuznetsov."

Katya throws a wicked elbow into my ribs. "How about we not talk about mistakes of the past? You couldn't pay me a million dollars to even look at Viktor—" But then she cuts herself off, her eyes locked on something over my shoulder.

Suddenly, she turns away so she can fluff her hair and adjust her lipstick. Since she doesn't drag the neckline of her shirt low enough for some tasteful cleavage, I know we've moved out of *there's a man I want to impress* territory into *there's a woman I need to intimidate*.

I wave Mila over and then hiss to Katya, "Be nice."

"I'm always nice," she mutters out of the side of her mouth.

She's not, and the warning glare I toss her way makes it clear that I know it.

She sighs and raises her hands in surrender, but I swear I hear her muttering under her breath. "… fraternizing… look at her… some nerve…"

I manage to drown her out and plaster a big smile on my face as Mila steps onto the patio. "Mila, come meet Katya.

Officially," I add. "In a way that doesn't involve being chased by security guards right after."

Katya laughs, but it sounds like she's being strangled. To her credit, she does offer Mila her hand. "Nice to meet you, Mila. Again. Sort of."

Mila smiles. "No hard feelings about crashing my wedding. It's all water under the bridge."

Wow. This is going well.

"Well, of course you wouldn't have hard feelings. You weren't the one being cheated on, were you?"

I bite back a sigh. *So close. We were so, so close.*

As if he can smell the catfight brewing, Shura shifts closer to us. He tosses Remi's Frisbee across the yard, but I know he's eavesdropping, ready to intervene.

"I can't believe you still care," I moan. "This is Viktor we're talking about. You just said you would spend another second near him even if you were offered millions of—"

"It's the principle of the thing," Katya cuts me off. "You don't steal another woman's man! Even if that man is a worthless pile of shit."

I'm ready to strangle my best friend, but Mila just laughs. "I get why you're pissed, Katya. You have every right to be. But you're making some big assumptions here."

Katya flips her short, blonde bob. "Which *are...?*"

"You're assuming I knew that he had a steady girlfriend and that I pursued him anyway. I assure you, I didn't. Nor did Viktor rush to tell me about your existence when he cornered me the day we... er... got involved."

Katya studies her with narrowed eyes. "He really didn't mention me?"

"No, and I'm sure he doesn't mention me to even a fraction of the women he brings home. I promise you, all of his latest conquests look very surprised when I walk into the room and catch them in the act."

Katya is speechless, and I want to applaud Mila. Give her some kind of award for accomplishing a task I believed to be impossible.

Finally, Katya picks her jaw up off the floor. "He cheats on you?"

"Constantly. Since the moment we got married. Probably even while we were engaged." She shrugs. "Viktor is a born cheater, Katya. That's never going to change."

"And you don't care? He's your husband."

Mila waves the title away like it's meaningless. I notice the way her eyes flicker to the corner of the pool where Leonty is rounding the corner with Olaf. "As long as he's occupied with his skanks, that leaves me free to live my life and fuck whomever I damn well please."

"It's a pleasure to meet you, Mila," Katya says, a small smile appearing at the corners of her mouth. "Call me Kat."

∼

"I think the first meeting of the *I Hate Viktor Club* has been a smashing success, don't you?"

"Oh, indeed," I concur in my best (read as: worst) British accent.

"Rousing, truly." Mila dusts the cake crumbs off her chic, fawn-colored dress—clothes being another topic over which Mila and Katya had bonded—and gets to her feet. I haven't missed how her eyes shift over to Leonty every few minutes.

Five minutes after Mila says goodbye and dips back into the main house, Leonty claims he needs to look into something in the garage and takes off in the same direction.

Katya's eyes are trained on him as he walks away. "Well, that answers that question. Those two are getting it on, aren't they?"

Since there's no point in denying it, I nod.

"Get it, girl! Not that I can blame her." Her gaze veers towards Shura, who's skulking in the corner of the gardens with Remi and Misha. "You do have extremely hot bodyguards."

I expect this from Katya. What I don't expect is the searching looks Shura keeps throwing her way when he thinks no one is looking.

"Well, I should be going, too." Katya sighs and heaves herself to her feet. "The picnic was a great idea, hon. We should do it again soon."

But she's not really focused on me when she says it because Shura is striding across the lawn directly towards us. "There's no need to get up, Ms. Natalia," he offers when he's close enough to be heard. "I'll walk Ms. Katya to the door. I have to… check on something in the garage myself."

"Busy day in the garage," I mumble under my breath.

He doesn't hear me, and Katya is too busy blushing to pay me any attention. The only goodbye I get is a last-minute wave over her shoulder after Shura has already led her halfway across the lawn.

I can't even bring myself to be annoyed. My friends are in love. Or, in Kat's case, in lust. I'm happy for them. Even if it means I end up sitting on a picnic blanket surrounded by half-eaten food, utterly alone.

It's been a wonderful evening. I've been surrounded by people—people I actually like—for hours now. And yet it takes all of five seconds by myself to feel loneliness settle on my chest like a boulder.

Pathetic, Natalia. Really pathetic.

I consider walking over to talk with Misha and play with Remi, but they seem content to play together in their own little corner of the garden.

Everyone has coupled up right under my nose.

"That just leaves you and me, little peanut," I whisper to my stomach with only the slightest hint of bitterness.

It's actually sad how quickly I perk up when I see Yelena's stocky silhouette bobbing in my direction. "Finished with your picnic?" she asks as she approaches.

"Yes, it was delicious. Thank you so much."

"Let me clear up, then. I gotta be fast, while the damn dog is still distracted."

Remi hasn't taken to Yelena like he has with the boys. To be fair, she hasn't really made an effort with him. *"I'm not a dog person,"* she's said more than once.

"The dog will be distracted a while longer," I say. "Why don't you sit with me for a bit?"

She squints out into the gloomy distance. "I really should be getting these things inside."

"Oh, come on, Yelena. Keep me company. And look—there's some of your favorite blueberry scones left."

I push the basket right under her nose and, with a reluctant eye roll, she takes one. "You're just lonely and settling for me."

I cringe. "I wouldn't go so far as to say—"

"And who can blame you?" Yelena charges on like I haven't spoken. "Trapped here by yourself more often than not. Nothing but an animal and a delinquent for company. Forced to watch while your friends live their lives and meet their matches… It must be frustrating."

"Enough with the encouraging pep talk," I drawl. "It's too much, really."

"He should be doing more for you."

I'm surprised by her directness. And by my own instinct to defend Andrey.

"He's doing exactly what he said he would. Andrey never promised me anything more than protection and comfort. I'm the fool who—" I stop short and stare sadly into Yelena's knowing eyes. "—I'm the one who wanted more."

"It's only natural, darling."

"It's stupid, is what it is. Stupid and naïve. I can't blame him for not being interested."

"He is interested," Yelena insists. "He's just scared. After everything that happened with Maria…"

Maria. I always had a feeling that there was someone else. But just like that, the woman in Andrey's past has a name.

It's weird being jealous of a woman I've never met. I have a million questions, but I don't want to lurk and sniff around on the periphery of Andrey's life. When I learn more about him, I want it to be because he wants to tell me. Not because Yelena felt like gossiping.

"Maria was—"

"Maria was important to Andrey," I interject gently. "I can tell. And if she still is, I'm sure he will tell me in time."

Yelena reaches over and pats my arm. "You're a good girl, Natalia. You deserve more." I wait for her to elaborate, but she falls silent and picks at her blueberry scone. "These were my husband's favorites, too."

There's an ache in her voice that I recognize all too well. "When did he pass away?"

"Shortly after Andrey took over as *pakhan*, actually," she admits. "It was years ago. He was young, thrown into the deep end without warning... He made a mistake," she continues. "My husband died."

She doesn't make a direct connection between Andrey and her husband's death, but I can hear it in all the words she doesn't say.

Andrey's inexperience cost Yelena her husband.

"I'm so sorry."

"He knew the risks." She says it robotically, like she's repeated the phrase so often that it's lost all meaning. "That's when I came to work for Andrey full-time. He wanted to give me a stipend, of course, so that I could retire comfortably. But I don't accept money for free. Never have, never will. I told him if he was going to give me money, then I would work for it. And I've been here ever since."

I can't even begin to wrap my head around the kind of mentality it would take to work for someone you felt was responsible—no matter how indirectly—for your husband's death.

Then again, Yelena may be old and bent, but she's tough. She's got grit and strength and the kind of perseverance that has me convinced she'll outlive us all.

"I lost my parents, you know. The pain never really goes away, does it?"

She meets my eyes for a fraction of a second. The agony there is deep and unwavering. "No. No, it does not."

"I guess you just have to endure the pain."

To my surprise, Yelena shakes her head. "Endure? No. I believe in moving forward. In action. In purpose. Without that, we may as well have died with them."

40

ANDREY

Laughter filters in through the open windows. If I turn around, I'll be able to see them all, spread across the lawn, Remi frolicking between the girls while Leonty and Shura pretend they're on duty.

It's been two weekends straight of picnics and movie marathons and dinners. Last Saturday, there was a barbeque. I watched from my office as Shura overcooked the steaks and Leonty mixed way-too-strong drinks for the ladies. Yelena kept Natalia in lemonade since she couldn't partake.

Misha was there, too, though always lingering on the periphery, watchful and quiet. Even Olaf, Leif, and Anatoly made their way out to join at one point or another.

I kept my distance so they could have their fun, but now, I have half a mind to order Shura and Leonty into my office right now to remind them that they're supposed to be overseeing this shit, not participating in it.

I'm still trying to block out the sounds of uproarious laughter when my door opens and Natalia walks in.

I rise to my feet, taken aback to see her here at all. Ever since her little seduction ploy in the pool house, she's seemed as keen as I am to keep a healthy distance between us.

"Hi," she greets awkwardly. "Can I come in?"

"You already did." I pretend to be preoccupied by the expanse of papers demanding my attention "Shouldn't you be out there hosting?"

More laughter rolls in from the lawn and Natalia peers out the window. "Wow, you can really hear everything from in here. Have we been distracting you?"

"I've barely noticed. I stay focused on what's important."

Not you. Not anything beyond my work and making sure my child is safe.

As if she can hear my train of thought, Natalia juts out her hip. "You know, you could join us," she spits in a way that isn't really an invitation at all.

"I'm busy, Natalia."

"Of course you are." She turns to the door again. "I'd hate to keep you from all of your important—"

"Did you need something?" I ask. "I assume you came here for a reason."

She swallows, her eyes flitting towards the open window yet again. "I'm taking next Friday off work."

"And?" I pick up a file to peruse, though I don't read a word.

"And I thought we could have lunch. Or dinner, I guess. Whatever's more convenient for you." My silence has Natalia rushing to fill in the blanks. "It wouldn't be a date or anything. It's just a meal. I think we should talk."

But she's holding herself so stiffly that I have to assume that accepting her invitation would, in fact, mean something.

Talking is never just talking with Natalia.

"I'll be busy on Friday."

She stares at me. I don't meet her eyes, but I feel her sharp gaze practically sawing into my skull. Finally, she sighs. "Yeah, I figured. Forget it. Bye, Andrey."

With that, she backs out of the office, leaving me wondering what the hell she wanted from me.

I'm still trying to figure it out an hour later when Shura and Leonty walk into my office. "You wanted to see us?" Shura asks.

He has the good sense to look nervous. Leonty is buzzed and too pussy-whipped to gauge that I'm annoyed as hell at both of them.

"Enjoyed your little party, did you?"

Shura clears his throat. "It wasn't a party. Leonty and I were just—"

"I know exactly what you and Leonty were doing," I snap, forcing him into silence. "How reassuring it is to know that my men aren't afraid of grunt work. I'm sure those bellinis you were guzzling made you so much more effective at your duties."

"Wait—are you pissed at us?" Leonty asks, finally catching on.

Shura squares his jaw. "You tasked us with watching Natalia. That's what we're doing."

"If I remember correctly, you weren't appointed to her security detail."

"No, but I do oversee it. In any case, I had a free evening and, if *I* remember correctly, I can spend my free time however I choose."

"Fine." I turn on Leonty. "What the fuck is your excuse?"

"Listen, Andrey," he starts, "I don't want you to think I'm slacking. I appreciate that you went to bat for me with Viktor. I'm not about to repay that by dropping the ball."

"Glad to hear it. Let's hear your latest report then," I growl. "Anything happening at her work that I should know about?"

Leonty wipes his palms on the seat of his pants. "Uh, work has been relatively quiet. I don't know. She's just been… yeah, quiet."

"Uncomfortable? Is it Byron?"

"No, Byron is behaving himself."

"Then what is it?" I growl, more than a little aware that I could know exactly what Natalia's day-to-day life is like if I asked her.

"It's just little things I've picked up on." He shrugs. "She eats by herself and she stays at her desk more. People go out of their way to keep their distance from her. But I'm there to make sure she's safe, not to make sure she's popular with her coworkers."

I grit my teeth and turn back to Shura. "Has Natalia mentioned anything to you?"

"Nothing at all," he swears.

I could ask Mila, but she's made it clear she doesn't like reporting on Natalia anymore, especially now that she, Natalia, and Katya are all close. I should be happy that Natalia has more friends in this house, but it would be easier if her friends weren't my former informants.

"Where is Viktor?" I ask, scraping the bottom of the barrel for information I care about.

"He's booked a room at the Red Palace," Shura informs me.

"Fucking typical. Probably whoring his way through half the staff. Alright." I turn back to my work. "If that's all—"

"Why did you turn down her dinner invitation?" blurts Shura.

Slowly, I raise my eyes, giving him ample opportunity to recant the question. But the silence stretches and deepens, getting darker and thornier with every passing second.

"Because I'm busy," I snarl at last.

Shura meets my gaze. "I happen to know you're not."

"You don't know a fucking thing about my schedule. Some of us don't have time for parties by the pool." I point to the door. "Out. Both of you."

They rise and shuffle out. But I don't miss the glance that Leonty and Shura exchange before they leave the office.

How is it that, in the space of a few short weeks, she has managed to bewitch everyone in this fucking house? And how exactly did *I* become the odd man out?

That evening, once dusk has fallen and the gardens are finally quiet, I make my way to the pool house.

Thanks to the canine pest, I'm forced to keep my distance, just in case he sniffs me out and alerts Natalia to my presence. It's just as well, really—I have no desire to get too close.

Every time I've made that mistake, I've let my guard drop.

I settle myself by the pool, just under cover of one of the larger trees. Even if she happens to look out, I'll be disguised in shadow. But I know she won't look out. She can play the piano for hours without stopping.

I close my eyes and let the music wash over me. It's the only sliver of peace in my life at the moment—these nights by the pool, listening to her play.

A half hour passes in what feels like seconds when Natalia stops playing to answer her phone. Her voice carries through the open window.

"Aunt Annie! Guess what I was doing when you called?" she laughs, standing to pace across the floor in front of the window. "Nope. Not even close. Getting colder. Okay, I'll tell you… I was playing the piano!"

She smiles, and she's beautiful. Forget the stupid dog; I want a closer look. But before I can stand up, she turns back to the piano. "Okay, hold on. Let me put you on speaker and then you can listen."

She places the phone on the surface of the baby grand and starts a new song. This one is light and happy. It's the most upbeat tune I've ever heard her play, and I've been out here all week listening to her find her way through one song after the next.

"What do you think?" she asks once she's done playing.

"Oh, sweetheart!" Aunt Annie's voice is exactly what I would have expected. Soft, maternal, like a caramel sweet warmed in a pocket. "That was wonderful. You haven't lost your touch. Where did you get a piano?"

"Um, Andrey… He gave me a baby grand."

"I told you I liked him. When do I finally get to meet him?"

I expect Natalia to make excuses. Maybe tell her what an arrogant ass I am. Warn her that she doesn't actually want to meet me at all.

"He's so busy," Natalia says instead. "He works really hard."

"I suppose he must if he can buy you pianos and trained support animals! Then at least tell me when I can see you," Annie continues. "We haven't met since you told me you were pregnant."

"How about next week?" Natalia offers. "I'll check with—I'll check my schedule."

"Wonderful. And the baby? How's my little grandchild doing?"

Natalia gets to her feet and grabs the phone but thankfully, she doesn't take her aunt off the speaker. "Grand*daughter*, you mean?"

Annie shrieks with delight and the rest of the conversation sort of slides into the background.

I sit there, under the shadows, staring at the silhouette of the beautiful woman carrying my child, wondering how I could possibly have found myself on the outskirts of this pregnancy.

I should have been there for the gender reveal. I meant to call the doctor yesterday after her appointment. But there was a Nikolai sighting in Chinatown. Two of my men were on his tail before he disappeared into thin air. I was busy. Again.

When I tune back into the conversation, Natalia is saying goodnight to her aunt.

"Enjoy your happiness, my beautiful girl," her aunt croons. "You deserve it more than anyone I know."

Is Natalia happy? I want her to be. I hope she is.

But as Natalia puts her phone away and sits back down at the piano, her smile disappears. She drops her head into her hands and cries.

I stand and walk away.

41

ANDREY

I'm pouring myself a cup of black coffee the following morning when Shura walks into the kitchen, carrying his own mug. He offers me nothing but a small nod.

Things have been strained between us since my chat with Leonty and him in the office. Regardless, when I gesture for him to sit, he takes the chair next to me without a fuss.

"How was dinner?"

Shura takes a long, thoughtful sip of coffee. "Good."

He knows I want more information, and he's withholding. *Asshole*.

"And here I was, thinking I was special to be invited." I smirk just to make sure Shura knows I don't really care.

Natalia invited everyone in my inner circle to the dinner I refused to attend—why should that bother me? I watched from the darkness of my office as they all returned, laughing and joking. I felt like a voyeur—poised on the outskirts of

Natalia's life, observing hungrily but refusing to get any closer. Still, I couldn't look away.

"Natalia would probably say you were special," Shura points out. "But then, she's that way."

He's right; she is.

Somehow, Natalia has created a family amidst the rigid control of my Bratva. Yelena seems to have renewed purpose for the first time in years and Shura has been smiling a lot more freely.

But the biggest change in character has come from Misha.

The boy has gained some weight in recent weeks. There's color on his cheeks and a healthy glow in his skin. Apart from Natalia, Remi has bonded closely with Misha, and I can't help but suspect that's because the dog sees Misha as an extension of Natalia herself.

Everyone who gets close to Natalia gains something from the proximity.

Everyone but me.

I frown like I have no idea what he's talking about. "She's what way?"

"Kind."

If I hadn't seen him ogle Katya a few too many times, I might have suspected him of having feelings for Natalia. As it stands, he just gazes off into the gardens with a bored indifference on his face.

"And Misha behaved?" I ask.

"I misjudged the boy," Shura answers gruffly. "We all did. He's alright, really."

"Did Natalia help you see that, too?"

Shura turns to me slowly, his dark eyes troubled. "She was right. He's just a child, but we treated him like an enemy. Is it such a surprise that he acted the way he did? It's what I would have done. Hell, it *is* what I did."

His arm moves instinctively to his right leg. I've seen the ugly burn mark only a handful of times, but it's still seared in my memory. That kind of scarring doesn't happen without some serious pain and trauma behind it.

"I think last night was the first time the kid ever tried birthday cake."

I process the words belatedly. "Why were you eating birthday cake?"

Shura takes another long sip of coffee. "Because it was Natalia's birthday."

Oh, fuck.

I feel my pulse in my temples like a drumbeat announcing just how badly I fucked up. "You didn't mention that to me."

"I didn't realize I was supposed to. Would it have changed your mind about joining us?"

An old memory plays out in my mind. A flash of red and black streamers. White cake with ridiculous rainbow candles sticking out of the top. A laughing Maria decked out in a shimmering red dress with a high slit.

"Thirty years around the sun!" she exclaimed, cutting into her thick cake. *"And here's to a hundred more!"*

She didn't get a hundred more years, though.

She barely got six months.

"No," I rasp, pushing away the memory with difficulty. "It wouldn't have."

Shura nods as though he had expected nothing less. With a disappointed sigh, he gets to his feet and leaves the kitchen, taking his coffee with him.

I'm alone for only a couple minutes before I notice Natalia walking across the lawn, Remi prancing at her heels. She makes straight for the kitchen.

"Good morning, Andrey," she says with a crisp formality when she slips through the French doors. "Mind if I join you?"

I nod towards the chair and she drops into it, touching the gold locket around her neck as though it will give her courage.

Courage for what, I have no idea.

I have nothing to say, so the kitchen is silent.

"I want to go see my aunt," she blurts. "She lives a little outside of the city, but I'll take my whole security squad if that makes you feel better. I just really need to see her."

She says it all quickly, like maybe I won't be able to refuse her if she gets it out fast enough. She's breathing in, preparing her counterarguments, I'm sure, when I nod. "Okay."

Her mouth opens and closes in shock before a cautious smile slips across her face. "Great, 'cause I was thinking I would head over there today."

I check the time on my Patek Philippe. "Well, I suppose I can push a few things around. Shall we leave in half an hour?"

Her mouth falls right back open again. "Erm... you wanna come with me?"

I don't *want* to come with her. The same way I don't *want* to pay for security. The same way I don't *want* to regularly threaten my enemies into compliance to maintain my control.

This is a business matter, pure and simple. Protecting valuable assets. Allocating resources.

"Extra security never hurts. And besides, I'm sure your aunt must be curious about the man you're living with."

Natalia blinks. "Um, yeah. She is, actually."

"Well, then we might as well get the first meeting over with."

She bounces up to her feet so fast that Remi jumps back in shock. "Come on, Remi!" she cries delightedly. "We're going for a little drive!"

"No!" I call out after her as she and Remi disappear through the back door. "We're not taking the dog!"

∽

Thirty minutes later, a massive German Shepherd is drooling on the shoulder of my shirt and getting hair all over my Aston Martin.

"The dog rides in the back or not at all."

Natalia frowns at me, but lovingly cradles Remi's head. "Oh, come on, he'll behave. He just wants to be close to me."

"Then keep him far from me," I warn. "Or we put him in the Wrangler with the boys. Your choice."

Natalia rolls her eyes, but orders Remi to lie down in the backseat. Showing he was every bit worth the fortune I spent, he obeys.

"I'll have to get the car detailed after this."

"You can afford it." Natalia smirks. "Aunt Annie hasn't met Remi yet. I had to bring him along."

"The dog will survive one outing without you."

She looks innocently at me. "But he's my emotional support animal. What if I have a sudden attack of PTSD?"

"I'll be with you," I remind her.

"No offense, but you're a lot less cuddly than he is."

I give Remi a disgruntled glare in the rearview mirror, and I swear he licks his chops.

Natalia is twisted towards me the entire drive, but only so she can keep one hand on Remi's neck at all times.

Jealous of a fucking dog. Give me a break.

An hour later, we pull up to Aunt Annie's place. It's a narrow house, wedged between two others like an afterthought, though the bright yellow paint makes it stand out like a friendly face in a crowd of strangers. Fairy lights run the length of her fence and glittery baubles dangle from the emaciated tree in her tiny front yard. As the boys follow me up the narrow sidewalk, I can't help but wonder if we're all even going to fit inside this shack.

I almost lose my balance on the crooked front steps that lead to the door. When I look down, I realize what caught my toe: tiny handprints pressed into the concrete. The second step has larger prints. The third step, larger still.

"Mine," Natalia explains when she notices me looking. "Ages two, four, and six. It was Dad's idea."

Natalia was here as a little girl.

I see the place through a child's eyes, and just like that, it's magical. Natalia must have loved it.

Before I can ask her, a woman's voice shrieks through the thin walls of the house. "Nic-Nat!"

The door swings open, and Aunt Annie is much tinier than I expected. A full head shorter than Natalia and skinny as a whip. But her wiry hands clamp down on either side of Natalia's face with force. "Baby girl, I've missed you." She looks down and gasps. "And there's the stomach! Oh, you're glowing."

Natalia waves away the compliment and turns to me. "Aunt Annie, this is Andrey. Andrey, this is the woman who raised me."

"A pleasure," I greet, offering Aunt Annie my hand.

She smacks it away. "Oh, there's no need for stuffy old handshakes. Give me a hug." As her arms clasp around me—as far as they can go, at least—she whistles. "Well, aren't you a big man?"

"Aunt Annie!" Natalia chides, the faintest trace of embarrassment blossoming on her cheeks. She waves to the security team. "This is one half of my own personal boy band—the blonde one is Leonty; the blonder one is Leif. The other two are taking a day off. Oh, and how could I forget my main man?"

I grit my teeth in annoyance as she calls Remi forward, then grit my teeth again when I realize how ridiculous that is.

Natalia notices nothing of the war raging inside me as she presents the beast to Aunt Annie like the damn canine is the star of the show. "May I present Remington Boone? Remi for short."

Aunt Annie pops a squat in front of Remi and offers him her palm, which is shrewdly filled with dog treats. This isn't the woman's first rodeo, apparently. Remi accepts wholeheartedly, devouring the treats and then licking the hell out of the woman's face for good measure as Annie and Natalia both laugh and laugh and laugh.

Then Leif, Leonty, and I squeeze our way down the narrow passageway and into a living room that is somehow narrower. It's packed to the gills with all manner of random objects—crystal balls, assorted coffee mugs, things crocheted into shapes I barely recognize—and looks out into the backyard, where a beautiful cherry tree stands shedding pink petals on the grass.

Natalia veers straight for the windows. "How's my cherry tree doing?" she croons as though she expects the tree to talk back.

Everyone takes off in different directions. Remi races out into the garden through the open screen door and Leif and Leonty join him, eager for a bit more breathing room. Aunt Annie seems to have disappeared, too.

"She'll be in the kitchen getting snacks," Natalia explains when she sees me searching. "She won't be able to have a proper conversation until she's certain everyone is well-fed."

I can't help but smile. This is what it would have been like to have a proper mother. Someone who vandalizes their own home in order to commemorate a child's handprints.

Someone who fusses over snacks for their kids' friends, who hugs instead of shaking hands.

Someone who gives love away freely, as though it costs them absolutely nothing. As if the mere act of giving it away makes them that much richer with the stuff.

I never knew what that was like.

Aunt Annie appears moments later with a tray groaning under the weight of enough pastries to feed my whole damn Bratva. She takes it into the garden and leaves it there for Leif and Leonty, then brings a second, equally laden tray into the living room.

"Cherry pie!" Natalia cries out and claps delightedly. "Bless you, Aunt Annie. You're a saint."

But Aunt Annie doesn't reply. Her gaze is fixed firmly on me. She's wearing a little smile that's polite but discerning.

And I understand right away.

She may be welcoming and gracious. She may be sweet and attentive. But she still hasn't made up her mind about me. She still hasn't determined if I'm good enough for her Natalia.

I can't say I blame her.

42

NATALIA

Under the pretense of helping Aunt Annie with the dishes, I slip into the kitchen.

She's standing at the sink, letting the water run while she gazes through the window into the backyard. Andrey joined Remi and the boys back there a few minutes ago, and I know she's watching him.

I also know that she knows that *I know* she's watching him.

When I can't take it anymore, I finally blurt, "Well? What do you think?"

"He's charming, smart, polite." Her eyes flit to me. "Bit ugly, though. Couldn't you have found a better-looking man, Nat?"

I burst out laughing. No one in their right mind could ever accuse Andrey of being ugly.

When the room falls quiet again, I watch her rinse our lemonade glasses, and wait.

"Honestly," Aunt Annie says after a few minutes, "he reminds me a little of you."

I flick a towel at her butt. "Don't be rude."

She's not laughing, though. "Right after we lost your mom and dad, you held yourself the same way. Like you were trying to keep everyone—the whole damn world—at arm's length."

I peek through the window to find Andrey, only to realize he's already looking my way. So I glance away and try to pretend like I was admiring the cherry tree, though I don't think I'm fooling anyone.

"He seems like a man who's carrying the weight of the world on his shoulders," Aunt Annie presses on.

I've sensed the same thing, but I assumed it had more to do with me than him. He's too big, too larger-than-life, to rely on the same kinds of defense mechanisms that I've always relied on. *Run. Hide. Show no one what you're feeling.*

"He's responsible for a lot of people," I explain softly.

Remi is nipping at Andrey's ankles now and he bends to scratch the pup behind the ears. It sends a little shiver of affection through me.

When I turn, my aunt is studying me carefully. She's always had the ability to see straight to the heart of me. One look from her, and I'm laid bare.

"Can I ask you something?"

I wince, even as I nod. "Shoot."

"Do you have feelings for him?"

I want to lie. It's poised on the tip of my tongue. But there's no point in it. Not only because Aunt Annie would see right through it, but also because she sacrificed her life to raise me after my parents died. I don't want to repay her with dishonesty.

"Lately, I've been feeling like… yes? Maybe. I think."

She nods solemnly. "I don't blame you. He's the kind of man who would be easy to fall for."

"I can't have him, though," I blurt. "I shouldn't. I can't."

Aunt Annie lifts her eyebrows with interest. "Why not?"

"I…" It's harder than I imagined to say it. "I don't think he feels the same way about me."

It's her turn to direct her gaze out the window, down to where Andrey leans against the trunk of a tree I've climbed I-don't-even-know how many times. He's cool and resolute in its shadow like he belongs there. Like he's always belonged there.

She watches him for a long time before she speaks again. "Have you given him the chance to know the real you?"

"What do you mean?"

"I mean, have you been protecting your secrets? Hiding your past?"

"No more than he does," I say defensively.

Aunt Annie's smile, just like her gaze, is cryptic and all-knowing. "Well, no wonder the two of you move around each other like magnets with the same poles. Just like I thought," she says quietly, "you two are alike."

"We aren't," I insist. "It's not like that."

Aunt Annie cups my cheek fondly. "If you say so, Nic-Nat. Now, how about another piece of pie?"

∽

On the way out, Andrey seems to know what he's in for. He doesn't offer Aunt Annie his hand, but instead leans in and gives her a one-armed hug.

I'm holding the door open for Remi to bound down the steps, but when I turn back around, I realize that they're still hugging. Andrey's neck is craned to the side as though Aunt Annie is whispering a secret to him.

A moment later, they split apart.

I glance at my aunt questioningly, but she simply smiles and plants a kiss on my forehead. "You take care of that baby now. And don't be a stranger, my girl."

Once Remi is secure in the back seat, I get into the car and roll down the window to wave some more. I don't stop waving until we've turned the corner and Aunt Annie disappears behind a sheath of maple leaves.

I wait, nervous, for Andrey to break the silence. He barely glances at me as we leave the neighborhood in our rearview mirror.

After twenty minutes of excruciating silence, I'm the first to crack. "So… that was my aunt."

One corner of Andrey's mouth curls up in a smile. "Give me credit for figuring out that much, *lastochka*."

My heart flutters wildly. *Get a grip, girl. We're just talking.*

The thing is, Aunt Annie's remarks have burrowed their way into my consciousness now. And it's got me thinking—

What if he's more like me than I realize?

What if he's holding onto his pain the same way I hold onto mine?

What if extending some trust is all it'll take to get him to trust me in return?

I twist back to pet Remi, but my eyes don't venture past Andrey's profile. Past the golden afternoon sunlight setting him in sharp, handsome relief. "Thanks for coming with me."

His hand tightens on the wheel. "You're welcome."

"She means a lot to me, my aunt," I continue.

"You two seem close."

My heart is hammering hard against my chest. Talking about this—any of it—feels like stripping naked in front of a crowd of strangers.

But, I remind myself, *Andrey is not a stranger. Not unless you force him to be.*

"I don't think I would have survived without her."

"You're tougher than you think."

"You didn't see me after my parents died." I swallow hard, my throat painfully dry. "I was... destroyed, honestly. I spent those first six months in a sort of daze. I wanted to die. I thought that was the only way to be with them again."

He looks over, those startling gray eyes boring into my face and making my skin tingle with heat.

I can't think when he's looking at me like that, so I turn to the windshield before I continue. "I couldn't function. I barely ate or slept. Couldn't go to school. It was the first time I experienced a catatonic episode. You saw what that was like."

His eyes are back on the road, but I can tell he's listening with rapt attention. Even Remi has stopped moving. It's as if he senses the tension in the air.

"Aunt Annie quit her job to homeschool me. Four times a week, I went to a child psychiatrist that the state recommended. Between those sessions and Aunt Annie's dedication, I started showing signs of life again." I glance at him out of the corner of my eye. "She still thinks it's the therapy that helped. But I know that she was the reason I got better. Her love, her care, her unfailing faith that I would come back." I exhale. "I hope to be the kind of mother she is."

"You will be." He says it so confidently. No doubts.

"How can you know that?"

"I've watched you with Misha," he says. "I've seen how patient you are with him, how protective. You're just as much of a force of nature as your aunt, Natalia. You just don't know it yet."

I don't know what to say to that, so I don't say anything.

We round one corner, then another. Eventually, we link up with the highway and settle into a droning, thrumming cruise.

"She reminds me a little of my own mother," Andrey finally says, cutting through the silence again. "Back when she was young."

My head swivels in his direction. Has Andrey Kuznetsov actually volunteered information about his personal life? Is there some kind of invisible torture taking place that I'm not aware of?

I sit very still, as though the slightest movement will send him retreating back behind his protective barricades.

"Arina had the same kind of maternal softness. It made you underestimate just how shrewd she really was."

"Arina," I repeat under my breath. "What happened to her?"

"She's been a patient at Drogheda Mental Institution for the past eleven years."

"Oh my." I draw in a breath. "I-I've… seen it a few times. On walks. It's a beautiful property."

"From the outside, maybe," Andrey says flatly. "But at the end of the day, no matter how beautiful, a mental institution is a mental institution. She's trapped there."

Something about the way he says that makes my heart ache. "I'm sorry."

"I'm the one who should be sorry."

He swallows like he didn't mean to say that and, honestly, I'm not so sure I was meant to hear it. Just to be safe, I pretend like I haven't.

But I can't stay silent, not when my curiosity is fit to burst. "Do you visit her often?"

"Not as often as I should." He swallows again, like this whole conversation is surprising him as much as it is me. "But I try to go as much as I can. I just don't know how much good it does her."

"Can she recognize you?"

"Some days, yes. Other days, she thinks I'm… someone else."

"Who?"

Those steely silver eyes flash to my face and then back to the road. "A man she fears and despises. The same man that's responsible for her lifetime sentence in Drogheda."

I don't know how, but I already know the answer to the question I'm about to ask. "Your father?"

Andrey nods. "My father."

He says it with so much venom that I find myself reaching towards him, fingers outstretched, longing to give him some kind of comfort. My hand lands on his thigh, close to his knee. He doesn't acknowledge my invasion of his space—but he doesn't throw me off, either.

Progress.

"Does she know you're going to be a father?"

Andrey's hands twitch on the wheel. "I did tell her," he rasps. "But I'm not sure she can process new information anymore. I'm not sure she'll remember."

"But you told her. That makes a difference."

"Does it?" He looks at me like he genuinely wants to know.

I nod firmly. "You haven't given up on her. Whenever she's lucid—whenever she's herself again—she'll know that. In her heart, even if not in her head."

He turns back to the road, and we finish the drive in silence.

But my hand remains on his leg the entire way home.

43

NATALIA

"If Abby asks me about Andrey, I give you permission to execute her," I tell Remi, dropping to give him his morning scratch behind the ears.

His tongue lolls out of his mouth, and I know in theory he's fully capable of turning Abby inside out, but he's so cute that it's hard to believe right now.

"Good thing you don't speak English," I say, leading him towards the door. "I'm not sure you'd understand my sarcasm."

Especially since it's barely sarcastic. Abby is the only person who talks to me at work anymore—if you don't count Byron, which I barely do since Andrey traumatized him. Byron is afraid to look at me wrong, lest he face Andrey's wrath. And Abby only wants to talk about Andrey. Work hours have not exactly been a fountain of joy the last few weeks.

I open the door of the pool house to let Remi out—and nearly step on a tiny box sitting on the welcome mat.

"What the…?"

It's wrapped in white ribbon, a small card flapping from the bow. I glance over at the pool, where two of my burly bodyguards are approaching, looking sleepy. Neither one seems to be aware of my little gift.

Flipping the card over, I read the neatly scrawled words.

Happy Birthday. I'm sorry I missed it.

It's not signed, but I know exactly who it's from. Smiling, I pull the lid off the box to find a gorgeous gold pendant sitting on the black velvet cushion.

Etched with cherries.

A burst of laughter escapes me and Remi's ears perk up. He cocks his head to the side as if waiting for an explanation.

I shake my head in amusement. "Oh, he's good."

Remi lets out a confused bark.

"I said no more presents—" I hold up the pendant. "—and then he goes and gives me something I can't refuse. Crafty."

Remi barks a couple more times.

"Hold on a second." I rush inside to slip the pendant onto a thin chain and fasten it around my neck. When I get back outside, Leonty and Anatoly are waiting. "Let's go, boys!"

"You're too cheery for a Monday," Leonty notes.

Anatoly nods in agreement. "Yeah. What's up with you? You're never this happy to be going to work."

I tuck the pendant out of sight beneath my blouse and do my best to control the smile on my face. "Yeah, well: new week, new attitude."

But "new week, new attitude" is not the philosophy my colleagues have embraced this fine Monday. They still eye Remi warily like he really might execute them on the spot, and then turn those same wary eyes on me.

Word has gotten around that I'm with Andrey Kuznetsov, and no one can figure out why I'm still showing up to work every day.

The old me would've been bothered. But somehow, with my new pendant sitting right over my heart, it's bearable.

Between that and the lingering feelings from my first real conversation with Andrey, I kinda feel untouchable as I skip around the office, keeping my head down and getting my work done. And when Byron asks me to join him in his office for lunch rather than eat hunched over my keyboard like normal, the world is so fricking peachy that I accept without a second thought.

"Byron!" I exclaim when I see my favorite pepper fried chicken with ranch dipping sauce from Burning Bird on his desk. "You shouldn't have."

"I know you've been having a hard time lately," he explains. "I wanted to do something to cheer you up."

I'm as cheered up as I could be, but I will never turn down fried chicken. I sit down and let him push my chair into the desk. "Thank you so much."

He pulls his chair closer and sits down next to me. A little closer than necessary, but I've got my fried chicken goggles on.

"Just trying to be a gentleman." He says it almost like he's trying to insinuate that there are other men in my life who are far from gentlemanly.

I suppress a smile and accept the drink he offers me. "Well, you've certainly been that. Honestly, you're a good friend."

"'Friend...'" He repeats the word bitterly.

I pretend like I didn't hear as I reach for the pepper chicken. "Hm, it smells—"

"Natalia."

My hand freezes on the aluminum foil wrapping. Dread prickles down my spine. Swallowing, I turn to him. "Yes, Byron?"

"We've known each other a long time now."

I wipe my sweaty palms on the front of my skirt. "We have. Two years, I think."

"Longer," he insists. "Almost three."

I give him a weak smile. "Has it been that long?"

His hand finds its way to my knee and I freeze. My eyes fall to the spot where his fingers are curling around my flesh. Squeezing. Kneading. He's leaving behind little red divots everywhere he touches, like bedbugs.

"I don't think it's a secret how I feel about you."

Mayday, mayday. Houston, we have a problem...

Where are my freaking bodyguards when I need them?

"Byron... listen—"

"I know what you're going to say." Byron's face contorts into a scowl. "*Him*. Well, fuck him, Natalia. He doesn't deserve you. You need a man who truly appreciates you."

It's distracting how tightly he's gripping my leg. It's starting to hurt, honestly. "Byron… I'm carrying his child."

"I don't care! You said you weren't with him. I don't care that you're having his baby. That's how much I want you."

My stomach twists. But not because of anything he's saying. Well, not just because of what he's saying.

It's because, as he speaks, his hand moves higher and higher up my thigh, nudging my skirt out of the way.

"Byron, stop!"

"We could be great together, Natalia."

My skin crawls as he reaches my inner thigh. Finally regaining some control over my body, I slap his hand away and get to my feet. "What the hell do you think you're doing?"

His mouth falls open like a dumbstruck fish. "I'm just trying to make you understand—"

"What I understand is that you're my boss and you just put your hand up my skirt! It's inappropriate."

He shakes his head. "I know I'm your boss, but that doesn't mean this can't work."

"This was supposed to be lunch." The smell of the chicken is still taunting me. I'm starving, and I have a strong feeling I'm not going to be eating a bite. "I don't want anything more than that, Byron."

He narrows his eyes until they're just slivers of black, the blue entirely gone. "You think this is inappropriate?"

"It is," I say softly. "I'm sorry, but—"

"So getting fucked on my desk by that psychopath is appropriate, but this isn't?"

Byron advances on me, moving closer even as I back away. My heart is thundering in my chest and cold sweat is prickling at the base of my spine.

"Scared of me, now?" he taunts. "Am I being 'inappropriate'?"

"You're not yourself, Byron," I squeak out.

"You don't know me the way you think you do," he hisses. "Just like I thought I knew you, walking around the office, all sweet and smiley, pretending to be a nice girl. You're not a nice girl. Nice girls don't do the kinds of things you've done to me."

"I'm sorry if I ever led you on. Believe me, it was never my intention. I was under the impression we were colleagues and friends. End of story." His eyes flash furiously as two veins in his temples pulse. "I'm leaving now."

My back is to him when he speaks. "Got what you wanted from me and now, you're just gonna walk away, huh?"

My instincts are screaming at me not to take the bait. But my sense of pride wins out over reason.

"What is that supposed to mean?" I ask, whirling around.

His smile is ugly. "The rumor mill has been churning since you fucked Kuznetsov in my office. Another employee would have gotten the sack for doing what you did. Who do you think shielded you from HR all these weeks? Who do you think kept the truth from reaching Mr. Ewes?"

My jaw drops. "That's why you didn't fire me? You were trying to manipulate me?"

"I was trying to protect you!" he roars. "Do you know what they're calling you in the office? Do you know what they say about you? They're calling you the office slut! Compared to you, Abby looks like the Virgin Mary."

I'm expecting it and still, it hurts. "Well, everyone is entitled to their opinions."

"I don't know why I wasted my time on you," he snarls as I rip open the door and step into the hall, praying it closes before the rest of his insult can reach me.

It doesn't shut fast enough.

"You're nothing but a two-bit whore who's willing to sacrifice her pride for a man with a fat wallet."

44

NATALIA

"Nat, are you sure you're okay?" It's the third time Leonty has asked.

I wasn't fine the first time. I'd walked out of Mr. Ewes's office thirty seconds earlier, still reeling from the aftermath of the meeting. My ears were still ringing. I felt numb to everything except the complete and utter mortification I felt, so I barely even heard Leonty; I just nodded and followed him to the car.

On the long drive across town, I replayed the conversation in my head again and again and grew progressively less fine. *Byron told me what happened, Ms. Boone. And worse, there are security cameras all over the building. I expected more of you.*

Now, I'm nauseous and on the verge of tears, but I give Leonty a tight-lipped smile. "I'm fine."

I beeline for the pool house, Remi close at my heels. *You can cry when you get to the pool house. You can cry when you get to the—*

"Natalia?"

I grind to a standstill. All at once, every bit of frustration and resentment coursing through me finds a target.

Andrey appears from around the corner. It looks like he's been out all day. His skin has a sun-kissed glow and his hair is windswept to perfection. He's beautiful.

But today, his good looks don't affect me at all. They only serve as a reminder that the world dances to the tune of men like him, while saving the consequences for women like me.

"Not now, Andrey."

"I just wanted to ask if you got my…" He trails off at the look on my face, his eyes narrowing shrewdly. "What's wrong?"

"Nothing."

Leonty defers to his boss and slips away while Andrey moves closer. "I don't think so, *lastochka*. Tell me what's wrong."

"Just the consequences of my actions. Our actions, I guess." Blinking back tears, I try to blurt it fast. "I'm suspended from work until further notice."

His eyes flare wide. "Why?"

"Because you got jealous and threatened my boss," I spit. "Because I was weak and had sex with you on his desk."

I hate that this is every bit my fault, too. I hate that I can't pin this all on Andrey, no matter how much I want to.

"God," I screech, "I can't even blame Byron. I mean, he reported me for the wrong reasons, but he had every right to do it from the very start. We had sex on his desk, Andrey! There are cameras!"

Remi is squinting at me, his ears pressed down with worry.

"Natalia."

At the sound of Andrey's voice, even Remi cowers. He bares his teeth, a low growl emanating from behind them.

Andrey ignores him. "Byron did this?"

He reaches for me, and Remi snarls.

Andrey flicks an irritated glare at my guard dog. "I can fix this."

Twisting around, I jab a finger into his chest. "Stay out of this. You've done enough."

Remi barks loudly and jumps in between us. I'm not sure if I'm more nervous of him or Andrey. Both of them look more than capable of murder.

"Remi," I say, "it's okay. '*Sidet.*'"

Andrey fixes me with a penetrating stare that's hard to break. "Come with me to my office."

"Not the first time I've heard that today," I huff. "I don't want to."

Andrey ignores me and turns for the door. "Now."

With the word echoing in my ears, I find myself following Andrey through the house and into his office. He closes the door behind me, shutting Remi out. His wet nose pokes under the gap, a frustrated growl rumbling through the wood.

"If you think you can manipulate me again—" I gasp, swallowing the words as he pushes me back against the door.

Andrey's entire body presses hard against mine. His fingers trace the column of my throat. "You're mad at me."

His silver eyes are fixed on me. They're distracting, but it's not like there's anything else to look at, anyway. Andrey is too close. Too big.

Too much. So much that I lost my mind and let him fuck me at work. What the hell was I thinking?

Andrey presses me more firmly against the door, and I remember all at once what I was thinking: *God, he feels good.*

"Yes, I'm mad," I hiss. "I'm mad at you and myself and Byron and—*everything!*"

He follows the chain of my necklace down and down, his fingers dipping below the collar of my blouse to pull the golden cherries out. "The trinkets I give you can't make up for that. I understand. You need an outlet for your anger."

I frown. "I don't…"

He takes a step back as Remi starts clawing at it. I don't have the presence of mind to console him right now. My attention is wholly caught by Andrey's hypnotic gaze.

"You want to rage at me?" he asks. "You want to slap me? You want to shout curses and break my stuff?" He gestures around at this office. "Go right ahead."

I fist my hands at my side. "What are you talking about?"

"There's no point in suppressing your anger. My advice? Let it out."

My tongue slides unconsciously over my lips. There's a lot of fragile things in Andrey's office. Would it make me better to shatter them? To watch his expensive things break at my feet the way my life has fallen apart?

"I can't… I don't want… That's not what I want," I stutter.

"Yes, it is. You're pissed off at me. So be pissed off at me." When I don't say anything, he steps back into my space. "Or would you rather I fuck the rage out of you?"

My breath catches as his eyes sparkle with promise. *This is what got me in trouble the first time.*

But there's a reason I keep coming back to Andrey time and time again. It feels good.

I nod, almost imperceptibly, but Andrey notices. He notices everything.

With one quick move, he spins me around and presses me against the cool wood of the door. Rough hands shove my skirt down my thighs where it pools at my feet.

His fingers graze over my exposed skin, his breath suddenly ragged and hot against my neck. "Surrender to the anger, little bird."

Then I feel him—his girth, his weight, his thickness sliding against my skin and between my thighs.

I bent at the waist, pressing my hips back against him, my palms flat against the textured surface of the wood.

"What do you say, *lastochka*? Are you ready to surrender?"

His hardness nudges at my opening without actually pushing past my lips. I know the only way he's going to give me what I want is if I ask for it.

"Fuck me," I whisper. "I need it."

With a satisfied chuckle, Andrey plunges inside me. I slap my hands on the wood, crying out as he buries himself into me as deep as he can go.

Remi barks on the other side of the door, clawing at the wood, but I can barely think in English, let alone the Russian I need to calm Remi down.

"You and me," Andrey pants. "We'll always come back to this. To each other. We need it."

I want to tell him he's a liar. I want to tell him I can live without this. But Andrey's hands come down over mine, his body shadowing mine against the door. We're molded together as he fucks me from behind with all the aggression and frustration I walked into the room with.

But now, the emotions are channeled into this beautiful, perfect thing.

The entire day will be worth it if only I can fall apart around him. If only I can feel him pulse into me.

"Yes," I groan. "Yes… harder, harder… *fuck*."

Andrey doesn't hold back. He doesn't know the meaning of "gentle." He just fucks me as though he's got nothing left to lose.

And I close my eyes and surrender.

45

ANDREY

The neon sign sits against a hot pink backsplash. *Hot Chick.* No points for subtlety.

Even from the outside, it smells like cheap booze and desperation. The kind of place my brother loves to frequent. To further prove my point, the halls are wreathed with smoke and the floors are filthy, but I'm not here for the ambience.

Byron Wells is playing darts by the bar. His back is to me, so he doesn't see me take a seat around the nearby billiards table. Just as I grab the menu on the table, a chorus of cheers echoes from behind the pillar.

"Nice shot, By!"

"You the man."

"You're killin' it tonight."

Tilting back in my chair, I peer around the corner.

Byron is reclining on a barstool like it's a throne, both his elbows planted on the bar counter. His hair is slicked back with a thick wad of gel and he's wearing a silk shirt unbuttoned to mid-chest.

"It's been a good day all around." No one asks, but he adds, "Scored a nice li'l victory at work."

"Does this victory have something to do with that hot ass little assistant of yours?" one of his friends asks.

"Maybe." Byron shrugs coyly. "Maybe not."

"She finally put out?"

I can't even pretend to be interested in the menu anymore. When the waitress walks over, I wave her away. She stalks off looking disappointed.

"Not yet," Byron says. "But she will."

So much confidence. It's just another nail in his coffin.

But one of his friends is looking skeptical. "This the same woman who's been playing hard to get all this time? What changed?"

"She finally realized my worth," Byron crows. "She wants a powerful man, and that's what I am. It's only a matter of time before I'm bending her over my desk and showing her how powerful I can be."

Without even realizing it, I'm on my feet. I didn't mean for this to become such a public spectacle, but fuck it—I'll act first and figure out damage control later.

But before I can advance on him, Byron pushes himself to standing. "Gotta take a leak. Be right back."

Fucking perfect. The simple act of following him across the bar to the men's room sends a surge of adrenaline shooting through me.

This feels good.

This feels right.

This feels like the old days, before the political ploys and the shadow wars. Back when I had one simple task and it was just a matter of executing it to perfection.

The lights flicker ominously as I slip into the bathroom. I take one quick scan, confirm that Byron and I are the only ones here, and barricade the door shut.

If all goes well, this shouldn't take more than ten minutes.

Five, if he dies quickly.

To save myself the mess, I let him finish at the urinal and shift over to the sink. It's not until he's washing his hands that he gives me a casual glance in the mirror, followed by a violent double-take.

His face is deathly pale as he whips around to face me. "W-what are you doing here?"

"I'm ranking the sleaziest bars in New York City. When I saw you in here, I knew I found the winner."

He shrinks away from me, leaning into the counter so far that the running water drenches his sleeves. "L-Listen, man—"

I take a step towards him and sweat beads across his forehead in the dim light. "I gave you a warning, didn't I?"

He's shaking his head frantically. "No, no... I didn't do anything! Mr. Ewes is the one that—"

I head-butt him so hard that his eyes roll back in their sockets. The clack of bone on bone is viciously satisfying.

"No," he sobs through a mouth that doesn't want to work right. "I didn't…"

"Shut the fuck up, *mudak*." I snatch him by the back of his neck, nails digging into his sweaty flesh as I force him into one of the bathroom stalls. The water sitting at the bottom of the toilet is fittingly murky.

Just what this fucker deserves.

"No, no, no… plea—"

His cries are cut off as his head disappears into the toilet. Water sloshes around him as he struggles to breathe, but it's easy to keep him down. So easy to hold him here and let his life drain away.

But not yet.

Wrenching him back up for a moment, I speak while he gasps and splutters wordlessly. "You picked the wrong woman to mess with."

"Please!" he screams.

But his panicked eyes only fuel my disgust. "She's the last woman you will ever prey on."

And with that, I dunk his head back into the dirty piss water. This time, I don't let go of him until he's stopped struggling, until his body goes limp and his head bobs peacefully in the water.

Good fucking riddance.

Straightening up, I close the cubicle door and give my hands a thorough wash before I open the door. There's a disgruntled older man waiting outside, aiming an evil eye in my direction. Ignoring him, I pass the bar on my way out.

"Where's By?" I hear one of his friends asking.

"He's plastered. He probably fell in…"

With a satisfied smirk, I leave behind the oppressive bar. The air outside is clean and fresh compared with the smoke and grime of the bar. But I can't appreciate it just yet.

I have one more score to settle before the night is over. Thankfully, Richard Ewes's brownstone is only a short drive away.

∽

Shura is leaning against the passenger side door of his Escalade when I drive up.

"Well?" I ask once I've joined him.

"He's asleep in his bed," Shura informs me. "And you're in luck: he's alone tonight. The wife's in Kentucky visiting her parents."

"Security system?"

"I disabled it a few minutes ago. You're free to walk in."

I clap him on the back. "Good man."

Shura sighs grimly as I make my way up the steps to the brownstone. He volunteered to be my backup for tonight, and I know why. Despite his hard, brusque exterior, Natalia has succeeded in worming her way into his heart, too.

He doesn't want to see her hurt any more than I do.

I let myself into Richard's house as easily as if it were my own. It's clean and utterly bland, like it was ripped from the pages of a suburban furniture catalog.

I pass a side table bearing several framed photographs, all of the same couple: a self-satisfied Richard with a much younger woman on his arm.

Men like him are all the same: So. Fucking. Predictable.

I climb up one flight of stairs and find the master bedroom on my right.

Richard is sprawled across the bed, the duvet thrown to the side to reveal his pudgy, naked body. I wrinkle my nose in disgust at the sight of his tiny, shriveled penis lying limply against a shroud of blonde curly pubic hair.

But it's a fitting way for this to play out.

I use zip-ties to strap the bastard to his headboard. As I'm lashing down his second hand, he starts to stir. I finish the ties, then drag the ostentatious armchair by the window to his bedside and wait as he blinks himself awake.

"Sorry to drop in so late, Richard—" He whirls towards me, the whites of his eyes gleaming with panic. "—but we have important matters to discuss."

"What the—" he gasps, looking around the shadowy room as though it'll offer him some explanation. "Andrey?"

I cross my legs and click my tongue impatiently. "I really don't have time to wait for you to catch up, Richard."

He starts straining against the zip-ties. "You can't just... This is my *house*! I could have you arrested!"

I smile coldly. "Go ahead. Call the police."

He thrashes against the ties for only a few seconds before he realizes just how fucked this situation is for him. He's not a stupid man, not like Byron. Just an unfortunate one.

"What do you want?" he whimpers.

"You suspended Natalia."

"You had sex with her in the office in full sight of a camera! What choice did I have?"

"And what about Byron Wells?"

Richard sags. "What about him?"

"I had my men do a little digging into Byron's history in your company. Apparently, there have been quite a few sexual harassment complaints lodged against him over the years. By quite a few different women."

"I... Er, that is..." he splutters, spit flying everywhere.

"Get to the point fast, Richard—you're losing me."

He swallows hard. His Adam's apple bobs violently. "What happened with you and Natalia has nothing to do with Byron. They're completely different situations."

"I agree. The incident between Natalia and me in the office was completely consensual. The situation with Byron was not."

"There is footage of—"

"I don't give a fuck what footage you have," I growl. Richard flushes red, then purple, then white with abject fear. "I don't care if I fucked Natalia on your damn desk. It still doesn't explain why she gets consequences while Byron gets a free pass."

"Human Resources will want to do an internal review and—"

I hold up my hand and Richard's jaw snaps shut. "I don't give a shit about the specifics. I don't care about the damn process. I want this situation fixed—and you are going to fix it for me."

"I can't… I—"

"You're the CEO of the company; you can do whatever you want. And trust me, Richard, you're gonna want to make me happy. Because if I'm not happy, I'm gonna come back here." I look around the room, taking in the jewelry dish on the other side of the bed. "Maybe next time, you can introduce me to your pretty little wife."

He blanches. "Don't hurt her!" he begs.

"I have no intention of hurting her. But I might make her watch me hurt you. Just depends on how much you piss me off."

His eyeballs look like they're going to pop out of their sockets. For the second time tonight, the stink of ammonia hits my nostrils like a sledgehammer. A dark stain spreads across the bed around Richard's crotch.

Honestly, it's almost enough to make me crave a showdown with Nikolai.

At least the man has a smidgeon more pride. At least he will pose a slightly bigger challenge.

This… this is like shooting fish in a barrel.

"Really, Richard." I wrinkle my nose. "There's no need to be afraid. Not as long as you do exactly what I ask of you."

He nods, tears rolling unchecked down his cheeks. "Alright. Okay. What do you want from me?"

I get to my feet. "First thing tomorrow, you will reinstate Natalia and wipe clean any black marks on her record. You will also give her a raise and an apology for your glaring lapse in judgment." I crack my knuckles and then my neck. "Personally, I think Natalia can do much better than your shitty little operation. But as long as she wants to work for you, I expect her to have a job there. Is that understood?"

"Yes."

"Then we're in agreement." I pull out a knife, causing Richard to piss himself a little more. "Get a hold of yourself, man. I'm just going to cut you loose."

The moment his hands are free, he snatches his duvet and fumbles to cover himself. Smirking, I walk to the door.

"Wait!" I glance at him over my shoulder and listen. "What do you want me to do about Byron?"

"You don't have to worry about Byron. I've already taken care of that problem for you." I smile and pull the door closed. "You're welcome."

46

NATALIA

"Nice, huh?" Leonty asks.

I take in the sunlight filtering in through the bay windows and the view of the property. "It's great," I agree. "But I still don't know why you brought me here."

Leonty's looking down at the garden as he replies, "Because your baby is gonna need a nursery."

This room would be perfect for a nursery—but that also means I would have to move into the main house at some point, too. Loathe as I am to admit it, I've become attached to the pool house.

It's a convenient loophole to keep from having to admit that Andrey and I live together.

We're under two separate roofs. We're neighbors more than anything.

But if my baby is going to be in a nursery in the big house, where does that leave me? Where does that leave *us*?

"Maybe we could add an extension onto the pool house?" I suggest. "Create a little nook for the baby?"

Leonty purses his lips. "Let me know how that conversation flies with the head honcho."

"Wuss."

"I don't see you rushing off to bring up the idea to him. You're just leaving it to me. Coward."

I chuckle. Takes one to know one, I guess.

Ever since my suspension from work and subsequent, suspiciously quick, reinstatement, I've wanted to ask Andrey what part he had to play in all of it. Because he must have done something.

Mr. Ewes reversed his decision in under twenty-four hours, and I not only escaped an HR review, but earned a raise.

Also, where in the hell did Byron go? I mean, the man disappeared without so much as a goodbye party in the breakroom. The only explanation I got was the same one as the rest of Sunshield: *Mr. Wells has decided to hand in his resignation and pursue alternative career prospects.*

Nobody bought that.

Least of all me.

Not after Andrey had basically assured me that he would "take care of everything." I could just ask Andrey, but truth be told, I'm terrified of what he might say.

"Andrey is busy, okay?" I say. "I don't want to bother him."

"Since when?"

Glowering, I join him at the windows. "Since he might have killed my boss for sexually harassing me."

Leonty's smile withers. "Would you just let it go already? You've got a good thing going here, Nat. Just enjoy it."

God, how I wish I could. "Do you think he killed him?"

Leonty shrugs, which, let me tell you, is not comforting at all. "Personally, I don't think you should be wasting your time worrying about that asshole. He's not in your life anymore. End of story. What you should be focused on is getting this room ready for the little princess."

He tries to pat my stomach, but I swat him away. "Don't patronize me."

Chuckling, he makes for the door. "I was told to let you know that this room is yours to design. So let your imagination run wild."

Then he disappears.

"Idiot," I mutter, turning back to the windows.

I left Remi with Misha in the gardens earlier, but I don't see any sign of them right now.

Almost as though I've conjured them out of thin air, I hear Remi's bark. A few moments later, the dog skitters into the room with Misha just behind him. They both slip and slide on the polished hardwood floors, laughing hysterically.

Misha sobers and dips his head as soon as he sees me, his hands folded behind his back. "Leonty said you were up here." He still walks into every room like he might be thrown out of it by the scruff. Another symptom of his rough childhood, I'm sure.

Though he's been tight-lipped about the details so far. I spent hours trying to wheedle some information out of him. In the end, it was Mila that made me realize that I was beating a dead horse.

"He's not ready to talk about his past yet. Instead of forcing the topic, just give him the space to trust you. One day, when he is ready to talk, he'll know he can come to you."

It was good advice. As soon as I stopped pushing him for information about himself, he relaxed around me. Sometimes, he even seeks me out.

"This is going to be the baby's nursery. What do you think?"

Remi explores the room in large, frantic circles, sniffing every nook and cranny. Misha, on the other hand, takes his time. He looks around with those watchful eyes, turning on the spot as though he's scared to take up space.

"What do you think?" he lobs back at me.

"I asked ya first."

His smile is shy. "It's… nice."

"What if we painted the walls a nice bright yellow?" I wonder out loud. "Or maybe wallpaper on one side with a forest motif? And then do this wall in green?"

Misha looks utterly lost. "Um… yeah. Whatever you like."

Remi butts his head against the back of Misha's legs. He drops to his knees to pet the needy dog. I can't help but smile at the two of them. It's amazing how far they've come. Just goes to show what you can achieve with a little love.

I gesture for Misha to join me at the window seat. He sits on the far end of the cushion while Remi resumes his circling inspections.

"Will you help me paint?" I ask.

At that, the boy's eyes snap to mine. "You want me to help?"

"Of course."

His face flushes and he looks down quickly. "I… I don't know how much longer I'll be around, though." His furrowed forehead suggests that he's been worrying about this for some time now.

"Is there somewhere you need to be, Misha?" I ask. "A home you want to go back to? A family who might be waiting for you…?"

He refuses to look at me. "No one's looking for me."

My heart splinters. But then again, I already knew that. It's been months and no one has come knocking.

"If there's someone you want to find," I say softly, "I could help you locate—"

"No!"

I pull back, startled by the fierceness in his voice and the sudden pallor in his skin.

"Sorry, it's just… I don't want to be found." He sighs. "If they know I'm alive, they'll know I failed. And they told me that if I failed, either Andrey would kill me or they would."

"But Andrey hasn't killed you," I remind him. "And he's not going to, either."

Misha squirms uncomfortably. "I know. I was wrong about him."

"Misha, is there any place you have left to go?"

He shakes his head and I detect the fear in his eyes at the mere suggestion. Slowly, the same way I coach strangers to approach Remi, I reach out and touch Misha's leg. He flinches, but doesn't shove me away.

"Well, then I'm the lucky one," I declare. "Because that means I get to enjoy the pleasure of your company."

Misha blinks at me like the idea is absurd. Like no one has ever said anything so nice to him.

Which cracks my heart a little more.

"Do you want to stay here with—?"

"I like staying here," Misha says before I can finish asking the question. "I like being around you."

I smile and squeeze his knee. "You're safe here, Misha. You know that, right?"

He nods, his smile withering. "But Andrey won't want me here forever."

Determination surges through my bones. I'm no longer interested in avoiding a hard conversation with Andrey. Not when Misha's peace of mind hangs in the balance.

"Don't you worry about Andrey," I assure him. "Leave him to me."

47

NATALIA

I press my shoulders back and knock on Andrey's office door, ready to be cool, calm, and collected.

But when the door whips open, it's Shura standing there.

I sag. "Where's Andrey?"

"He's in the gym."

With a nod of thanks, I'm already turning away when Shura clears his throat. I've never seen him look so awkward. "I was just wondering if… er… When will Katya be visiting next?"

I suppress a smile. I know how Katya feels about Shura; I just wasn't sure if he reciprocated. The sheen of nervous sweat on his forehead makes things a little clearer.

"Soon," I assure him. "She wants to come over and see the nursery."

He shrugs like he could care less. "I have some records she wanted to borrow. That's all."

"I could just give you her number, if you want? That way, I don't have to be your middleman."

"Oh? Well, um…" His face flushes. "I suppose so. If it makes things easier for you."

"I'll drop you her contact."

I'm humming the wedding march and grinning like a loon as I walk to the gym in search of Andrey.

But an eyeful of Andrey, shirtless and sweating, as he rails against a punching bag in the far corner of the gym, wipes the smile and every safe-for-work thought away.

He's wearing a pair of black shorts and matching black hand wraps as he bounces on the balls of his feet, circling the punching bag with a kind of brutal grace I've never seen before. When he unleashes his fists on the poor bag, threatening to rip it right off its hook, I think I'm watching poetry in motion.

Gingerly, I approach, marveling at the way his muscles ripple with every movement. He has muscles in places I didn't even know you could have muscles.

Forget cool and calm—I'm officially hot and bothered. And who could even blame me? He's perfection. I want to run a finger over the topography of his thighs, mapping them so future generations can know what a perfect specimen looked like.

And don't even get me started on his—

"Natalia?"

I freeze like a kid caught with her hand in the cookie jar. My face is flaming, but I square my shoulders and meet his eyes. "We need to talk."

Nice, approves my inner coach. *Very stern. Very imposing.*

"What's this about?"

I should answer him, but my attention is fixed on a single drop of sweat sliding down the V-cut of his abs until it disappears below his waistband. Only when it's gone do I blink back to his face, determined to keep things on track. "It's about Misha."

Andrey starts unwinding his hand wraps but his eyes stay trained on me. "Okay. What about him?"

Things have been reasonably calm between us ever since the whole suspension debacle. We haven't slept together, but we haven't fought, either. It's been… nice. I don't want to ruin a good thing, but I'm set on getting my way here. If that means another fight, then so be it.

"I want to keep him."

So much for easing him into the idea. I'm just a big, dumb bull stomping around in Andrey's china shop.

"You want to keep him?" The incredulity in his tone is exactly how I did not want this conversation to start.

Although, calling it a "hostage negotiation" at this stage might be more accurate.

"That came out wrong." Taking a deep breath, I try again. "Do you know what that kid has been through?"

"Considering I put him through some of it, I have an idea."

"He didn't explicitly say so, but I'm pretty sure he was born into some sort of…" I lower my voice. "—human trafficking ring."

I wait for some sort of reaction, but Andrey just keeps undoing his hand wraps, the long, sweaty loop of fabric piling up at his feet.

"Do you understand what I'm saying?" I press. "He mentioned his mother briefly, and I think… Andrey, I think she was sold—"

"She was a prostitute."

I jerk back, frowning at him. "Wait, how do you know?"

"The boy's been in my home for months now. Did you really think I wasn't digging into his background? Did you really think I wouldn't want to find out everything there is to know about where he came from?"

"So… you know where his mother is?"

He shakes his head. "Dead, most likely."

"Oh my." My heart breaks for Misha. But then something strikes me. "Wait… does he know?"

"I'm not sure. Apparently, they were separated when he was only seven or eight."

Seven or eight. It's the same age I was when I lost my parents. I want to wrap Misha in a tight hug and never let him go.

"Why were they separated?"

"From what I understand, Star—we couldn't find her birth name—was sold to the highest bidder at an auction years ago. The man who purchased her wasn't interested in paying for her son as well."

My chest feels heavy. It's hard to breathe. "Oh my God."

"Misha was kept with the pimps and trained to be an errand boy of sorts."

"That's—" I can't find a word bad enough to describe what I'm hearing. "Despicable!"

Andrey's eyes soften. "I know it doesn't seem this way, but Misha was one of the lucky ones."

"How can you say that?" I scoff. "His mother was sold like a cow at auction! And he was forced into child slave labor!"

Andrey takes a cautious step towards me, leaving the black wraps behind him like shed snakeskins. "When a woman in that kind of scenario is unfortunate enough to have a child, one of two things usually happens."

I go deathly still in anticipation of what I'm about to hear. I have a feeling it won't be pretty.

"Either that child is killed. That's the best-case scenario," he informs me, taking no pleasure in the information. "Because the children that live get sold to the kind of men who hunt for that kind of thing."

He lets the information settle between us. He watches me, waiting for my mind to go to the darkest possible reality… because that's where Misha grew up.

"People like that can't really exist," I breathe. "They're monsters."

He meets my eyes and nods. "Which is why I've done my best to take out as many of them as possible."

For the first time since I was introduced to Andrey's wild and violent world, I ask myself if maybe I judged him too harshly. I thought it was all bad guys. Not black-and-white, but black-and-blacker.

Now, though, I'm seeing shades of gray.

Sure, Andrey deals in murder and money, but at least he's not buying or selling human beings. At least he's not ripping sons from their mothers or raping innocent children.

He may not be a hero.

But he's not the villain, either.

"Do you know how Misha's mother died?"

He shakes his head. "Her trail goes cold after her last purchase. She definitely wasn't sold again, which means she probably died at the hands of her last owner."

I drop my face into my hands. It's all so horrible.

Then a new thought occurs to me, and I bolt up. "The man that sold Misha's mother… Is he the same man that sent him to spy on you?"

"Yes. Nikolai Rostov." Andrey's jaw tightens, but he reaches out to brush the tips of his fingers against my cheek. "Why do you think I wanted you to move in here with me, Natalia? Why do you think I gave you a full security detail and a guard dog? We're not dealing with some petty threat here. Nikolai Rostov is—"

"A monster," I finish for him. I grab his hands without thinking about it. I don't even care that they're callused and sweaty. "Don't you see, Andrey? This is all the more reason we should keep Misha with us! He has no one. We're all he has."

"'We'?"

Another blush creeps up my cheeks, but I don't care. So what if I embarrass myself? It's for Misha's sake. He deserves it.

"Please, Andrey. He's just a kid. A kid who never had a chance. I'll take responsibility for him, if that makes a difference. I just... I can't bear the thought of him—" I break off as the sobs I've been holding in finally catch up to me. I'm not sure how I ended up sitting on Andrey's lap, but my cheek is pressed to his shoulder and his hand is on my back.

"Hush now, little bird. It's okay."

"It's not okay," I mutter through my tears. "None of it is okay."

"You can't carry the weight of the world on your shoulders."

His voice is soothing, but I won't relax until I get what I came here for. I pull back so I can look in his eyes—so he can look into mine. "He needs someone, Andrey. Just like I did when I lost both my parents to that... that bastard. I can't turn my back on him. Please don't ask me to."

His hand is tracing up and down my spine slowly. "Alright. I won't stand in your way."

I'm instantly cautious of the victory. "So he can stay?"

Andrey nods, his eyes flashing with some unknown emotion. "He can stay."

And finally, I let myself breathe. I let myself be comforted.

Because I believe Andrey.

More importantly, I realize... I *trust* him.

48

ANDREY

For the first time since he was captured by my men, I seek out the boy.

Misha is reading in his room. It's just a book, but the way he jumps and tries to hide it when he sees me standing in the doorway makes it seem like illegal contraband.

"What have you got there?"

"Nothing," he answers a little too quickly.

I hold out a hand, waiting. His face sours, but he retrieves the book from under the pillow where he stashed it. He doesn't meet my eyes as he forks it over.

I'm expecting a dirty magazine or a mass murderer's manifesto, but it's just a flimsy paper copy of *The Ugly Duckling*. I flip through the pages, looking for something stashed between them, but there's nothing.

The words are in large, bolded text. It's the kind of easy reader book you'd give a child just learning to read. Nothing more, nothing less.

I look from the cover to Misha's face. "We have a library if you want something else." I don't immediately understand the flush that rises to his cheeks. And then it hits me: "You can't read."

"I can read," he snaps. He sucks in his cheeks, chewing on the insides. "I'm just… not very good." His voice wobbles, but it doesn't break.

Not for the first time, I understand what Natalia sees in him. He's made of tougher stuff than most.

Throwing the book onto his bed, I gesture for him to follow me. "Come on, let's go for a walk."

He doesn't move. "Where?"

"Just around the property."

"With Natalia and Remi?" He looks past me into the hallway, the hope in his eyes dimming when he sees it's empty.

"Just me today, Misha."

Judging from the look on his face, he's not reassured in the least, but he does follow me out of his room.

The silence continues until we're outside. I don't have to worry about being interrupted; Natalia and Remi are at work for the day. Then again, maybe it might have been better to include Natalia in this conversation. Misha likes her. He *trusts* her.

I suppose I'll have to rely on my own instincts to guide me through this one.

We walk for several more minutes before I finally break the silence. "Misha, do you know why you were sent to spy on me?"

The boy's head rises and his chin juts out stubbornly. "I wasn't sent to spy; I was bait." He spits the word like it's beneath him. Given what I've seen of him the last few weeks, I tend to agree. Nikolai severely underestimated the asset he had on his hands.

"I don't have any more information to give you," Misha adds brusquely. "I've already told Shura everything I know."

"I know that." I step closer and clap a hand on his shoulder. "I know Nikolai Rostov, Misha. He would never have considered you important enough to share information with. You were only a pawn to sacrifice. So that, if you were caught, it wouldn't matter, because you'd have nothing worthwhile to divulge."

He works his jaw back and forth until I'm sure his teeth are dust. His hands start to tremble with a rage I know all too well.

With a sigh, I lead him over to the old stone bench. He perches on the far corner of it, his hands tucked beneath his thighs so I can't see them tremble.

"If I were to set you free, where would you go?"

Misha's jaw trembles for a moment before he composes himself with the resolve of someone who had to grow up far too young. "I don't know."

"Where would you go if you could go anywhere you wanted to?"

"I… I don't know," he repeats. His hands are fisted so tightly his knuckles are white.

The circus, he could've said. *Disney World. The fucking moon.*

He didn't even have enough of a childhood to dream.

"And what if I said you didn't have to go?" I look in his eyes, trying to drum up some of the magic Natalia has. The quality that draws people in and holds them close. "What if I told you that you could stay here if you wanted?"

He doesn't even hesitate. "I would stay."

It's the first clear answer I've gotten out of him since he was captured. I can't explain the surge of satisfaction that it sends coursing through me. "Natalia thinks that this is the best place for you."

There's a ghostly smile fighting its way to Misha's lips. "So I get to stay here? With Natalia?"

"She seems to think that you'll be a great help with the baby."

He finally lets the smile crack through the surface. "I'm good with babies. I used to look after the smaller kids in the compound."

My gut twists. "There were others?"

"Not many. I was always the oldest. I think that's why they kept me around. They needed someone to babysit."

His voice cracks as he speaks. Reflected in his eyes are the ghosts of all those little ones who came into his care with little explanation and left with even less. A graveyard of unfinished stories, unanswered questions. I shudder at the sight.

Did he love them? Did he help them? Did he know they were marked for death from the beginning?

"That's all in the past now, Misha. You don't have to babysit anyone if you don't want to."

He stuffs his hands into his pants pockets and turns to the side so that only his profile is visible to me. He's fighting emotion and I'm impressed with how well he masters it.

The boy has potential. A lot of potential.

"But living here comes with conditions."

He doesn't so much as flinch. Apparently, this is something he does understand—nothing in life is free. "Okay."

"You have to go to school, for one."

"No. I can't do school." For the first time, he looks genuinely panicked. "I'm stupid."

I clasp a hand on his shoulder and he freezes at the unexpected contact. "I've seen stupid in my life. You're not it."

"I can't go to school. I'll never fit in there. I'm not... I'm not like other kids." He looks down, wringing his hands together into worried knots. "I'd rather just stay here. I'll stay here and work—be useful to you and Natalia."

My chest is alive with a million nameless emotions now. But one thing rises above the fray, one certainty.

Natalia is right. He deserves more.

49

NATALIA

"No, Natalia. Out! Out now!" Yelena literally shoves me out of the laundry room, her face twisted into a no-nonsense scowl.

"Yelena, it's just the laundry!" I complain. "I can help with the laundry."

She pulls the laundry room door shut behind her and puts her hands on her hips. "Those detergents are full of chemicals, and I don't want you breathing in the toxins."

I can't help but pout. "I can help! And then you can tell me more stories about your childhood in Russia."

"Another day," she says, her scowl softening ever so slightly. "Right now, I have to get the laundry done. Where are your two shadows?"

"Misha is in a tutoring session."

"Which means Remi is with him," Yelena finishes knowingly.

Remi must be able to sense how much Misha hates his study sessions, because he refuses to leave Misha's side while he's working at the table. Remi curls up under the desk, and it's so damn sweet that I don't even mind being abandoned.

Even though I'm desperate for some company. Which is why I'm begging to do laundry.

"Find Mila then," Yelena suggests.

"Mila is out with Leonty."

"Katya?"

"Katya is busy, too," I grumble. "If you just let me into the laundry room, I promise I won't touch the det—"

Yelena slips into the laundry room and closes the door before I can even finish.

So much for that.

I've spent plenty of lonely days in this house, so I don't know what makes today so unbearable. Or, maybe I do know why…which makes it all even more unbearable.

The sad, pitiful fact is that I'm jealous of my friends. Mila is out with Leonty and Katya is with Shura. My two friends are out being wined and dined by handsome men, and I'm left behind to twiddle my thumbs and daydream.

I wander through the house, lowkey hoping that I might run into a certain silver-eyed distraction. But the manor is dishearteningly empty.

I'm nearly desperate enough to go hang with the Bratva boys who aren't out wooing my friends. Except I already know Anatoly and Leif are in the gym, pumping iron and slapping each other in the back of the head for shits and giggles. And no amount of boredom is worth enduring that.

I'm about to give up and retreat back to my fortress of solitude in the pool house when the sound of an engine catches my attention.

Mila is back!

I careen through the house towards Mila's wing of the house, prepared to drop to my knees and beg Leonty and Mila to let me third wheel with them.

I don't see Leonty's car in the drive and the entryway is quiet, so I keep moving to Mila's room. It crosses my mind that I could be about to walk in on my friend and bodyguard getting it on, but desperate times and all that.

Unfortunately, Mila's room is empty.

"Huh." Hands on my hips, I spin in a slow circle like I might be able to make a friend appear.

Suddenly, the door behind me swings open.

"It's about freaking ti—" The words die on my lips, replaced by only one. "Viktor."

His eyes are bloodshot and hooded, and his attention is sluggish. If I hadn't spoken, he probably wouldn't have even noticed I was here.

"Who're you?" he slurs.

He's clear across the room, but I can smell the booze coming off him. Booze and smoke and filth I don't even have the words for. If Yelena didn't want me near laundry detergent, she's certainly going to have something to say about my proximity to *this* walking trigger warning.

"I was just... waiting for Mila," I mumble uncomfortably. "I'm gonna head back to the pool house."

Suddenly, his eyes go wide. Recognition flickers across his face.

"Natalia." There's a strange new silkiness in his voice. He runs a greasy hand through his even greasier hair. "It's been too long."

If you ask me, it hasn't been nearly long enough.

His eyes slip down to my belly. There's no denying my pregnancy anymore, but this is the first time I've felt so self-conscious about it. I feel vulnerable.

"You're glowing," he remarks.

If that hideous drawl is supposed to be charming, he ought to go back to the drawing board.

"Er, thanks." I move to leave, but he's blocking my path out of here. His blue eyes are clearer suddenly, brighter and full of intention.

"Going so soon?" Viktor asks. "Don't break my heart. We've barely had a chance to catch up."

My skin crawls. It's amazing how violated I feel just standing here under his gaze. I take a miniscule step back. "Maybe another time. I'm a little tired."

"We are family now, after all," he says, plowing right over my protests. "I should get to know my future sister-in-law."

"I'm not your future anything, Viktor. Andrey and I aren't together."

Viktor takes a step forward. "Then my brother is a fool. I would have made you mine in a heartbeat." He lurches forward and plants his hands on either side of the table I'm standing in front of, trapping me between his arms.

"Viktor—"

"Hush." His breath is vile and the erection pressing into my thigh is even more so. I cower against the table to keep some distance between our bodies.

"Please," I whisper, afraid to scream the way I want to for fear of escalating things. "This is wrong."

"'Wrong'?" Viktor chuckles. His foul breath is making me lightheaded. "What's wrong about this? You're not with my brother. You just said it yourself."

"I am carrying his child, though."

"So what?" he scoffs. "Does that mean he owns you? Does he own your body, Natalia?"

His hands trail over my stomach, and I slap them away. "Get off of me!"

"It's okay," he croons, holding me tighter. His fingers dig into my hips. "My brother won't mind. He lets my bride fuck whoever she wants. I'm sure Mila has told you all about it."

I press a hand to his chest, trying to force his eyes to mine. Trying to make him see me as a human, not an object. "Viktor, I didn't make that decision. None of that has anything to do with me."

"I beg to differ, pretty girl. It has everything to do with you. If Andrey can do whatever the fuck he wants, I should be allowed the same right."

Oh, God. This is really happening. If I don't stop, Viktor is going to...

I squeeze my eyes closed as Viktor suckles his wet mouth to my neck.

I can't fight him. I'm trapped with a predator who is more than capable of taking what he wants from me. I need help.

I want to scream.

I'm about to.

Then I notice movement in the doorway, and my stomach plummets.

Misha is staring at me, wide-eyed and horrified. He understands exactly what is happening, and somehow, that makes it all so much worse.

He takes one step forward, but I shake my head gently.

Viktor will kill him if he comes in here. Misha is tough, but he's just a boy. If Misha intervenes, Viktor will hurt him. And tough as I know Misha can be, I also know that he won't stand a chance against a full-grown man. Especially one with as much rage as Viktor.

Go, I mouth to him. *Please.*

For a second, I don't think he's going to listen.

Then he turns around and runs.

I sigh in relief, and Viktor groans. "I knew you'd like it. I'm gonna fuck my brother right out of your system."

50

ANDREY

"I've dug as much as I dared, boss." Gedeon is whispering into the phone. I have no idea where he is right now, but there must be other people nearby. "Asking too many questions could raise suspicions. I don't wanna blow my cover."

Gedeon is undercover on the far periphery of Nikolai Rostov's operation, picking up scraps of info that turn out to be red herrings or smoke in the wind more often than not. Still, it took careful planning and some serious stealth to get him even that close. I'm reluctant to jeopardize that for the sake of a brooding teenager.

So, discouraging as that is, it's what I expected.

"You made the right call," I say with a sigh. "If there was anything worth knowing, I'm sure we'd know it by now. But keep your eyes open just in case."

I hang up with Gedeon and try to get back to work, but Remi keeps barking outside.

It's the first time I've heard him all day. Ever since Misha started his tutoring, the two of them spend all of their time in the makeshift classroom I had set up for him.

I turn around, expecting to see Natalia and Misha out there fawning over the beast, but Remi is alone. *Weird.* Since the moment Remi arrived on the property, he's been glued to either Natalia or Misha. So where are they?

As if in answer to my question, my door bursts open and Misha careens into my office, sweating and panting.

"N-Natalia," is all he manages to get out.

It's enough.

"Where is she?"

Misha turns and starts running again. He's fast, but I keep up easily, following the boy all the way through the house to Mila's wing.

I know things are serious because Misha, despite being calm and level-headed since he arrived here, is frantic. Still, I'm expecting a medical episode—low blood sugar or something to do with the baby.

What I'm not expecting is to find my sack-of-shit brother groping the pregnant mother of my child.

Rage like I've never known floods through me, turning my vision red.

I'm not murderous. That word doesn't do it justice. It would make light of the way I want to shred my brother into pieces and burn them. The way I want to wipe him off the face of the Earth so no one will ever remember his name.

Natalia whimpers, angling as far away from Viktor as she can. Her face is ashen, frozen in horror at the hands of the motherfucker I'm forced to call my brother. Viktor is so intent on his prey that he doesn't notice his audience.

Huge mistake.

I grab his neck with every intention of snapping it in my palm and rip him away. Natalia wilts, crumpling to the floor where Misha hurries to catch her.

She's safe, I tell myself. It's the only way I can look away from her and deal with the human scum at my feet.

Viktor is bleary-eyed and dazed. *Drunk.* It's no excuse, though. I've made too many excuses for him over the years, but never again.

He opens his mouth, perhaps to apologize or beg for his life. I have no idea which and I don't give two fucks.

Before he can do either, I drag him to his feet, only to knock him down again with a solid blow to his face.

He buckles, following the momentum of my blow all the way to the tile floor where blood puddles around his head.

Satisfying as the punch was, it's not nearly enough to satiate me. *There'll be time for that later,* I console myself before turning to Natalia. *She comes first.*

Natalia is trembling on the floor, an arm thrown over her stomach, the other wrapped around Misha. He is holding her up, but he's also shaking, speaking so quickly I almost can't catch the words.

"—my fault. I'm so sorry. If Remi was with you, then—" He chokes in a breath. "Remi should have been with you. He's your dog."

It's a testament to the love that Natalia feels for Misha that she fights through her own fear to reassure him. She grabs his face. "No, Misha. None of this is your fault."

The boy is sobbing now, tears flowing like rivers down both cheeks. "But if Remi had been with you—"

"Stop." Her voice is weak, but the command comes through loud and clear. She raises a trembling hand to cup Misha's face. "This is not your fault."

Her eyes flicker to Viktor's limp body, but I squat down between them, blocking my brother from view. Misha flinches back as though he's waiting for me to disagree with Natalia and blame him.

"Natalia's right, Misha." My voice is thick with anger, but it's not directed at the boy. "This is not on you. This is on him."

I turn to Natalia and take her hand. Her beautiful green eyes are cloudy, fighting to rise above the shock of her assault. "Did he hurt you?"

"H-he tried… Misha came just in time." Her eyes veer back to him and she makes a brave attempt at a smile. "You saved me, Misha."

The boy doesn't look convinced.

"What the hell?!"

I turn around to find Mila and Leonty standing in the doorway. Leonty's gaze is focused on me, but Mila only has eyes for the unconscious bastard on the floor.

"What did he do?" she breathes.

I can't tell them. If I do, I'll kill him here and now. Instead, I gently pull Natalia to her feet and pass her to Misha. "Take her to the pool house," I tell him. I nod at Mila. "You go with them."

Mila and Misha help Natalia out of the room, leaving Leonty and me with Viktor's unconscious body.

"He didn't," Leonty growls, shaking his head. "Even he isn't that stupid."

But he is.

"Round up the men," I instruct. "I want him moved to the gym."

Leonty doesn't bother asking further questions. He knows what's coming. It's not a tradition that's typical for members of the *pakhan's* family, but Viktor has just forfeited his right to immunity.

He'll suffer like he's nobody to me.

I'm carving my way across the house, more than ready to have this done, when I notice Yelena skulking in the archway. "What happened?" she asks.

I'm not in the mood for explanations, but she cared for Viktor since he was a boy, too. She has always been a kind of mother to him.

"Viktor thought he'd get back at me by cornering Natalia."

She gasps. "Did he…?"

"No. I got there before he could."

She nods once, pivots on her heel, and walks towards the pool house faster than I knew she was capable of.

I let her go.

I have a brother to torture.

When I enter the gym, Viktor is stirring on the rubber flooring, surrounded by my men. Natalia's entire security detail is here. So are Yuri and Efrem. Shura stands removed from the rest of them, his arms so tense that I can see the veins running through them.

"Efrem," I bark, "wake him up."

Efrem flings a bucket of frigid water onto Viktor's face, and he splutters awake.

Water drips from the end of his crooked nose and blood is congealed along the side of his face. He squints into the light, but he sees only me. I'm kneeling down, close enough I can still smell the liquor on his breath.

One glance around the room is enough for Viktor to realize there's no way out. He's surrounded by men who will kill him without hesitation as soon as I give the order.

His chest rises and falls erratically as he looks at me... and waits. When it becomes clear that no one's going to breathe a word until he does, he opens his mouth.

Nothing but hot air comes out.

He tries again. "I am your brother," he finally croaks.

"And you think that will protect you?"

"This is beneath you," he says. "It's beneath me. This tradition is reserved for—"

"Traitors," I spit.

His eyes narrow. "I have done nothing."

"You put your hands on what's mine."

His face ripples with anger. "You let my wife fuck *that—*" He points at Leonty without looking at him. "—traitorous piece of shit and you claim this is my fault! You've made me a laughingstock! You've fucking ruined me!"

It's clear that the last few weeks haven't been kind to Viktor. He looks like an empty shell of the man he used to be. But any pity I might've had is nonexistent in the face of what I just witnessed.

"I never needed to lift a finger to turn you into a laughingstock, Viktor. You did that all by yourself. If you want to blame someone for ruining you, look in the fucking mirror."

Drool slicks his chin as he draws himself up on his knees as tall as he can. "I know my worth."

"Then you'll know that disposing of you would cost me nothing. In fact, I would only stand to gain." I get to my feet. "So don't fucking tempt me."

The whites of his eyes have disappeared behind thick, red veins.

"I know things," he blurts out, more spit flying from his mouth. "I know your secrets, brother. Don't forget that."

"Are you threatening me?" I ask in pure disbelief.

"I'm reminding you that I have the power to destroy you if I wanted to."

I take two steps forward, forcing Viktor to crane his neck back to look at me. I squat down in front of him and take his hand. "Then it's incumbent on me to remind you—" My hand tightens around Viktor's wrist and his eyes flare with panic.

"—that you have no power at all here anymore. You made sure of that the moment you touched my woman."

Grabbing his index finger, I snap it back hard.

He screams.

His wail pierces through the quiet of the gym. But I've already moved onto the next finger. And the next. I don't stop until all five are mangled and useless.

If he acts fast, he might be able to put them back together. But they'll never be fully functional again.

He's still howling with a mixture of rage and alarm when I kick him back against the rubber flooring. I gaze down at him with revulsion. "You're no longer welcome in this manor. You're no longer welcome in my sight. Stay the fuck away from me and you might live."

Viktor is clutching his hand at the wrist, staring at his mangled hand. But I know he can hear me over his steady whimpering.

"You were right about one thing, though," I concede after a moment of thought. "You are my brother. So I will allow you to live in my safehouse in Hunts Point."

His desperate eyes meet mine. "You're exiling me?"

"A little rough living won't kill you. In fact, it might finally make a man out of you." I start to walk away as Viktor makes an attempt to sit up again. My *vors* close in on him, but I know they'll wait for my command.

"Andrey!" Viktor screams. "Andrey! You can't do this."

"You can begin," I tell my men from the doorway. "Just don't kill him."

I let the door fall shut on Viktor's hysterical screams.

51

NATALIA

The pain pulls at me like quicksand. I'm waist-deep in it, but I don't have the energy to fight. Part of me doesn't even want to.

Make it end, I think. *I don't want to hurt anymore.*

Then there's a furry muzzle pressing into my side, reminding me he's still with me even hours later. The gentle murmurs of familiar voices. Light and darkness folding into one another, shadows that come in waves, then flow back out again.

Pain and grief. Mila and Misha and Andrey.

Crippling anxiety until I can barely breathe. Leonty and Shura and Andrey.

Depression so dark I can't see through it to the other side. And Andrey.

And Andrey.

And Andrey.

"Has she eaten anything today?"

I want to ask him, *How long have I been like this?* But my mouth won't obey.

"I managed to feed her some soup," Mila responds, her voice coming to me through a haze I can't dispel. "And, like, half a sandwich. Ish."

"Take Remi outside. He needs a walk." Andrey's voice is as commanding as ever, but there's an edge to it that reminds me of shattering glass.

"Remi won't move off her bed. I tried this morning. He refuses to leave her side."

"Get Misha. Remi will move for him."

Eventually, the soft, furry weight at my side disappears. *Good. He'll need some fresh air. They both do.*

Everyone is taken care of. They don't need me. Maybe everyone would be better off if—

"Okay, *lastochka*," Andrey whispers in my ear. "It's time to come back now."

His hands move gently over my body, and there isn't a single part of me that is scared. His touch is soothing and gentle. Nothing like—

No.

It hurts too much to think about. It's easier to forget.

But Andrey won't let me. He peels away my clothes like he's afraid I might crumble, and passes a hot towel over my body. It fills me with an aching tranquility.

Life can't be all bad if there are moments like this sprinkled in, can it?

For the first time in too long to remember, I open my eyes.

And Andrey is there, his steady presence, the hypnotic brilliance of his silver-eyed gaze. I blink a few times, marveling that the world is right here in front of me, close enough to touch.

"There you are, little bird," Andrey whispers softly. "I knew you were in there somewhere."

Andrey dries me off and dresses me in clean clothes. Then he tucks me back under the blankets, and Andrey is everywhere.

My cheek is pillowed on his chest. His arms are wrapped tightly around me, and I feel safe. Safe enough to tunnel my way out of the quicksand and take my first few tentative steps out onto solid ground.

"Andrey," I croak. "Wh…where is everyone?"

"I had Shura and Leonty take Misha and Remi out for a few hours. They needed to get out of the manor. Kat and Mila joined them."

The image of all of them together makes me want to smile, but I can't. Not yet. "It's nice that they have each other," I breathe, almost too softly to be heard.

Andrey lifts me up and holds a glass to my lips. "You need to drink something."

I don't realize how thirsty I am until the water hits my tongue. I drink until the glass is gone. When Andrey offers to get me more, I cling to his shirt, silently begging him to stay. "How long have I been out?"

"Three days." His lips brush against my temple. "Do you remember what happened?"

I look down at my hands. My skin is chalky. God only knows how bad the rest of me looks. "Yeah. I remember everything."

"I'm sorry, Natalia."

I've never heard Andrey so broken. That, more than anything, wakes me up. "You had nothing to do with it."

"Viktor is my brother. I should have seen this coming." I flinch at the mention of Viktor's name, and Andrey rests a calming hand on my knee. "He's far away now, Natalia. He won't be able to hurt you anymore."

The silence that falls between us is heavy, drenched with the memory of what could have happened if Misha hadn't been in the right place at the right time.

"How is Misha?"

Andrey doesn't quite meet my eyes when he answers. "Struggling. He feels as though he failed you."

"He didn't. He got me help." I swallow down the emotion crawling up my throat. "He got me you."

"I know that, but he wishes he'd done more."

"Viktor would've hurt Misha for interfering. He has to know —I'll talk to Misha when he gets back," I say. "I'll explain everything."

"Maybe you should start by explaining it to me." Andrey tightens his hold, protecting me from whatever he's going to say next. "You froze, Natalia."

It feels like an accusation. I want to put some distance

between us. But I also don't want to move away from his warmth.

"What are you trying to say?"

"That you're not seven years old anymore, stuck in a car while horrible things happen outside of your window."

It feels like a punch to the gut, a breath of fresh air, and a bucket of ice water all rolled into one.

"I need you to be able to fight. I need you to be able to—" His voice breaks, and he reaches for my hand, squeezing it like he's the one sinking into quicksand. "If I hadn't come for you, I don't know what would have happened."

"I know. I know I can't do that, but I don't know how to stop," I whisper. "Every time something bad happens, I revert back to that scared little girl."

His hand curls around my jaw, turning me to face him. "Tell me the story."

Tears fill my eyes at the mere thought. I don't like talking about that day, but here, with Andrey, I feel safe. Protected.

It's my story to tell and it's time to tell it.

"We were driving home and it was late. I was supposed to be asleep, but I had to pee, and Dad stopped at a gas station."

I can still see the little station, silhouetted against the dark sky. Half of the lights in the parking lot didn't work. The ones that did were flickering. It looked like a scene from a horror movie.

It turned into one.

"My mom took me inside to the bathroom and then to get

snacks while Dad filled the tank. Then, we switched. He went inside, and I climbed into the car."

Is this the first time I've told this story out loud? It might be. I'm surprised by how many details I can remember. I can hear the lights, the neon signs buzzing. The rumble of the refrigerators. The crackle of empty chip bags blowing in the wind like tumbleweeds.

Andrey's fingers slip through mine, and I cling to him, forcing myself to stay here in this moment.

"I'd just gotten back into the car when this… this man approached us. Mom was trying to talk to him, and then he grabbed her." I blow out a harsh breath, trying to ease the pressure in my chest. "I could hear her screaming, '*Lock the doors, lock the doors!*'"

Tears pour down my cheeks now, but I will myself to keep going. Andrey here, warm and present next to me, gives me enough strength to power through the knot in my throat.

"Dad ran towards us yelling. I remember thinking he was going to fix everything. Then I saw the gun."

I shudder so violently that Andrey tightens his grip on me.

"The first shot was so loud that I covered my ears with my hands. I wish I'd closed my eyes, instead. Then I wouldn't have seen my father—"

I break off, choking on my own words.

"I'm sorry, *lastochka*," Andrey whispers in my ear. "No child should have to watch their parents die."

My jaw trembles. But now that I've started the story, I need to finish it.

"Dad dropped and my mom screamed. It was the worst sound I've ever heard in my life. She tried to run to him, but the man shot her, too." I look at Andrey hopelessly. "We were only an hour outside of New York. We were so close to home… but I needed to use the bathroom…"

"You are not to blame," he whispers in my ear. "Just like Misha isn't to blame for what happened with Viktor."

I close my eyes and see them again. My mother and her dimpled smile. My father with his untrimmed beard and his round glasses.

Andrey cradles me in his arms, gazing down at my face while he strokes my cheek. "You're braver than you know, Natalia."

"What if you're wrong?"

I expect him to tell me that he knows me better than I know myself. And maybe that's true. Maybe he does.

But he doesn't say that. But instead, he drops a kiss on my forehead and murmurs, "Then I'll be brave enough for the both of us."

52

ANDREY

It's been a long time since I woke up next to a woman. And as I do, I wait for the guilt to set in. For the reservations to launch me out of the bed and as far from her presence as I can manage.

But neither happens.

Strange.

It gets slightly less strange when I look down at her face. Then it makes sense. It's easy to be captivated by how peaceful she looks, curled up on my side, her eyes fluttering in a dream, her lips parted. She's a painting come to life. A living, breathing masterpiece that's somehow landed—quite literally—in my lap.

Only a fool would turn away something this precious.

Natalia stirs slowly, blinking into consciousness as she rolls onto her back, a curtain of dark hair falling against her face. I push it aside and she looks at me.

"Andrey," she breathes. "You stayed."

"I stayed."

"I was scared you'd slip away in the middle of the night while I slept."

"I'll be honest: it crossed my mind."

"Because of Maria?"

I freeze, shocked to hear that name from Natalia's lips. "Who—"

"I'm not going to tell you who mentioned her to me," she interrupts. "Rest assured, it was purely accidental and I know no more than her name. Although—" Her mouth turns down apologetically. "—I have made a few guesses."

I clear my throat. "What have you guessed?"

Her eyebrows knit together. "That Maria was very important to you. That you lost her a long time ago. And that, maybe, she's part of the reason you keep me at arm's length all the time."

As she speaks, goosebumps erupt all over her arms despite how warm and cozy it is in bed.

"Perceptive," I acknowledge.

Her hand grazes my chest, right over my thudding heart. "Am I right?"

I look down at her. "Except for the part where it was my fault that she died in the first place."

A startled gasp escapes her. "That's not true."

"Trust me: I wish it weren't."

"It would have been an accident then," she states. "Just a mistake."

I'm not sure what I've done to earn her trust. Or her faith in me. I feel undeserving of both. "My mistake was thinking I could live a normal life," I explain in halting syllables. "My mistake was being foolish enough to think that I could have the best of both worlds."

She sits up a little, resting her head against my arm. "Was it him again?" she asks, pointedly avoiding Nikolai's name. "Did he kill her?"

"I don't know. I was so lost in rage that I killed every man there before I could question any of them. I'll never know who sent them or what the purpose of their mission was. Those questions will haunt me for the rest of my life."

"Oh, Andrey…" she whispers, tears glistening in her eyes.

My voice goes raspy as I lapse back into the memories. "It was a weekend run to Michigan. I was meant to be in and out in a few days. Easy, no fuss, no complications. I'm the one who convinced her to come with me. It was just the two of us in the villa. No security because she was determined to have privacy and, fool that I was, I decided to make her *happy*."

"You couldn't have known…"

"That's the thing: I *should* have known. I was the newly-minted *pakhan* of the Kuznetsov Bratva. Of course there were eyes on me. Of course my enemies had doubled. I was a fool to think that my new position didn't come with a new and unique set of dangers."

Her grip on my chest tightens. It grounds me. Steadies me.

"There were five or six men, I think—I can't remember now. I was outnumbered and unprepared. And proud. I tried to fight them off on my own."

"One versus six," Natalia gasps. "How did you survive?"

My jaw clenches. "Ironically, Maria saved me. The moment I saw her die, I was filled with this black fury, an uncontrollable hatred. Her death gave me the surge I needed to kill them."

She shudders, drawing me back to her molten green eyes. They're wet with tears. "I'm so sorry, Andrey."

There's a lump in my throat that I haven't allowed myself to feel in quite a while. Somehow, though, her presence makes it bearable.

"So am I."

"That's why you've been so overbearing with my security."

I brush a stray tear from her cheek. "I don't repeat my mistakes, *lastochka*. I'm not willing to risk your safety after what happened with Maria."

Natalia props herself up against the headboard and pulls me towards her. She cradles me close, holding me the same way I held her through the worst of her catatonia. We don't speak, but she presses a kiss to my cheek every few minutes, a small reminder that she's still here.

And fuck, does it feel good.

After a long time, she strokes her fingers through my hair and kisses my lips. It's soft and fleeting and full of promise.

"How about some breakfast?" she suggests.

The idea of leaving the pool house twists my stomach in uncomfortable knots. Leaving these four walls might break whatever spell has allowed the two of us to let down our guards and simply exist together.

"Or I can whip us up something right here," Natalia suggests as if we're on the same wavelength. "If you don't mind enduring my subpar cooking."

"How can I say no to an offer like that?"

She slips out of bed, giving me a full view of her perfect body before she pulls on her silk robe.

"I hope you have a strong stomach," she warns before disappearing into the kitchen. "I might've oversold my cooking skills."

～

It's the smell of burning that draws me to the kitchen five minutes later.

"This is my kitchen, Andrey," she warns with a spatula aimed at me like a sword. "My kitchen means my rules."

I lift my hands in surrender. "I'm simply offering to be your sous chef. Do you need anything?"

I scan the kitchen for the source of the rancid smell. At the same time, Natalia spots it. "Oh, no! The eggs!"

The fire is on full blast, flames licking up the sides of the pan so the edge of the eggs are turning black, but the center is still a sloppy mess.

Natalia yanks the pan off the stove and is headed for the trash, but I slip it out of her hands.

"This is salvageable."

I kick down the heat, scoop out the worst of the burnt bits, and give the eggs a good mix.

"Of course you're good at this, too," she grumbles behind me. "This is embarrassing."

I can't help but laugh. "No, it's not."

"I almost set eggs on fire." She wrings her hands in front of her waist. "I was just nervous. I've never cooked for a man before. Or in this kitchen, and—"

I grab her by the hips and reel her in towards me. She folds into my body with a gasp and I catch her lips with mine. When we pull apart, her cheeks are flushed.

"Luckily, I have a strong stomach." I turn her towards the stove. "You finish cooking for me. I'll eat them even if they catch on fire."

In the end, the eggs are rubbery, but edible. Natalia and I eat them together. The windows and curtains remain closed. The pool house remains our own little world.

We don't let ourselves talk about the people who are no doubt congregated in the main house, probably wondering what the hell is going on between us. We let it be just the two of us.

It's not until mid-day that Natalia sighs into my chest. "I should go see how Misha and Remi are doing."

I plant a kiss on the top of her head. "I suppose I should talk to my men."

We hesitate, waiting to see if there's any way we can put it off and stay here.

But duty calls. It always does. My obligations have never ended simply because I wanted them to.

"Everyone will want to know how you're doing."

Natalia cringes. "I must have freaked them out."

"Only because they love you."

"Andrey…" She squeezes my wrist, holding me in the pool house for another second longer. "Thank you. For everything"

"Put your money where your mouth is." I unwrap myself from her arms and get to my feet. "You can thank me by having dinner with me."

She brightens. "Tonight?"

"Tonight." I wink. "Wear something pretty."

53

ANDREY

She steps onto the porch, and even the breeze goes still to admire her.

Her hair is a silky waterfall cascading over one shoulder. The cherry pendant I gave her for her birthday dangles from a thin chain around her neck, catching the moonlight until it seems to glow.

"Remi was not happy to be left behind," she informs me as I hold the passenger side door open for her.

"That dog has hogged your company for long enough. It's my turn tonight."

Her lips curve up as she slides into the Porsche without mentioning the blacked-out Wrangler looming behind us.

Leonty and Leif have specific instructions to be as discreet as possible tonight. Shura will be at the restaurant, too, scoping out the perimeters, making sure everything's safe. With any luck, we won't even notice they're there.

The ride is smooth and quiet. Natalia's thigh is warm beneath my palm as I drive, and the scent of her perfume floats through the car, just subtle enough to make me wonder if I'm dreaming the whole thing up.

She holds her chin high as we emerge from the car, proud and defiant, though she lets me lead her into the restaurant. Just like the perfume, I wonder if I'm imagining the tremor in her hand.

It's as though she's determined to prove that she belongs here.

Whether "here" means at this restaurant or at my side, however, I don't know.

She spends an inordinate amount of time talking to the waiter, and when he finally leaves, it's with three pages of his notepad filled with damn near every item on the menu.

The door to the kitchen clicks shut and she winces. "I overdid it, didn't I?"

"You're pregnant. You get to order whatever you want."

"I'll never be able to finish half of it." She twirls a lock of hair between her fingers. "Mom had a rule about wasting food. If we couldn't finish it ourselves, we had to make sure someone else could. There was a homeless shelter nearby. We used to drive down after every holiday with all our leftovers."

"Then that's what we'll do," I say. "I know a bridge not far from here with a homeless camp beneath it. We'll go by after dinner."

She blinks at me, lips parted, head cocked to the side. I'm just as confused, to be honest. The offer flowed naturally from my lips; I didn't say it to mock her or patronize her or even to flatter my way into her bed tonight.

It just felt right.

When the first appetizers hit the table, Natalia samples each dish, but leaves most of it untouched.

It makes me wonder if she's purposely eating less so the homeless people she hasn't even met yet can have more. I'm happy to take care of them on her behalf, but my primary goal tonight is to take care of her.

"What did your parents do?" I ask when the first courses have been cleared away.

"Dad was a music teacher," she says. "He was the one who taught me the piano. He played a whole bunch of different instruments, though. Guitar, flute, accordion. Even fiddled around with drums a little. Mom was a temp. That's how she met my dad. She took a position at the school he worked at."

Her eyes are brighter than usual as she talks about her parents. I get the feeling she doesn't do it very often.

"She stopped working when she got pregnant with me, though," Natalia continues. "She said that was always her dream job."

"She wanted to be a mother?"

She tries to return my smile, but her chin quivers. "She didn't get to finish that job, though."

"Arina was a good mother, too," I say quietly, losing myself to nearly forgotten memories. "But like yours, she didn't get to enjoy it as long as she should have."

Natalia's eyes are flecked with diamonds—a combination of the lights above and her own unshed tears. "What happened to her? If you don't mind me asking, I mean."

My instinct has always been to deflect. My mother is a soft, vulnerable underbelly I don't let anyone see.

But I don't feel that with Natalia.

I want to know her, and I want her to know me. And I have no idea why.

"She married a cruel man."

"Your father, you mean."

I nod. "Sometimes I think it might have been kinder if he'd just killed her," I admit—something I've never spoken aloud before. "Instead, he wore her down. He twisted and deformed everything good about her until it was unrecognizable. Until she didn't even know herself. She's buried so deep in her own mind now that no one can pull her out."

"Why? Why would he do it?"

"Because we loved her," I explain. "Because Viktor and I loved her more than we would ever respect him."

Every smile that we aimed at her, every bubble of laughter that she pulled from us—Slavik took as a personal affront. The very sound seemed to offend him.

Natalia's eyes are fixed on me. Her knuckles are white as she squeezes my hand. "He probably knew that, one day, you and Viktor would stand between him and Arina. That you wouldn't let him hurt her anymore."

"Well, we both failed in that regard," I growl bitterly.

Natalia's grip on my hand just gets tighter. "You were a child."

"I grew up, Natalia. And I played right into his hands. His plan worked. He was successful in driving a wedge between us."

Her eyes shine with tears, and I hate that I made her cry. This night isn't about me. It was meant to be for her.

"I apologize. I shouldn't have—"

"No!" she snaps. "No, I'm glad you shared that with me. It… it helps me understand you better."

"I'm not sure I'm worth understanding."

"Of course you are," she says gently. "Everyone is worth understanding, Andrey. Most people are redeemable."

"That's a little too optimistic for a *mudak* like me, little bird."

"You're no *mudak*, whatever that means," she insists, her pronunciation surprisingly on point. "You wanna know why?"

"Tell me."

"Because you didn't hurt Misha, even though it would have been easier to get rid of him. You tried to find his family even though you knew it was a pointless search. You protected Leonty from Viktor and you gave Mila the freedom she's craved her entire life. You take care of your men and you stop monsters from hunting innocent women and hurting innocent children."

I stay silent, my breath held captive in my throat as she continues.

"I know you think I'm naïve and maybe, sometimes, I am." She squares her jaw as though she's waiting for me to agree with her. When I don't, she forges ahead. "But I'm not nearly as naïve as you think I am. I know you're not the hero in this story, Andrey Kuznetsov. But I don't think you're the villain, either. No matter how hard you try to be."

54

NATALIA

"Can I get the birria beef sandwich to go, please?"

The waitress eyes my half-full plate of carbonara. "Of course, ma'am."

Katya and Mila share a pointed look before Kat whistles. "A second lunch for later? You're really taking the 'eating for two' thing to heart, huh?"

"It's not for me; it's for Andrey. He usually works through lunch and forgets to eat, so I want to bring him…" I trail off when they exchange yet another look. "What? You two keep doing this thing. It's driving me insane."

"Well," Kat says, folding her hands on the table in front of her, "Mila and I couldn't help but notice that you've been remarkably happy these past few days."

Mila nods her agreement. "Ever since you and Andrey had your little lockdown in the pool house. Did your mental breakdown bring you together?"

"Hey!"

Mila shamelessly refuses to take it back. "Come on, Nat. You barely moved for days. It was fucking terrifying."

Katya nods in reluctant agreement.

"Don't get me wrong," Mila continues. "I don't blame you at all. Dealing with a drunk, angry Viktor is no joke. I have the scars to prove it. It's enough to drive even the strongest woman into disassociation."

She's being generous. I happen to know that neither Katya nor Mila would have shut down the way I did.

"It was a bad moment," I admit.

"No, babe," Mila argues, "a 'bad moment' is the snakeskin coat I decided to wear to my twenty-first birthday party."

Katya jumps in with relish. "A 'bad moment' is realizing that you already used the last condom in your purse and the hot guy you've been chasing for a month is all out, too."

"A bad moment is—"

"I get it!"

"We're getting side-tracked," Katya says, steering us back to the original topic. "The point is, you've been doing really well since then."

"And we can't help wondering why." Mila wags her brows.

In case she isn't being obvious enough, Katya asks, "Are you and Andrey a thing now or what?"

I glance down to my phone in hopes it'll save me from getting backed into this particular corner. It hasn't pinged once since we sat down to lunch, but that doesn't stop me from hoping.

Nope. Nothing.

Disappointment claws at my chest, and I meet my friends' eyes. "We're not together, but we're... getting along."

Katya sags. "Seriously? We were so damn sure—"

"He's spent every night at the pool house!" Mila says. "You two have to be a thing."

I purse my lips at Mila. "I thought you were done spying on me."

She shrugs. "I happen to be sleeping with one of your bodyguards. It's pillow talk."

I slash my arms through the air. "I didn't come out to lunch to be interrogated. Let's talk about something else. Literally anything. Nice weather we're having. How 'bout those Yankees? Any new movies—"

Mila turns to Katya. "There are stages of grief, but are there stages of love, too?"

"If there are, denial must be the first step in both," Katya declares.

I groan and bury my face in my hands. "I regret the day I introduced the two of you."

Mila ignores me. "I'll just ask Leonty to be more alert when he's on night duty around the pool—"

"Yes, he's sleeping over," I cave. "But no, we're not sleeping together. We're sleeping, but we aren't *sleeping* sleeping. No sex. Okay?"

They exchange another glance.

"How is that humanly possible?" Katya asks. "Didn't he take you out for some big, romantic dinner the other night?"

I can't help but smile at the memory. "I don't think I'd go that far. But it was really nice. We compared parental horror stories, a rousing game of 'What's Worse, A Dead Dad Or A Shitty One'? The best part is that everybody loses. Then we drove our leftover food to a homeless encampment and passed it around."

Another incredulous glance.

Katya turns her frown on me. "Okay, you're right—that is not even remotely romantic."

"I guess you had to be there." I lean forward. "Look, Shura and Leonty aren't like Andrey. They're open and ready to put themselves out there. Andrey is… reserved. He keeps everything inside. Getting some details out of him is a big step forward."

Mila and Katya exchange another look.

"You two do that again and I'm gonna shove your faces into the butter dish," I warn.

"Okay, I believe her about the no sex thing," Katya announces a bit too loudly. "Natalia gets cranky when she isn't getting any action."

Action. Like that's the missing piece. How do I make them see that sex with Andrey has always been easier than breathing?

But this stuff—talking, sharing, opening up to one another—that's always been the complicated bit.

Katya and Mila are conducting another telepathic conversation as they try to puzzle me out, and the fact they've gone from sworn enemies to friends in such a short amount of time is almost enough to make me believe in miracles.

If they can grow together, maybe Andrey and I can get along, too.

No matter what my friends say about the two of us, that's as much as I'm willing to hope. Sure, he's been attentive and patient and kind. Sure, he's opened up to me. He may even enjoy sleeping with me on occasion.

But love?

Lord knows I've made plenty of mistakes when it comes to Andrey Kuznetsov—but I won't make that one.

Falling in love with him would be the worst mistake of all.

∽

I walk into Andrey's office with his to-go container, expecting to find him poring over paperwork at his desk.

Instead, I find two guns where the paperwork ought to be.

What the hell?

I hear him in the adjoining bathroom, but I can't take my eyes off the guns, glinting under the sunlight streaming in through his open windows. When Andrey emerges, I blurt, "There are guns on your desk."

His jaw tightens. "How was lunch?"

"Good. Why are there guns on your desk?"

He buttons his shirt cuffs and walks over to me. "I have a meeting in half an hour."

"And that requires guns?"

"It's just insurance, *lastochka*. Nothing to worry about."

His smile is cool and confident, but it has my heart beating erratically, chasing out all the air in my lungs.

"Who, me? Why would I worry?" My voice shifts up a couple of octaves. "I'm sure it's perfectly normal to go to meetings armed. Remind me to clean my bazooka for the board meeting next week. Oh, and I'm getting tea with Annie next weekend, so I should probably make sure my AK-47 is—"

"Hey." His hand curls against the side of my cheek. "My normal is different than yours. And just because I've got guns on me doesn't mean I'm going to need them."

"But there's a chance you might?"

He hesitates. "Only a very small one."

"What's this meeting about?"

It's the first time I've asked him a direct question about his work. I half-expect him to shut me down and tell me to go back to the pool house. Part of me thinks that might be the right call. The less I know, the better.

"You want to know?" he asks.

I nod, trying to convince us both.

"I'm meeting with some investors to discuss a cross-country expansion. It's just a logistics chat."

My gaze flickers back to the guns on the table. "Will you be going alone?"

"Shura, Efrem, and Yuri will be with me. Vaska might join, too."

I chew on my bottom lip. This is exactly why I can't fall in love with a man like Andrey. He's always walking into danger, dodging death, ducking enemy fire. I wouldn't survive being worried about him all the time.

"Don't worry, little bird." He presses a kiss to my mouth. "I've handled a lot worse with a lot less."

I watch, terrified as he tucks the guns away—one in the waistband of his pants, the second in his jacket pocket. Then he turns and points to the takeout container. "You brought me something?"

"Uh, a sandwich from the restaurant… You usually work through lunch and I…"

Andrey is looking at me like he's just figured something out. His eyes are bright and my heart is thrumming, and—*shit.*

It's already too late.

"Wait here," I order, whirling out of his office and running down the hall.

He calls after me, but I keep moving. I rush to the pool house, retrieve what I need, and then fly back to the office as fast as I can.

He's still waiting by the entrance for me. "Where'd you go?"

"I went to get this." Grabbing his hand, I fold something into the center.

He stares down at the golden necklace in his palm. "This is your locket."

"My mom's locket, yes. I want you to keep it with you. Think of it as… as a good luck charm. A protection amulet." I shrug. "Whatever you want to call it."

He lifts his gaze to mine. "This is your amulet, Natalia."

"And I'm giving it to you."

Because it's all I can do. As stupid and ultimately useless as this gesture is, it's the only thing I can do for him. It's still more than I got to do for my parents.

"And you should know…" My voice trembles. "… it means a lot to me. So, you have to bring it back for me. I want the necklace personally delivered. By *you*. In one piece."

His smile is knowing as his fingers close around the locket. He fastens the chain around his neck and tucks it out of sight beneath his shirt. Then he kisses my forehead before he dips down to kiss my belly, as well.

"I'll bring it back safe and sound."

Then Andrey is gone.

Leaving me with a gaping chasm of dread in the pit of my stomach.

55

ANDREY

Shura and Vaska are already waiting at the entrance of The Capital Hotel when I arrive.

Shura's impassive scowl is in direct contrast to Vaska's ear-to-ear grin. Bastard looks like Christmas came early. After weeks of bed rest, followed by months of rehabilitation, I don't blame him. It must feel like a blessing to be on his feet again.

We clasp hands. "Vaska—you look good, brother."

He's practically foaming at the mouth, bouncing from heel to heel with excitement. "I feel good, sir. It's about time I saw some action."

If all goes well, there won't be any action today, but I keep that to myself as I lead my men through The Capital's arched doorways.

I don't need to ask Shura if our prospective partners have arrived. The number of security teams I pass as we make our way to the Executive Lounge tells me that all three men are here, punctual as ever.

I assign my men to positions at the various doors before I step into the lounge with only Shura at my side.

The large, opulent room is empty, apart from the three men who rise to their feet when I enter. It took a lot of effort and a fuck ton of bribery to get these three to the table. Like Vaska, though, I'm damn near giddy with excitement at what we stand on the precipice of accomplishing.

Cevdet Bakirtzis controls a trafficking pipeline that runs through the Midwest. He inherited his mafia after his father's death when he was only twenty-three years old. But he single-handedly expanded the empire across Chicago and Denver. He's the main reason my shipments get to their chosen destinations without a problem.

Luca Giordano has cornered the drug market all along the West Coast. Very Italian and very proud, he was the last to come around to a partnership with me, but once he saw how fruitful it would be with him, even he couldn't resist.

Bujar Mustafi was the easiest to convince. The soft-spoken Albanian used to be in production himself before my superior product and cheaper cost effectively cut him off at the knees. He rallied fast and fell into step as a smuggler who controls most of the South, his tendrils snaking into damn near every town between here and the Florida Keys.

"Ah, the young *pakhan* is finally here," Cevdet booms, offering me a meaty hand.

He likes to get in ahead of the game, Cevdet does. That usually involves a lot of snide jabs at the expense of both Bujar and Luca, but he's well-behaved thus far. Every man present knows that their own operations depend on the moving cogs in our shared partnership.

One way or another, I'm walking out of here with what I want.

It's up to them if that's through business or through blood.

The table is already littered with coffee mugs. The smell of bourbon is emanating from Luca's gold-trimmed cup.

"I apologize, gentlemen. I didn't realize I was late to the party."

"You're not late," Cevdet announces. "I'm always early."

"And since Cevdet is always early, Bujar and I decided not to let him show us up," Luca quips.

Cevdet twirls a finger through his massive handlebar mustache and laughs heartily. Luca's laughter is more of a wheeze, whereas you'd be hard-pressed to hear Bujar's laugh at all.

They're a motley crew. But an effective one.

Which is how I know that Nikolai Rostov would stand to gain a lot by destroying the alliance I've managed to create.

"I hate to dive straight into business," I say, "but we might as well get it out of the way."

Bujar is the only one who looks like he appreciates the straightforwardness. His thin lips tighten with satisfaction as he sits up a little straighter.

"Oh, very well," Luca mutters as he picks up his coffee-spiked bourbon. "You Russians can't carry a casual conversation to save your lives. I assume we're here to talk about the Rostov *stronzo*?"

My eyes narrow. "I came to discuss shipments. It seems you know something I don't, Luca. Care to share with the class?"

Luca smiles, flashing his freshly-whitened teeth for my benefit. "Now, now, Andrey, there's no need to be testy. I'm unequivocally your man."

"Are you?" I ask, half-amused and half-annoyed. "Because you did entertain a meeting with Nikolai once."

He waves away the fact. "I had to make sure you weren't short-changing me. I am a businessman at the end of the day, Andrey. I have to know who is offering the better deal."

Although his features remain inscrutable, Bujar's mouth twitches under his dark beard.

"Good to know that your loyalties can be so easily swayed by the highest bidder, Luca."

The Italian rolls his eyes. "I have no desire to become entangled in Rostov's repulsive skin trade. Quite apart from having moral qualms about it, the constant body trail would be bad for business."

"Has he tried to contact you again?"

Luca is busy primping his expensive Italian suit. "Not in over a year. And as I informed you all then, I told him to fuck the hell off. My answer will be no different if he makes another attempt."

Luca has always been slippery, but despite Shura's reservations about the man, I do trust him. He may treat the whole operation as a game, but he's got as much skin in it as the rest of us.

"Ha! Rostov wouldn't ever dare approach me," Cevdet claims

proudly. "He knows exactly where I stand on the skin trade. No family man would ever entertain scum like Rostov."

Undoubtedly, he's also thinking of all the Bakirtzis assets that are interlinked with the success of my Bratva. Like Luca, he's as self-serving as they come.

But loyalty is loyalty, regardless of the motive.

"As for me, I'm not even on Rostov's radar," Bujar declares. "He doesn't see me as a big player. Simply a cog in the wheel."

"I doubt that, Bujar," I murmur. "Nikolai has eyes everywhere. And he's never turned down a free meal."

Cevdet turns to me thoughtfully. "You think he'll try to approach each of us?"

"His moves are getting harder and harder to predict," I admit grudgingly. "He's become a ghost in the last year. Which leads me to believe he's planning something."

I glance at Shura, who's stationed by the window, his spine rigid as ever. But I know he's analyzing everything we've discussed so far.

"I doubt Nikolai will approach any of you," Shura says when I gesture for him to chime in. "Our alliance is too strong to pick apart now. Our investments run too deep and he knows that everyone here has his reasons for spurning what he has to offer."

"I sense a 'but' coming," Luca says. "You think he's shoring up alliances?"

"He will if he's smart. He has to match our strength," I say. "Finding new friends is the only way he has a prayer of lasting."

"Who does he have to turn to?" Cevdet scoffs before answering his own question. "No one of consequence. All the major players are sitting in this room."

Luca and Bujar nod their agreement. But one glance at Shura tells me he's the only one here who thinks the way I do.

Nikolai Rostov is not to be underestimated.

"Before we jump into the expansion, I have to clear up some rumors that have been circulating," Cevdet blurts suddenly, turning his blue eyes on me.

I wave to give him the floor.

He waggles feathery brows in my direction. "Is our young *pakhan* going to be a father soon?"

This time, I take pains to avoid Shura's face. I've made no public announcement, which means the eyes trained on my family are closer than I suspected. There's no point in lying, though. Honesty begets honesty. Sooner or later, the truth will emerge. These men might as well hear it from my lips.

"Yes," I say. "The rumors are true."

Luca immediately declares a toast must be made and Bujar offers me a congratulatory nod. But Cevdet is impatient for more information.

"And am I correct in assuming that, if there had been a wedding, we would have received invitations?"

"Of course, Cevdet. There has been no wedding. Nor will there be."

At that, the mood turns tense.

Cevdet is the only one brave enough to ask the question on

all of their minds. "Is that because you're biding your time? Or is it because the woman is... unimportant?"

"She's the mother of my child. There's nothing more to be said."

The dismissal is clear. All three men arrange their faces into polite respect and Cevdet pivots into the safe territory of the expansion.

I'm the only one who can't stop thinking about what I said and how I said it.

∽

Two hours and several more cups of coffee later, I'm saying my goodbyes.

Cevdet hangs back, always determined to have the last word. "Given the current climate, if you need additional protection, I can provide it," he says, lowering his usually booming voice into something approximating a whisper.

I regard him carefully. "A kind offer, Cevdet, but I happen to know that your men don't come cheap."

"For you, my friend, I would provide the service free of charge."

That takes me back. "Why?"

He runs his tongue over his mustachioed top lip. "I have three daughters, Andrey. And I would go to any trouble to make sure they're safe. I can recognize that same instinct in other men. I recognized it in you, try as you might to hide it."

Fucking hell—am I that transparent?

"She is important to you and—No, no, don't bother denying it. She *is* important to you. Which means she has a target on her back." He claps a hand on my shoulder. "Nikolai Rostov is the type of man who would sell his own mother for spare change. He has no honor. But you do. That means something to me."

I incline my head in gratitude. "That's generous of you, Cevdet. I will consider your offer carefully."

"We must protect what's ours, Andrey," he says, reverting to his usual ear-splitting volume. "It is our most sacred duty."

And with that, he follows Luca and Bujar out through the gilded doors.

56

NATALIA

It was clear from the moment Andrey burst into the pool house and declared that we were all going out to dinner that he was happy about something. I can only imagine that his meeting went well.

Not that we've been alone long enough to talk about it. Since the moment we sat down to eat, he has been carrying the conversation, laughing the loudest, talking the most, making sure everyone is involved.

Still, his hand finds mine under the table. He drapes an arm over the back of my chair. When the drinks come out, he checks to make sure mine is virgin before he hands it back to me with a wink.

I've never seen him like this before—with me or anyone else.

Andrey speaks of the Bratva as a family, but I always assumed it was in the corporate sense. *We're a big family here. We have a unique culture. We care about your wellbeing—unless it affects our bottom line.*

But Andrey is *friends* with the men in his employ.

He makes his way around the room, laughing, joking, and swapping stories. He spends a full ten minutes ragging on Anatoly for the silk floral shirt he's wearing. When Leonty jumps on board, Anatoly threatens to strangle him with his own napkin, and the three men dissolve into laughter.

"Yelena, the dumplings are for you," Andrey announces, waving the plate under her nose. "I know you love them."

"I can't have another," the old woman groans. "I have to watch my weight."

"Watch it another night. It isn't going anywhere." Andrey grins wickedly.

"Andrey!" I gasp, smacking him on the elbow with the back of my hand.

"Cheeky little bastard," Yelena hisses before grabbing the dumplings he's offering her.

Even Misha seems to be in high spirits. He's sitting on my right, one hand protectively cupped over Remi's head as the poor dog whines every so often. He's not a fan of all the noise, but perched between Misha's legs, he's tolerating it pretty well.

The only one who seems to be having less fun than Remi is Shura. But I'm assuming that has less to do with the noise and more with the fact that Katya isn't here. She sent me a text earlier saying she wouldn't be able to make it.

When the men burst into laughter again, Misha flinches. His face is as taut and anxious as ever, but that is his default position. The kid's been conditioned to be wary for too long for that to go away overnight.

I nudge Misha gently. "You doing okay?"

"I'm fine."

"Did you eat enough?"

His smile breaks through for a moment. "I've never eaten so much in my entire life. Remi loved it, too."

Misha and I have been passing Remi little tidbits under the table throughout the dinner. It's probably the only reason Remi endured all this noise.

"How are your lessons going?"

"Okay, I guess."

The slump of his shoulders says otherwise.

"Is Mr. Akayev not treating you right?" I've met his personal tutor a few times now, a taciturn Russian in his late sixties. I wish Andrey would've chosen someone softer, warmer, but I can't deny that the man knows his stuff.

Misha looks alarmed that I would even suggest such a thing. "He's fine. Maybe a little impatient, but he's okay. It's the work."

I put my hand on his shoulder. "How about you come over to the pool house tomorrow and we recap what you've learned so far? Maybe I can help."

"Yeah?"

"I always learned best when I liked my teachers. And my two favorite teachers in the whole world were my mom and dad."

Misha frowns, and I immediately regret bringing it up.

Why did I go and mention my wonderful parents to a boy who's never had any inkling of what it's like to have even one functional parent, let alone two? It's like wagging a juicy steak in front of a starving man. *Look what you can never have.* I feel like a bitch.

I pat him on the arm as Remi whines for attention. Misha dips his head down to let Remi nuzzle his face, and I turn to Andrey, whose eyes are finally fixed on me.

His hand slides up my thigh under the table. He doesn't seem to mind that we're surrounded by people—and when his hand is warm against my skin, I don't mind, either.

"You already have a full-time job, *lastochka*," he points out softly. "Why take on the role of teacher, too?"

"Because he needs me."

Andrey doesn't say anything, but he steals glances at me for the remainder of the night.

When we get back to the manor and Remi ambles off to bed with Misha, Andrey takes my hand. Going to the pool house has become something of a routine for us now. But tonight feels different.

My heart is fluttering in my chest as we step through the door. Wordlessly, we move to the bedroom, walking into something that feels as inevitable as breathing.

Andrey only lets go of me to undress, his eyes still tracing over me like he's making sure I don't disappear.

But there's no chance of that.

His tie puddles on the armchair, followed by his suit jacket. Cufflinks, his watch, his shirt—he places each item carefully in the chair, and I watch as moonlight ripples down the broad expanse of his back, a familiar tingle low in my belly.

It isn't until he's standing in his black boxer briefs that he turns and looks at me, eyebrows furrowed. "What's wrong, little bird?"

What's wrong is that Mila and Katya were right: I've been in denial. I thought I could have Andrey without needing him. I thought I could be close to him without it changing me.

But I'm more tangled up in the father of my baby than I might ever be able to undo.

For tonight at least, I want him to feel the same way.

"Do you trust me?" The words barrel out of my mouth before I can second-guess them.

"Yes," he answers.

"Then lie down."

I'm stiff with nerves as I move to my closet and pull out two Hermes scarves that he gifted me. They felt too luxurious to wear, but I've found the perfect use for them now.

Andrey is watching me with a singular focus from the bed. When I climb over him and press one of his wrists to the bedpost, he doesn't fight. Not as I wrap the scarf around his hand. Not even as I pull the knot tight.

When I move to the other side, he offers me his hand willingly.

Once he's bound to the headboard, I shimmy his boxers off and have all the proof I need that he's interested. He springs free, hard and ready, and I have to resist the urge to taste him.

I have other plans tonight.

I move to the end of the bed and slip out of my clothes, hoping that my courage doesn't fail me halfway through. Once I'm naked, I straddle him, running my hands up and down his sculpted chest. It feels nice to have time to enjoy him—no rush.

"You have never looked as beautiful as you do right now." His voice is a rasp, but his words are soft and sincere.

"You really think so?" I ask, sliding my hands over my stomach. "Even with the bump?"

"Especially with the bump." He exhales slowly. "I want to be the one touching you like that. Do you know how fucking sexy you look with my baby in your belly? If I'd known what we were starting in that elevator… If I'd—" He swallows as his cock twitches. "I wouldn't have waited for all the stuff that had to happen in between. I would've gotten you pregnant then and there."

"That's how you feel now, but then?" I wrinkle my nose. "We were strangers. You wouldn't have wanted it."

The dark expanse of his eyes tells me how much he wants it now. "Maybe if you'd asked nicely."

A naughty little lightbulb pings on over my head. *Do I dare?*

I decide that I do.

"Pretend that I don't then."

"Pretend what?"

"Pretend I'm not pregnant. Pretend you don't know me. Pretend… just for tonight… that this is the beginning of our story."

"Natalia, I—"

"Hush." I press a finger over his lips and then drop my voice into a sultry purr as I grind down his body. "Andrey, I want a baby. I want you to give me one."

His forehead creases with confusion as his eyes drop to my belly. I continue to grind myself against his erection, chasing the delightful pressure that's building between my legs.

"Please," I croon, working him against my entrance. "I want you to fuck a baby into me."

Understanding flickers across his face, and he growls with want even as he shakes his head. "No. No, it's not the right time."

I pout, working the length of him between my legs, back and forth, again and again.

His cock is twitching, impatient to get this show on the road. As for me, I'm savoring this feeling: the heady mix of power combined with desire.

"I'll give you a baby one day," he continues without taking his eyes from my face. "But not now. Not yet."

"Well then." I slap my palms against his chest. "If you won't give me what I want, I'll just have to take it."

"*Lastochka…*" he growls.

I lift my hips higher and align his cock with my slit. I'm so wet that his cock slips inside me with zero pressure.

"I didn't want to have to do it this way," I trill in fake apology. "But you're leaving me no choice."

With that, I sit down on his cock.

"Fuck," I moan as he disappears into me. I'm already so close to coming and we've barely even begun.

He looks like he's not far from the edge himself. His hazy, desire-dappled eyes are focused on me. His hands strain against the scarves, but I did a good job with the knots. He's gonna have a hard time freeing himself without my help.

"You're not getting away that easily," I grit out, riding my hips back and forth. "I'm not stopping until you give me a baby. You're gonna stay right here, tied up and at my mercy, until you've got a baby in me."

"You really want my baby in you?" His jaw is clenched, his hands balling into fists as I steal my pleasure from him.

I arch my back as the intensity builds. "More than anything. I want you to fill me up. I want to be yours—inside and out."

Broken curses spill from his lips. "I want to touch you."

Every time he strains against the ties, I buck my hips harder, I bounce faster. I'm not capable of forming words anymore. I'm not capable of doing anything other than riding him, taking us both to the conclusion we need.

"Oh, God," I whimper. "I'm so close, Andrey. I want you to finish inside of me. Fill me up. *Please*."

With a roar, he comes deep inside of me, taking me over the edge with him.

Ripples of heat and pleasure ravage my body until I can't sit up. I fall against his chest, his thundering heartbeat in my ear.

"Jesus Christ, woman," Andrey says breathlessly after long, silent minutes have passed. "Where the hell have you been all my life?"

57

ANDREY

Natalia's phone buzzes as I pull along the curb in front of her office, and she lunges for it like it's her last lifeline. When she drops it in her lap with a frown a second later, I know it wasn't who she hoped.

"Katya still hasn't responded?"

Natalia shakes her head, chewing at the inside of her lip. "She hasn't responded all weekend."

"Maybe she's busy?"

Fuck knows we've been busy. In bed, in the shower, on the kitchen counter. I'm actually not sure when Natalia had time to text Katya. Her hands and/or mouth have usually been pretty thoroughly occupied.

"Shura hasn't spoken to her, either," she says. "No one has heard from her in days."

"They probably just had a fight," I suggest. That would explain Shura's bad mood the last couple of days.

"No, Katya doesn't do the silent treatment. When she's pissed, she screams. We'd know if they got in a fight."

I squeeze her hand reassuringly. "Go to work and try not to worry. I'll look into it."

"You think there's something to look into?" she asks in a panic.

"Just to be safe. I'm sure it's nothing, but I'll go check on her."

Natalia doesn't look convinced, but I am. After a weekend of fucking Natalia absolutely silly, the world seems rosy and harmless and easy to bend to my will. With a hand on the small of Natalia's back, I usher her into the office building.

The moment she's inside, though, I turn to Leonty. "Don't let her out of your sight."

His smile falters. "Something wrong, boss?"

"I'm not sure yet. Just make sure you have eyes on her at all times."

~

It takes a full minute of pounding on Shura's apartment door before he finally answers. His scowl is far from welcoming. "I'm off today."

No, he's pouting. I knew he'd be hiding out here. He rarely uses the apartment, but we couldn't drag him out of it for two weeks after his divorce. The fact he's here now means Katya really is giving him the cold shoulder.

"You're off when I say you're off."

He throws the door open with a grumble and slumps into the living room. "What do you need?"

"When was the last time you spoke to Katya?"

He whips around, worry eating away his frown lines. "Why? Did Natalia say something? Did she reach out? The last time we spoke was the day you took everyone out to dinner. I was with her earlier that evening and…"

I wait for him to finish his thought, but he seems stuck on a memory. "Shura?"

He snaps out of his reverie and focuses on me. "It wasn't a fight. She was just a little annoyed at me when I left."

"Why?"

Grinding his teeth together, he lets loose a frustrated hiss. "Apparently, I'm not 'transparent' enough for her. She claimed she had no idea how I feel about her."

He glares at me as though daring me to laugh.

"I spend fucking time with her, don't I?" he explodes when I say nothing. "I take her out, buy her shit, wine and dine her in expensive damn restaurants. What the fuck is that if not —" He breaks off, clicking his tongue against the roof of his mouth.

If anyone can understand where Shura's coming from, it's me. For men like us, giving someone our time means everything. We lavish them with gifts and our attention, but we don't talk about our feelings.

"I got pissed and told her that if she didn't realize by now how I felt about her, then she was the stupid one."

I raise my eyebrows. "Charming."

"I'm not good at this shit, 'Drey," he mutters. "I'm good at fucking and fighting. After Melania, I didn't think I'd ever find myself in this position again."

"You and me both, brother."

Our eyes meet. Understanding flits between us.

"Even if she's giving you the silent treatment," I say wearily, "it doesn't explain why she's ignoring Natalia."

Shura pales. "She hasn't talked to Nat, either?"

"No. And she's—"

"I'm going over to her place." Shura already has keys in hand and is storming towards the door.

"Before we resort to breaking and entering, let's check in at her office first," I suggest. "According to Natalia, she should be there about now."

Shura growls with impatience, but he agrees with a curt nod.

Fifteen minutes later, when he's sprinting out of Katya's office alone, I know something is wrong.

By the time he gets to the car, I'm already on the phone with Leonty. "Pull Natalia out of work and meet us at Katya's apartment," I order.

"She's not there," Shura pants, buckling himself into the passenger seat. "She didn't call in sick or anything. No one has seen her."

The man is a nervous wreck as we hurtle towards Katya's apartment. Every time we get caught at a light or stuck in a bit of traffic, he looks like he's about to rip his hair clean out.

As soon as I pull up to her building, Shura makes a beeline to the fifth floor. I follow behind him and find him battering his fist against the door of Unit #506.

"Katya! If you're in there, open the fucking door now!"

Glancing down the deserted corridor, I notice someone peering out of the door at the far end. The moment she sees me, she pulls her face in and the door snaps shut.

"Shura," I caution, "I'm not sure we want to draw attention to ourselves like this."

"She's not in there," he declares, whipping around. "We'll have to break down the door."

"First, you need to calm down."

"'Calm down'?" he growls, his eyes bulging. "Would you be able to calm down if your woman was in danger?"

Thankfully, before I can even attempt to lie, we hear footsteps on the stairs below. I peer down over the banister to see Natalia running up with Leonty at her back.

She appears on the landing, panting and clutching her side. "Well? Is she here?"

Shura shakes his head, the vein in his forehead throbbing.

"Move aside," Natalia commands as she steps between us. "I've got a spare key."

One quick flick of her wrist and the door swings open. Shura steps in behind her.

"Katya! Kat?"

But I know Katya's not here.

The air in the apartment is stuffy and stale. There's a rancid stench coming from the garbage can, which hasn't been taken out in a few days at least.

Natalia seems to be thinking along the same lines. "She hasn't taken out the trash. She *always* takes out the trash before she leaves. She got maggots once and swore she'd never let it happen again."

Shura disappears into Katya's bedroom, but my eyes stay fixed on Natalia. She looks as pale as Shura.

"Andrey," she croaks, turning to me, "something is not right. She travels for work sometimes, but she would've told me about it. And she would've answered my calls."

I take her hand and pull her to me. Katya's disappearance and Shura's panic makes me want to keep Natalia as close as possible.

"Don't worry. We'll find her."

Before she gets any words out, Shura is stomping back into the small living room. "Her passport was in her bedside drawer," he announces, holding it up. "Her suitcase is still under her bed, too. She only has the one, so—"

"Someone took her," Natalia gasps.

They look at each other, horrified. I'm not sure who to reassure first.

"First things first," I say, taking control. "We've got to get back to the manor. I'll get the whole tech team on her trail ASAP."

Shura's eyes meet mine. "Andrey—"

"Breathe, brother," I tell him firmly. "I *will* find her. Have I ever let you down before?"

His jaw tightens fiercely. "Never."

"Then trust me."

58

NATALIA

Mila and I have been sitting on the patio for so long that my legs are going numb. She doesn't wander and neither does Remi—both of them stay touching me at all times. Even when Misha meanders down to the pool, Remi sits glued to my side, sensing that my need is greater at the moment.

The tech room is close enough that we can hear Shura shouting through the walls. "Why the fuck haven't you found her yet?! Tracking her cell phone shouldn't take this damn long!"

It's been hours of this—quiet stretches of nothing, then Shura losing his shit, then Andrey kicking him out again.

Someone steps onto the patio. Mila and I look up hopefully, praying it's Andrey with news. But it's just Leonty, looking somber and on edge as he walks around to us.

"Have you two eaten anything?"

Mila shakes her head for the both of us. "Not hungry. How's it going in there?"

"Shura's got the tech team shitting themselves. Andrey forbade him from coming back in there." Leonty sighs. "I think Shura knows he's not helping. He went quiet and stormed off."

Mila's hand tightens around mine. "He's just scared. Men like him aren't used to being scared."

Patting Remi's head, I slowly push myself off the patio swing. My legs complain with pins and needles, but I ignore the feeling and stretch.

I limp around slowly until the feeling comes back. I oughta move or run or, better yet, sleep, but I'm terrified I'll miss something if I go. So I pace the same four feet back and forth and back and forth.

Remi follows behind me, and even Misha is on the same page. He's on his tenth or hundredth or thousandth circle around the pool.

"They have to find something soon, right?" I ask no one in particular.

Leonty sits down next to Mila and wraps an arm around her. "If anyone can get Katya back, it's Andrey."

Misha climbs up onto the porch and strokes Remi's head absentmindedly. I touch his shoulder, if only because it's so much easier to put on a brave face when you're trying to be strong for someone else.

"I'm sure we'll hear someth—"

Before I can finish my sentence, a commotion explodes inside the house.

Without hesitating, I sprint into the manor and push my way into the tech room. Andrey is standing with his back to me, leaning over one of his men as they both peer at a large screen.

I can make neither heads nor tails of what they're looking at. Complex computer code ripples across the monitor, a string of numbers that makes absolutely no sense until—

Coordinates, I realize. *It's a set of coordinates.*

Andrey looks at me with a grim steel in his eyes. Then his gaze flits over my shoulder. "Leonty, go get Shura. We know where she is."

I slip further into the room and squeeze Andrey's hand. "Is it really her?""

"I think so. Her phone was dumped several miles from her apartment, but we managed to hack into surveillance footage and security systems in the area. They've got her in an abandoned flop house on the outskirts of the city."

He presses a button on the keyboard and the numbers disappear, affording me a grainy view of a depressing building losing a long war with weeds, graffiti, and despair.

"She's in *there?*"

"She's being guarded. We haven't determined how many yet."

"Is Nikolai behind this?" I ask.

"It can't be anyone else."

"I don't understand, though," I protest. "What would Nikolai stand to gain from kidnapping Katya? How does he even know about Katya when he barely knows about me?"

Andrey's eyes are troubled when he forces them to mine. "He must know more than we think he does."

That sends a tremor of fear shooting through me. But before I can process it, Shura's storming into the room. "Where is she?"

Andrey points. "We have a location. Are you ready?"

Shura is already backing out of the room. "We leave in ten."

He disappears and Leonty follows him out. I cling to Andrey's arm, too many fears to choose from swirling in my head.

Andrey seems to know exactly what I'm thinking. "I will be careful, *lastochka*. You have nothing to fear."

Oh, how wrong he is.

"Andrey, please…"

"I'll get her back safely."

"I need *you* to be safe, too."

His eyes soften as he pulls me to him, pressing a tender kiss to my lips. "I'm still wearing your locket, little bird. How can I not be?"

With that, he's gone, leaving me with nothing to do but wait.

I retreat back to the patio where Mila's still sitting with Misha and Remi. Leonty must've filled her in before he left, because she's ashen-faced and picking at her cuticles.

This time, I take her hand and pull it onto my lap. She gives me a distracted smile that betrays just how worried she is.

"Do you ever get used to this?" I ask. "Waiting here when you know the people you love are in danger?"

"I wouldn't know. I never had anyone I cared about before now," she admits softly. "I never had anyone to wait for."

Her voice breaks on the last word. I squeeze her hand tighter.

Misha looks at the two of us, something unreadable crossing his face. Then he bolts to his feet. "I should've gone with them."

"No!" Mila and I cry at the same time.

"It's too dangerous, Misha," I add. "And you're—"

"Don't tell me I'm a child. I'm not like other kids my age." His eyes flash defiantly and, despite the fact that I know he's right, I can't fathom letting him walk into any danger.

"But you're still a kid. You deserve to be protected."

From danger. From the realities of this world. Misha shouldn't even know this kind of dark underbelly exists.

"I want to earn my place. I want to be the one protecting the people I care about."

The frustration in his voice is obvious. And it terrifies me.

Nervous as I was to see Andrey go and scared as I am that he'll be hurt—imagining Misha out there in the field, exposed to guns and enemies and death, hurts so much worse.

My hand curls protectively around my stomach. It's the same feeling I get every time I consider that my child won't be safe in this world.

I've never let myself really think about it.

But it's here now.

And it isn't going away.

"Maybe one day, you'll get to," I tell him slowly, mostly to keep my voice from shaking. "If that's your choice. But not until you're a man. Not until you're old enough to understand the risk you're taking."

"I understand now."

"How can you?" I argue as Mila shifts uncomfortably at my side. "You're only fourteen. You've faced a lot in your life, but you don't have to anymore. You can be a kid now."

His jaw flexes with all the teenage angst he's been bottling up. "I'll do what I want."

"Not while I'm taking care of you."

He whirls on me, red-faced. "What gives *you* the right to tell me what to do? Who the fuck do you think you are?"

"Your mother!"

Mila sucks in a breath, but Misha and I are frozen, staring at each other as the words ricochet between us. I open my mouth to take it back, but… I can't.

No—I won't.

Instead, I kneel in front of him. "I know I'm not your *real* mother, Misha. But I do sometimes feel like I am." His face is blank, unreadable. I have no idea what he's thinking, so I speak the truth. "You are mine to protect. *Mine*." I blink back tears. "You may hate me for it, but…at least you'll be safe."

Without warning, he throws his arms around me and hugs me tight. As soon as I hold him close, some missing piece of my heart clicks into place. Things feel *right* in a way I've never felt before.

When Misha and I finally pull apart, Mila's dabbing her eyes with the corner of her blouse. Pretty sure Misha's eyes are wet, too, because he grunts something about taking another walk around the pool and darts off without meeting my gaze.

Mila takes my hand once more and we sit like that. Neither of us move for a long, long time. Remi pants, Misha does laps around the pool, and nobody breathes a word.

~

I don't know how long we've been still as statues before my phone shatters the silence. "It's Andrey." My hands are shaking so badly that I almost drop it. "Hello?"

"We've got her, *lastochka*," Andrey's voice is restrained but triumphant. "She's shaken but unharmed."

"Oh, thank God!" My lungs expand with the first real breath I've taken since the moment we opened Kat's apartment door.

My phone starts beeping with an incoming call. It's Aunt Annie. But I swipe it away and concentrate on Andrey's voice. Mila is standing now, too, a smile on her face.

"Did they put up a fight?"

"They—"

The steady *beep-beep-beep* of another incoming call has me pulling my ear from the phone, losing Andrey's answer.

Aunt Annie again.

I decline the call a second time and put the phone back to my ear. "I'm sorry—what were you saying? Were there a lot of men?"

"Only four, it turns out. She wasn't as well-guarded as we thought. We were in and out in under twenty minutes."

I can hear the concern in his voice. He's questioning why the rescue mission was so easy.

Beep-beep-beep. Okay. Now, I'm worried.

"Andrey, I'm sorry, Aunt Annie's calling. It's the third time…"

"It's okay. We'll talk when I get home."

Home. He's coming home.

I hang up and call Aunt Annie back. The call connects.

"Hello, Natalia."

I go cold, goosebumps rippling down my arms because…

That's not Aunt Annie.

The voice on the other end of the line is silky smooth and deeply masculine. And he knows my name.

"Who is this? Where is my aunt?"

Mila stands up, mouthing questions at me I can't answer. My heart is thrumming erratically again. The relief I felt a moment ago has all but disappeared.

"She's at St. Vincent's Hospital. You might want to rush over." The words are tinged with sick amusement. "She's not doing so well."

"Who are you?!" I scream, sending Mila running into the house for help before she even knows what's happening.

"My name is Slavik," he says with a little chuckle. "Say hello to my son for me, will you?"

Then the line goes dead.

59

NATALIA

Anatoly and Olaf are in the front, careening through traffic towards the hospital. Mila is next to me, talking to Misha.

He shouldn't even be here. I should've made him stay home. But would he even be safe at home? Would any of us?

"Natalia?"

The second I hear Andrey's voice, tears fill my eyes. The loose grip I've had on my emotions gives way, and tears pour down my face.

"They got her. They hurt Aunt Annie."

I have no idea how he manages to understand me, but his voice is deadly calm when he asks me a single question. "Who got to her, *lastochka*?"

"Your father," I whisper. "Slavik."

There's a beat of silence. I'm bracing myself for the disbelief, the incredulity. I'm resigned to the precious minutes I'll waste trying to convince him that I can still go to the hospital and that he doesn't need to bury me in some underground bunker in Siberia.

But as it turns out, Andrey doesn't need convincing.

"Stay safe," he growls. "I'll handle the rest."

∼

When we arrive at the hospital, Anatoly accompanies all of us into the emergency room. People aim annoyed looks at Remi, but I'm prepared to sic him on anyone who gets in my way.

Once I give them Aunt Annie's name, we're led to a room on the fourth floor.

I don't remember getting into the elevator or walking down the hallway. Just that, the next thing I know, I'm standing in front of this woman who has always been a strong, dependable force of nature, who is now lying in a narrow bed with tubes sticking out of her arms…

And a blazing red rope burn seared into her neck.

"Oh, God. Aunt Annie," I croak.

She stirs, blinking up at me. Her voice—what's left of it—is a nasty rattle in her throat. "My Nic-Nat…"

I grab her hand as tears gush down my cheeks. "I'm sorry," I whisper. "I'm so sorry."

"Oh, sweetheart," she whispers with difficulty. "I was so scared…"

"Of course you were."

She shakes her head, her eyes bulging out of their sockets, making her thin face look even more gaunt. "Not for me, child. For *you*."

"Me?"

She nods, her eyes floating to the door. "The men that attacked me asked a lot of questions about you. And the baby."

My legs are shaking, so I cling to the railing of the bed to keep from toppling over. "Who were they? Why did they do this?"

"They were waiting in the house for me," she explains, wincing on every other word, but talking through the pain anyway.

"Did they say who sent them?"

She shakes her head.

"Was there a man named Slavik there?"

She frowns, her shoulders rising and falling in a weak shrug. "They didn't introduce themselves properly, I'm afraid."

Why would they? She didn't need to know their names if they planned to kill her.

The rope burn around her neck makes my own throat feel tight. "You're safe now," I assure her. "I promise. No one will hurt you anymore."

Her fingers tighten around my hand. "Sweetheart, do you know what you've gotten yourself into?"

No. The answer is a firm, resounding no.

But how can I possibly say that to her? How can I possibly give her more worry and pain on top of what she's already carrying? *All because of me...*

"Andrey will keep us safe, Aunt Annie."

She doesn't look convinced or relieved. She's still looking at me as though I'm the one in the hospital bed. As though I'm the one who was almost strangled to death.

We're interrupted when a nurse walks in with a new dose of painkillers. I back away and let her administer the drugs.

Everything feels like it's moving in slow motion. I'm no longer in my body. No longer connected to it.

I recognize the sense of panic that precedes one of my episodes. It's kicking in already. It will take only the smallest trigger to send me careening back into numbness and catatonia.

Not now. Aunt Annie needs you.

Misha needs you.

Katya needs you.

I wipe away my tears hastily and fumble around in my pocket for my phone. Andrey should be here. Where is he?

But according to my lockscreen, I've got no new messages or calls.

Moving makes it easier to stave off the shock and anxiety. I pace as I call Andrey, desperate to hear his deep, calm voice.

"Natalia."

Oh, thank God.

"They tried to *strangle* her. She could have died! Where are you?"

"My father is back." His voice is neither gentle nor reassuring. He's speaking to me like I'm one of the men he commands. "I have to contain the situation before it gets out of hand."

"*Before* it gets out of hand?" I cry. "He tried to kill my aunt! I'd say it's already out of hand, Andrey!"

He refuses to reveal even a hint of what he's thinking when he asks, "How is she?"

"Hurt and terrified!" I screech, earning me a reproachful look from the woman behind the nurse's station.

"This is my fault." It sounds far too cold to count as an apology. "I should have had a team on her. I didn't think she was in any danger."

"Andrey, please," I implore. "I need you…"

Desperation is the only thing that allows me to be so vulnerable. I'm going down either way—I might as well be honest on the way out.

"Shura is with Katya, but Leonty is on his way to the hospital now. He should be there shortly."

I don't understand. I didn't ask for Leonty. Or Shura. I asked for *him*.

"Andrey—"

"Slavik returning is not something I anticipated. He may be my father, but he's a dangerous man. I need to sort this out first."

I clutch the phone tighter, a flimsy lifeline. But before I can say anything…

He hangs up.

I freeze, held captive by dead air and the burgeoning feeling of isolation.

"Excuse me, ma'am?" I turn to the blonde, curly-haired nurse. "Your aunt has just been sedated. She's going to need plenty of rest. Her blood pressure is pretty high and, given her age, we're gonna have to monitor that closely."

I blink fast, wishing there was an adult in the room with me who knew how to handle things like this. "Um… but she's out of danger? She's going to be okay?"

The nurse frowns, which isn't at all reassuring. "As I said, her blood pressure is high. Until it drops, she's not out of the woods yet."

I mean to take a step towards my aunt, but my feet don't cooperate and instead, I go barreling into the nurse. She steadies me with both hands. "Ma'am, are you alright? Let me get you a chair."

"No, no," I insist. "I'm okay."

I *have* to be okay. How can I expect to be there for my family if I fall apart at the slightest sign of conflict or pressure?

I stumble over to Aunt Annie's bedside and take her hand again. Her palm is limp and cool against mine. She turns her head to me, but her eyes are blurry from the drugs and fatigue.

She mumbles something, but I don't understand a word of it.

"What was that?" I ask, dropping my ear to her lips. "Aunt Annie?"

"It'll be the drugs," the nurse informs me as she heads for the door. "It's perfectly normal. She'll be out soon."

But when the nurse is gone, I try again. "Aunt Annie?"

"You're not safe, Nat." Her chest rises and falls with the effort.

"Don't worry about me. I'll be fine. I'm protected."

Aunt Annie's eyes widen for a moment as though she's remembering something. "He said… he said…"

The noose around my neck feels like it's tightening. "Who said? What did he say?"

She passes out before she can tell me.

60

ANDREY

The manor is uncharacteristically quiet.

No chatter.

No barking.

No laughter.

I used to think I preferred it this way.

What the fuck was I thinking?

"Where's Viktor?" I hurl the question at Shura the moment he walks out of the guest bedroom that Katya's settled in.

"Viktor? Fuck Viktor," Shura spits. "What does he have to do with this?"

He's doing better since we managed to get Katya back, but his fists are still balled tight. He's waiting for a fight to break out at any moment.

It's not enough to have Katya back—he needs to know who

ordered the hit on her. He needs to find them and kill them to make sure it never happens again.

I understand the instinct.

"More than we realized." I slam my fist against the doorframe, letting the pain focus me. "When I kicked him out, I thought he'd tuck his tail and cower like the little rat he is… But I was wrong."

I should have known that cornered rats tend to bite.

Shura pulls the door shut, deadly focused on me. "What do you mean? Why the hell would Viktor target Katya? What does he stand to gain from taking her?"

"The same thing he'd stand to gain from attacking Natalia's aunt in her home," I say. "We're scattered all over the city and trying to pick up the fucking pieces."

Shura's eyes narrow. "Viktor doesn't have the balls to do something this elaborate."

"I agree. But he's not the mastermind behind it. He's just the puppet—as per fucking usual."

I can practically hear his mind whizzing as he connects the dots. "You think he's working with Nikolai?"

I snort. "Nikolai is too smart to get into bed with someone as useless as my brother. No, if he forms an alliance, it's gonna be with someone who's bringing something to the table."

"But who—"

"Slavik."

"The *fuck*? Slavik?!"

Normally, I would've told Shura the second Natalia called me, but he was caring for Katya. I didn't want to interrupt.

Now, there's no other choice.

I nod. "He's back. He called Natalia personally. He took the credit for putting Annie in the hospital."

Shura runs a hand through his thinning hair. "Fuck. I thought we were rid of him."

"You and me both," I say darkly. "His return complicates everything."

Shura's gaze goes distant as the gravity of the situation sinks in. "If Nikolai realizes that Slavik is back, brother… all hell will break loose."

"Which is why he won't find out."

He hisses through his teeth. "That's going to be next to impossible to contain. We don't even know why Slavik is here. Do you think it's a temporary visit?"

"If it's not, we'll convince him to make it one." I grab my keys. "Come on."

I march towards the door, eager to sort out this situation before any more shit hits the fan. When I glance over my shoulder, though, I realize Shura isn't following.

"What… what about Katya?" he asks.

Blyat'. He must really love the woman if there's even a question of him staying with her instead of coming with me.

"Need I remind you who abducted her in the first place?" I snarl. "You think any of our women are safe with Slavik around?"

He nods crisply before I even finish the question. "You're right. Obviously, you're—Fuck. Okay, I'm coming." He follows after me, back straight, chin high, ready for war.

Good. I'll need the best of him.

So will the women who depend on us.

~

As I pull us out of the driveway, I call Drogheda. I placed Arina within the institution well after Slavik left, but given my brother's complete lack of moral fiber, I have to assume her location has been compromised.

Once the receptionist at Drogheda is made aware of who I am, she transfers me immediately to the chief psychiatric administrator.

"Dr. Fernando."

"Mr. Kuznetsov," he starts, his voice already shaking, "is there something I—"

"I have an issue, and I'm sure you'll do everything in your power to see that it's solved."

He rushes to assure me he will do exactly that, still tripping over every syllable. I can hear the frantic wheeze of breath rattling in and out of his chest.

It's a pleasant reminder that, although there are a handful of men on this earth who seem to think they can kill me and take what's mine, the rest of them are content to lie down and let me step right over them.

As it should be.

"My father is back in town after an extended absence. Considering he and my mother are still legally married, he has certain legal rights where her medical care is concerned."

There's a pregnant silence while I let Dr. Fernando fill in the blanks. "You wish for me to bar him from seeing her?"

"Bar him. Withhold information. Expel him from the property if you have to. He is not to be allowed admission into Drogheda."

Dr. Fernando's swallow is audible. "Th-the thing is, Mr. Kuznetsov, legally speaking, he has, as you said, certain rights—"

"If he gets within a country fucking mile of my mother, it's your neck I'm coming for. Is that enough motivation for you?"

"O-of course, Mr. Kuznetsov."

"Good. If Slavik tries to make contact, I expect you to inform me immediately."

"O-of cou—"

I hang up and make a sharp turn that has Shura gripping his arm rest. "You really think he'll target Arina?"

"I'm not taking any chances. Just to be safe, station some men on the premises."

Shura pulls out his phone and starts typing. "Where exactly are we going?"

"Hunts Point. The quickest way to find Slavik is to find Viktor. Rats flock together, Shura. If we get one, we'll get them all."

My phone continues to buzz throughout the drive, though I ignore it as we pull up in front of the laundromat. Distant gunshots pop off. Homeless wanderers groan and shuffle down the sidewalks, though the wiser ones beat a hasty exit when they see me approach.

The laundromat hasn't run a single laundry cycle in the two years I've owned it. Out front, the air is rich with the smell of rot and decay. Inside, the windows are dark and the mattress in the back of the room is in disarray, a stained sheet twisted in a heap on the floor. Empty bottles line the far end of the room. A moldy burrito lies on a paper late in the center of a flaking card table.

All surefire signs that my brother was here.

"He hasn't been back in a couple of days," Shura observes, wrinkling his nose against the stench.

"He'll have left us some sort of message," I say. "Slavik didn't come back just to avoid me."

As we step into the rear office, I come face to face with the "message" my father has left me.

It's in the form of none other than Fyodor Navalny, my father's right-hand man.

Seated behind the ancient, crumbling desk, he looks like he did a decade ago—big, beefy, grizzled into something barely human. He's perhaps a little grayer around the temples and the beard, but no less fierce for it.

"Fyodor," I greet, hiding my rage behind a forced smile. "It's been a long time."

"It has, young master."

Young master. The word choice is not an accident.

Fyodor is reminding me of my place now that Slavik is back. He's reminding me that the hierarchy has changed.

I grin a little wider. This time, I don't have to force it. "It's *pakhan* now, Fyodor. It has been since Slavik fled the country with his loyalists and his whore."

Fyodor doesn't react. "I assume you're here to speak to your brother."

"I figured it was the easiest way to see Slavik."

"Then you'd be right," Fyodor rasps, his voice grating like sandpaper. "You can follow me. I'll take you to the *pakhan*."

More power games. A younger Andrey might've taken the bait. Might've raged and seethed at my father's petty insults. I'm older now. I have more to lose.

And less room in my head for the old bastard who tried to mold me in his image.

"That won't be necessary."

Fyodor is halfway out of his seat when I speak. As I do, he freezes. "Excuse me?"

"Slavik has gone through a lot of trouble to get my attention, but a phone call would have sufficed. Then again, he's always been a showman, hasn't he?" I pause, enjoying the flash of irritation on Fyodor's face. "If my father is so desperate for an audience with me, he knows where to find me. I do have some errands to run today, though, so... let's give him an hour, yes? If that won't work, I'm afraid I won't have any more time for the foreseeable future. Please pass along my apologies to the old man."

With that, I turn and leave.

It's a distinct pleasure to turn my back on a man who used to do the worst of my father's fucked-up bidding. To not fear him in the least as I go.

Shura is pale-faced as he climbs into the Escalade beside me.

"Why the fuck would you invite the bastard to the manor?" Shura growls.

"Because Slavik needs to understand that I'm not intimidated by him." My hands tighten on the steering wheel. "And there's no fucking way I was going to go crawling to him. It's my Bratva now. It's time my father learned that lesson."

61

ANDREY

There was never a doubt in my mind that Slavik would show up. He's too curious, too greedy, too fucking pompous not to seize the chance to come to the manor.

I watch from the front parlor as four SUVs stop at the base of the driveway and my brother and father climb out.

They're accompanied by a dozen men, all decked out with earpieces and guns. For reasons I'll never understand, the men who walked onto that jet plane and left with my father to Russia have remained by his side all these years. I'd commend them if it didn't mean more people I might have to kill.

Viktor's suit hangs loosely on him. There are dark circles under his eyes and his cheeks are hollow. *Must be hard to eat with that mangled right hand of his,* I think as he shoves his bandaged hand into his pocket.

"I'll do the honors of letting our 'guests' inside." Shura scowls before trudging to the foyer. Just as he disappears through the door, my phone starts to ring.

It's not Natalia this time. It's Leonty.

"Whatever it is, make it fast," I bark. "I'm busy."

"Er, it's Natalia," he says quickly. "She's… Brother, she's not doing—"

Heavy footsteps grow louder. "Leonty, you'll have to handle it for now. Mila's with you, isn't she?"

"Yes, but—"

"And Remi?"

"Yes, sir, but—"

"That's what they're there for: to help her. Use your best judgment. I have to go."

I hang up on his strangled protest and turn my phone to silent. Guilt weighs on my shoulder, but the stakes are high. I can't afford to be distracted.

Natalia will be a lot worse off if I don't take this meeting.

Slavik is an imminent threat. Letting him move unchecked could have consequences that stretch far beyond the safety of my family alone. My entire empire could be compromised.

I pocket my phone as the door opens. Shura enters first, holding the door for my father and brother. As soon as they are through, he slams the door closed on the rest of my father's men.

Fyodor hisses from the hallway, but Shura bolts the door with a smug smile.

"Was that necessary?" Slavik drawls.

"It's for the *pakhan* to decide what's necessary," Shura replies coldly. "Not you."

Viktor glowers. "How dare you? Do I need to remind you—"

Slavik holds up a hand and Viktor goes silent. "That's okay, Viktor. Loyalty is to be commended. No matter how misplaced."

"Sit down," I order, suddenly impatient to get them out of my house as soon as possible.

Slavik claims the biggest armchair. "How interesting to be asked to sit in my own home. As though I were a guest."

I take the sofa directly opposite him. Up close, I can see the changes. He's fitter than I would have expected for a man closing in on his seventies. The mess of hair he used to sport is gone now, replaced by a close-shaved crewcut that makes him look younger and more severe at the same time.

Viktor stands at Slavik's back like a nervous guard dog, shifting his weight from foot to foot.

"Sit, brother," I tell him. "Your remaining hand is safe from me today."

Viktor opens his mouth to snap back, but Slavik clears his throat and jabs his chin towards a chair. Viktor holds his tongue and sits down.

Good boy. Heel for your master.

"It was poor form, punishing your brother that way," Slavik admonishes me coolly. "I'm told his hand will never be fully functional again."

"I thought that would be preferable to him being dead."

"You made an invalid of your brother for a cheap piece of pussy?" He shakes his head in quiet disapproval. "We are

Kuznetsovs! We don't fuck riffraff. We certainly don't knock them up."

My smile dies as my jaw clenches.

Seeing that, my father sighs. "I shouldn't need to say we don't let ourselves come to care about riffraff, either—but it seems you might need to relearn that lesson."

It was a slight slip of my mask, but it was enough. I won't let it happen again.

"She's carrying my child. That is all."

"I think not. I see what she really is: a weakness." He leans back, arms folded, legs crossed, perfectly at ease. "I thought I taught you better. I thought you were smarter than your brother." Viktor flinches, though if Slavik notices, he shows no sign of it. "Love…" The word twists on his tongue. He makes it sound dirty, ugly. *Wrong.* "—is nothing more than a liability."

"The only liabilities I see are the two men standing in front of me."

Viktor hisses. Slavik leans forward and steeples his fingers together. "I don't remember you complaining when I handed you my empire and smoked the competition in a single move."

"Don't act like a saint, father. You didn't rat out the Rostovs for my benefit."

"Why else would I have done it?" He's barely blinking. The effect is unsettling.

"You tell me. Petty revenge is my best guess, knowing you. Nikolai must have offended you. Did he not kneel to kiss the ring fast enough? Did he do a poor job licking your boots? I know how fragile your ego can be. It's the same for all weak men."

The smile slides off his face, turning his gray eyes icy once more. "You dare to sit in my house, use my title, command my men, and call *me* weak?"

"You've been gone a long time, so you must be confused." I lean forward to mirror his posture, resting my elbows on my knees. "This is not your fucking house and it's not your fucking Bratva. Don't you get it, old man? You're not in charge anymore."

Slavik sinks back, never taking his eyes off me. His fingers run through his thick beard again and again. "I acknowledge that you've done well in my absence, Andryusha. You've built on my legacy, and you will get the credit for it once I reclaim my rightful place."

"You and I have very different ideas of where your 'rightful place' is."

He carries on, ignoring me. "Out of gratitude and respect for everything you've done, you can keep your men and this house. I will even let you keep the whore, if that's what you truly want."

"I don't want anything you have to offer. Not when it means falling into step behind you."

"I am your father. You will be *pakhan* again one day. After I am done."

"I owe you nothing."

"You owe me everything!" he roars, face purpling as spit flies past his lips.

I stay perfectly calm. "The man I am and the *pakhan* I am… It has nothing, absolutely fucking *nothing* to do with you." I crack my neck. "You want proof? Look at the useless dead weight kneeling at your side."

His eyes narrow. Viktor tenses. For a moment, the silence feels like it's on the cusp of breaking into bloodshed and chaos.

Then the moment passes.

"This has been an enlightening conversation, son," Slavik states as he pushes himself to his feet. "It's good to know where we stand."

I square my jaw. "Am I right in assuming you're here to stay?"

"Oh, yes. Russia was a good respite, but this is home."

Snapping his fingers, he motions Viktor to follow him. My brother's eyes dart to mine, clearly embarrassed by his treatment, but unable to do a goddamn thing about it.

My fool of a sibling picked the wrong side.

"I hope you know what you're doing, Slavik," I call after them. "It's not just me you have to deal with. Nikolai won't take kindly to your return, either."

Slavik looks supremely unconcerned. "I'm not worried about the Rostov boy. He's just another ant that requires squashing. He'll die the way they always do: squirming beneath the heel of my boot."

With that, he departs.

Shura follows Viktor and Slavik out, and I turn back to the window. I'm confident in my power and my men. The problem is that Slavik seems just as confident.

What makes him so damn sure he'll get back control of the Kuznetsov Bratva?

What does he know? What has Viktor told him?

The door flies open before any answers present themselves. Shura is breathless, and the look on his face sends my heart plunging into my stomach.

"It's Natalia."

∽

The moment I step into the hallway, I smell it. Beneath the antiseptic and the over-bleached hospital bedding…

Blood.

Olaf's limp body is lying in the threshold of the door. I jump over him and nearly trip over Anatoly's corpse.

"No, no, no!"

As I search the room frantically, I find Remi lying behind the armchair, eyes closed, tongue lolling out of his mouth.

I turn the room upside down, but I already know there's no point.

She's gone.

62

NATALIA

It's the pain that wakes me.

A dull, nagging pain. I'm achy all over, the same way I used to feel after a night out with Katya. Back then, the culprit was obvious: tequila. It's not as obvious this time around.

I'm stiff, but when I try to move to ease the pain, my hands and legs are unwilling to obey.

No, not unwilling—un*able*.

My eyes fly open, and I feel the zip ties cutting into my skin before I see them. I take in the small room in one panicked sweep. Sickly, yellow walls. Narrow windows covered in moth-eaten curtains.

I draw in a ragged breath, and the air is dank and stale.

"Anatoly! Olaf!"

My guards were just outside the door, but that was a different door. A different room. Still, I call out for anything familiar.

Emerald Malice

"Remi? Remi!"

Remi doesn't answer with a whine or a bark, and my voice echoes pathetically in the empty space.

Every second that passes brings my fuzzy memories into sharper focus.

And that hurts worst of all.

A knock at the hospital room door. Anatoly and Olaf standing in the way.

Then everything descended into chaos.

Anatoly and Olaf dropped to the floor, and Remi took their place, snarling and baring his fangs—doing his job.

Then... nothing.

I don't remember what happened between that moment and this one, but my grim surroundings tell me it wasn't anything good.

I glance down at my stomach and pray no one hurt my baby in that blank space I can't remember. Almost in answer, I feel a fluttering kick, earnest and comforting. Despite everything, I smile.

At least my child is safe. At least my little girl is a fighter.

Given what's coming, she might have to be.

Without warning, the door unlocks. A man strolls in like it's any other day. He's tall and broad-shouldered...

And strangely familiar.

"I've seen you before." My voice is hoarse, and I cough. *How long have I been here?* "Where have I seen you before?"

He grabs a chair along the wall and slides it closer to me. Swinging it around, he straddles it backward and crosses his arms over the top.

"You don't remember?" He sounds almost disappointed. "I'm offended. I thought I made an impression. A couple of them, actually."

I take him in again—strong, pointed jaw; hooked nose; bright, hazel eyes. I shake my head, the answer coming to me but still not making any sense. "You're the guy… the guy who spilled our drinks at Burning Bird."

His grin makes me shiver. "A first impression is hard to undo. I guess I bought you and Katya those drinks for nothing." He shrugs, an easy smile on his face. "I'm not usually that clumsy. I was just so eager to meet you, Natalia."

My body is cold, goose-pimpled with dread. "You're Nikolai Rostov."

He's like an optical illusion in front of me. I tell myself there's no way, but the moment the words are out of my mouth, I can't see anything else.

He is Nikolai Rostov—and he's been here the whole time.

His smirk only gets wider. "Pleasure to meet you, Mrs. Kuznetsov."

"What did you do to my bodyguards?" I spit. "And my dog?"

And Andrey. Where's Andrey? And Mila… Katya… Misha…

The faces of the people I love flicker like a slideshow through my mind, and I grow colder as each one passes.

"I don't know about the bodyguards, to be honest," Nikolai answers with a neutral shrug. "I can tell you the dog isn't dead, though. I don't kill animals if I can avoid it. Nasty business, that."

"But killing people is okay with you?" I hiss, unable to contain my disgust. "Selling women and children is just fucking dandy, but animal cruelty is where you draw the line? Am I hearing that correctly?"

"You're a lot feistier than I anticipated. I can see why you managed to make an impression on Andrey." He studies me closely. "Why you're with that asshole, however, I'll never understand."

"He's no asshole, Nikolai Rostov. *You* are."

"I'm sure you believe that. He's probably spent a lot of time filling your head with lies."

"You don't sell women and children, then?"

For a fraction of a second, the most terrifying, inhuman rage I've ever seen flies across his face. One blink later, it's gone. His face falls into somber lines—the very picture of sadness.

I don't trust it for a second.

"You don't know me, Natalia. You know only the sick, twisted version of me that Andrey has fed you. He's painted me out as the villain, but all I am is a son—a son trying to avenge his parents." I frown, and Nikolai jumps on my confusion. "He's left that part out of the story, has he, pretty lamb?"

Humming under his breath, he rises and circles behind me. I stiffen when I hear the unmistakable *shiiink* of a blade being unsheathed.

He bends low, and I'm waiting for the blade to press to my neck. For this nightmare to end in blood and darkness.

Then the ties around my wrists and ankles fall loose. Blood rushes back into my extremities, and I damn near moan with relief.

Nikolai saunters back around and reclaims his seat, tucking the knife away out of sight. "I'm not a bad man, Natalia. Far from it." He eyes me carefully. Sizing me up, maybe, though God only knows why. "I know about your parents. About how they died… Do you still love them?"

I scowl at him. He has no right to talk about my family, but what choice do I have other than to play along? "You don't just stop loving people just because you lose them."

The hazel in his eyes melts and boils. I swear there are demons in him begging to come out.

He once again clears his throat and looks human once more. "I can't say I ever felt the same about the people who birthed me. They made it very clear that they loved drugs more than me."

He rolls up the sleeves of his shirt. I suck in a sharp breath.

His skin is peppered with cigarette burns and tiny scars notched from elbow to wrist. He doesn't explain them, but I get the feeling that some stories are better left unspoken.

"I lived on the streets more often than not. It felt safer than staying in that house with those parasites. I'd have ended up there sooner or later, anyway. My mother overdosed; my father went to jail. I became what I had to be: a street rat doing unspeakable things to survive. Sometimes, I had to let other people do unspeakable things to me to survive."

Horror prickles at the edges of my mind, but I won't let myself feel bad for him.

Not until I know what he's done to the people I love.

"Until I met Elia Rostov." He smiles, remembering it all fondly. "Elia had a gun pointed at his head when I met him. I still don't know why I intervened. I suppose you could call it fate, though a more cynical soul might say I was just a desperate boy snooping where I didn't belong. But I killed the *mudak* who was about to shoot Elia in the back of the head. Ripped his throat clean out with my bare hands, funny enough. And Elia... oh, he *liked* that. He liked that a lot."

Nikolai licks his lips, as if the memory tastes good. His voice simmers.

"It was the first time in my life someone had looked at me and seen the potential there. The boy I once was died that day, and Nikolai Rostov was born. I took Elia's name—his mark." He touches the black tattoo on his left forearm. At first glance, I think I see a snake caught in the mouth of a bird. But as Nikolai twists his arm, I see the snake's tail wrapped around the bird's throat, strangling it to death from the inside out.

I swallow, my throat as dry as sandpaper. "What does Andrey have to do with this?"

"Everything!" he snarls with such ferocity that I flinch back in my seat. "Andrey and his father wanted everything Elia had built. Those Kuznetsovs are greedy, hungry leeches. But you didn't know that, did you, dear? None of us did, at first." Nikolai reaches out and rubs a thumb along the line of my jaw. "They say such beautiful words and offer such beautiful pictures of the future. You know exactly what I mean. I see it in your eyes." He licks his lips again. A darting, snake's tongue. "And that's precisely what they did to my adopted family. They came to us offering peace. *Cooperation.*"

His voice is low and steady, so quiet I lean in.

"We shook hands on it!" he roars, spit flecking his lips and dotting my face. I slam back against my chair. "And then... *and then...* when the time came to pass the baton, Andrey went back on everything he'd sworn he would do. He overthrew his own father, exiled him out of the country, and assumed the mantle of Bratva *pakhan*. He went back on the agreement he made with my father and sold my parents out to the FBI."

My heart is beating fast. Not because I believe anything he's telling me—but because *he* evidently does.

"That was not Andrey," I insist. "He wouldn't. He didn't— He's not a liar."

Nikolai's smile is cruel, pitying. "Oh? Did he tell you that?"

"He doesn't have to. I know him. He would never go back on his word. If anyone ratted out your parents, it was Slavik."

I have no proof of this whatsoever, but I just *know*.

"Yes, that's what I thought, too." Nikolai sighs. "And don't get me wrong: Slavik is as dishonorable as his unworthy son. Apples rot right next to the trees that birthed them. Slavik is far from innocent. But why would he go to the trouble of selling out my parents just to leave the country—not to mention his entire fucking legacy—behind?" His tongue clicks. "No, Andrey Kuznetsov is the only one who stood to gain. He *did* gain."

"You believe what you want to believe."

He arches a brow, sliding closer. "I could say the same about you, pretty lamb."

"I'm no lamb," I snap fiercely. "I don't just follow blindly."

"Is that so?"

Silence might be worse than anything Nikolai has to say. If I stop long enough to think, I might lose myself again. And this time, I don't have anyone to care for me until I'm ready to come back.

I have to take care of myself.

I have to protect my baby.

"You expect me to trust a man who would sell children into sex slavery?"

"You think the drug industry is any different?" he demands. "It destroys families just as fast as the skin trade. Trust me, I know. I lost two parents to the Kuznetsov drug ring."

My blood goes cold. "W-what?"

He smiles patronizingly. "Do you think there are any drugs sold in this city that don't come directly from that *mudak* you defend? Every dime bag of weed, every last fucking line of coke, every syringe brimming with devil's poison… Andrey touches all of it. Profits from all of it. I didn't lose just one set of parents to him—I lost *two*." Nikolai gets to his feet slowly. "You know what it's like to lose parents, Natalia. You understand the pain."

His face is creased with loss. For the shortest of moments, I do feel his pain.

But I'm not so far gone that I can't see what he's trying to do.

"Don't feed me sob stories!" I cry out. "If you're really capable of feeling anything at all, then you would never have thrown Misha into the lion's den without any regard for his safety!"

He hesitates for a moment, his eyebrows twisting together to form a bridge across his forehead. "Misha?"

"Of course you don't even remember him. He was the errand boy you sent because he was worthless to you. A pawn you didn't care about sacrificing. Someone unimportant. Expendable."

Nikolai's eyes flare with something: recognition, perhaps?

"You hated the way you were treated; you hated being forced to survive on the streets. But that's exactly what you're doing to *other* women, *other* children—"

"Foolish woman!" he seethes, causing my jaw to snap shut. "I'm giving them second chances. New beginnings. Those women and children I sell have nothing and no one. Without me, they'd be roadkill. With me, they can have a purpose."

"As *what*?" I scoff in horror. "Some old pervert's mistress? A punching bag for some rich sadist?"

"It's a better fate than death on the side of the road."

"I'd much rather die on the side of the road than be the possession of sick men like you."

Nikolai stares at me silently for a long time. "He really has done a number on you, hasn't he?" He slips a hand into his pocket and fear rockets down my spine. If he pulls out that knife, I won't be able to fight back. I won't even be able to run.

But he doesn't pull out a weapon. Instead, I find myself faced with a shiny black smartphone.

"You seem to be under the impression that you've picked the hero. Which would make me the monster in your story. I've got news for you: Andrey and I… we're *both* monsters."

He raises the camera and snaps a picture of me.

"You'll figure that out soon enough."

63

ANDREY

I used to think it was just a horror story for the men in this city to scare children with—*The Slaughterhouse.*

But it's real.

The Slaughterhouse is Nikolai's playroom. The place where human flesh is traded for money and the highest bidder always wins.

I'm in the middle of destroying the furniture in my office when Shura, Efrem, Vaska and Yuri thunder in. "Jesus Christ, Andrey!" Shura exclaims when he sees the carnage. "What the fuck is going on?"

I shove my phone in his face. I know Natalia's picture is still there, but I can't bring myself to look at it again.

Not that I need to. Her red, raw wrists and pale face will be in the back of my mind until the day I die.

The texts, too, are imprinted in my mind. I repeat them to myself as Shura's eyes scan the thread, horror leaching his face of color.

Emerald Malice

NIKOLAI: *I have your pretty little lamb.*

NIKOLAI: *You have one hour to show your face. Otherwise I'll have to take the little lamb to The Slaughterhouse.*

"Nikolai has her," Shura breathes.

My men stand to attention. The men I have left, anyway. Anatoly is dead. Olaf is fighting, but the doctors don't know if he'll make it through the night.

They died trying to save Natalia.

To honor them, I'll finish what they started.

"We don't have time to waste," I growl. Truth be told, the ten seconds I just used to destroy my office were ten seconds I could have used to close the distance between Natalia and me.

Every second counts. Every move matters.

"We head out in five," I snarl, rushing down the hall.

As I get ready, I order some men to stay behind to protect Misha, Katya, and Mila. The rest of us speed out of the manor, arrowing toward the location Nikolai sent.

"He sent you the location, brother." Shura's face is tight and doleful as I speed through the streets. "This is a trick."

"You think I don't fucking know that?"

His jaw drops indignantly. "Then why—"

"Because he has my woman!" I roar. "What would you do?"

Shura's jaw snaps shut, and he doesn't breathe another word until we're standing outside the deserted-looking house on the far edge of the city.

"What's the game plan?" Shura rasps, loading his weapon.

"The game plan is to get in there, find Natalia, and get her the fuck out."

"He knows we're here," he reminds me. "This house is a ticking time bomb. You really think it's gonna be that easy?"

"No," I say grimly as I load a second gun and stuff it in the back of my pants. "I don't."

But I don't have another choice.

Before, I had only my life to lose. Now, I'd gladly trade that if it meant Natalia and my daughter could be safe. And I will, if it comes to it. Without a second thought.

Which is why, with my men at my back and flanking the house, I charge in.

The house is dark and musty. Dust fills the air after I kick the door in. Before it can settle, gunshots ring out. I spot the shooter behind a rotted-out sofa, and he drops with a single shot to the head. Shura takes out another near the fireplace. A third fires, but falls back with a hole the size of my fist in his chest.

Sheetrock dust and gunpowder combine into a haze so thick no one can see, but we don't stop moving, don't stop shooting. Men on both sides drop and scream as bullets wail through the air, but we press on.

I turn a corner and a shot screams past close enough to singe the skin of my scalp. But close enough isn't close enough.

I fire and drop the man like the waste of space he is. Anyone working for Nikolai after what he's done isn't worth my mercy.

I duck behind a rotting half-wall and check my watch. How much time do I have left? Twenty minutes? Fifteen?

My men clear the sitting room, and I spot the staircase.

I race towards it, launching myself at two Rostov soldiers blocking my path. I tackle them both to the ground, killing one with a bullet to the face and breaking the other one's neck with my knee.

"Andrey!" Shura roars from the bottom of the staircase. "Wait!"

But I don't wait. *Fuck* waiting.

More men are posted at the top, but my body is moving faster than my brain can keep up with. Maybe it's why it takes me half a flight of stairs to notice the pain in my side.

I've been hit, it seems.

Irrelevant.

I charge down the hallway, pouring blood from the wound in my ribs. A door looms at the end, and I crash through it like holy fucking lightning.

Then I grind to a halt.

Nikolai is in front of me. I can still hear gunfire downstairs, but Nikolai is calm.

Unbelievably calm, given he's unarmed and I have every intention of ripping his head from his body.

He half-turns to me, nodding to the gun I have aimed at his chest. "I'd put that away if I were you," he says. "Shooting me might set her off."

A whimper to my right draws my attention, and my knees nearly buckle.

Natalia is sitting in a chair—alive, whole, perfect. Except…

"No."

"Oh, yes," Nikolai hisses, his eyes narrowing with triumph. "Time to make a choice, Andrey Kuznetsov."

Shura was wrong: the house isn't the ticking time bomb.

Natalia is—by virtue of the explosive strapped to her chest, counting down the time remaining to detonation.

"You have thirteen minutes left."

64

ANDREY

"Isn't this fun?" Nikolai eyes my gun with amusement, knowing as well as I do that it's useless. "If we're going to kill people, it might as well be poetic. Don't you agree, pretty lamb?"

Natalia is pale as ash and shaking like a leaf

"Don't you dare fucking speak to her!" I snarl.

"You're in no position to be giving orders, Andrey," he replies coolly. "As a matter of fact, I'd be very careful about how you speak to me."

"One bullet is all it would take, Rostov. One fucking bullet."

He sighs like this whole charade is boring him. "And just like that, another precious minute lost to idle chatter and idler threats. Only twelve left. Life does move so fast, doesn't it?" He kicks away the ratty old carpet at his feet to reveal a trap door. When he opens it, it reveals a set of stairs that descend into a pool of darkness below.

Nikolai takes the first step and pauses. "You can come after me if you want, but your lady would pay the price, I'm afraid."

My gaze slides to Natalia. She looks beyond terrified, but she's still here with me. Her eyes are focused and present. I wonder if that's a good thing or not. If we do make it out of here, the memories of this nightmare might drown her.

He takes another step, his eyes dancing with amusement I desperately want to shatter with a bullet. Several bullets, preferably.

"It's up to you, Andrey. What's more important to you: your woman or winning?"

The fight continues to rage around us. Footsteps thunder down the hall and more guns bark and chatter downstairs.

My men are out there fighting and Natalia is strapped to a bomb. They'll all be gone if I don't save her.

Not that there was ever another choice, anyway.

I turn my back on Nikolai and drop to my knees in front of Natalia. Nikolai's triumphant laugh rings out before the trap door thuds closed, sealing away the sound.

"Andrey..." Natalia's eyes are wide as she stares at me. Her lips are chalky white.

"You're going to be fine, *lastochka*." I circle her chair and clock every detail I can see. Three colored wires weave in and out of the vest.

Blue.

Yellow.

Red.

Only one is safe to cut. Only one will stop the bomb from detonating before the twelve—no, fuck—*eleven* minutes are up.

Natalia is shaking, the chair rattling against the wood floor from the force of her tremors. "Go, Andrey. Just g-go. It's too late."

"Don't you do that," I snarl. "Don't you fucking give up."

"Please," she rasps. "We don't both have to die…"

Suddenly, the door flies open.

I lunge for the gun, ready to fight tooth and nail for the opportunity to snip one of these wires. At least then, Natalia and I would die together. At least she wouldn't watch me die in front of her.

But it's only Shura, followed by a blood-splattered Leonty and Efrem.

"Fuck…" Shura mutters, inching forward cautiously. "Is that what I think it is?"

Our eyes meet. I know I'm asking a lot from him, but the alternative is not an option. And when he gives me a solemn nod in return, I know he will be with us to the end.

"Leonty, Efrem—get our men out of the house." I glance at the timer on the vest.

Nine minutes.

Leonty stiffens. "I'm not leaving."

"Don't fucking question me. I gave you an order and I expect it to be followed."

When he still doesn't yield, I grab him and pull him so close that only he'll be able to hear what I have to say. "If Shura is unsuccessful, everyone on this block will be reduced to ash. Go, brother. You have Mila to think of now."

That, at last, seems to get through to him. He slumps in resignation and turns towards the door, but I grab him again. "Leonty, you're my cousin. I trust you. If this goes wrong, avenge me and my family."

He shakes his head. "I… Andrey, you're not going to—"

I don't have time for empty optimism. Neither does Natalia.

I push him out of the room and slam the door.

Shura's kneeling next to her, plucking at the wires of the vest and muttering softly to himself.

Seven minutes.

Natalia's eyes are trained on the floor. They're wide and empty, her jaw slack. I drop down in front of her and cup her face. "Come back to me, little bird."

She blinks through a fog I can't see, finally focusing her eyes on mine.

"I'm sorry." I clasp her hand tightly, hoping she knows how much I mean it. "I should have come to you first and dealt with Slavik later."

She blinks again and a tear falls down her cheek. I lean forward and catch it between my lips. *Five minutes.*

"Andrey, please," she whispers. "Take Shura… Just *go*."

Shura's still muttering under his breath, so I answer for the both of us. "We're all leaving, *lastochka*. You included. Mila and Katya are waiting for you at the manor. So is Misha. And Remi."

More tears spill down her cheeks.

Four minutes.

"M-Misha…" she sobs. "He doesn't need to lose another person."

"Exactly. We're his family now. And we have to go back for him."

My hand goes to her belly. I feel the baby—my daughter—kick fiercely. As though she recognizes me. As though she agrees with me.

Three minutes.

"I-I'm scared…"

I'm desperate to look at Shura, to ask how it's going. Has he narrowed it down?

Pick a color, brother. Time is running short.

"There's nothing to be scared of." I dig into my shirt and pull out her locket. I've worn it faithfully ever since she gave it to me. "See? I'm wearing your gift."

I reach around Natalia's throat and touch the pendant I gave her. "I'm wearing yours and you're wearing mine. They'll keep us safe. We have nothing to be afraid of."

She smiles through her tears, her eyes scanning over my face again and again. Like she's determined to take in as much as she can… just in case.

One minute.

As seconds wither and die, I feel my hope die with them. If Shura can't figure this out, there's no way out.

Forty-three seconds.

Forty-two.

Forty-one.

"Andrey." Her voice is strangely, alarmingly calm. I can smell death in the room with us. I wonder if she can, too. "I want you to know something."

I've been prepared to die since I was a teenager. I accepted the likelihood that my life would be short a long time again. So I know the fear in my gut is not for myself.

It's for her.

Even if I have to go, why does she? My death will cost the world nothing. But hers? The earth will lose something precious if Natalia is not here to walk it.

All the people she's drawn in and held close—Remi, Misha, Mila, Katya, even my fucking guards—they'll be worse without her. Even the gardens won't be the same without Natalia's laugh to fill them.

Thirty seconds.

"You can tell me tomorrow," I rasp. "Tomorrow, when we're back in the manor and Remi is playing with Misha in the garden."

"I love you, Andrey." She smiles sadly, and my chest constricts.

Her hope is gone. She thinks this is the end.

I grab her hand and bring it to my mouth, breathing her in for what might be the last time. As far as dying goes, this is better than I ever imagined for myself. It's better than I deserve.

Twenty seconds.

"Natalia—"

"*Yes!*" Shura's triumphant voice cuts through the room.

Seventeen seconds.

Seventeen seconds.

Seventeen seconds.

The flashing countdown on Natalia's chest is frozen, but I still can't let myself believe it.

Until Shura stands up, a blue wire held above his head and a wild look in his eyes.

"You did it," I breathe. "You fucking did it."

Natalia lets out a strangled cry, and I tear the vest off her and drop it to the floor. She rises on trembling legs and then falls into my arms, sobbing on my shoulder.

I rise to my feet, taking her with me. I curl her in my arms and walk out of the room, leaving the stink of death behind us.

65

NATALIA

The relief is stale by the time we get to the car.

Andrey wraps me in a blanket in the back of the Escalade, but I shove it aside, bolting up out of the seat. "Where's Katya?"

She was abducted by Nikolai. Or maybe it was Slavik. The fact I don't know does nothing to slow my racing heart. Bad guys morph into each other, into the shadows, stretching and melting and reforming again and again. I can't keep track of whose blood is on whose hands.

"Misha," I say again, the cry strangled in my throat. "Where is he? And Remi?"

Were they in the hospital room with me?

Does Nikolai still have them?

Are they alive?

"Aunt Annie…?" I croak, exhausted with this never-ending list.

Fear tugs at the back of my mind, pulling me deeper into a spiral I know I won't claw my way out of. Not this time.

This is too much. There's too much pain, too much fear. I'm alive, but there are too many people still left to lose.

I can feel the quicksand calling to me. The temptation to step into it and disappear has never been stronger.

Andrey wraps me in his arms and cradles me against his chest. His heartbeat is a steady drum in my ear. "Mila and Katya are waiting for you at the manor. They're excited to see you."

I cross their names off the list in my mind. They're okay.

"But Misha—"

"Misha is at home taking care of Remi," he says with a dark chuckle. "That dog went down with a chunk of flesh in his teeth. Somewhere out there, someone is limping around with half a calf because that beast loves you so much."

Remi is alive.

Misha is safe.

"Aunt Annie," I breathe again, unable to believe I could be so lucky and she'll be safe, too.

Andrey smooths my hair away from my forehead and presses a kiss to my skin. "Annie is in the hospital. She's stable and doing better."

"She's still in danger, though," I whisper. "They came after her once. They'll do it again."

"That's why I'm moving her to a secure location," Andrey agrees. "A safehouse on the outskirts of the city that not even Viktor knows about. She'll have the best care and a private medical team on hand to monitor her every breath until she makes a full recovery."

I cross her name from the list, too.

And wait for the relief to hit me.

And wait.

And wait…

But there's nothing but emptiness.

Shura drives over a speed bump, and Andrey hisses under his breath. His hand presses to his hastily bandaged gunshot wound.

He acted like it was no worse than a mosquito bite—a mere annoyance, nothing more.

"What about you?" I press. "You need medical attention, too."

"The Bratva doctor is already on site. He'll tend to me when we get there." He gives me a bracing smile that I try hard to return.

Does he see through me?

For a moment, his face falls into hard lines, but then his hand drapes over my shoulders. "Don't worry, *lastochka*. This is nothing. A little scrape for the storybook, that's all."

The lie would be a lot more convincing if I didn't smell his blood. The metallic taint of it clings to his shirt, soaking through like a blooming red flower.

I turn away and press my hands to my stomach.

Our daughter kicks and flutters, a little reminder that I can't withdraw. No matter how much I want to shut this all off—

no matter how much I hate that so many people were hurt because they were close to me—I have to keep going.

For her.

When we stop at the manor, Leif opens the door and Leonty moves forward to help me out. Andrey and Shura are there, too, like it might really take four men to get me inside.

But I root myself to the spot.

"Where's Anatoly and Olaf?"

All four of the brave, strong men go pale.

They shift nervously, glancing from me to each other, and my heart lodges in my throat.

Andrey steps up. "Natalia, let's get inside. Maybe now's not the time—"

"Don't! Don't you dare fucking patronize me."

"Natalia—"

"Look me in the eye and tell me the truth. I deserve to know."

"'Drey," Shura mutters, "she's right. She deserves to know."

Andrey sighs. It might be the most vulnerability I've ever seen from him. Something in the darkness in his eyes and the exhausted slump of his shoulders.

"Olaf was injured, but he's going to be fine. He'll need bed rest for a few weeks, but otherwise, he'll make a full recovery."

I wait for him to continue, but he doesn't.

Leaving me to ask the question I know I don't want the answer to.

"And Anatoly?"

No one says anything.

"He's gone, isn't he?"

"It's not your fault," Andrey insists.

I turn to the house, my jaw clenched tight so it can't wobble. He's dead because of me. I don't deserve to cry.

Andrey grabs my arm and tries to guide me, but I tear my arm away.

I don't deserve his comfort.

"I want to see Remi," I demand weakly. "Take me there."

Andrey hesitates, so I make my way toward the infirmary, one slow, aching step at a time.

Inside, I find Misha sitting on a chair, chin slumped to his chest and snoring softly. His hand rests on Remi's head.

The boy looks exhausted.

The dog looks destroyed.

But both are breathing. *Thank God.*

Not wanting to wake them, I slip back out as quietly as I can, a grateful sob still caught in my throat.

Andrey is waiting in the hallway for me. "Come," he says softly. "You need a check-up, just to make sure everything's alright with the baby. The doctor is waiting."

I whirl around to face him. "You're the one who needs a doctor. You've been shot!"

"I'll get my wound checked once I've made sure you're okay."

One of his men is dead because of me, and he's worried whether *I'm* okay. Guilt claws at my chest. "I'm fine. Stop worrying about me!"

Easy, Nat. He's just trying to help.

I blow out a ragged breath and start over. "I won't be able to relax until you get that wound sorted out, Andrey. You're still bleeding."

He doesn't so much as glance down at the wound. "I want to be with you."

"I'm not letting you anywhere near me until you get yourself sorted out."

I won't lose him, too. I can't.

"Very well," he sighs, gesturing to a door farther down the hall. "Dr. Abdulov is right through that door. I'll get checked out and you can see Katya and Mila. They've been waiting for you."

Then, to my surprise, he bends down and kisses me softly on the lips.

It's too soft and tender for all the horrible things that have happened in the last few hours. I feel guilty for enjoying it. He's dripping with blood and Remi is a ragged mess of bandages in the other room and Misha looks like he hasn't slept in weeks and Annie is all by herself in the hospital and Anatoly is dead, he's fucking *dead,* for God's sake, and here I am, enjoying a kiss.

It's selfish.

It's wrong.

I pull away, feeling another wave of guilt for that, too.

There are no right choices anymore. I'm forever at an impossible crossroads, stuck looking at the paths "wrong" and "wronger."

"We're going to get through this, Natalia," he promises me, his hand floating towards the locket hanging against his chest.

I smile weakly and grab my own chain. I can't bring myself to say anything. If I do, I'll break.

So I just turn and walk away.

66

NATALIA

"Nat!"

I'm lying on the bed, ready for the ultrasound, when Kat and Mila burst into the room. Dr. Abdulov is unceremoniously shoved aside to make room for both women. To his credit, he does his best not to look too upset about it.

I accept Mila's hug, but my eyes are on Kat. She looks good considering that she was held hostage for… actually, I don't even know how long.

But I don't see any obvious signs of torture or abuse. Then again, I know better than anyone that the worst scars can't always be seen.

"Are you okay?" we ask in unison.

"You first," I insist, refusing to let go of her hand.

She nods and tries to talk, but her voice breaks. She swallows and tries again. "I'm fine. No one hurt me, but I was… scared."

"Did they talk to you? Did you see anyone you recognize?"

"If you mean Viktor, then no. And no one spoke to me. Even when I screamed and demanded answers, they just ignored me." She drops down heavily on the edge of my exam table. "I mean, I knew it had something to do with you, but no one would explain what it was."

I know she doesn't mean anything by it, but I feel the weight of those words. They settle on my chest and get heavier with each passing second.

"I'm so sorry, Kat—"

"Don't!" she snaps before I can even finish. "This is not on you. I'm just glad you're okay."

"And the baby," Mila adds. "Is the baby okay, too?"

"That's what we need to determine," Dr. Abdulov interjects with slight impatience. "All we need to do is check for the heartbeat and then you'll be free to continue your conversation."

Mila and Katya back away and let the doctor take the lead. He lifts my shirt and presses a heartbeat monitor against my stomach, poking and prodding until, finally, the room fills with the sound of the baby's heartbeat.

I could feel the little kicks on the drive over, but she'd gone uncharacteristically still since we got back to the manor. Until I hear it, I don't realize how worried I'd been that I wouldn't.

"She's okay," I splutter, feeling the tears rush down my cheeks. "She's okay."

Mila claps a hand over her chest and Katya grabs my hand.

The only problem is Dr. Abdulov is frowning, his forehead creasing the longer the heartbeat continues. That is definitely *not* the expression you want your doctor to have when he's staring at your unborn baby.

"Doctor? Is something wrong?"

Without changing his expression, he moves the wand around my belly, searching for something.

That's when I hear it, too.

The baby's heartbeat sounds strange. Like there's an echo.

Finally, Dr. Abdulov's face clears. As he sets the wand down, he smiles. "Everything is fine, Ms. Boone. But it seems you're having twins."

Katya and Mila explode in gasps and tears. Dr. Abdulov explains the positioning of the babies and how he found both heartbeats, but I can't hear a thing. The thunder of my pulse in my ears is drowning out everything else.

Twins.

Two babies. Twice as much to love.

So why is my chest filling with dread?

"Thank you, Doctor. Um, can I have a moment?" As he starts to rise, it takes all the energy I have to lunge forward to grab his wrist. "And can you not mention this to Andrey? I'd like to… I want to tell him myself."

He nods and leaves us alone.

The second the door is closed, I drop my head into my hands. My friends shift closer, and I wonder in a dull panic if they can hear my thoughts. If they know what I'm considering.

"Natty... I know that having twins is a lot, but you can handle this," Katya assures me. "I know you can."

"And we'll help you, you know," Mila adds.

"Exactly! We'll be on hand for babysitting duties whenever you need," Kat chimes in.

A crackle of dark laughter bursts through my lips as my hands drop. "If either one of you is even *alive* to babysit these twins."

Mila gasps, but Kat is already shaking her head. "I knew you would do this," she says. "I knew you'd find a way to blame yourself for what happened." Her jaw is squared now, her eyebrows pinched together. "Don't do this, Nat."

"They targeted all of you because they wanted to get to *me*," I rasp. "Even if I'm safe, the people I love won't be. That's what they told Aunt Annie. If you think the message wasn't supposed to get to me, then you're delusional."

Swinging my legs off the bed, I spring up, feeling lightheaded but pushing through it. I'm done shutting down when I should be fighting back.

Even if fighting back means...

Leaving.

"What's going on with you?" Katya asks, planting herself in front of the door.

I avoid her eyes. "It doesn't concern either one of you."

"She's thinking of leaving?" Mila guesses.

"No." Kat shakes her head. "Even Nat wouldn't be that much of a martyr to—" But her eyes slide to my guilty face, and she stops short, the words dying on her tongue. "Jesus Christ,

Nat. You are. You're thinking about it. You can't *leave*. Do you know how much danger you'll be in if you do?"

"None if I disappear. No one will be able to track me down. I can raise my children somewhere far away, somewhere they'll be safe. Away from the politics and the guns and the never-ending violence."

Away from Andrey.

My heart cracks, but I shut that thought out for now. Because the more I talk, the more I realize: I've made my decision.

I just have to make peace with it.

"Andrey will protect you!" Mila cries out.

"He can't protect me from everything. From everyone. Tonight has proven that. I mean, we're surrounded by enemies—Slavik, Viktor, Nikolai, God only knows who else. They're all out for blood, and I'm not prepared to sacrifice my children."

"But… Andrey," Mila tries again.

"It doesn't matter how I feel about him. It doesn't matter how he feels about me." I place both hands on my stomach. "This is about protecting my babies."

Mila and Katya glance at one another. They both look lost for words.

"Listen, I'm asking for nothing but your silence," I tell them. "You can disagree with me all you want. You can judge me. You can even hate me. Just don't rat me out to Andrey. *Please.*"

"Are you really going to do this?" Mila whispers.

"It might take some planning. And some time. But I know I have to try."

Then Katya inches forward, her bottom lip trembling. "I'm the one who put this idea in your head, aren't I? When I first found out you were pregnant, I said I'd leave with you. But I didn't know Andrey. I didn't know… I didn't have…"

"Shura," I finish for her, taking her hand.

She'd been willing to uproot her entire life and follow me out of the state to raise the baby when she first found out I was pregnant. Now, though, the circumstances have changed.

Everything has changed.

"You have Shura now. I know you can't come with me. I never expected you to."

She gives me a watery smile. "I wish I didn't… but—"

"You love him."

She nods. Then a disbelieving laugh bursts through her lips and she swipes away her tears. "God, that's embarrassing. What's happening to me?"

"He's a good man, Kat. I'm happy for you. I'm happy for both of you." I look at Mila over Kat's shoulder. "Leonty and Shura are lucky."

Mila's face crumples. "This feels like a goodbye. And it's not! It can't be."

"It's not goodbye." I think of all the preparations I need to make. I can't just waltz through the front door. Andrey would never let me go. I have to bide my time, wait for an opportunity to present itself. "Not yet, anyway."

"Hey!" Mila offers weakly. "Maybe in the meantime, Andrey will finish off Slavik and Nikolai and then you won't have to leave at all."

Katya nods along, but my hope died when I was looking into Nikolai's eyes, the bomb counting down to our deaths.

In that moment, I knew I was going to die and take Andrey and our babies with me.

That's where *love* was going to land us.

Still, I nod. "Yeah. Maybe."

"Everything is going to be fine. You aren't going anywhere," Katya says with forced cheer.

"But please don't say a word to—"

"We won't breathe a word of this to Andrey," Mila swears, cutting me off at the pass. "I promised no more spying."

I give her a thin smile.

"To *anyone*," Katya adds. "That includes Shura and Leonty."

I take their hands, holding them close for what might be the very last time. Neither of them looks happy, but they squeeze right back.

We all have hard choices to make.

I can only hope they're the right ones.

67

ANDREY

"Congratulations. The bullet missed all your major organs." Alexei dips his bloody hands into the bucket of water beside him to rinse them clean.

"I could have told you that. Actually, I did tell you that," I growl. "Just get the damn bandages on. I need to go check on Natalia."

Something is wrong with her. I saw it in the flickering of her eyes, the way she wouldn't hold my gaze for longer than a second or two.

Shura's not back yet, either. Between the two of them, my stomach is a mass of churning nerves.

Alexei is just finishing with the bandages when Shura finally walks into the dining room we're using as a makeshift infirmary.

"What's going on?" I push off the table and dismiss Alexei with a jerk of my chin.

Shura's bleak face doesn't provide much in the way of reassurance.

"What's wrong? Is she—"

"Natalia is fine. Physically speaking, at least." He sighs and scrubs a hand down his face. "But she's shaken."

"Obviously. But she's conscious. She's dealing with everything," I say, a desperate edge in my voice. "I call that progress."

I wait for Shura to agree, but his jaw is set and his eyes are dark. "She wants to leave."

I stare at him, waiting for the words to make sense. Waiting for him to explain himself.

They don't. He doesn't.

"What the fuck does that mean?" I snap. "I brought the doctor here. She's being taken care of. We don't need to leave. There's nowhere to—"

"'Drey, she wants to *leave*," he repeats. "I overheard her talking to Mila and Katya. She plans to run."

She wants to leave. Leave here. Leave me. Leave *us*.

I want to be angry. But how can I be?

After everything she's been through—after everything she's in danger of losing, it makes sense that her first instinct would be to get as far away from the toxic asshole who dragged her into his blood-soaked world.

"Katya and Mila promised they would keep her secret, but it was obvious that neither one was exactly gung-ho about the shit," he continues. "They tried to convince her to stay."

Leave. Leave. She wants to leave. That shit repeats in my head like a broken record.

The world without her is dark.

Without her scent…

Without her body next to mine in bed…

If Natalia leaves…

I don't know what will become of me.

"Drey?"

I turn towards the windows where the roof of the pool house is partially visible. The manor will be empty without her.

So will I.

"I can't exactly blame her," I admit softly.

"The fuck are you talking about?" Shura barks. "This is her home. You are her family."

"Maybe it'd be better if I wasn't." My own voice is a weak, rasping shell of itself. "Let's face it: the people closest to me always end up hurt."

"If you're talking about Maria—"

I whirl on him, eyes wild. "Of course I'm talking about Maria. She died because of me!"

"Drey, brother—"

"She was pregnant, you know? When she died. She was pregnant with my baby."

Shura's jaw snaps shut. His cheeks hollow as he takes that in. I'm not surprised at his reaction. I've kept that piece of information to myself for a long fucking time.

"How... How do you know that?" he croaks at last.

"I found the positive pregnancy test in her purse hours after her funeral. Three of them, actually. They all said the same thing."

Shura gingerly lowers himself into a chair at the dining table. "Fuck."

"The thought of letting Natalia go is unbearable," I whisper. "But what's worse would be losing her altogether. At least this way, I'll know she's out there somewhere, alive and well."

"With your child."

The thought cuts deep, but I know how to carry on while wounded. I've been doing it all my life.

"Maybe the best thing I can do for my child is to stay away from her. From both of them."

Shura looks indignant on my behalf. "You'd just let her go. Just like that?"

"Not 'just like that.' She'll need to be watched over, protected."

If I send my men and Natalia ever sees them, she'll know I'm keeping tabs on her. It will have to be men she doesn't recognize—men with no connection to me. Shadows to guide her from now until the end of our days.

"If any of our men offer to come with her, she's going to know immediately that it's because *you* ordered them to," Shura says, his thoughts traveling the same path as mine. I see the moment he reaches the end of the sidewalk because he looks horrified.

But we're long past having good options. All that's left is bad and worse.

"You're going to entrust Natalia and the baby to mercenaries? To strangers?"

I shrug. "They can watch her from afar. Send me pictures and updates when I ask for them. Keep me notified of any developments that occur along the way."

Shura's mouth opens and shuts soundlessly. "You're going to watch your daughter grow up through… through fucking *pictures?*"

I feel that exact same disgust in every cell of my body. The wrongness of it all.

"Show me the better way," I beg him. "Show me what else I should do."

He doesn't answer.

We both know he can't.

68

ANDREY

I find her sitting under the shade of the trees by the pool house. I steal a few minutes to watch her unnoticed—the way her hair ripples softly in the wind. The way she plays with her pendant absentmindedly, watching every tree and blade of grass and bird as though she's trying to commit it all to memory.

I'm not surprised, then, when she finds me watching her.

Nor when the sad lines of her face rearrange into a weak smile that she can't hold. By the time I make it over to her and sit down, she's frowning in thought again.

I want to reach out and smooth the line between her brows, but I'm careful to leave plenty of space between us. It doesn't do a damn thing to dim the urge to touch her.

I shove that urge down and lock it up tightly, though.

Because if I touch her... I might never let go.

"All bandaged up?" Her voice is light, casual. If I didn't know what she was planning, I might overlook the way her breath hitches.

I raise my shirt to display my bandages. "Like I said, just a little scrape."

"We have very different opinions about what constitutes a 'little scrape.'"

I lower my shirt. "You don't have to worry about me, Natalia. I can take care of myself."

"So can I, you know?" Her eyes meet mine for a moment before she tears them away again. "I know that hasn't always been the case, but—"

"You're stronger than you look. Yes, I know." This time, she does smile. The sadness doesn't quite leave her eyes, though. "How was the doctor's appointment?"

"It went well. The baby is fine." She gazes out towards the house. "What are you going to do, Andrey? Now that your father's back, I mean."

"The only thing I can do: fight."

She nods as though she expected the answer. "You have Nikolai to deal with, too."

"I'll have to deal with Slavik first."

Much as it pains me to admit, I need to make sure my own house is secure before I deal with Nikolai. I won't be able to defeat him if Slavik is trying to undermine me at every turn.

"Nikolai told me… He said that you ratted out his parents to the FBI and went back on the truce you'd negotiated with them?"

"That was Slavik."

She nods sadly. "That's what I told him. I knew you'd never go back on your word. But he seemed to think that you were the one who had everything to gain."

"That's how it looked to me, too. For months after Slavik left, I wondered why he would do all of that and then leave the Bratva to me. Still, I was foolish enough to believe that I'd never see him again. I should have known that my father never does anything without insurance."

Her eyebrows knit together. "You think he always meant to come back?"

"I think he wanted to make provisions for a return in case it didn't work out in Russia."

"So… he didn't leave for the quiet life then?"

I snort. "He doesn't know the fucking meaning of 'the quiet life.' Slavik thought he could shore up power in Russia. He tried hard for years, as far as my intel suggested. But it's a different world over there. He was a small fish in a very large pond."

"I bet his ego couldn't take that."

I smile darkly. "No. Didn't dim his light too much, though. He's confident that my men will defect to him when he declares his intentions."

Her eyes widen with alarm. "Is that likely?"

"I'm sure a few will." I drag a hand through my hair. "There's nothing I can do about that."

"But that means you're vulnerable. That means there are people you trust who could betray you."

Unable to stop myself, I turn to her, cupping her face and drawing her eyes to mine. "Like I said, *lastochka*, don't you worry about me."

She flinches out of my reach and laces her fingers together. "Misha wants to be a part of the Bratva," she says, the words leaving her lips reluctantly.

I sigh and my hand falls limply to my lap. It burns and tingles from the little contact. "I'm aware."

"You'll train him?"

"When he's ready."

"He's not just a soldier, Andrey. He's not just another pawn to be sacrificed. He's—"

"I know, little bird. He will choose his own path. And he will have a home and a family here if that's what he wants."

We're both skirting dangerously close to the secret we're both trying to hide from each other. There's a tangible goodbye in the air, a sense of finality that wavers unwillingly between us.

"I'm sorry for not showing up for you, Natalia," I tell her suddenly.

"You already apologized for that."

"It wasn't nearly enough. I told you I would protect you, and when you needed me most, I wasn't there."

"You have a Bratva to lead," she offers. "You have hundreds of men fighting for you. I know I can't always be the priority."

It tears me apart to hear her say that. Because the truth is, she *should* be the priority. Every fucking time. The fact that she thinks otherwise is on me.

But considering our circumstances, that reality is no longer an option.

I have to push her away in order to protect her.

She has to leave me behind in order to protect our child.

I grit my teeth and force the lie out. "I have to focus all my efforts on Slavik and Viktor now. That means I won't be around very much."

She looks like she's battling tears but when she looks at me, her eyes are dry. "I figured."

"I won't be coming to the pool house at night, either. So, if you want to lock your doors, you should."

She swallows as something ripples across her eyes. "I understand."

Slowly, I rise to my feet. She watches my movements, but she doesn't mimic them. And fucking hell, this moment is harder than it ever should've been.

I can't say goodbye to her properly. I can't reassure her the way I want to. In the absence of all the things I can't say to her, I give her one last promise.

"I'm going to make sure your aunt is safe and protected, Natalia. No one will ever hurt her again. You have my word."

Her lips tremble, her eyes turn watery, but still, she doesn't shed a tear. "I know that, too, Andrey."

69

NATALIA

The moment Andrey is out of sight, I crumble.

I sob like a baby, curled up on the deck chair. I wrap my arms tightly around my shivering body, afraid I'll fall to literal pieces.

I want to call Andrey back so he can hold me. I want to talk to Mila and Katya, to try to feel even an ounce of the hope they seem to have that everything will be okay.

But I can't. I have to do this alone.

I haven't even left yet and already, I'm so unbearably lonely.

The sound of approaching footsteps has me darting upright and wiping the tears hastily from my face.

Of all the people I imagine might be coming, Yelena is the last person I expect to see mounting the steep steps with muffled complaints.

She heaves to a stop in front of me, squinting down at my

face. I may have wiped away my tears but I can feel how red and puffy my eyes are. I won't fool her.

"Are you okay, *dorogoya?*

I shrug. "As okay as can be expected."

She claims the pool chair next to mine. Her arthritic old fingers cup my knee as she offers me a sad, sympathetic smile. "Everything's alright now. Your aunt and your friends are safe. And you're home again."

"Slavik, Viktor, and Nikolai are still out there," I point out. "And they're coming for me, Yelena. I can feel it in my bones. If not me, they'll want my baby."

I think about the way Nikolai looked at my stomach. Like it was something evil and unholy growing inside of me. Not a baby, but a beast. Something to be slaughtered before it grew too big to be controlled.

I expect more words of comfort from Yelena. I expect more assurances that everything will work out for the best, that Andrey will magically sort everything out and there will be a happily ever after at the end of this story.

But Yelena says no such thing.

She does the opposite, actually. She bites down on her bottom lip as though she's trying to stop herself from saying something damaging.

Then she sighs. "I don't want to lie to you, child."

"W-what do you mean?"

"This life—the Bratva life—it's a hard one. Especially when you have a family." She looks out towards the trees and I imagine she's picturing her own family. The husband she lost to someone else's war.

I don't know what to say, so I take her hand and squeeze it. "I'm sorry, Yelena."

She shrugs. "It was the life he chose. And this is the life I chose. I have no regrets."

"Andrey thinks he can protect us," I whisper, placing a hand on my stomach.

"All men think that," Yelena scoffs. "But it's just a lie they tell themselves. Andrey is no more capable of protecting you than he was of protecting my husband."

The sudden lash of bitterness in her voice takes me back. Not once, in all the time I've known her, has she betrayed the slightest bit of resentment towards Andrey. But I can see it now, lying just beneath the surface of her maternal kindliness.

Festering. Like a rotten wound.

"I ask myself sometimes why I stayed here, after everything that happened. You might've wondered the same thing, yes?" I don't answer, but she carries on. "I suppose I thought I could keep the memory of my husband close if I stayed a part of the world he died for."

The silence thuds and pulses. It stretches forever and collapses into the blink of an eye. I feel the words in my mouth before I've even decided to say them.

"Yelena…?"

She stares back, unblinking. As though she already knows what I'm about to ask her.

All my love,

Natalia

Folding up the note, I stash it in the drawer of the writing cabinet and join Yelena outside on the patio.

"I've arranged it," she says bluntly. "It's all fixed."

I know I should be asking more questions. *Fixed with who? How did you arrange this so fast? Where do I go? How will I live?*

But I settle on the question that seems the most urgent.

"When?"

Her answer is immediate. "Right now."

70

NATALIA

"We have to be quick and quiet," Yelena explains, dragging me towards the back of the house. "I'm going to need to take you through the servants' entry. Then I can sneak you through the side gate."

"But there are cameras everywhere. What about—"

"I've disabled them," she interrupts. "They won't know until it's too late."

Too late. Too late to say goodbye. Too late to undo the deaths I've caused.

I don't realize I'm slowing down until Yelena snatches up my hand in both of hers and squeezes hard enough to frighten me. "Listen to me, child. You don't have time. No time for questions, no time to get your things, no time to say goodbyes. We need to go." Her eyes are wide. "Now or never."

She doesn't wait for me to answer. Keeping a vise grip on my forearm, she starts to drag me into the manor.

"Yelena," I whisper as we slip inside, "why are you doing this? Why are you helping me?"

"Because I don't want you to go through what I went through." Her hand is so tight around my wrist that it's starting to hurt. "Because I don't want you to lose the twins, and I certainly don't want them to lose you."

God, the twins. Two souls coming to life inside of me. Two little babies that are relying on me to protect them, to keep them safe so they can have a chance to—

Wait.

Wait.

I grind to a halt and rip my hand free of Yelena's claws. "Yelena, how did you know I was having twins?"

Outside, the sun is shining and birds are chirping.

But in this hallway, I feel a kind of chill I've never felt in my life.

She blinks the question away in irritation. "You told me. Now, come—"

I don't let her grab me again. "No, I didn't. I just found out myself."

The sweat on her brow drips down the crook of her gnarled nose. "You did tell me, child," she hisses impatiently. "You're confused. Now, *come*. We're wasting precious time."

Why was Yelena so quick to help me?

Why is she in such a rush?

The questions I didn't stop to ask outside are stacking up in front of me, becoming too big to summit.

"Come, Natalia!" she growls. "If you don't make that car, you'll have missed your chance to save your children."

What's wrong with you? You trusted her all this time. What's changed now?

I don't have time to find answers before the infirmary door opens just down the hall and Misha walks out, rubbing his drowsy eyes.

Yelena drops my hand immediately.

"Natalia!" Misha rushes forward and throws his arms around me.

"Misha…" I croak, breathing in the familiar warmth of his downy hair.

"You're safe! I was so scared."

I draw back a little and cup his face. "I'm fine. Andrey and Shura got me out in time. How are you?"

"I'm fine. I was with Remi. He's doing better."

The smile on his face gives me hope. "You'll look after him, won't you?"

Misha frowns. I bite my tongue, cursing myself internally. His gaze slides from me to Yelena, who's lingering in my periphery, wringing her hands anxiously.

"Why do I need to look after him?" Misha asks. "Where are you going?"

"Nowhere!" Yelena answers for me. It would have been better if she'd just let me handle this. Her words are far too harsh. Misha is too perceptive. "She needs rest, some peace and quiet."

His eyebrows pinch together and they refuse to iron out. "Let me come with you."

"No, that's okay," I protest. "You should rest, too."

"I've been resting for hours. I want to do something. Let me walk with you."

He's not looking at me when he asks, though.

He's looking at Yelena.

"Misha, please. Just trust me. Go to your room and get some proper rest. On a real bed. You're dead on your feet."

He shakes his head, looking from me to Yelena again and again. "Something is going on. You're going to do something you shouldn't be doing."

"*Prygat!*" Yelena snaps. "This doesn't concern you, boy."

"Yelena!" I gasp at the venom in her voice.

She whirls towards me, spittle flying as she jabs a finger at Misha. "Don't trust him, Natalia. The boy's a spy! He's been informing on you for months, I know it!"

"Yelena, that's enough. Misha isn't a spy."

But she is backing away from him, glaring at him like he's the devil himself. "You're blinded by your kind heart, Natalia. The boy is Nikolai's man."

Misha hasn't moved since she accused him. His face is pale and his hands are balled into fists. "Natalia, get away from her," he spits.

"What in the—? Both of you, stop," I beg. "This is what Nikolai does. He's turning us against one another and he's not even here. Don't give him that kind of power."

But I might as well be screaming into the void for all the good it does me. Yelena and Misha aren't listening.

Misha's eyes narrow, and he shifts closer to me. "Remi never liked Yelena. You remember that, right? He always growls whenever she's close. Just like he did in the hospital when that 'nurse' showed up."

He's not lying. Remi and Yelena never warmed to each other.

"Misha," I try again, "please, just trust—"

"Enough of this!"

I glance back just in time to see Yelena swing something large and heavy towards us. I jump out of the way and Misha stumbles back, but the butt of the antique fire poker stabs him in the shoulder.

He lets out a strangled cry and drops to the floor, blood already bubbling up from the wound.

"Yelena!" I scream. "What the hell?!"

But Yelena isn't listening. She's advancing on Misha with the poker raised, ready to strike again.

I grab a hold of it and try to pry it out of her hands, but for an old woman, she's fucking *strong.*

"Have you completely lost your mind?" I cry, no longer caring if we're overheard. "He's a child!"

"And you're a fool!" Yelena shrieks. "If you don't come with me now, all will be lost." She drops the poker and snares my wrist again, fingers pressing down hard on the bruises she left there.

"Yelena, you're hurting me—"

"We don't have time. We must—"

But her words are cut off by the crack of ceramic as it splinters against the back of her head.

Yelena's eyes roll backwards and she collapses to the ground, just as thundering footsteps echo down the hall.

Seconds later, Andrey, Shura, and Leonty flood into the living room. "What the fuck happened here?" Andrey demands, gawking at Yelena's form with an unreadable look on his face.

I can barely make my lips form the words. "Misha cracked a vase over her head."

Misha's temples are slick with sweat. He's shaking from head to toe, but he doesn't look remotely apologetic. "Yeah," he confesses. "And I'd do it again."

Shura and Leonty scoop up Yelena's limp form and move her to the sofa. Andrey's face is pure wrath as he turns on Misha. He looks terrifying. If I were Misha, I'd be shitting my pants.

But Misha presses his bleeding shoulder back, wincing only slightly, and meets Andrey's eyes. Neither one says a word.

I jump in between them. "Andrey—"

He doesn't look at me, but he does hold up a hand. Despite myself, I fall silent. He's radiating a dangerous energy and it's impossible to ignore.

"Why?" he snarls.

"She was up to something," Misha says evenly. "I don't trust her."

Shura places a pillow under Yelena's head and straightens up to look over at the confrontation unfolding before us. "She's been with us a lot longer than you, boy."

Misha whirls around, glaring indignantly between Andrey and Shura. "That doesn't make her trustworthy. She accused me of being a spy, but I think *she's* the spy."

"Why do either of you have to be a spy?" I cry out. "Misha, you misunderstood what was happening, okay? This is all just a big, stupid mistake!"

"She was trying to get you to leave!" Misha insists, blowing my cover in one simple sentence. "She was trying to smuggle you out of here. Why would she do that when this is the safest place for you?"

My jaw falls open as every pair of eyes in the room swivels to me. I find myself grappling for words, searching desperately for an alibi.

"Nat…" Leonty's voice is soft and disbelieving. "Is that true?"

Yelena stirs and Misha looks at her with disgust. He'd kill her right now if we let him.

"It was my idea to leave," I choke out. "If you're gonna blame anyone, blame me."

Leonty is the only one who looks remotely shocked by my admission. Shura and Andrey are expressionless.

"I still don't trust her!" Misha exclaims, breaking the tense silence. "She was always whispering and creeping around at weird hours. I saw her talking to someone on a phone in the laundry room once. She got mad when she saw me there."

My stomach roils. Andrey sees the discomfort on my face and scowls. "What is it, Natalia?"

"I… uh… it could be nothing." Swallowing hard, I glance at Yelena, who's moaning softly on the couch, not quite conscious yet. "She just… She never liked me coming into the laundry room. She claimed it was because of all the chemicals."

Andrey and Shura exchange a glance, having a silent conversation. A moment later, Andrey points his chin and Shura nods, disappearing through the open archway in the direction of the kitchen.

"I'm not lying," Misha insists. "And I'm not a spy. I just—"

"It's okay, Misha," Andrey interrupts. "I believe you."

"You do?"

"Let me be clear: I believe you're not a spy. I believe that you believe everything you just told us." Andrey's eyes are still cold. "But that doesn't mean you're right."

Misha's shoulders slump. He opens his mouth to retort, but before he can say anything, Shura enters the living room.

He's carrying a small, black phone in his hand.

"I found this stashed at the back of the laundry cabinet," he says darkly.

I feel like I'm going to be sick. I glance down at my wrist and see the bruises Yelena left there. Five purple ovals marking my skin.

"Anything on there?" Andrey asks.

"Only one outgoing call on the contact log. It was placed about forty-five minutes ago."

"Call the number," Andrey orders.

Shura dials and transfers the call to speaker. The rings echo harshly, magnified in the taut stillness. And then, someone picks up.

"Yelena," a deep, familiar voice hisses, "where the fuck are you? You were supposed to have delivered her by now."

Shock and rage ripples across Andrey's face as he takes the phone from Shura's hand.

"Yelena!" the voice barks again. "Where—"

Andrey smashes the phone onto the floor and stomps it into pieces. "Fuck!" he roars so loudly that Yelena's eyes fly open. She scrambles around in a panic, but her limbs are sluggish and her mouth flaps without any words coming out.

Andrey descends on her like a nightmare. "How long? How fucking long have you been spying for my father?"

Of course. That's why the caller's voice sounded so familiar. It was the same voice that told me my aunt was in the hospital.

Slavik did this.

Yelena looks towards me as though I can explain what's happening. For a moment, I feel only pity for her. For this bitter, old woman surrounded by three hulking men who might kill her if she says one wrong word.

Then her eyes slide to the arm I've got wrapped protectively around Misha.

Her face twists and morphs. The tender, maternal woman I had come to know is gone.

Now that I'm searching for it, I see the anger there—the rage so deep and sudden that I clutch Misha closer like I can protect him from it.

"From day one," she spits at last. She lets out a cackle of hard laughter. "You cost me my family. And you were egotistical enough to believe that I would simply accept it."

Andrey's jaw shifts. "This is about Yegor."

"Yegor died fighting for his Bratva," Shura declares. "For his *pakhan*."

Yelena glowers at him. "My husband died following the orders of an inexperienced, foolish boy who didn't know what he was doing."

Andrey is quiet for a while. No one else dares to breathe. My heartbeat stills in my chest when he unsheathes a knife from his hip and toys with it. Twists it this way and that.

He's never looked colder.

Without looking up, he orders, "Leonty, get Misha and Natalia out of here."

Misha tries to steer my hand, but I'm frozen on the spot. "You can't just kill her."

"She's a traitor. She was going to deliver you straight to my psychopathic father. She's been spying on me, on you, on all of us," he seethes, his control slipping. "After all this fucking time… death is a kindness. This is the Bratva way."

"Then find a better way!"

"*Lastochka—*"

"Enough!" It's Yelena who yells, cutting through our argument in a shrill voice strained with pain. She lifts herself off the couch with difficulty and looks towards me. "I don't need you to defend me, girl."

"I'm not defending you," I throw back at her with disgust. "You deserve to be punished. But I don't believe in senseless violence or unnecessary murder."

"No?" Yelena asks, a vicious smile curling over her lips. "Well, I do."

I see a flash of silver at her side and suddenly, she's lunging at me.

I have only enough time to step back, Misha's arms tightening around me, as the mouth of her gun rises and rises until I'm looking down the barrel.

Andrey moves first.

He grabs Yelena by the hair. Her eyes bulge cartoonishly as he yanks her backward, twisting her arm at the same time. The handgun she's carrying drops, skitters across the floor, and settles to a stop at my feet.

Using her hair to steer, Andrey twists her around to face him. Then he slashes his blade across her throat, sending blood spurting out in nauseating red bouts.

Yelena is dead before she hits the ground.

Bile rises in my throat. I taste the acid on my tongue. Her blood is painted across Andrey's face and hands as he turns to me. "Natalia…" he rasps, taking a step in my direction.

It happened so damn fast. So… easily.

A few seconds and a life was extinguished, just like that.

As fast as my father's.

As fast as my mother's.

Horror claws its way up my spine and I back away from Andrey. "Don't come any closer."

My voice is clear and strong. But my whole body is shaking violently. The blood on his face distorts him into a monster that I cannot recognize. A beast I cannot love.

He steps over the dead woman at his feet and keeps moving towards me.

Dreams melt into a reality so thick and viscous that I can't tell where one stops and the other begins. The next thing I know, I'm picking up the gun at my feet…

And pointing it directly at Andrey.

It's not just him I don't recognize—I don't recognize myself, either.

My world has been ripped off its axis. Up is down and down is up. My loved ones are enemies. Away is safe, and here is…

Here is death. Death and blood.

"Natalia, I know you're scared, but you have to trust me. Put down the gun." He takes another step forward.

"Stay away from me!" I scream, flying back in panic.

But my heel catches the baseboard and, in my surprise, my hand clenches automatically.

The gun fires.

Andrey glances down at his torso in surprise as blood begins to bloom on the white of his shirt.

The knife clatters from his hand and he drops to his knees. Misha and Leonty and Shura close in around him.

My entire world coalesces down to a single word. A single instinct.

Run.

Or death will catch you, too.

TO BE CONTINUED

Andrey and Natalia's story concludes in Book 2 of the Kuznetsov Bratva duet, EMERALD VICES.

Check it out!

ALSO BY NICOLE FOX

Novikov Bratva

Ivory Ashes

Ivory Oath

Egorov Bratva

Tangled Innocence

Tangled Decadence

Zakrevsky Bratva

Requiem of Sin

Sonata of Lies

Rhapsody of Pain

Bugrov Bratva

Midnight Purgatory

Midnight Sanctuary

Oryolov Bratva

Cruel Paradise

Cruel Promise

Pushkin Bratva

Cognac Villain

Cognac Vixen

Viktorov Bratva

Whiskey Poison

Whiskey Pain

Orlov Bratva
Champagne Venom
Champagne Wrath

Uvarov Bratva
Sapphire Scars
Sapphire Tears

Vlasov Bratva
Arrogant Monster
Arrogant Mistake

Zhukova Bratva
Tarnished Tyrant
Tarnished Queen

Stepanov Bratva
Satin Sinner
Satin Princess

Makarova Bratva
Shattered Altar
Shattered Cradle

Solovev Bratva
Ravaged Crown
Ravaged Throne

Vorobev Bratva
Velvet Devil
Velvet Angel

Romanoff Bratva

Immaculate Deception
Immaculate Corruption

Kovalyov Bratva
Gilded Cage
Gilded Tears
Jaded Soul
Jaded Devil
Ripped Veil
Ripped Lace

Mazzeo Mafia Duet
Liar's Lullaby (Book 1)
Sinner's Lullaby (Book 2)

Bratva Crime Syndicate
Can be read in any order!
Lies He Told Me
Scars He Gave Me
Sins He Taught Me

Belluci Mafia Trilogy
Corrupted Angel (Book 1)
Corrupted Queen (Book 2)
Corrupted Empire (Book 3)

De Maggio Mafia Duet
Devil in a Suit (Book 1)
Devil at the Altar (Book 2)

Kornilov Bratva Duet
Married to the Don (Book 1)

Til Death Do Us Part (Book 2)

Heirs to the Bratva Empire

Can be read in any order!

Kostya

Maksim

Andrei

Princes of Ravenlake Academy (Bully Romance)

Can be read as standalones!

Cruel Prep

Cruel Academy

Cruel Elite

Tsezar Bratva

Nightfall (Book 1)

Daybreak (Book 2)

Russian Crime Brotherhood

Can be read in any order!

Owned by the Mob Boss

Unprotected with the Mob Boss

Knocked Up by the Mob Boss

Sold to the Mob Boss

Stolen by the Mob Boss

Trapped with the Mob Boss

Volkov Bratva

Broken Vows (Book 1)

Broken Hope (Book 2)

Broken Sins *(standalone)*

Other Standalones

Vin: A Mafia Romance

Box Sets

Bratva Mob Bosses (Russian Crime Brotherhood Books 1-6)

Tsezar Bratva (Tsezar Bratva Duet Books 1-2)

Heirs to the Bratva Empire

The Mafia Dons Collection

The Don's Corruption

Printed in Great Britain
by Amazon